~

Roses and Ruins

Roses and Ruins

GREEN HAVEN SERIES

KL AUSTIN

Roses & Ruin

Book Cover by Jessica Smith at Unbound Bookish Design

Logo by Jules Seelman at JS Designs Co.

Edits by Emma and Scott Editorial

First edition 2026

ISBN Paperback 979-8-9948771-1-1

ISBN EBook 979-8-9948771-0-4

Manufactured in the United States of America

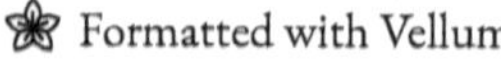 Formatted with Vellum

Chapter One

CORDELIA

Ten minutes done, just two to go.

I focus on stirring the next layer of resin for the Underwoods' wedding in three weeks. This is the final layer to pour over the LED lights nestled in the Mr. & Mrs. frame, decorated with dried white and pink flowers to echo their wedding theme.

Once I finish this layer, I can mix up the navy blue and pink resin tomorrow and finish the whole thing. I let out a heavy sigh as I finish stirring. Ever since I started adding the personal touch of the epoxy resin Mr. & Mrs. sign with the flowers, colors, and lights a little over a year ago to match a couple's wedding theme, my life has been measured in twelve-minute increments. I glance out the window that's over the table in my craft shed, taking in the sprawling valley and the mountains that surround us. I will never get over how beautiful it is here, and how incredibly lucky I got with this place. While we have the main barn that can comfortably hold up to three hundred for a wedding, we also have a couple of smaller sheds and outbuildings on the property. I left the old silo, hoping to do something with it one day. But I don't know what yet. For now, the guests like to include it in pictures. With the other buildings, the only one worth saving was this one.

It's roughly two hundred square feet. I kept a bunch of the wood from the other buildings and made a wall and bought the hardware for a barndoor, turning one side, length-wise, into my office while the majority of the shed is for arts and crafts.

"I really need to invest in one of those automatic stirring stations for this," I say aloud.

"You've been saying that for over a year, Cordy. If you don't buy yourself one, I'm getting you one for Christmas," Harper says from her perch on the smaller table. Harper and I have been best friends since we met twelve years ago. She is the exact opposite of me in appearance. Where I have all the curves, she's the tiniest thing, aside from being well-endowed for her frame, but her over-the-top personality makes up for her petite build tenfold. She's been a social media manager for a couple of companies for the last five years, including mine, and is starting to branch out into being an influencer. With long, icy blonde hair and big gray-blue eyes, she's more than stunning. Setting her phone down for the first time in the last hour, she asks, "What time is the construction guy supposed to be here for that estimate?"

"He should be here any minute, assuming he is on time." The last two couldn't be here on the right day, let alone on time, so my hopes aren't too high this time. As I finish up my mixing, I flick the switch on the string lights for the third time, just to make sure they were working before it was too late to do anything about it. Once I pour the mix into the frame, I set aside the silicone measuring cups to dry. I give the frame a couple of taps to release the air bubbles to the surface and toss my gloves into the trash.

"I think someone just pulled up," Harper said, hopping off the table and walking to the window, "Yup, a big truck just pulled up—Oh em gee! Is that the construction guy?"

I pull the chopstick from my hair, letting it fall in big, dark waves, and I walk over to the window next to the door. Reading the side of the truck, Campbell's Construction, I mutter, "Yup..." My voice trails off as my gaze shifts to the man walking around the front of his truck. Towering well over six feet, his muscular frame is a sight to behold. His jeans pull taut over his legs, hinting at powerful thighs, and his blue t-shirt stretches across his broad chest, while his biceps look like they might burst the seams. His light brown hair is trimmed short on the sides, a white baseball cap shading his face, with dark sunglasses resting above a neatly trimmed beard. His muscles ripple as he reaches into his pocket, pulls his cell phone out, and taps the screen before bringing it to his ear.

BUZZZ!

Harper and I both jump, grabbing each other's arms as my cell phone starts dancing across the table.

"For fuck's sake," I breathe out. Releasing Harper's arm, I take the two short steps to the table and grab my phone. "Hello?"

"This is Dean, from Campbell's Construction. Is this Miss Rivers?" Naturally, his voice is pure sex appeal, deep and smoky.

"Yeah—" my voice comes out a little too breathy, so I shake my head and try again, "Yes, it is."

A faint smile tugs at his lips as I glance back out the window, "I'm here at the site. Near the small barn you said to meet you at."

"Oh, I will be right out!" I hang up my phone and toss the torch to Harper, "Can you finish this?"

Harper sighs dramatically, "Fine, but if you think this will keep me away from that impressive male specimen out there for more than five minutes..." She narrows her eyes and lets the threat hang unspoken.

"Got it," I try to hide my snicker.

I turn around and push open the door, walking outside. "Hey, Dean. I'm Cordelia Rivers, owner of Glass River." I offer my hand.

Dean pauses for a second before sliding his sunglasses off, revealing the most stunning blue-green eyes, like the ocean after a storm. He takes my hand in his, and a jolt of electricity rushes up my arm as butterflies swarm my stomach.

"Pleased to meet you." His voice is like smooth whiskey, rich and warm, making my thighs involuntarily clench.

He holds my hand just a second longer than necessary before clearing his throat. "So, what are we looking at for you today?"

Focus, Cordy! Use your words.

"Um, yeah. So I was looking to add on a couple of things." I gesture toward the old barn I bought and transformed into one of Western North Carolina's most sought-after wedding venues when I moved here three years ago. "I was looking into adding some rose bushes under the upper deck off the side, and putting in a couple of cute swings. I also want to add a second staircase on the opposite side, bringing both stairs around to meet on another lower deck, something grand-looking. I keep going back and forth with paving that walkway, but I like the rustic look of gravel against all the glass. However, I know that it makes walking in heels a little difficult, so adding the wooden deck might be nice."

Dean is using his cell phone to take some pictures and nodding. "Agreed. The glass and the gravel are a good contrast, adding interest instead of making it seem too modern, which keeps it more whimsical. All you've mentioned sounds simple enough."

I smile. "I do have one more thing."

I start walking toward the river that runs through the property. Taking a deep inhale of the spring air, I cast my eyes toward the cotton candy clouds floating through the sky. I stop about a hundred feet from the bank. "I want a giant pergola or lanai here. Something that can be used to do weddings outside. I have a couple of arches that we set up, but I want something more permanent." I glance at Dean, "I know there's a risk of flooding with the river being here, but if we set it far enough back, I think it will be safe," I say. I have a vision, but I also know that he's the professional and can tell me if I need to reassess anything for safety and longevity. My eyes shift to him, and I find him already watching me. *He really is breathtaking.*

He slips his sunglasses back on and turns his gaze toward the river. "Flooding is always a risk this close to water, but I think we can build something that could withstand it. Be a little more expensive, but if it won't wash away—"

"It's worth it," I finish for him, smiling.

"Exactly." As he snaps a couple more pictures of the area, I take it all in. I love this spot immensely, with the mountains acting like sentries guarding this valley. The river flows quietly, softly burbling in the background, creating a feeling of peace, something I don't have much of. I think this is why I love this spot, it brings a sense of tranquility and contentment. When Dean turns, we walk back toward the parking lot.

"Give me a day or two to write up the estimate," he says. "If you're good with the price, I'll get some visual examples mocked up for you."

Before I can answer him, I hear Harper.

"Hi there, handsome," Harper purrs, leaning against the front of the truck. I barely contain my eye roll at her boldness. The truck is huge, and it's making Harper look more doll-like than usual.

Sighing, I say, "Dean, this is Harper. She's my best friend and the social media manager of the place for me. Harper, this is Dean."

Harper pushes off the truck and saunters over, offering her hand, "Pleased to meet you, Dean," she says with a smile that isn't quite as flirty as I would have expected it to be.

"Likewise," Dean shakes her hand and turns back to me, "Well, I will be in touch, Miss Rivers."

"Please, call me Cordelia."

"Cordelia." He taps a finger to the brim of his hat, his eyes holding mine for just a moment too long with an intensity that makes my face heat, before climbing into his truck.

Harper leans against my arm with a dreamy sigh as we watch him drive away. "If a guy that looked like that was eye-fucking me as hard as he was you just now, I'd be down at the courthouse signing a marriage license."

"Harper! He was not!"

"Mmmhmm," she hums, knocking her hip into mine as she walks off. "You keep telling yourself that. Maybe eventually you will believe it."

I flick my gaze skyward, trying to ignore the feelings bubbling inside me.

Chapter Two

DEAN

I thought my heart had stopped when Cordelia stepped into the sunlight. Paint-splattered work boots, skin-tight jeans that didn't leave anything to the imagination, and a light green sweater hanging off her shoulder, revealing a black bra strap and just the edge of delicate black lace. The woman was perfection in all the ways I could only dream about, having curves that should come with a warning sign.

Long dark hair and sparkling green eyes above perfectly full lips that I just wanted to run my thumb over and devour.

"Fuck." I mutter, adjusting myself as much as I can while driving. My dick has been painfully hard since she took the first two steps in front of me, giving me the perfect view of that ass in those jeans. When she showed me the spot for the pergola and the breeze caught her hair, carrying her perfume—roses—I nearly came in my pants like a goddamn teenager with no self-control.

This is going to be a problem.

Thirty excruciatingly painful minutes later, I pull into my spot at my office. I walk inside to find my younger brother, Graham, sitting at my desk, in my chair, with his boots propped up like he owns the place.

"How'd the meeting out in the middle of nowhere go?" Graham asks, putting his hands behind his head and leaning back.

"Get. Out. Of. My. Chair," I growl through clenched teeth, "Now."

Laughing, he swings his boots down and stands. "Sorry, man, it's just such a comfy chair."

"That's why it's mine." I drop into the seat, eyeing him. "If you wanna take on more responsibility, I will gladly buy you one of your own."

He smirks, but I don't let up. I've been bugging him to take on more so I can do less for the last two years. I'm not old, not yet anyway, but I am getting to the point where I want to have more of a life outside of this company I started when I was fifteen, almost thirty years ago now.

"It would mean more money for you, too," I add. "Which would only help you out with Madison."

"Madison and I are fine. Besides, if I take on more, that's less time with her. She's twelve, almost thirteen. I can't leave her on her own too much right now. Yesterday, she told me about a boy she has a crush on. Said he's 'the most perfect and beautiful boy' she has ever seen, while sighing heavily and staring off into the distance. She's never going to have a boyfriend. I'm going to ship her off to an all-girls boarding school in Switzerland or something."

I throw my head back, laughing. Hell, I needed a good laugh after the morning I had.

"Look, how about the first time a boy comes over, I'll bring Murph and all our guns, and we can just be sitting on the porch out front cleaning them?" I ask, still chuckling.

"YES! Thank you! We were awful at sixteen, man. I'm terrified of what she is going to bring home. Maybe she will decide she's into girls? Is it too late for that?" Graham runs his fingers through his hair, which is badly in need of a cut, holding it back from his face.

"I don't know if that would be any better, in all honesty."

Graham leans back into his chair, exhaling. "Fuck, man. Being a girl dad is rough. But wait, you can't just change the subject like that. How did it go at the wedding venue?"

Goddamn it. "Fine," I grunt.

Graham raises an eyebrow, a smirk tugging his mouth. "So, is she pretty? She sounded pretty on the voicemail."

Turning away from him, I switch on my computer, pulling up the program to upload the pictures I took.

"Oh no. No. No no no... You like her!"

"Graham, get the fuck out of my office unless you plan to do some actual work. I have been taking care of your ass since we were teenagers, I'm not above kicking you out if all you're going to do is act like a child."

Graham raises his hands and takes a step back. "Oh, this is good. I can't wait to see how this plays out. You never let a woman get to you like this." He chuckles but leaves my office.

I shake my head as the door closes to the trailer, thankful that Graham didn't take my overly harsh words personally. He's always been carefree and just lets the bad roll off his back.

I get to work on writing up the estimate, trying and failing to push away the image of her legs wrapped around me, her long dark hair fisted in my hand.

I've been a bachelor since high school. Never wanted to deal with the drama of a relationship. I keep a small list of women in my contacts who understand the no-strings deal that comes from being with me. After our mom died in a car accident when I was seventeen, our dad didn't last much longer. Two years later, he was gone, too. Died of a broken heart, people said. Graham was seventeen then. Luckily, Mom was smart with money. She'd taken out life insurance on her and Dad. That gave me the foundation for this company. I think a lot of the town took pity on me and started hiring me for jobs to help out. But once they saw the quality of my work, the jobs kept coming. By twenty-seven, I had fifty employees on my payroll.

Graham used his share of the insurance money to put himself

through college, earning a business degree. Probably the first and last time he ever listened to me.

I give him shit, but he really does a lot for the company. He handles the taxes, accounting, and the business end of things, with the exception of the payroll, which I still manage.

When he got his girlfriend pregnant at twenty-eight, he was the happiest man on the planet. She wasn't. Samantha wasn't made to be a mother, and after she had Madison, she split. Signed over everything to Graham and never looked back. Graham and I have sat through more tea parties than I can count. And yes, I've worn a princess crown and a feather boa while she painted my nails pink and put blue eyeshadow on my face. That girl has us both wrapped around her little finger, and it's been that way for almost thirteen years now. I never wanted kids, and watching Graham do it alone over the years has only reinforced that decision.

An hour later, I've downloaded the photos and saved my notes on everything she wants. I close the file and shut down the computer, needing to get outside—do something—to keep my mind off the green-eyed goddess from this morning.

"Hey, Dean! You coming out for beers tomorrow night?" Graham calls as he approaches with Wade and Matt trailing behind him.

"Before you say no," he adds quickly, "Let me remind you that you are always preaching about everyone being a team player."

Oh, I see what this is about. I nod. "Yeah, I can do that. We don't have a job site to be at early Saturday, so it shouldn't be a problem."

"Excellent!" Graham grins as the guys all fist-bump each other.

I fire up my truck, clean up my tools, and lock up the office trailer before heading home.

I pull into my driveway of my childhood home, the place that's been my ongoing renovation project for the last twenty years. Maybe one day I'll actually finish all the changes, but it always felt like something was missing, so I kept going. I gutted the kitchen to the studs, and redid it with a breakfast bar cut into the living room wall, Carrara marble countertops, and tile backsplash throughout. Including up to the ceiling behind the stove. Dark gray lower cabinets and cream colored uppers, stainless steel appliances and a light gray hardwood floor. Then came the sunroom addition: folding glass doors on every wall with a hot tub inside. After that, I tackled the bathrooms. I remodeled both full baths and eventually converted the half bath and laundry room between the kitchen and garage into a full bath, adding a stand-up shower for those days I come home filthy and don't want to track it through the whole house.

Hanging my keys on the hook by the door, I head to my room, strip out of my work clothes, and turn on the shower. I wait for it to warm before stepping in. The second I close my eyes under the water, all I can see are those emerald green eyes staring at me. Before I know it, I've got my dick in my hand, giving it a few slow strokes. *Fuck, I shouldn't be doing this while thinking of her.* But I don't stop myself. I keep going, picturing her hair wrapped around my fist and her lips around my length—

Fuck!

I finish in my hand, letting the water wash it— and what's left of my sanity—down the drain.

Chapter Three

CORDELIA

Driving through downtown toward Music and Margaritas, the cutest bar in town with the best music selection, I can't help but smile a little sadly at everything the last ten years have brought me.

I love it here.

Ten years ago, Harper and I took a girls' trip to Asheville, North Carolina, right at peak fall color season. We both fell in love with the place, already planning our next trip back within twenty-four hours of arriving. But everything changed when the best part of my life was destroyed. I needed to escape. Harper, just getting started with the social media work, had the flexibility to go anywhere. With both her boys in college on the other side of the country, she packed up and moved with me a year after everything fell apart.

I always figured she was just happy to be done with the life she'd had back in Ohio. We never looked back. We loaded all our most important possessions into our Jeeps, and we started over in Green Haven, a small town just south of Asheville. We rented a tiny apartment, found the wedding venue, and threw ourselves into the renovation. Harper and I handled everything that we could ourselves, and for the bigger project, like the giant glass wall of windows, we roped in a local handyman, the son of the owner of the local hardware store. We pestered the owner with so many questions by the fourth visit that he made his son come out to help.

It took nearly a year to get the venue up and running. With Harper's expert social media skills, we had weddings booked nearly every weekend that first year and now we are booked through this year and halfway through next. Business has picked up so much that we have started double-booking some weekends. This new micro wedding trend has been amazing for filling in morning and early afternoon, with larger weddings in the evenings. Even some weeknights are booked now, especially in the fall. With the mountain and river in the background, everyone wants that view. And honestly? It's stunning.

I usually never meet the girls on a Friday or Saturday night—weddings require early starts—but the team I finally hired to help with set up and clean up has been a godsend.

We usually meet on Wednesdays for Wine Nights and all the local gossip.

Harper and I first met Faye, owner of the boutique hotel, The Rosewood, our first night in town. We were desperate for a place to crash those first couple nights, and she welcomed us like old friends. Faye took over her grandmother's little B&B and revamped it into a lush, modern boutique hotel.

Gwen owns Scarlett Sage, a small shop across the street from The Rosewood. It quickly became a favorite of ours. Gwen sources the cutest clothes from the best designers. Faye and Gwen were friends before we came along, and then after we got here, our duos merged, and now the four of us are inseparable.

These weekly meet-ups are our ritual; catching up on life, laughing, and sharing stories. But after yesterday, Harper sent out a 911 in the group chat.

And so, here I am, going out on a Friday night for the first time in probably eight years.

I pull into one of the last open parking spots at Music and

Margaritas, and glance at the clock. 7:15. Great, fifteen minutes late, which means Harper's definitely spilled everything.

Groaning, I get out of my Jeep and head inside. I can hear the notes from an old Garth Brooks song playing in the air as I reach for the door. The lights are dim, as usual, with close to a hundred neon signs lining the walls. Some are the typical beer and drink signs, but others are music references. Max, one of the owners, is the biggest music buff in the whole town. Under the pink glowing music note sign is an old jukebox that still plays records. Max swears that the music sounds better on vinyl. He's not entirely wrong, as everyone is almost always playing music from there instead of the digital one that hangs on the wall.

I spot the girls at our usual table, steeling myself for the oncoming interrogation. I take a deep breath and realize that I can smell sugar in the air before I wave and walk over.

"Dean?! Dean Campbell??!!" Faye practically screeches, leaping off her barstool.

Faye is my height, and we've been mistaken for sisters more than once. We both have sharp cheekbones and striking green eyes. But while she's a perfect honey blonde with highlights kind of girl, I have always preferred keeping my hair dark as night.

I shoot a pointed look at Harper and narrow my eyes. "Seriously, Harper, you couldn't have waited fifteen minutes?"

"Hey, not my fault you were late," she says with a smug smile, taking a sip of her wine.

"Okay, I'm going to need all of the details," Faye says as she settles back into her stool.

"Um, I called his company for a quote, and he came out, took a look at the place, and said he would get back to me in a couple of days." I slide my wine glass toward me and take a larger sip than is socially acceptable. I already know this is going to turn into a full-blown interrogation, and there are no steamy details to give.

"Guys, seriously, that was all that happened. Harper is convinced he was staring at me with heart eyes. Maybe you should talk to her about the details."

"It wasn't just heart eyes, it was lust-filled eyes," Harper says confidently.

I roll my eyes and reach for my glass of wine again, seriously considering downing the whole thing in one go.

"Ok, so you met, he seemed attracted, and you are too, and you will probably be seeing more of him in the near future?" Gwen asks matter-of-factly.

Gwen has some of the brightest blue eyes you'll ever see, and she always keeps a streak or two of blue in her blonde hair to highlight them. She's also the tallest of the four of us and has curves that could make Marilyn Monroe jealous. She knows it and isn't shy about using them to her advantage.

"Um.. I never said I was attracted."

"Sweetie, every woman in this town finds that man attractive," Faye says with a knowing smile.

"Yep," Harper and Gwen chime in together.

"We are going to need far more wine for this conversation. I cannot with you three." I stand and make my way up to the bar, where I spot Rita and Max, owners of Music and Margaritas, deep in animated conversation.

They've been married for over thirty years and built this bar to be a reflection of who they are. They both love music and enjoy sharing that with everyone around them. They also happen to make some of the best drinks in the city. Lately, cakes have become Rita's new thing.

"Rita, no. You are not walking around serving people random slices of cake!" Max says, exasperated.

"And why not? I can't eat all this cake, and I know you can't either! What am I supposed to do? Throw it away and waste it?!"

I knew I smelled sugar in the air.

"Fine, but I'm not carrying it around for you. I have drinks to help make."

"Hey, Rita, did you say cake?" I asked, leaning over the bar.

"Cordelia! Oh dear, you heard that?"

"I think this half of the bar did, and now I think everyone's waiting for cake," I say with a wink. I've had her cakes before, and they're heaven on a plate.

"I made that lemon blueberry cheesecake cake again," she says proudly, "but I also tried a new recipe that I think you will love."

"I need the whole thing. Stat." I'm practically drooling. That cake is my absolute favorite—a light, fluffy layer cake with lemon blueberry cheesecake layered with fresh lemon zest and blueberries on top. It is also one of the most dangerous things I've ever tasted.

"And we are gonna need another bottle—maybe three—for our table."

"I'll bring out two bottles of wine and four slices of cake for you ladies," Rita replies with a wink of her own.

"You are my favorite, Rita!"

As I return to the table, I announce, "Rita is bringing more wine and cake."

Harper's eyes go wide, "That chocolate cake that I would commit ungodly acts for?"

Laughing, I nod. "I would assume so. She knows what you like."

"Ok, so back to the point of this evening," Gwen says, steering the conversation back. "You seriously don't think he's attractive? He has those Daddy vibes going on with the gray at the temples, and the man clearly knows how to work with his hands. I bet he's amazing in bed."

I choke on my wine and sputter, "Geez, Gwen! Fine. Yes, the man is attractive. No, I haven't thought about it beyond that."

"Cordy," Faye starts gently. "It's been at least three years since you had a decent guy in your life. You've got to start putting yourself back out there."

Faye can be annoyingly intuitive and must've caught the slight tremor in my voice.

"Nope. Nope nope nope. It has been more like six years," Harper cuts in, unapologetically blunt. "Because we don't count Jason. He wasn't a relationship. He was solace."

I roll my eyes, "Jason should count. He was literally the only one—besides you—that was there whenever I needed someone. And he still is."

"I know we weren't there for the beginning," Gwen says softly, "But we've been here through the end of it. And we know you don't like talking about it, but Harper has filled in some pieces over the last couple years."

She reaches across the table and places her hand on mine, giving it a gentle squeeze.

"Cordy, we're not going to sit here and pretend we know how it feels. We can't even imagine. But what happened with Evan... he's the worst kind of guy. Not everyone is like him. There are good ones out there. I mean, I haven't found one, but I refuse to believe they don't exist."

"Gwen is right," Harper says. "Cordelia, you own a wedding venue for crying out loud. You can't tell me you don't believe in happily ever after."

I glance down at my wine glass, slowly twisting it between my fingers. "Look, girls, I appreciate the sentiment, I really do. But I still feel like I can't breathe sometimes. I know it'll take time to heal. And I will put myself back out there... when I think I can handle it."

Harper starts to say something, but thankfully Rita appears at that exact moment, saving me from whatever emotional truth bomb was about to be dropped. She begins passing out different slices of cake to each of us and placing two fresh bottles of wine on the table.

I know I need to move on—to try to let myself feel whole again, and maybe, someday, allow myself to love—but the idea of handing that much of myself over to someone...of giving them any kind of power over me...it terrifies me.

I was a wreck for a long time.

There were moments I'm sure Harper worried I'd hurt myself just to make the pain stop. Not that I ever would, but the feeling of your heart shattering over and over, your lungs desperate for air, your whole body locked in grief, that's a kind of torture no one warns you about. Those months... Hell, I think I single-handedly kept the local liquor store in business with how much I drank, trying to numb the constant ache. I honestly don't know what would've happened if Harper hadn't stepped in, literally throwing a bucket of cold water on me. She made me put my big girl panties on. She reminded me of the dreams I'd talked about since we first met, and of the new dreams that still needed to come true. She shoved me into a shower, ordered food, and put on the first *Sex and the City* movie. We sat there, a bottle of wine between us, crying as we watched Carrie's world fall apart. It took over a year to get to the point that I was at that day. When your world collapses, and you're the only one who can make the necessary decisions, you don't get the luxury of falling apart. Not until it's done. But this? This one is never done.

Once the dust is starting to settle, once there's nothing left but silence and grief, that's when you break.

Harper and I spent a month planning out our next steps. Then we packed up our lives, loaded everything into our Jeeps, and drove to a fresh start. One where I didn't have to worry about people around me knowing my tragic story.

"Oh, the chocolate cheesecake is simply amazing, Rita!" Harper groans through a mouthful of cake, pulling me out of my thoughts.

Chuckling, Rita replies, "Of course, honey, I know it's your favorite. Just like I know the honey lavender cheesecake will be your new favorite." She nods to a slice in front of me with a proud smile. "I've also got a box for each of you in the fridge—three slices each of your favorites. Don't forget to get them before you leave."

Faye takes a bite of the raspberry lemon coconut cake and immediately starts making the most inappropriate sex noises I have ever heard.

"Faye, my God, what is wrong with you?" Gwen asks, laughing.

"If you take a bite of that cassata cake already, you'd understand."

I finally take a bite of mine and let out a loud groan. "Oh my God. This makes that lemon blueberry cheesecake cake feel like ancient history. I want to marry this cake."

"I'm actually scared to even eat this in front of you all after hearing the way you're reacting," Gwen says, eyeing us with mock suspicion.

We all stare at her because we know she still hasn't tried one of Rita's cakes yet.

"Fine! I'll try it. I'm gonna have to try to get two of my walks in tomorrow for this." She raises her fork and takes a bite, and I swear I see her soul leave her body.

"Ohhh! How did I live without this? Can I get more?"

We all burst out laughing.

"Girl, just wait," Harper grins, "This cake thing is just getting started. I cannot wait to see what she makes next."

Chapter Four

DEAN

"If I make this shot, Boss is buying everyone a round!" Ray calls out, lining up a shot he definitely shouldn't be able to make.

The whole room erupts as he sinks the 8 ball into the middle pocket.

"I think I was just hustled," I mutter, rubbing a hand over my face as the guys cheer and fist bump around me.

"If you came out with us more often, you'd know to never play against him," Graham says, slapping me on the back.

"Yeah, yeah. Come help me carry all the beers back over here." I turn towards the bar, and Graham follows.

Music and Margaritas is a favorite around here. The guys love the pool table and they love Max. He can bullshit with these guys all night, and they eat it up.

"Well well, look what the cat dragged in!" Rita says with a grin as she places a second bottle of wine on a tray alongside four slices of what looks like pie cake heaven. "Haven't seen you in a while, Dean. How've you been?"

"Oh not too bad, Rita, and you're looking as beautiful as ever," I say with a wink.

"Flattery won't get you a discount on a full round of beers for that crew," she laughs, "But I can give you a slice of cake."

"What kind do you have there?" I ask, eyeing the purple-swirled cheesecake on the tray.

"Well, I have—""

"Dean Campbell!" Max's voice booms as he walks out of the kitchen. "How you been, son?"

"Dean here just lost a round of pool and now he gotta pay up —with a full round for the guys," Graham adds, chuckling.

"Max will help you get those. I'll bring the cake in a minute," Rita says as she lifts the tray and heads toward the front of the bar.

"Ray?" Max asks, already grabbing glasses.

"Yup," I say, hanging my head in defeat.

"Yeah, he'll do that. Kid's too talented for his own damn good." Max starts filling pints. "Seven drafts, right? You want a tray to carry them all?"

"That would be great, Max. Thanks."

Just as Max places the last beer in the tray, Rita steps behind the bar. "I'm gonna bring over some cake for you boys."

"Thank you, Rita!" Graham calls after her.

I pick up the tray and follow Graham back to the pool tables, where we've claimed a high top table just big enough for all our drinks. The main bar and seating area takes up the whole front of the building, with the bar occupying the majority of the back. Off to the left side, making the area for the customers an almost L shape, is where Max set up the pool tables and dart boards. As the guys grab their beers, Rita sets her tray on top of the now-empty one and starts passing out slices of cake to everyone.

"Is picking out the perfect piece of cake for every person you meet your superpower, Rita?" Graham asks, digging into his chocolate cheesecake. "Cuz, if not, it should be. This is so good."

Rita grins, "Ya know, it just might be." Then she turns to me. "This honey lavender cheesecake is for you, Dean. You'll love it. Promise." With a wink, she grabs the two empty trays and heads back to the bar.

"So, is it her superpower or what?" Graham asks around a mouthful of cheesecake.

I eye the cake skeptically before taking a bite. "Alright, I'm impressed. This is really good. Wow!"

Just as the music drops to a lull, we hear a burst of laughter coming from the front of the bar. I can't see much from where I'm sitting, but Wade clearly can.

"Now that is a table full of gorgeous females," he says, his eyes locked on the front.

All the guys turn to look and all nod in agreement.

"I might have to go introduce myself to that dark-haired one," Wade says with a grin.

I lean over the table to steal a glance—and immediately go still.

It's Cordelia.

I grip my beer tighter, knuckles going white, and clench my jaw. Graham must pick up on the shift in my energy.

"Dude, you good?" He asks quietly. Then, "Shit, is that her? The lady from the wedding venue?"

I push back from the table, focused only on her. I barely register Graham chuckling behind me.

"Wade," he calls, "I don't think you stand a chance with that one."

I don't even remember deciding to move. One moment I'm sitting, the next I'm walking toward their table like I'm being pulled by a magnet.

Cordelia's clearly out with friends. I recognize Harper from the other day. The other two look familiar, but I can't place them. Cordelia looks stunning. Her face is flushed from laughter, her green eyes sparkling. She's in jeans again, but this time with black stiletto knee-high boots and a red one-shoulder sweater. Her long dark waves are down again, falling around her shoulders.

Harper spots me first and gasps audibly, her eyes going wide. That gets the attention of the other two, who turn to look at me with shocked expressions. Then Cordelia turns toward me. Her laughter fades from her rose petal lips, replaced by surprise as her eyes meet mine.

"Dean," she says, barely above a whisper. "What are you doing here?"

"Hi, Cordelia," I say, a smile tugging at the corner of my mouth. "It's nice to see you too."

"Oh, I'm sorry. That was really rude of me," Cordelia says quickly. "I just haven't seen you here before, is all." She glances at her friends, then brings her eyes back to me.

I rest my hands on the edge of their table, right next to hers, "The guys from work dragged me out. We were in the back playing pool, then I saw you over here..." I trail off realizing I have no clue what I'm doing or what I'm even supposed to say to her now.

"Hi, Dean!" Harper chirps, jumping in. "Good to see you again. These are our friends, Faye and Gwen."

"Ladies," I nod in greeting, noticing the smirks on their faces before turning my attention back to Cordelia.

God, this woman couldn't be more perfect if I built her from scratch in a lab.

A soft blush creeps up from her chest to her neck, and I can't look away from her eyes.

Fuck. Think, Dean! I silently scold myself.

"I, uh...I was working on those mockups and realized I never got your email. I was going to give you a call, but it was the end of the day, and I wasn't sure if I was going to be catching you at a bad time." *Jesus, could I sound like more of an idiot?*

"Oh, is everything ok?" she asks, reaching for her purse and rummaging through it.

"Yeah, everything's fine, just wanted to clarify a couple things."

She smiles, handing me a small business card. "Here's my card, it's got both my cell and email."

Our fingers brush as I take it from her, and a jolt shoots up my arm—and straight down to my groin.

No, not now, man, down.

"Perfect," I say, clearing my throat. "I'll send the mockups over to you in the morning if that works?"

"Ya know," Faye cuts in with a sly smile, "if you wanted to meet in person, Cordy is always at Corner Coffee by 8:30 every Saturday morning."

Cordelia shoots her a look sharp enough to cut glass. Faye grins back, completely unfazed.

"Oh really?" I ask, raising a brow. "I'm usually there around seven. Sounds like we've just been missing each other. I'll buy you a coffee tomorrow? We can go over the mockups together?"

I sound way too hopeful.

Cordelia glances down at her hands on the table, then slowly looks back up at me. Her emerald eyes meet mine, soft but uncertain. "Um.. yeah. I can do that. Eight?"

"Sounds perfect. I'll see you tomorrow morning." I tap the table lightly. "Have a good night, ladies."

"Nice to meet you, Dean!" Faye calls after me.

"You too," I say, looking up. Gwen gives me a small wave.

Harper just winks at me, that knowing smirk plastered across her face.

I get back over to the guys, kicking Graham out of his seat before downing the nearly full beer I left at the table.

"Damn, that bad?" he asks.

"I have to go."

"Wait! Did it really go that bad?" Graham asks, pushing me back into the chair before I can escape.

I let out a deep sigh, "No, it didn't. Actually, it didn't go badly at all. I walked over there and had no idea how I got there or what the hell I was even going to say!"

Graham laughs, slapping me on the back. "You were over there for a few minutes. Was it all awkward staring at her, or did you use your big boy words?"

I shoot him a glare. "I made up some bullshit about needing her input on the mockups and not having her email."

Then I drop my head into my hands, shaking it slowly. "She

gave me her card. And her friend—one of them—said she's always at Corner Coffee on Saturdays. We're meeting there at eight tomorrow morning to go over some stuff."

"Wait, I thought you didn't get a chance to start anything for the mockups?"

"Exactly. Which is why I need to leave. Now."

Graham grins. "Good luck, man! You're gonna have a late night. Unless you want help? I've got to leave in the next twenty minutes to relieve the babysitter anyways. I can grab Madison and head over. You know she loves hanging out at your place."

I nod, grateful. "Yeah. I could use a little help digging myself out of this mess. I don't even know how I ended up here."

Graham chuckles, "Go pay your bar tab and say your good-byes. I'll grab Mads and meet you at your place."

I make my way around the table, telling the guys to have a good night and that I'll see them Monday morning. I close out my tab and say goodbye to Max and Rita and head out through the patio intentionally. Because if I see Cordelia again right now, there's no telling what I'll say.

* * *

"I think these are the last two Coronas."

I glance up from saving and closing my laptop to see Graham shutting the fridge and adding lime wedges to our drinks. We've just wrapped up the mockups after three solid hours. I'm pretty sure Madison is passed out on my couch, some teen chick flick still playing in the background.

"You wound me, little brother. Questioning my bachelor-ness like that," I say, linking my fingers behind my head and leaning back in my seat. "I've got two cases in the garage fridge."

"Oh, thank fuck, I was worried for a minute," Graham smirks, handing me a bottle.

I take the beer, sip slowly, and my eyes linger on the bumblebee tattoo on his forearm. I remember exactly when he got it. Madison was almost a year old and never stopped moving. We started calling her our busy bee, and two days later, Graham got that tattoo. It's still the only one he doesn't bother to hide. The rest stay tucked under his shirts and pants. I once asked him why he bothered getting tattoos if he was going to keep them covered. He told me he used to get judgmental looks from preschool and kindergarten teachers—figured it was easier to avoid the conversation.

But lately, I've noticed that's starting to change. Over the last year, he's been rolling his sleeves up more, letting the ink show. A small thing, but it says a lot.

"You're a good dad, Graham, you know that?" I say, voice low. "You got dealt a shit hand, but you stepped up. I just wanted you to know, I'm proud of you. And thank you for your help tonight."

He runs his hand over the ink. "Of course, man. Anytime." He sighs, long and deep. "I know I give you shit about taking over more with the company..."

He trails off for a moment, then continues.

"But I will. I realized something on the drive over, listening to Mads go on about everything. How hard it is doing this alone. You never once complained about stepping into that role for me. I know this company is your baby, and I don't wanna screw it up. You gave up so much for me. And you deserve to have your own life now."

He pauses again, eyes steady on mine.

"I hope... whatever this is with Cordelia? I hope it turns into what you need it to be."

I stare at him for a moment. "Fuck, man. Stepping up for you was never a question. You're my brother. When you're ready, the payroll and schedule are yours to manage. And when that time comes, I'm making you a 50/50 partner."

He looks up, stunned.

"You've got a daughter who's gonna be learning to drive soon, needing her own car, and let's not even talk about college. You need to be prepared."

I sigh, pushing the bottle aside.

"As for Cordelia… I don't know what it's going to be. But I do know what I want it to be."

"Well, fuck, man," Graham mutters, shaking his head. "Didn't know we were gonna get all emotional over here."

I laugh softly, but there's warmth in my chest.

Because for the first time in a long time… it feels like things are finally falling into place.

Chapter Five

CORDELIA

Stepping out of the shower, I check the time—just enough to dry my hair before I need to leave for coffee with Dean and go over the mockups. Thankfully.

Normally, I would throw on yoga pants and twist my hair in a messy bun for my Saturday morning coffee run. But thanks to Faye, I had to get up early and actually care about how I look. Early-morning Saturday coffee now apparently requires effort. I know she means well, pushing me to put myself back out there, encouraging me to look for even the smallest bright spot in my life, and to focus on that. And maybe, she's right. Maybe it's time. But there are so many ways this could go wrong, and I'm just not sure I'm ready.

Everyone heals at a different pace. I know Harper wants me to take the next step—not just moving five states away and coming back to North Carolina after more than twenty years, but actually moving on. Starting again. Feeling something.

Letting out a deep sigh, I shake my head, trying to push the spiraling thoughts away and focus on the task at hand: getting ready for this meeting.

Because that's all this is.

A meeting.

Not a date.

This is most assuredly NOT a date.

Forty-five minutes later, I walk into Corner Coffee. I love the smell of a coffeehouse. Yes, it smells like coffee and tea, but the smell of fresh coffee is like the promise of a new day, a fresh start. When you first walk in the door, you have the counter directly in front of you with the giant chalkboard listing out all the options. To the right, they set up three rows of long high-top tables, all with outlets in them. I've made this spot my cubicle for the day on more than one occasion. To the left are all the two and four-top tables. The left side goes around the counter, to the side where you pick up your made drinks after ordering, and you can't quite see the front door if you sit all the way in the back. Everything is in shades of brown like coffee beans, from the walls to the counter, to the tables and chairs. I try to take a quick glance around past the regulars I see on Saturday mornings, but before I can, I hear Rachel.

"Hey Cordy!"

"Hey, Rachel. How have you been?" I ask with a warm smile.

Rachel's mom is the owner, Jules, while still in high school, she is one of the few teenagers I know who actually enjoys early mornings and helping her mom out on weekends. Just like Brian always did. I mentally shake the thoughts away and focus on what Rachel is saying.

"I'm good! Excited for my senior year to finally be over. I think I convinced Mom to let me road trip to California after graduation with a couple of friends, before we start college."

"That sounds amazing!" I say, heart pinching just slightly. "You'll make so many memories. Trips like that... they stay with you forever. You and the girls will never forget it." I pause. "Just... be careful, okay?"

I try to keep the emotion out of my voice. I try not to think about how Brian and I will never plan another road trip.

Rachel laughs, rolling her eyes and gives a dramatic wave of her hand. "You sound just like my mom." Her laugh still lingers in her voice before asking, "Want your usual?"

"Always, yes, please," I reply, smiling. "And hey, consider taking a self-defense class, maybe even a firearms safety and shooting class. I know, I know, I sound like your mom again. But, Rachel, you really can't be too careful."

She leans across the counter and gently grabs my hand.

"I know. I already talked to Sheriff Murphy about it. He told me about the rules for carrying across state lines, and he's going to help us figure it all out. He's even looking into putting together a self-defense class just for girls."

She lets go of my hand and starts prepping my cinnamon honey latte. "I promise, we want to have fun, but we want to be safe, too."

Her eyes meet mine, full of understanding—and something more. Like maybe she knows a little more than she should. Wouldn't be surprising. High schoolers are more than fluent in social media.

"Good, I'm glad to hear that."

I glance toward the corner of the café as I walk to the end of the counter, where Rachel will bring my drink.

Dean is already here, seated with his iPad set up, eyes locked on me.

"Good morning, Cordelia."

Just the sound of his voice sends a shiver down my spine and heat pooling low in my stomach.

Fuck.

"Hey, Dean. Fancy seeing you here," I say with a smile, walking over to his table.

He actually stands and pulls a chair out for me.

The man stands up.

"Thank you," I murmur as I take the seat. "Very gentlemanly of you."

He flashes me a smile that could short-circuit traffic lights. And my heart does a little tap dance in my chest.

"Of course. My mom always said to treat a lady the way I treat her. Said if I did that, I'd never do the wrong thing."

"She sounds like a smart lady."

"She was," Dean replies, sitting back in his seat.

My heart tugs at the soft ache in his voice. I set my purse down on the table just as Rachel walks up with my latte. I definitely don't miss the fact that he said *was*. Past tense.

"Here ya go!" Rachel says, clearly trying and failing to hide the smirk on her face.

"Thanks, Rach."

"So," Dean says, unlocking his iPad and pulling up the mockups, "I figured we could just get started?"

I know these are just sketches of what my dream might look like, but it's everything I envisioned right there on the screen. He captured it all: the swing, the rose bushes, and he even added climbing roses to the pergola by the river.

I gasp. "Dean!"

He chuckles softly. "Good or bad?"

"It's flawless," I breathe. "Exactly what I imagined down to details I never even said out loud."

Tears prick the corners of my eyes.

"Oh, don't cry," he says quickly, eyes wide with a hint of panic. "I never know what to do when a gorgeous woman is crying."

He looks torn between bolting and wrapping his arm around me.

I laugh through the tears and fan my eyes. "Really, they're happy tears. I promise. I just... wasn't expecting to see everything I've imagined for so long. To see it in front of me, real. Tangible. It makes me believe I could actually have it one day."

I pause to steady my voice.

"I never thought this was going to be a possibility."

Dean smiles gently, then scoots his chair a little closer and leans over his iPad.

"There's one more I want you to see," he says. His voice softens, and there's a flicker of something I can't quite name in his eyes—reverence, maybe. Or something deeper.

"This one is different," he adds. "I had an idea for the pergola, so it's the only one done with color."

He swipes to the next rendering and turns the iPad toward me.

And suddenly, the tears shift.

No longer the happy, joyful tears of moments ago, these are the ones I keep to myself. The kind I hide.

On the screen is the same beautiful riverside landscape... but in front of it stands a striking black pergola, white draping dipping between the slats of the roof like silk. And climbing around the beams: red and gold roses.

Marine Corps red and gold.

I gasp and clap my hands over my mouth. The emotion wells up so fast it steals my breath. I blink furiously, trying to hold it all in. *Not here, not now.*

"If you don't like them—" Dean starts, concern in his voice.

"No!" I cut in quickly. "No, I love them."

I lower my trembling hand, trying to keep my voice steady even as it shakes. "Dean, I can't even.. I don't—It's perfect." I look up, my eyes glassy and full.

"Can we do this? Exactly like this?"

Dean's eyes flick between mine, searching, trying to read what's going through my head. I can see the concern etched in his expression, even if he's trying to play it cool.

He reaches across the table and places his hand gently over mine, giving it a soft squeeze.

"I can absolutely make it look exactly like this."

I glance back at the iPad, the colors still vivid. "Thank you," I say quietly.

Dean leans back slightly but keeps his focus on me. "I don't know where the idea for the colors came from, but while I was designing the plans, this image just popped into my head and... I had to make this one in color." He looks at me again, his voice gentler now. "It just felt like it needed to exist."

Oh, Dean. If you only knew what this meant to me.

But if I stay here much longer, I will lose it.

I clear my throat, "I hate to cut this short, but I just remembered I need to check on something this morning."

He sits back, nodding. "No worries. I'll touch base this week so we can nail down start dates, order materials, and get the timeline figured out."

I rise from my chair and grab my coffee. Dean stands too, because of course he does. He's just that kind of man.

"Thank you," I say again. "And I'm sorry for cutting this short. I really do love it. Really."

I look up at him, locking eyes—his are more green than blue today. I want him to see the truth in mine. To feel how much it means.

"It's fine," he says, a smile forming. "This was kind of a last-minute meeting anyway. It was really good seeing you, Cordelia. I hope you have a good day."

"You too, Dean. Thank you again." I offer him a small smile before turning to leave.

I head straight to Sebastian's. I think this has turned into a Whiskey type of morning.

I park my Jeep and walk through the open bay door. Inside, Sebastian is leaning into the engine bay of an old 70s Challenger.

"Hey, Sebastian."

He turns his head over his shoulder, that signature wide grin stretching across his face. "Hey, Cordy!" He straightens up and grabs a shop rag, wiping his hands before pulling me into a warm hug. Then he pulls back, eyes studying mine.

"You look like you're not here for me," he says softly. "You need Whiskey, don't you?"

I nod once.

"You know where she is, and her keys are in the usual spot."

He tips his head toward the keyboard on the wall, where he keeps all his customers' keys hanging.

"I'll be here when you're done."

"Thanks, Sebastian."

I turn and walk over, grab the keys for Whiskey, and start heading back toward the bay door.

"She's running again," he calls out just as I reach the threshold.

I freeze.

Turning back, I see he's already returned to the engine bay, like he didn't just drop an emotional bomb on me. My heart leaps, and I break into a full sprint—in wedges—across the gravel lot, nearly twisting my ankle twice. But I don't stop. I round the corner and there she is.

"Hey, Whiskey, I missed you."

I run my hand over the hood of the '95 Mustang. Fully restored. Cam. Headers. Matte black vinyl wrap gleaming like liquid shadow under the rising sun.

"I hear you woke up," I whisper.

As soon as I open the door, my eyes linger on the raised EGA embossed under the vinyl in the roof, the giant eagle, globe and anchor. It's subtle, but powerful. I pour myself in and shut the door, the cabin wrapping around me like armor. Fingers trembling, I slide the key into the ignition and grip the steering wheel. I take a deep breath, push in the clutch, and slowly exhale as I turn the key.

She rumbles to life.

"Oh, hey there, girl."

I keep her in neutral and ease off the clutch. She lets out a deep growl. Low, guttural, alive.

"I know you need new tires before we can really let loose, but... can we just sit here for a minute?"

Whiskey answers with another rumble, almost like she understands.

I lean back in the seat, still holding the wheel. Letting the sound wrap around me like a lullaby. A comfort I haven't felt in far too long.

Brian would have loved you so much. You have become everything he wanted you to become and then some.

I smile to myself. And then the tears come. I sit there in Whiskey, fully sobbing, for twenty minutes.

Once my tears finally slow, I shut off the engine and climb out of the car. I close the door gently and rest my head against the roof for a moment, grounding myself in the cool metal and low hum of peace still buzzing in my chest. Then I make my way back inside the shop.

As I come around the corner, I see Sebastian seated in a chair, another one pulled up beside him that I recognize from his office. He's got a beer in hand and tilts the open bottle slightly toward the open chair, in a silent invitation. There's a can of Cayman Jack Margarita waiting beside it. Fresh beads of condensation forming along the cool can. I walk over and practically thunk into the chair, body still heavy from the emotional release. I lean over to grab the can, but before I can open it, Sebastian takes it from me, cracks it open, and hands it back to me. Then he grabs a clean shop rag and hands that over, too.

I must look like a raccoon with mascara streaked down my face. I didn't even think to check the mirror before coming back in.

I wipe at my cheeks and eyes in silence. We stay like that for a minute, in the silence.

"She's running really well," Sebastian finally says, voice low and steady. "Tires'll be here in three days. Honestly, I don't know how you were driving her around with those back tires. They're practically racing slicks. It's dangerous."

I let out a soft sigh, "I know, but... I didn't drive her that much. Never seemed all that important."

I take a long sip from the can, letting the cool, sharp citrus ground me again.

And just like that, I'm remembering how I found Sebastian.

. . .

I had reached out to a couple of Brian's old friends, asking if they knew anyone in the general area. I was willing to drive up to two hours if it meant finding the right person. One of his friends got back to me almost immediately. He said his uncle was a Marine a while back and had opened a shop in his hometown, which just happened to be my new town. The shop specialized in classic cars but worked on everything.

He told me to mention his name and I would be treated like family.

Two days later, I stopped by and asked if I could speak with Sebastian. The woman at the desk smiled and went to get him.

"Hey, I'm Sebastian. What can I do for you, ma'am?" he said as he walked up to the counter.

The 'ma'ams' always got me right in the heartstrings.

"Hi, I'm Cordelia Rivers. Your nephew, Lew, recommended I come see you. I've got a Mustang that probably needs new brakes—and a few other things. She's way overdue for a checkup. Lew spoke really highly of you. Said you would be the best person for the job."

"Yeah, he gave me a call, told me you'd be stopping in." He paused for a second, his voice softening, "Ma'am, please let me tell you—"

I cut him off with a wave of my hand. "Please... don't."

He didn't push. He just nodded like he understood.

Then he came around the counter and offered me his hand, "You got the Mustang with you?"

I took his hand, smiled, and nodded.

From that moment, we fell into an easy rhythm. The kind of friendship that didn't need much explanation. He seemed to understand my reluctance to talk about the big things. But when he saw Whiskey, he knew immediately.

"She was his?"

"She was supposed to be," I said softly. "Everything he ever told

me he wanted her to be, she is. Just not a drift car, I'm not going to be a drift queen anytime soon, and she's too important to risk."

"I assume you've got another car? She's way too nice to be driving in shitty weather."

I nodded.

"Alright then," he said, clapping his hands. "Let's go. I'll drop you off at home and have a little talk with her. She's got stories to tell me."

"Just like that?" I was surprised.

He smiled, "Just like that. You're family."

I ducked my head, blinking back the sudden burn in my eyes. Taking a deep breath, I looked up at him.

"Thank you, Sebastian."

I shake myself out of the memory, glancing at Sebastian.

"Have I ever told you how much it meant to me that I never had to say anything? That you just understood and never brought it up to anyone?" My voice softens. "I don't like it when people look at me differently."

Sebastian turns his head.

"Cordy, I would never. You know that. I'm one of the few people who can even begin to understand... and I know that you needed that. You needed peace when no one else could give it to you. You have that here."

I give him a watery smile and glance past him at the sign on the wall behind the Challenger: 'Could it be that time of the month again? Replace that O2 sensor today!'

"Peace... and extremely raunchy humor."

He grins, that signature I'm-way-too-proud-of-this-joke smile tugging at the corners of his mouth.

"Yeah, you like that one? It's new."

I laugh, wiping a finger beneath my eye. "Yeah. Sounds like something Brian would have said."

Sebastian lifts his bottle and tips it toward me in a quiet toast.

"Semper Fi," he says before knocking back the rest of his beer.

Chapter Six

DEAN

It's been a week since I last saw Cordelia. She's been answering all emails promptly— even enthusiastically—reassuring me that she loves the plans for her venue. But I keep thinking about the look in her eyes when she saw the rendering with the roses. It was like she was staring at a ghost. Even after she said she loved it, her smile never quite reached her eyes. And then she took off so quickly. It's been replaying in my head ever since. I've gone over every word I said, every moment we shared at the table, trying to figure out what I did, or didn't do, that made her react that way.

But I can't.

So I've done the only thing I can do: keep moving forward.

She signed all the documents, so I've started pushing ahead, ordering materials and finalizing logistics. We are set to begin in two weeks, once we wrap up another project. Usually, I'd pull a few guys off current sites to get a head start. But with her business, timing is everything. She made it clear that we can't be on-site during scheduled weddings, and that means we'll need to be in and out with absolute precision. The guys are going to love it; two, maybe even three weeks of short Fridays and guaranteed weekends off.

Right now, I'm just finalizing the flower order with a local lawn and garden company when my phone buzzes.

Graham.

I hit the speaker button as I answer the call. "What do you want at ten a.m. on a Saturday morning?"

"'Hey Graham, how are you today?' Oh, I'm fine, thanks for asking, brother. How are you this fine morning?" I can practically hear the smirk through the speaker.

I roll my eyes, hit send on the flower order email, and close my iPad. "I'm fine. Just finished up the flower order for Cordelia's project."

"Oh! That's excellent. When are we supposed to start? Or... have you already started?"

"You really need to grow up one day. We start in two weeks. You'd know this if you'd actually paid attention at the meeting yesterday morning."

"Sorry about that. Madison was having a fashion emergency, and I had to explain to her that just because someone else is wearing the same outfit doesn't mean I need to leave work and bring her a new one. I literally cannot with this girl. She's not even a teenager yet. It's only going to get worse."

"Lucky for you, I've got a soft spot for my niece."

"Anyways..."

"And there it is."

"There, what is?" Graham asks incredulously.

"I knew this wasn't a 'shoot the shit' phone call. I knew you wanted something."

"Hurtful, brother. I just wanted to say hi and see if you had plans this afternoon."

I sigh, already knowing my Saturday is about to be hijacked. "No plans. Just mowing the lawn and maybe grilling up some steaks later."

"Excellent. I can help with the lawn, and Madison can do the leaf blower. We'll be done in half the time and still have plenty of time to clean up before the boys come over. Lachlan's bringing the steaks, Bast is bringing ice and drinks. I grabbed some pasta salad—"

"I got stuff to make Rice Krispies treats, Uncle Dean!" Madison yells in the background.

I chuckle. I hadn't planned on company, but I can't say no to that kid. And if I'm getting free steaks and cold drinks in exchange for manning the grill? I'm in.

"Sounds like a right good time. When will you two be here?"

"Oh, um ... about that..." Graham trails off—just as I hear my front door creak open and Madison's voice echoing through the house.

"Uncle Dean! Where are you?"

I hit end on the call, laughing, and yell back, "Kitchen, kiddo!"

Madison comes bouncing in, her hair flying in every direction. "Uncle Dean! Can I go in the pool?" she asks as she launches herself into my arms for a hug.

Graham strolls in behind her, bags in hand. "We've gotta help with yard work and make the Rice Krispies treats first. Then you can swim, Mads. Gotta earn it." He shoots her a pointed look as he sets the bags on the counter.

I add, "I just opened the pool up last weekend, so it might still be a little chilly."

Madison pouts, but once I tell her she gets to use the leaf blower, her mood shifts immediately.

I pull out a pot and some butter, and Graham tosses me the marshmallows.

"Get a wooden spoon, and come show your uncle how it's done," I grin at Madison.

Once the Rice Krispies treats are in the fridge to set, we head outside. I show Madison how to use the leaf blower as she's practically vibrating with excitement, and we get to work. We get the yard done in no time.

Before I can tell Madison 'good job,' the girl is cannonballing into the pool.

Graham shakes his head while I laugh, grabbing the last of the tools to put away.

We finish up, grab a couple of drinks, and settle into the chairs around the pool. It's nothing fancy, just a simple above-ground setup, with the deeper end dug into the ground. I built a wooden pool deck around the shallow end last summer, added a couple of barstools, a short staircase, and a small bar along one side. Nothing extravagant, but it does the job.

About two hours later, Lachlan and Bast show up, steaks in hand and a cooler filled with ice and drinks. We grew up with both of them. Lachlan's the local sheriff now, and Bast did fifteen years in the Marine Corps before an injury forced him to retire. He moved back home and opened a mechanic shop of his own, which he still runs today.

"When do you guys wanna eat?" I ask after everyone's settled in around the patio.

"I'm good for a little bit. Maybe start it up in an hour?" Lachlan says, cracking open a Corona and adding a lime before taking a seat.

"I'm good with that," Bast agrees, grabbing his own drink and settling into one of the chairs.

"It's been too long since the four of us sat around and caught up," Lachlan adds. Lachlan has always had an air of sophistication to him, along with the chiseled jaw line that all the ladies love. He's getting a little gray in the temple, more and more in the last couple of years. But his eyes are what really have always gotten the attention, with one that is almost an aquamarine color and the other a warm brown.

"Yeah, seriously," Bast says, taking a long pull from his bottle. "So... anything new with you guys?"

"Well," Graham chimes in, grinning like an idiot. "Dean here has been making googly eyes at his new client for the last week."

"For fuck's sake, Graham, I have not been," I grumble. "I can appreciate a beautiful woman without making googly eyes at her. Go grab me a drink, you little shit."

Laughing, Graham gets up and heads to the cooler. He returns with two drinks, adds limes to both, and slides one across the table to me with a smirk.

"So," Lachlan says, raising a brow, "who's this beautiful woman you're not making googly eyes at?"

"New client. She wanted a quote for some additions to her wedding venue. Owns a place just outside of town—gorgeous property, runs right along the river."

"Cordelia Rivers?" Lachlan asks, tone shifting slightly.

I glance up at him, surprised. "Yeah... how did you know that?"

"Pulled her over not long after she moved here, actually," Lachlan says, leaning back in his chair. "You know that spot where that rockslide wiped out the road a few years ago? Well, the county never got the speed limit sign back up." He shrugs. "She was going a little fast. I let her go, don't worry. It wasn't her fault."

I chuckle, "Always the good guy, huh?"

"It is a heavy burden," he says, nodding solemnly and tipping his bottle toward me before taking a swig. "But I carry it well."

He glances at Bast. "Hey, did I see her Mustang over at your shop the other day?"

Bast is quiet. Too quiet. He's staring at his bottle, slowly turning it between his fingers, like he's lost in thought. That's not like him. Bast is usually steady, clipped, and straight to the point. But now he's unreadable.

What the hell does he know about Cordelia?

"Yeah," he says finally, voice low. "I just had to find a couple of wires some mice decided looked tasty, along with some new tires and a new clutch."

He still doesn't look at me, just keeps spinning that damn bottle like it's going to give him answers.

Interesting.

"I showed her the plans last weekend—all laid out—and when I got to the last one, the only one I did in color... I don't want to say she freaked out, but something definitely shifted. I have no idea why."

I'm watching Bast out of the corner of my eye, waiting for a reaction, but it's Graham who speaks first.

"The one with the red and yellow roses next to the pergola?"

Bast straightens just slightly. Subtle enough that no one would notice unless they were watching him, as I am.

"Yeah, that's the one," I say, answering Graham's question about the red and yellow roses.

Still, Bast says nothing. Just keeps spinning that damn bottle between his fingers.

"Maybe those are just the colors she wanted," Lachlan offers casually. "And she was surprised you picked the same ones?"

"Maybe."

But I don't believe it. Not really.

Graham must sense my unease, because he shifts the conversation in another direction. I sit back, letting the voices around me fade as my thoughts drift.

I've known these guys since before high school. They practically helped me raise Graham. We've never kept secrets from each other, not once. But Bast? He's holding something back. I can feel it in my bones. What that is, I don't know. He knows something about Cordelia. And it's not just knowledge; it's something he's protecting. Or maybe...

Maybe he has feelings for her?

It would track. Bast has always had a thing for beautiful women with strong spirits and good taste in muscle cars. But no, this doesn't feel like that. This silence? It's protective. Like whatever he knows isn't his to share, maybe.

"What do you think, Dean?"

Graham's voice cuts through the fog of my thoughts.

"What do I think about what?" I ask, blinking back to the present.

Graham and Lachlan both laugh.

"See what I mean, Lachlan?" Graham says with a grin. "Dude

is so in his head over this girl. Better make that venue perfect, 'cause I think there's gonna be a need for it in your future."

Before I can tell him where to stick that grin, Madison calls out from the pool.

"Dad, I'm hungry!"

Thank fuck for that girl.

"I'll get the steaks started, Maddy Girl!"

She beams at me. "Thanks, Uncle Dean! You are the best; I don't even care what my dad says about you!"

I head inside, still laughing as I hear Graham sputter and spit his drink out at Madison's latest antics. I start pulling the steaks from the fridge, grabbing seasonings and supplies, when I hear the door creak behind me.

Bast steps in.

He sets his beer down on the counter, placing both hands on either side of it, and stands silent for a beat.

"Red and yellow roses, huh?"

"Yep."

He makes a low noise in his throat—half exhale, half grunt. "You showed her that last Saturday?"

"Yeah," I reply, still working. "We met early for coffee to go over the plans."

"And what made you decide on those colors?"

Ok, this is starting to feel like a prelude to a 'What are your intentions with my daughter?' conversation.

I stop what I'm doing and turn to face him.

"It just came to me, man. I was sketching the plans, and I could see it so clearly in my head, I had to put it on paper. And before you ask, yeah, that's exactly what I told her, too."

Bast lowers his head, sighs, then straightens and takes a swig of his beer.

"That's good." He pauses, then adds, "And before you ask, this isn't my story to tell. Hell, it's not even one she's ever told me. I just know the tip of the iceberg, and I can guess at the rest. But it's 100% hers to tell. I won't be the one to open that door."

He meets my eyes, expression unreadable.

"What I will say is I was probably one of the first friends she made when she got to town. I won't discuss you with her unless she asks, and I won't discuss her with you unless I feel it is something that I can share with you. But if this is something you're actually serious about? Then I've got your back. I'll lend you an ear when you need it. Because you will need it."

His voice drops an octave, steady and solemn.

"You need to be patient with her, Dean. This isn't going to be a short-term thing. If she lets you in, it's for the long haul. So if you're not ready for that, walk away now."

Whoa. What just happened?

I can't remember the last time Bast said this much in one breath. Maybe back when he got out of the Marines and started the shop. That was the only other time he spoke like this— passionate, steady, and deadly serious.

"Bast," I say, meeting his gaze. "I promise you, if she lets me in, I'm in—all the way. I don't know what it is about her, but she's different. I haven't had someone rent space in my head like this in a long time. I don't even know how long, if ever. I'll respect your friendship with her. I won't ask for anything you're not willing to give. I promise."

I hold out my hand, and Bast looks me square in the eye to the point I'm almost starting to squirm with unease. Then he grabs my hand and pulls me in for a hug.

"Good," he mutters, then grabs his beer and heads for the door.

Just before he disappears, I swear I hear him say under his breath—

"She won't survive another broken heart."

Chapter Seven

CORDELIA

It's been four weeks since I met Dean in the coffee shop.

Four weeks of emails and texts about the Glass renovations, and I haven't been able to stop thinking about the way he looked at me when he thought he'd done something wrong with the drawing of the roses. It's been years since I felt anything break through the ice around my heart. Don't get me wrong, watching all the couples exchange vows and promise each other has made a few tears fall. But feeling something? Really feeling it? That hasn't happened in a long time. And now, I'm unsure what to do with this new development. I sure as hell am going to avoid those stormy eyes if it's the last thing I do.

The heart is a tricky thing. No matter how deep the pain goes, it still seems to beat for hope and love, no matter how much you tell yourself you don't deserve it.

I'm sitting in my tiny on-site office—a glorified broom closet tucked inside the art and craft shed—trying to map out the construction schedule. A storm delayed us by two days, and now I'm ensuring the work won't interfere with this weekend's wedding.

"Hmm... if I offer the McRedmonds a $1000 refund since they'll lose some of the grounds for photos during the work, I think the rest will be fine. I know she was looking forward to the river in the background, though..." I let out a frustrated groan. "Ughh! Why did it have to storm?! Everything was lining up so perfectly."

I'm so lost in my own spiraling thoughts, I don't even notice the door opening.

"I can tell my team to knock out the river area first, if that helps you at all."

I whip my head up and immediately lock eyes with him. He's leaning against my door frame with his arms crossed, looking completely at ease.

Those stormy eyes that have haunted my dreams for weeks.

"Dean! I'm sorry, I—"

"Cordelia," he says gently, cutting me off. "You're fine—nothing to be sorry about. You've got a business to run, one that relies heavily on a picture-perfect backdrop. Honestly, the storm was a blessing in disguise. My other team wrapped up early because of it, which means I've got a full crew. We'll make up for the lost time and still hit your deadline."

I just stare at him.

How is it possible that someone who's known me for mere hours can walk in and silence the mental hurricane in my head with a few calm sentences?

"In fact," Dean continues, "I've got the guys scheduled for twelve-hour days. I know you have weddings on Fridays and Saturdays over the next couple of weeks, so we will clear out by Thursday afternoons. The crew's actually pretty pumped—they're looking forward to some three-day weekends. I think this job might end up spoiling them a bit." Dean finishes as he lifts his arm and rubs the back of his neck.

Fuck, that's a nice arm.

"Cordelia?"

"Huh?" I blink, shaking myself out of my daydream about those arms. "Oh my god. I am so sorry. I think my brain short-circuited when you said you'd be able to make up the lost time.

All the planning I've been stressing over just flew out the window."

Dean chuckles as he lowers his arm. "Well, I did make you a promise, and I like to keep those."

I slide my chair back and get up from my desk, "Thank you. It's so important the weddings over the next couple of weeks go smoothly. The business kind of depends on it.' If even one thing goes wrong with a wedding, I cannot even begin to tell you the holy hell a mother of the bride or groom will rain down."

Dean laughs. "Well, we definitely don't want any irate moms storming the venue. I also informed the crew that Thursday afternoons will be primarily dedicated to clean-up and finishing days. I don't want them leaving anything out that could ruin photos or a bride's dress."

I offer Dean a small smile as I walk up to him. "You thought of everything."

He takes a step back to allow me through the doorway. I start heading toward the main doors to take a look at everything when Dean speaks behind me.

"Cordelia, do you have any plans this week or weekend?"

I freeze for a second while my brain registers what he just asked.

"Um, I mean, other than being here and doing payroll, no, no plans," I say as I turn to face him.

Dean meets my gaze. "Would you want to have dinner with me one night?"

This is it.

This is that stupid moment Harper has been saying for years would come. The moment where I have to decide to stay living in the past or try to actually forge some semblance of a real life.

I'm not ready for this, I think to myself. Then I see that look on Brian's face right before he went skydiving flash through my mind—one of pure terror followed by the biggest smile—and I know I have to do this.

"Uh, I think I can make Thursday night work, if that's okay with you?"

"Thursday is perfect." He pauses. "I can pick you up if that's alright?"

"Yeah, that would be fine."

"Great." He smiles, and it's the kind that steals the air right out of my lungs. "I will text you the details. I should get out there and make sure everyone stays on task."

With that, Dean brushes past me and heads outside, leaving me rooted in place, heart pounding and head spinning.

I grab my phone out of my pocket and open my text thread with Harper.

> Me: I finally listened to you.

> Harper: YAY!! Wait. What did I say? I need to document this for future purposes.

> Me: I agreed to a date with Dean this week.

> Harper: *shocked face emoji* OMG *heart eyes emoji*

I can literally hear her squeal in my head. A second later, another text from Harper appears in the group chat.

> Harper: Cordy is going on a date with Dean this week, ladies! You both owe me $10!

> Gwen: Damn it! One week more and you would have owed me!

> Faye: Fuuuck! But YAY!

> Harper: I knew it would happen once they started on the venue. That man wasn't going to wait any longer.

Me: WTF?! Y'all placed bets on my non-existent love life?

Faye: Not like that. It was more about how long Dean would last.

Harper: And how long you would hold out.

Me: I don't like any of you right now

Gwen: Bullshit. You love us.

I roll my eyes and lock my phone, though I can't help the smile tugging at my lips.

Heading back into the office, I start closing my laptop and grabbing my purse. For the first time in weeks, I don't feel like I'm carrying the weight of a thousand wedding details. If Dean really follows through, I can finally stop trying to control every last detail.

As I swing my purse over my shoulder, I hear my phone chime with another text.

"Okay, what now?" I mutter, expecting more texts from the girls.

But it isn't the girls. It's Jason.

I freeze, staring at the screen, unable to open the message. Just seeing his name is enough to send a jolt of emotion coursing through me.

Without opening the message, I shove the phone back into my pocket.

I'm not going to deal with this while I'm here. I don't know what it is going to say, but I'd rather find out once I'm home.

I head out to my Jeep, throw my stuff into the passenger seat, and head to the driver's side when Dean's voice catches me off guard.

"Everything alright?"

I whirl around, startled, "Yeah, uh, just wrapped up everything that required my attention. I've got a couple of errands to run in town."

Dean studies my face, "Alright. I will let you know if anything comes up. Not that I expect anything to."

I nod, already opening the door. He reaches out and gently closes it for me once I'm inside, offering me a warm, easy smile.

I manage a small one in return, starting the engine, and watch him walk back to the crew.

I don't register a single thing on the drive home.

I open the garage when I get home, parking my Jeep in the driveway. Once I'm inside my kitchen, I throw my purse on the counter and take a couple of steadying breaths before opening my phone.

> Jason: Hey Cordy. Rumor has it that I will be back on the East Coast this fall.

I squeeze my eyes shut.

And just like that, he's everywhere.

The flag. The uniforms. The first tearful hug.

Then the unlikely friendship.

The stories. More tears. The grief.

The fateful "I don't want to be alone", the desperation for connection and understanding. Then the images of tattooed arms and Jason above me.

"Fuck!" I yell into the quiet and empty house.

The word echoes off the walls as I slide to the floor, phone still clutched in my hand.

I sit there, knees drawn up, heart breaking all over again. I don't even know how long I've been crying.

I know what he is asking; it's not the underlying offer of a release, but rather the actual offer of being able to see him and not do this over the phone this year.

He knows he has a standing invitation, and he isn't asking for one. He's telling me he will be here this year.

In person.

Finally, I type a reply.

Me: Hey Jason. Thanks for letting me know. Let me know how it plays out.

His reply is immediate.

Jason: You know how it goes. I will let you know once it's for sure.

I sit on the floor for a long time, unmoving. Trying to decide what to do and how, I decided to listen to Harper and say yes to the idea of something new. It would be the same day he texts me.

Me: Jason texted me.

Harper: Fuck.

Harper: What did he say?

Harper: Did you answer him?

Me: He thinks he will be back on the East Coast this year, or so he has heard.

Harper: The fucking odds. The day you agree to a date with the first man since him, he texts you.

Me: It was less than 10 minutes.

Harper: Where are you?

Harper: Never mind, used the stalker app. I will be there in less than 2 minutes.

True to her word, Harper comes flying into the kitchen through the garage door minutes later. Her eyes land on me, still on the floor. Without saying a word, she sinks next to me, wrapping her arms around me. I let it go of all of it. Again. Harper shushes me and holds me while the tears flow.

When I finally calm down, my voice is small. "For one tiny, fragile moment today, I felt like maybe I could breathe without this feeling in my heart. I know it wasn't Jason's fault, but fuck, Harper. It's coming up on five years. For a brief moment, I didn't feel it, and now I feel guilty. I hate this. I hate that this is my life. I hate that everything that makes me feel slightly happy is tinged in guilt."

"Cordelia, you know I love you. You know Brian wouldn't want this for you. I know you hate that saying. But you also know I'm right. He knows you will never forget him. He knows that you still need to have some kind of life. I will never begin to know what you feel, but I can imagine it, and it's terrifying and soul-crushing to even think about, let alone live it." Harper leans back, using a finger to push my forehead until I meet her eyes. "You, Cordelia Rivers, are the literal strongest woman I know, and you deserve to have someone to lean on fully and to share this burden with, in ways that I can't, in the ways that Jason can't. Do NOT feel guilty over doing something you need to do. It is one date, nothing more. Not yet, anyway," she adds with a smirk.

I let out a chuckle that is more a sob than a laugh. "I love you," I whisper.

"I know." Harper places a kiss on my forehead. "Now, you are going to pick yourself up, clean the mascara off under your eyes, and we are gonna go see Gwen and get you a new dress for your date."

She stands and helps me up, shoving me through the kitchen into the bathroom. I clean up the black tear tracks from my face, throw a brush of foundation over my face, and a swipe of mascara over my lashes.

We head out to my car, since Harper ran here from one street over, and swing by her house to get her purse. We get into town a few minutes later and grab a parking spot on the street, waving to Faye as we pass her open front doors before crossing the street to

Scarlet Sage. As we walk in the door, Gwen looks up and smiles, and then all our phones go off.

> Faye: Buying a new dress for the date??

> Me: Harper wouldn't have it any other way.

> Gwen: I'll send you pictures!

> Faye: You better!

After Gwen pulls a couple of new dresses, we all settle on a pretty deep navy blue wrap dress with long sleeves and a shimmer that makes it look like the night sky. It does incredible things for my figure.

> Harper: *picture attached*

> Faye: Perfection! Dean won't be able to keep his hands off you. *winky face*

Chapter Eight

CORDELIA

The rest of the week passes in a blur. Trying to decide how to deal with this situation with Jason since Dean is involved has led me down a rabbit hole of darkness, as it also means trying to explain my life to Dean. Something I don't talk about at all outside of Harper. Granted, Gwen and Faye know because Harper told them, but I don't discuss it. I hate the look people have in their eyes after they find out. When people look at you with that soft, pity-filled expression, it makes you feel more broken than you already are.

Thankfully, running a business and doing payroll have kept me distracted. They help to break up a lot of the self-destructive thoughts I was falling into.

If I'm being honest with myself, Dean has also helped. And by 'helped,' I mean he has had me reaching for the vibrator in my bedside drawer more than I care to admit, especially after last night when he texted me just as I was climbing into bed that he needed my address to pick me up for our date. Now it's all I can do to stop thinking about his ridiculous arms and how that scruff on his face would feel—*Nope, not going there.*

I take a breath and will my hand to stop shaking long enough to get my eyeliner on. Now, I'm not one of those girls who does the whole thick eyeliner and smoky eye thing. No, I prefer the more complicated, yet looks effortless route—simple, winged liquid eyeliner paired with a red lip. Classic. Chic. I get one eye perfect on the first try, but the second one, as usual, requires a little cleaning up with a cotton swab. After applying mascara, I decide to go with something a little less bold. I grab a soft yet bright pink lipstick. Deciding that the pink does, in fact, go well with the navy dress, I give my curled hair a quick finger comb to break up the curls a bit.

"Well, that is as good as it is going to get. Which doesn't look half bad," I say to my reflection.

I flip off the bathroom light as I hear a car pulling up outside. I take a quick peek out the front window and see Dean's truck pulling up. Not his work truck with his logo, no. It's a white 2500 Ram with black trim. I shake my head and laugh to myself. I grab my purse and head to the front door. I'd rather get outside before he can see inside, at all the little details that will cause questions, until I decide to talk to him about, well, everything. I'm locking the door as I hear his door open.

"Wow. You are a vision," Dean runs his hand down his face as I descend the front steps. His eyes locked on me, taking me in.

He's dressed in dark, fitted jeans and a white polo shirt, paired with a nice pair of what appear to be black Doc Martin boots. He did without a hat this time, and his hair is giving Captain America vibes, combed to the side with the front piece falling across his forehead.

"Thank you. You clean up rather well yourself, Dean."

"I notice we have similar tastes in vehicle colors," Dean says with a laugh, motioning between his truck and my Grand Cherokee. Both are white with black trim and details.

"I noticed that as well. Great minds, right?" I say with a smile.

He steps closer, offering his hand. I take it, and he leads me to the passenger side of his truck, opening the door and helping me in before gently closing it.

Once we get on the road, I glance over at him. "So where are we going?"

Dean smiles and flicks his gaze to me, "I was thinking we could try this little Italian place down off Main."

"TJ's?"

"Yeah."

"Oh, I love that one. They have the best garlic bread and house dressing. I wish they would bottle and sell it for home use."

Dean chuckles, "I've only ever had it when Graham, my brother, picks it up and brings it over. Never had it fresh, though."

I shift in my seat, turning slightly to face him more. His hand drops to rest casually on the center console, elbow bent, fingers drumming lightly.

We fall into easy small talk for the rest of the drive. Once we arrive at the restaurant, we are seated at a table in a quiet corner next to the window. We order drinks and salads while we browse the menu. Once we place our main entree order and our salads come out, the conversation flows. The whole time, I'm waiting for the questions that I always tiptoe around. The ones that, even five years later, I still don't know how to answer.

"So how did you and Harper end up here?" Dean finally asks.

"Well, long story short, we came here once on a girls' trip, well, to the Asheville area, and we fell in love with this place. Harper loves the ocean, and knowing that I wanted to open a wedding venue, we both knew that somewhere close to the water would be incredibly expensive. So she relented and agreed to come here. Only a few hours from the ocean, easy for a weekend trip when we can."

I take a drink of my iced tea and continue, "We both... had some things happen in our lives and were ready for a fresh start. We packed up everything, got a moving truck, and trailered her Jeep, Glinda, and drove mine. Which took forever because lifted Jeeps do not like mountains."

"Lifted Jeep?" Dean asks.

"Yeah, you met Aurora, my Grand Cherokee. Harper and I met through the off-road community and Jeeps. She has Glinda, her metallic yellow Wrangler. I have a green Wrangler, Elfie."

"You two named your Jeeps?" Dean asks with a chuckle.

"We did! We named them after seeing the Wicked musical before we ever met. Once we realized our Jeeps were named after best friends, we decided we had to be too. Been friends ever since. She loves doing all kinds of photo shoots with the two of them. Once she got into social media management about six years ago, she insisted that we both dress as our witchy counterparts for a shoot. That was probably one of the best Halloweens we have had in a long time." I have to stop there before more things start spilling out about why it was also the last real Halloween I have had.

Dean smiles, "Sounds like you two have a special bond. I must admit, I have not seen Wicked. I know that Madison, my niece, made my brother see it in the theater when it came out recently. I think I know all the songs from her singing them."

I laugh, "You mean all the songs from the first half."

Dean blinks. "The first half? What do you mean?"

"Yeah, it is split into two movies. The next one comes out this year, late fall, I think."

"Well, I hope you don't take this the wrong way, but I hope for my brother's sake you stick around and maybe take her to see it."

I put my hand over his on the table, "Dean, I kind of own a business here, I think I will be around. Regardless of how things go with us, I would love to take her. Watching someone experience that kind of magic for the first time? That's what it's all about."

Dean places his other hand over mine, and his smile is that heart-stopping one again.

"I know how I want things to go with us, but I'm also thrilled to hear that. I know you haven't met her, but the poor girl just has

Graham and me, and honestly, she could use some women in her life."

The waiter breaks the moment with our meals. Everything is delicious, as I had expected it to be. We keep up the conversation. He tells me about Madison and Graham and growing up here. Just enough is shared about each other to feel like we know each other. At the end of the date, he insists on paying, and when we get to my house, he walks me to the door.

"I'm not going to let you invite me in," Dean says gently. "Just want to make sure you get inside safe and sound."

I unlock my door and turn, offering a smile to him. "Thank you for tonight, Dean. I really had a good time. It was actually really nice to get out of my usual routine for once."

Dean takes my hand and places a kiss on the back of it before leaning in and brushing another one on my cheek. "I really hope to see you again soon, Cordelia," he whispers against my ear before pulling back, and adding, "You get inside and lock the door, ok?"

I nod, words not forming due to the instant shot of desire his lips have sent through me. I turn and step inside, gently closing the door and twisting the lock until I hear the click. I lean my head against the wood, and that's when I hear it. Just barely.

"Good girl," Dean rumbles through the door.

And damn do those words, coming from him, do things to me.

Chapter Nine

DEAN

Me: Is it too soon to plan another date?

Cordelia: No, but aren't you still in my driveway? Why didn't you ask me at the door?

Me: I might be… and I didn't want to seem overly eager.

Cordelia: I think we can plan something. I'd be open to that.

Me: Perfect, I will talk to you tomorrow, Cordelia. Have a good night.

Cordelia: You too, Dean. Let me know when you get home safe.

It's been two and a half days, and all I can think about is Cordelia and her rose scent, the way she looked in her dress, and how much I wish I had kissed her at her door. But I didn't want to come off as overly eager. Now it's Sunday morning, and I have the boys coming over, thanks to Graham. Again.

Me: What time are y'all gonna be here?

Lachlan: I think Graham told us noon?

Graham: Noon.

Graham: I might be over earlier than that. Madison has been talking my ear off about some boy at school, and I swear I can only take so much of her asking if an outfit looks ok, then changing twelve more times, and each time asking if it looks good. I can't deal with a teenager, guys. Please save me.

Lachlan: *laughing emoji*

Graham: Is it too late to put her in an all girls school?

Me: Back to that again, are we?

Bast: How do I always end up back in this group?

Graham: Because this is your life, and I will keep adding you back every time you leave.

Me: You can mute it, dude.

Graham: Don't tell him that!

Chuckling, I put my phone back in my pocket, knowing that Graham will send at least three more messages once he realizes that Bast actually put the group on mute.

I busy myself with cleaning up around the house and pulling

the cover off the hot tub, knowing that Madison will want to use either the hot tub or the pool again today. Once that's done, I grab a couple of beers and head out to the back patio to enjoy the last few minutes of peace before everyone arrives.

I can't help but let my mind wander back to the date the other night. Cordelia had many moments where it seemed as though she had to shake herself out of whatever thought had taken her away, and most of those moments occurred when I asked about her past and her decision to move here. It suggests that something significant happened to her, and she may not have entirely let it go or moved on. I know it's only been one date, but I still want to tear down her walls and get her to let me in. I know a thing or two about dealing with past trauma and how to move on with it. I only realized about ten years ago that everything that happened with our parents was actually trauma. It took watching Graham become a dad and the ways I reacted to it that made me aware. I met with a therapist for about two years and learned how to handle and filter my emotions about our parents.

Bast is the one who pushed me to go. The guy is more attuned with his feelings than most people. I know he went through his fair share during his time in the Marines. I recognize that Cordelia probably has something she is working through and might need someone in her corner. I want to be that person so badly. It's not that I feel like I need to fix it for her. But because I know how it feels not to want to burden those around you by asking for help.

"Fuck it," I say aloud. I pull my phone out and shoot off a quick message to her.

> Me: Hi Cordelia. Just wanted to say hi and see if you'd like to plan another date sometime soon?

I watch for the bubbles to tell me she's typing back after seeing the message be delivered, but before she reads it, I hear, "Uncle Dean? Where you at?"

I shove my phone in my pocket as I stand up, "Out back, Mads!" I call into the house.

Graham and Madison come through the open French doors onto the patio. Madison makes a straight line for me to hug me.

"Oh, she can hug you, but I'm not cool enough for hugs anymore, I guess," Graham says from behind her, exasperated.

I look down at her, and she rolls her eyes. Laughing, I reply, "Well, that's because you're Dad and I'm the cool uncle. Just the natural order of things, brother."

Madison releases her hug and points to the pool with a questioning look. "Yeah, go enjoy it."

"Thank you!" she calls as she runs back inside to change, I would assume.

"So," Graham starts, smirking as he grabs the second beer I'd brought out and pops the cap, "you going to tell me about your date now? Or should I wait until the guys get here and then you only have to give the embarrassing details once?"

Scoffing, I lean back in my chair. "Don't you have something better to do with your life than worry about my love life?"

"Nope, not a thing," he replies instantly, grinning.

"Mm-hmm, so you don't wanna talk about how you are still avoiding Main Street because you don't want to run into a certain shop owner?"

That wipes the smirk right off his face.

We had a small restoration project for a store on Main Street, located next to a boutique, about a year ago. Graham had to run over and let the owner know that we needed to cut into the original brick wall and wanted to ensure there wasn't anything on the wall that could fall due to the vibrations. I still don't know exactly what happened, but Graham came back flustered and had a blush going up his neck to his ears. He still won't tell me what happened.

Before he can stammer out a response, my phone dings. I grab it out of my pocket quickly, knowing damn well this is just going to steer the conversation back to me.

> Cordelia: I would love that. I have nothing going on tonight, but I think you might be busy.

Before I can even formulate a thought, let alone respond, I hear a deep rumble from the front of my house. Graham and I exchange a look, and I head through the doors to go to the front of the house. Just as I open the front door, I spot a black Mustang in the street out front, and Bast is walking away from it.

Bast just smirks as he walks past me into the house. "Hey Graham," he calls out casually, "you and Madison cool dropping me at home later? I didn't drive."

"Yeah, man, we got you." Graham is doing all he can not to start laughing.

That's when I see her, Cordelia, sitting in the driver's seat of the Mustang.

"Hey, Dean!" she calls and waves as she leans over the passenger side.

I jog up to the window and lean in, netting her sparkling green eyes with my own. "So this is how you know what I'm doing tonight? Stalking me now?" I don't really want to make that seem like I want her to be, but damn do I want her to be.

"Not intentionally, I wasn't," she replies with a small smile. "Sebastian called. She was done yesterday, but I had a call off for a wedding and I needed to be on site till late. He offered to bring her over to me if I agreed to give him a ride to where he needed to be. So, here I am. I didn't realize it was your house until we were halfway here."

Don't seem overly eager.

"Do you wanna come in? I'm about to fire up the grill."

"Maybe next time? I just really want to drive her a bit. She's been with Sebastian for a while, and I kinda missed her."

"Maybe this week? Got a free night?"

She looks away and considers with her finger tapping her lips. "Hmmm, I think I could do Tuesday if that works for you?"

YES! Internally, I am pumping my fist, but outwardly, I push myself to remain calm.

"That would be perfect. Six?"

"It's a date."

"It is." I start to push back to standing, "You be careful driving out there tonight. Nothing too crazy."

"Of course." Cordelia smiles. "I'll see you Tuesday."

She throws the Mustang into first, and the moment she shifts her eyes back out the windshield, she guns it, leaving a little bit of burnt rubber in front of my house. I don't know how long I stand there watching her drive off. Eventually, a beer appears in my peripheral vision. I blink, finding Bast standing there.

"Have I ever mentioned that you are my best and most favorite friend in the world?" I ask as I take the beer from him.

"Negative, but I'll be sure to rub that in Graham's face a bit."

"As you should." I chuckle.

ated with a flourish and decorative swirl below.

CORDELIA

A quiet thrill hums through me as I pull away from Dean's, Whiskey's engine purring beneath my hands. *Is it him, or having her back?*

Both, I decide, easing onto the road.

Driving Brian's Mustang is always bittersweet, but I always feel like he's riding shotgun, telling me he can drive her faster, and to punch it because she can handle it. Especially after all the upgrades we made. I nudge Whiskey into a steady roar, grateful for the empty roads stretching past Dean's rural home. I drive further out of town, deciding that I don't want to go home yet. I want to enjoy the last few days of cooler nights before summer gets here. As the trees blur past my windows, taking her into fourth and finally fifth gear. I hit play on my playlist, which I only listen to when I drive her. It's a mix of songs that speak to me and remind me of Brian, as well as a few of his favorites. I slow down and make the turn to head into the winding mountain road leading further from town, just as I Drive Your Truck by Lee Brice starts to play.

The past years have carved deep scars into me—losing a huge and defining part of my life and surviving all that came after that, it reshaped me. It changed me at a fundamental level. Every day, I wrestle to live fully. I know that. I know I hold back in many aspects of my life. Relocating after everything shattered me, especially as change terrifies me now, but having Harper help and be a rock for me is the only reason I was able to do this. I know it was a lot for Harper to uproot, but I'm so thankful she needed to get out of Avon with me.

Not that it was a small town by any means, but I don't think any city would have been big enough for her to make sure her ex would have left her alone and stopped following her. If I had stayed, I would have been clinging to a hollow past.

For over a year, I merely existed, drifting through the motions. Now, I'm trying to do more than just exist; I'm actually trying to live. I know I need to keep going. Maybe I need to take an actual chance on Dean, let him in. Tell him the whole story. Fuck, letting someone inside and see all the dark corners inside, what if he can't handle it? What if he decides I'm too *broken*? I'm not even sure if I could ever let myself feel love again. Evan couldn't handle it, and he saw it all. It still amazes me that people think you can bounce back from these things within months and move on. I know it would be different with Dean; he has more good in his little finger than Evan had throughout his whole soul, but—

Lost in thought, I slam on the brakes around the bend, skidding to a halt as two massive dogs block the road.

I grip the wheel tightly, breath getting caught in my throat.

"Oh, you aren't dogs. You're wolves." I notice the blood smeared across the muzzle of the smaller, lighter, almost silver colored one. The bigger of the two is as black as midnight. I look into the eyes of wolves, and they just stare back. Despite their appearance, they aren't growling, no teeth bared. They just aren't moving, guarding whatever it is they have in the road. Deciding that they probably aren't going to move as they want to protect their prey, I scan around me and realize that the road is wide enough to turn around. I know if someone comes along, though, and no one knows where I am, it could be a perilous situation. I glance over to the steep drop-off to the left of the road, then tap my phone, sending a pin to Sebastian and making a call, putting him on speaker. It rings twice, and he answers.

"Cordelia, are you ok? Something happen to Whiskey?" There's a note of concern, bordering on panic, in his voice.

"Whiskey is fine, at the moment." I let out a small, half-hearted chuckle, "I might be a different story. I sent you a pin drop with my location. Just stay on the phone with me for a minute and I'll explain," I tell him.

"Got the pin drop," Sebastian says, his tone becoming more comforting, "Hey guys, I'll be right back."

"I'm turning around right now. I came around this bend, and there were two massive wolves in the road. They didn't seem all that interested in moving out of the way, as they seemed to have taken something down. It's just this bend and the drop off. I didn't want something to happen, and no one knew I was out here," I explain. "Just stay on the phone with me while I get turned around, ok?"

"Damn, wolves? I hear them out there, here and there, but not enough to think that they might come this close. It's been a while since they showed up around here."

"Yeah, I've heard them once when I was out at Glass, alone and at night. I never did that again."

"You going home after you get out of there? If you wanted to decompress a bit, you can come back over here." He lowers his voice as he says the last bit.

"Is this your way of giving me permission to keep seeing Dean?" I tease him. I ease out of the last part of my three-point turn, glancing in my mirror to see the wolves haven't moved an inch, just watching.

"Yeah, Cordelia, I am."

"Sebastian... I—this is going to sound crazy. But this felt more like a message, not a threat. You know how Brian loved wolves. Do you think...?" I trail off.

Sebastian lets out a heavy sigh. "Short answer, yeah. Long answer, I think you owe this to yourself. You've been too hard on yourself; you think you do a great job of hiding what's going on. But I see it. I can see the emptiness in your eyes when you smile. It takes someone who has seen things and lost people to recognize the darkness in another. Do I think Brian was telling you to stop running? Yeah. And it's about damn time you listened to him. Come back here." Sebastian takes a deep breath before adding, "I also want to make sure you are actually ok."

I don't start driving right away; Bast's words hit me like a punch to the chest. I always knew he had his own demons, but this is the most he has ever admitted out loud.

"Ok," my voice is small as I answer.

"Good. You all turned around now?"

Instead of answering, I hit the gas and fly from first to second to third gear.

Bast chuckles, "I'm going to take that as a yes. See you soon. I'm gonna make Graham move his car. Whiskey doesn't get street parking."

"Thank you, Sebastian. For all of it, the last few years, this, just all of it."

"You never have to thank me." He hangs up the phone, and just like that, I am left to my own thoughts again.

I drive a little slower back out of here after my little wolf encounter, keeping my eyes bouncing between the road in front of me and the sides for more of them, or even something else.

I was a little annoyed for a minute at Sebastian for not telling me that he knew Dean, but I guess it never came up before today, so I let it go pretty quickly. Sebastian mentioned he knew him and was extremely close to him when I was taking him over to Dean's place earlier. He didn't warn me off, but said he may have had "a slightly intimidating" chat with Dean a while back. He apologized if he overstepped, but he didn't want me to be blindsided by the fact that they were friends or that he would stand up for me.

I know everyone always says that they are there for you when devastating things happen. "Anything you need," they promise. "Even if it's just to listen or sit in silence with you." The truth, though? They don't, and they aren't. They mean well, I'm sure, but they don't show up.

The people who stay and actually hold true to those words are the ones who didn't actually tell you they would do it; they just did it. They just show up for you, time after time. Sebastian came into my life after everything happened, and yet he never wavered in being a safe place to land. He is like this older brother I never had, cliché as it sounds. I can get over his protective instincts where I am concerned, since I know it comes from a place of love. He is always looking out for me. He even left work one day and lied to a postal worker about being my actual brother and living with me to sign for a certified letter that I didn't want to miss, which was being delivered while I was in Charlotte picking up some things for Glass from IKEA. He usually lets me set the pace and asks questions when I tell stories, but the questions aren't probing. They are innocuous questions, meant to keep me talking without making it evident that that is what he is doing.

As much as Harper is my best friend, one that I would do anything for, she doesn't bring that up as often. Maybe it's because both Sebastian and Brian were Marines. I know that he is the only one who, in the last four years, has wanted to hear the stories. Who lets me talk about him. I did therapy for a while after, and that was when I realized how much I needed to talk through it all, talk about the memories, and work through it all. To come to terms. Although I may never come to terms with what happened, it is a step in the right direction.

I know that the girls are right, that I shouldn't close myself off to having a real life, but it's so hard to see a future that is so different from the one I should have had. That Brian should have had.

As I near Dean's street, I shake myself out of my thoughts and work on putting on the mask I wear 95% of the time. People treat you so differently when they know the story, and I hate it.

I see Sebastian outside, and true to his word, the gray truck that was in the driveway is in the street now, leaving me a spot in the driveway for Whiskey.

I park in the driveway, engaging the e-brake as Sebastian walks up to me.

"What happened?"

"I was coming around one of the bends, and there were two wolves with bloody faces over what I think was a deer. One was almost silver in color, and the larger one was black as night. They didn't move. They just stared me down, almost like they were telling me I wasn't going the right way. I sound crazy, I know."

Sebastian wraps his arms around me, "Not crazy. Not even a little bit, because that would mean I'm crazy too. I think it was Brian's way of telling you to stop running." He pulled back and looked directly into my eyes. "Cordelia, I've never pushed you, but I'm going to right now. You can't keep running from your life. I won't tell you that he wouldn't want that because I know how much you hate that saying. But you gotta live your life like he lived. He didn't let moments pass him by. He ran at life with his arms wide and wanted to experience it all. Stop punishing yourself for something you had no control over."

A sob breaks from my chest as the realization of what I have been doing for five years crashes over me. I grip his arms so hard I'm sure I would have drawn blood if not for his long sleeves. "I know you're right, I do, but I'm scared. There is so much." I trail off as Dean comes out of his front door. He doesn't seem happy to see Sebastian with his arms around me, but he doesn't come closer, just leans against the post on the front porch, and crosses his arms, letting his gaze drift to the ground.

Sebastian turns to see him, then back to me, "You start by letting someone in." He drops his arms, turns, and walks back inside.

Fucking Marines and their tough love approach.

Dean doesn't move at first, just watches as Sebastian strides into the house before turning back to me. I fiddle with my keys and try to blink the tears back before I take a step toward him.

"Hey, beautiful. Didn't expect you back here, but it is a welcome surprise."

I close the distance and take one step up the front porch stairs. "Yeah, I had a little run-in with a couple of wolves and kinda freaked myself out a bit."

"Let me guess—a really large black one with a smaller, lighter gray one?"

Surprised, I rear back a little, "Yeah, he was almost silver."

Dean uncrosses his arms and offers me a hand, letting a low chuckle out as I place my hand in his, "I named those two Knight and Moon. Original, I know. I've seen them more times than I care to admit. There's something eerie and unsettling about those two. The first time I saw them was two days before my dad died. Then again, when Madison's mom showed up, saying she didn't want her. I saw them again the day before I met you." He tells me this as he guides me up the stairs and through his living room.

"What? Are they bad omens? Cuz they feel like bad omens based on what you just told me."

"No, but given how freakishly long they have been around, I think they are spirit guides of some sort. Trying to warn you or steer you onto the right path. Now, you hungry?"

I offer a small smile, "I could eat."

"Well, come on in. I'll make introductions. You want a beer or iced tea?"

"Iced tea would be great; I won't drink and then drive that car." I stop myself before I say anything else. I know I should tell him about Brian, but this doesn't seem like the right time to get into my grief.

As we approach the sliding doors, I can hear the conversations from outside.

"Hand to God, she tried to pay us in chickens. Live chickens." Everyone is laughing. "I told her if they could hang drywall, we might consider it."

Dean laughs as he steps through the open doors, "Graham, dude, enough about the chicken lady. That was four months ago."

I recognize the sheriff from when he pulled me over a couple of years ago, when he says, "I swear I get calls from her neighbors once a week that the damn rooster got out and I gotta go chase it back into her yard. She really does need to do something about that fence."

Dean steps closer to the table, directing me to a chair he pulls out for me, "Hey, guys, this is Cordelia. Cordelia, this is Graham, my brother, and Lachlan. You already know Bast and Madison; my niece is over there in the hot tub."

I glance at the hot tub and see that Madison is just soaking it all in and hasn't heard a word that was just said. "Hi, everyone." I offer a warm smile and a small wave and take my seat.

"I'll be right back with that tea," Dean says as he jogs back into the house.

Graham adjusts in his seat to turn more toward me before he leans on his elbows on the table and says, "So you're the reason Bast has been giving me shit all day about how he is Dean's favorite."

Sebastian and Lachlan both let out a laugh. I let out a nervous laugh, "Um, I'm not really following, but sure."

"It's because he brought you over here, and you're back here, and now I really won't ever hear the end of this." Graham drops his head to the table.

Dean places a glass of iced tea in front of me and gestures to the food on the table. "I just got done grilling it when you pulled up. You had good timing."

We all get some food, and Madison joins us after a little while as well. The conversation is easy, mostly about my venue, and the guys share stories of growing up and the trouble they all caused.

I hadn't realized how much I missed this feeling—genuine and effortless companionship.

Chapter Eleven

DEAN

I keep glancing at Cordelia next to me as she chats with my friends and brother, noticing how easily she seems to fit here. Not just with the guys, but in my space, in my home, in my life. I love having her here; her presence brings a vibrancy to everything that was previously lacking. This house, my sanctuary yet constant project, suddenly feels... still. I'm not sitting here thinking about the next project; I'm thinking about whether she likes it. If she would want changes. Would she change colors? How would she decorate it? I know I have the bachelor life down, and my house shows that, bare walls, nothing decorative, just functional. Just the basics, couch, TV, tables. It never felt complete. But with her here... it feels complete. Which is crazy, given we haven't known each other all that long. Madison bounces past me into the house, returning a moment later with the bag of stuff to make s'mores.

"Uncle Dean, can you get a fire going, pretty please?" Madison bats her eyelashes and puts all the innocence she can muster into her voice.

I ruffle her hair and stand up, "I can do that for you, I suppose." Then I swing her up and over my shoulder before threatening to throw her into the pool. She squeals and giggles, yelling to put her down.

I toss her into one of the lounge chairs, laughing as I start gathering the kindling and lighter. A few minutes later, I have a good fire going, and Madison is pulling up two chairs next to it. I grab the skewers for the marshmallows and hand them to her. As she walks past, she turns a third chair into her table, laying out the graham crackers and Reese's cups, and placing a marshmallow on each skewer. Thinking she is about to hand me one, I start to lift my hand, but she skips past me and goes right up to Cordelia.

"Do you wanna make a s'more with me? I laid out everything, and Dad says that Reese's make the best s'mores."

A flicker of emotion flashes across Cordelia's face—it was so quick I can't be sure, but it seemed like it was sadness—before she smooths it away and smiles, reaching for the offered marshmallow. "I'd really like that, thank you."

"Wow, what am I? Chopped liver?" Graham leans back in his chair with his arms wide, looking at his daughter like she just ripped his heart out.

"She's a girl. Girls go first." Madison spins on her heel and walks with Cordelia to the two chairs, with the chair turned table in between them.

I go back to the table and take my seat, swiping my beer and taking a drink. I can feel Lachlan and Bast staring at me, but I don't look at them; I focus on the two girls by the fire. She's naturally good with kids, which makes me wonder if she has any or if she wants any. I know I don't at this point in my life. I want a partner to share in the mundane, everyday tasks and to travel with. Fuck, I've always wanted to travel. I've had a passport for fifteen years and never used it once. I want to use it. I need to.

"Is the second date too soon to have the deep conversations?"

Graham scoffs, "You're asking the table of perpetual bachelors that question? I don't think we're qualified."

Bast leans forward in his chair, "No, it isn't. Not if you feel half of what your eyes show when you look at her."

I nod my head as I take another drink, letting Bast's words settle in my chest.

A little while later, after everyone has had a couple of s'mores, Madison's head starts dropping and bouncing back up as she begins to fight sleep. Graham gathers all of their stuff up, and I carry Madison out to the truck as she sleeps.

"She's a good one, Dean. I would suggest that you not fuck this up."

I close the truck door after depositing Madison into her seat and buckling her in. Turning to face Graham, I say softly, "I know she is. Something has drawn me to her from the moment I met her." I sigh. "I can feel that she's holding something back. I want her to open up and talk to me, let me in. I'm hoping that being here tonight might help that."

Graham nods and gives me a hug, "I hope so too, brother. Thanks for carrying Mads out here."

With that, Graham heads around and gets into his truck. I walk back up the porch steps and find Cordelia at the sink washing the plates and my grilling utensils. I get a flash of a future with her and me, cleaning up after parties with our friends, maybe even playful water fights in the kitchen. The kind that leads to us naked on the floor while I worship every inch of her. I shake off the images swirling in my head.

"You don't have to do that."

"I just wanted to help." She continues to clean the last couple of items in the sink, placing them into the dish rack to dry.

I can feel this electricity between us; she has to feel it too. At least I really hope she does.

Before I can say anything else, Bast walks inside. "Graham left when he was supposed to drop me off, didn't he?"

Cordelia giggles, "I get the feeling this isn't the first time that has happened?"

"No, and I doubt it will be the last. Scatterbrained fucker he is."

"I can give you a ride home," Cordelia offers.

"Nah, I got him. We just finished cleaning up outside,"

Lachlan says as he comes inside carrying an armful of empty beer bottles.

The guys say their goodbyes in the front yard, and Bast whispers something to Cordelia when he gives her a hug that makes her smile, but it doesn't quite reach her eyes.

"I guess I should be getting out of here, too. You probably have an early morning tomorrow."

"Cordelia, I would much rather lose sleep because you're here than lose it thinking about you later."

I offer my hand, and when she places her hand in mine, the contact sends a slow burn up my arm. As I guide her back inside from the porch, I realize she's letting me. She's not fighting me. She's letting me lead. Having her in my space all day has brought the feelings that have been steadily growing towards her to a head. I need to make sure she is on the same page; hell, I would be happy to know that she just wants to be around me more.

Once I close the door behind us, I turn to her, not letting go of her hand. I take a small step toward her, closing the distance between us. Her eyes are the most gorgeous shade of green, and this close I can see the little gold flecks in them.

"I really loved having you here tonight," I say, my voice low and rough with emotion. "And I would very much like to kiss you." I lift my free hand up and cup her face, my eyes on her full and pink lips. She leans into it, and her eyelids get heavy for a moment. She doesn't pull away or tell me to stop. I slowly duck down, and when I can feel her let out a small breath against my lips, parting hers, I crash my lips into hers.

Her lips are soft and plump, and she tastes like summer and chocolate. I swipe my tongue against her lips, and she allows me entry. Her whole body melts into mine, closing the remaining distance. I move my hand to the back of her neck, pulling her in tighter as she fists my shirt. When she lets out a small moan, I release her hand I was holding and place it on her lower back, pressing her further into me. Her body fits so perfectly with mine, and I know I will never get enough of this. I also realize that I can't—and won't—push her for more than this.

This is everything I need. I can wait for the rest. The rest of her heart, her soul, her body. When she's ready, I will be here.

I break the kiss and place my forehead against hers, both of us breathing heavily.

"Cordelia." Her name is a whisper on my lips, a prayer of what I want to come.

"I know. I feel it too." She takes a small half step back to look into my eyes. "But, I can't do more. Not yet. I need you to go slowly. Please." The please is so quiet, barely a whisper.

"I will move at a glacial pace if that is what it takes. But I couldn't let you leave tonight without making sure you know where I stand."

She nods and says, "Maybe not that slow, but just patience." Then she rests her head against my chest, and I wrap my arms around her and breathe in the soft scent of roses that clings to her skin. Trying to memorize the way her body feels against mine. I can go slow with her, as long as we keep going forward, but I'm going to savor every second she gives me in this moment that I can.

"Dean?"

"Yeah?" I say as I tuck a lock of hair behind her ear, reveling in the fact that she allows me to touch her.

"Thank you." She swallows and wets her lips before continuing. "I really enjoy spending time with you. And I want to see where this goes. I really do. I'm just..." She trails off, dropping her eyes.

I can feel the tension in her muscles. I don't feel the need to say anything and just let the silence envelope us while she gathers her thoughts.

"I'm just nervous. For a lot of reasons. I've had some... things... happen in my past that have left me rather emotionally scarred. I'm not ready to talk about them right now. But I think I would like to be, sooner rather than later. I've had Harper, but I haven't really had anyone else have my six—um, my back in a long time."

I notice the stumble, and I'm glad she hasn't brought her eyes up to meet mine because she would have noticed that I caught the slip.

Which means, whatever the reason for Bast's protectiveness is, it is probably related to the Marines.

I grab her chin and bring her eyes back up to mine.

"I will not force you to tell me anything—or do anything— that you are not ready to do. I've waited forty-five years for you; I can be patient a little longer. Just promise me one thing, Rosebud."

"Rosebud?" Cordelia asks with a tilt of her head.

"You always smell like roses," I shrug.

Cordelia smiles, "I like that. No one really ever gave me a nickname before. I mean, my friends call me Cordy, but it's not the same thing." She waves a hand, "Sorry, you were asking me something."

"I will give you all the nicknames you will let me give you." *Girlfriend. Fiancée. Wife. Lover. I want them all.* I press a kiss to her forehead. "Promise me that when you are ready, you will let me in? I won't push for it."

She searches my eyes for something, I'm not sure what, but she must find it.

"I can make that promise."

Chapter Twelve

CORDELIA

After saying goodbye to Dean last night, and another lingering kiss before getting in my car, I came home and spent the rest of the night going through both of my rechargeable vibrators. I must have given myself five orgasms throughout the night, all of them ending with Dean's name on my lips. A result of the intense dreams I kept waking up from, all involving Dean. Clearly, my subconscious was more on board with this new development in my life than I was. I finish placing both toys on their respective chargers, then make my bed.

I read something a long time ago, that no matter how you feel, always make your bed. It sets up your day to feel productive because you accomplished something first thing in the morning.

I make my way over to my dresser and grab my workout gear before brushing my teeth and throwing my hair in a high ponytail. I'm filling up my water bottle when Harper texts to make sure we are still doing yoga at her house. I let her know I am leaving my house in a couple of minutes to walk over. I grab my yoga mat and lock my door behind me as I head over.

As I make my way over to Harper's house, I keep replaying the whole evening over and over. Between getting Whiskey back, the wolves—*what the hell even was that?!*—and then dinner with the guys, my brain is in overload from the whole night. I am shaking myself out of it as I start up Harper's front walkway, knowing I need to forget about all of it completely. The girl is like a shark when it scents blood in the water. If she even catches an inkling that something—ANYTHING—happened last night, she will not relent.

Harper throws open her door just as I take the step up, "There you are! Took you long enough—" She stops abruptly, eyes squinting. "There's something different about you." She starts making a circle around me with her finger.

Fuck. I must not have schooled my features as well as I thought I was.

"I don't know what you're talking about," I say as I squeeze past her in the doorway.

Harper has lived in this house for almost a year now. After our brief stay at The Rosewood, we found a small apartment in one of the downtown buildings. Since Faye recommended us to him, he was willing to let us sign a month-to-month lease, as we knew we would be buying a house as soon as one became available. We found my home within the first year. Harper moved in with me and helped with all the bills until her little two-story bungalow popped up on the market a year ago. She moved on it fast and thankfully got it, since it was only one street over. We both wanted to be as close to neighbors as possible.

Her house is a mirror image of mine, steps in front of the door, but to the left. Her upstairs wasn't renovated to have a full bathroom in it, like mine was. Other than that, it's practically the same house. Both of our kitchens have been updated with better cabinets and granite countertops as well.

She hasn't done too much with it yet, but she did set up her living room with all her LED lights and horror movie paraphernalia. Her pride and joy is the table we made together right after she got the house. She wanted to utilize my epoxy resin skills by encasing a bunch of cheap horror movie replica items in her table. I think we spent almost a week mixing and pouring epoxy for this project, but I will say it looks amazing. We put props from all her favorite movies inside. *Halloween, Nightmare on Elm Street, Annabelle, Friday the 13th*, all the greats and classics.

"Cordelia Scarlett Rivers," Harper scolded.

Turning, I throw my arm, not holding my yoga mat out, "Really? The full government name?"

Harper's expression goes blank and yet chilling, "Don't. Lie. To. Me."

"Ok, Snape," I say as I turn and head for her back door to her deck. "Can we please do our yoga session, and then I will fill you in?" I add with a grumble, "You owe me coffee for this."

Harper lets out a squeal and claps her hands together, "Oh, you got it! I will order it for delivery when we start our Savasana, so it will be here when we are done." She grabs her phone from the table in the dining room on the way outside. "What do you want?"

"Cinnamon latte, iced. Since it feels like it's going to be eighty by the time we are done."

"Ok, I just have to hit send." She drops her phone into the grass next to her yoga mat. "Do I get any hints? Does it involve Dean?" Her voice gets all singsong-y when she says his name.

I lay out my mat, taking a cross-legged seat at the top of it, completely ignoring her question, "Stretchy or strength today?"

Harper narrows her eyes at me. "Fine, I will allow the subject change, for now." Harper takes a seat and says, "Stretchy. I think I tweaked something yesterday looking for my yellow bikini."

"The one with the purple polka dots? That's your favorite. What happened?"

"Not a clue. I haven't worn it since last summer, and I knew it was going to be warm today, so I was gonna pull it out last night and sunbathe later, but I can't find it. I checked under my bed, the dresser, my closet, and moved the washer and dryer. Nothing. Zilch. Nada."

That bathing suit is her favorite, as it features her two favorite colors, and she has had it for almost ten years. She takes meticulous care of her clothing, so I can't imagine she would misplace it. I mean, her whole second bedroom is her 'dressing room' because she has so many clothes.

"How did that go missing?" I ask as we begin to settle onto our mats.

"No idea. I can't help but wonder if it got mixed with some other clothes. I'm gonna have to go through all my clothes, and that's gonna take me a week to do."

"Well, I'm here. I can help."

"AFTER you tell me whatever secret you have."

"Yoga and caffeine first, then I will tell you," I promise.

We move through our poses, doing deep stretches for our shoulders, hips, and backs for an hour. As we start to settle into Child's Pose before our Savasana, Harper hits the order button for my coffee. I smile, knowing she has been waiting for this, and I plan to make her wait and drag it out as long as I can. I'm fully aware that I am an evil, evil friend.

Before I can even stand up, Harper starts with her questions. "Sooooo... What happened? And with whom?"

"Funny, I don't see my coffee."

"Ugh, I hate you coffee people. Can't you just be naturally perky in the mornings like me?"

I shoot her a pointed look, "Naturally perky? So you are telling me you didn't take a hit of the devil's lettuce this morning?"

"It is ALL NATURAL!"

"And coffee is made from ground beans. So it's all natural too!"

"Not the way you get it."

"Well, if you had a damn Keurig, it would be!"

"Agree to disagree." She waves me off before picking up her mat and rolling it up.

By the time I get my mat back in its straps to carry it home easier, I see the car pulling up with my coffee. I rush for her door, swinging it open and skipping down the step.

The kid doesn't notice me until I'm almost next to his car, and he startles when he sees me.

"Oh! I'm sorry!" I say with a laugh, "I just really, really need that coffee."

"I should have been paying better attention," the kid says breathlessly as he hands me my coffee.

"Thank you, thank you, thank you! I will make sure she tips you extra since I scared you." I wave as I go back into the house.

Harper is waiting for me as soon as I walk in, leaning against the wall, tapping her fingers against her crossed arms.

I point to my coffee, "You are gonna need to tip him extra, I scared him."

Sighing, she pulls out her phone, taps the screen, and adds to the tip as I take the first sip of the sweet nectar of the gods.

"So did you want help looking for your bikini?" I ask.

"Oh no. No, no, no, no, no. Spill it. Right now." She points to the couch, "Sit down, and spill."

Laughing, I sit down, "Spill what?"

"Cordeila! I know you are going to drag this out as long as you possibly can, but I am putting my foot down." She stomps her foot to try to make her point.

"Are you sure we shouldn't get Faye and Gwen over here first? They are going to want to hear this."

I can see her visibility shaking with her repressed rage.

"Ok!" I laugh, "Ok, I will tell you... Dean definitely knows what he is doing when it comes to kissing."

Harper screams. Not a little lady like scream, a full-bodied scream that will probably get the cops called. "Ohmygodohmygodohmygod!" she exclaims as she jumps onto the couch next to me. "Details. Go. Now."

I back it up to the beginning and go through the whole night, dropping off Sebastian, to the encounter with the wolves, to how I ended back at Dean's house, finally giving her all the details on the kiss.

Harper throws her head back against the couch, "I'm so jealous. I haven't been kissed in three years." She lets out a loud sigh before turning back to me. "So, did you wear out your vibrators? You did, didn't you?"

I can feel my cheeks heat, giving me away.

"Both of them?!"

"Is it getting hot in here? Did you turn the air on yet?"

"YOU DID!" She's doubled over, cackling. "Oh, this is so much better than I had hoped for. So you're seeing him again tomorrow?"

"That is the plan." I'm finishing off my coffee as I ask, "Did you want help looking for that bathing suit while I'm here? I just have to run out to Glass and do another epoxy pour and make sure the AC is working in the craft shed."

"No, no worries. I want to put all the spring stuff into the back and move the summer stuff out of the closet anyway. I'm sure it will turn up. Yoga Wednesday morning again, and then drinks as usual with the girls?"

"It's a date. And I will make you wait until Wednesday night with the girls for the Tuesday details."

I wink as I grab my Yoga mat and dart out her front door, closing it as she yells, "The fuck you will!"

Once I get home, I take a quick shower, opting not to wash my hair until tomorrow and leaving it in a messy bun on top of my head. I reach for my lotion, taking a moment to assess my appearance. I know I don't have the body I had in high school. I have larger hips and stretch marks. Gravity is winning the fight with my boobs as well. But at least all the ink looks good. I have a green and black dragon that stretches from the left side of my mid-back, ending with her tail wrapping around my thigh to almost my knee. Above her, flying high and out of reach, is a smaller red dragon on my right shoulder blade. It is by far the largest tattoo I have gotten, and the single most meaningful. I like them being a little hidden when I want them to be. This piece consistently receives attention in the summer, as it's the only time it truly shines. I have two on my feet, an orca, and a mermaid.

Harper introduced me to her artist, David, about eight years ago, and now he comes down once a year. Spends a day working on her and another on me, in exchange for free room and board while he goes up to Asheville for the art scene there. He actually sells a few paintings and has been hired by a couple of art galleries and coffee shops to do huge murals on their walls. We get extremely cheap tattoo work in exchange for him being allowed to stay with one of us. He is already scheduled to come down the first week in October and paint me a mural on the side of Glass that doesn't have any windows. He's seen the area and knows its wedding venue, but I'm leaving all the details in his hands. Full creative freedom. We are planning to change it every year. Keeps it unique and makes it more fun for the wedding parties, at least I think it will.

I know that if I haven't told Dean the whole story about my past and my life by the time David comes down, I will have to then, since we are tattooing Brian's handwriting across my collarbone.

Or you could just invite him to the Outer Banks and tell him then.

The thought comes out of nowhere.

I finish my routine and throw on minimal makeup before heading to Glass.

Twenty minutes later, I'm pulling into the parking lot, in front of my craft shed, when I see Dean making his way over.

"Hey, Rosebud," he says as he places a hand on my open car door and lowers his head for a quick kiss. "Sorry, I'm not sure of the rules with this, but I couldn't help myself."

I smile. "I'm not complaining."

"Good. So what are you doing up here today?"

"Finishing up an epoxy sign and making sure my AC is on in there. The epoxy won't set properly if it's over roughly seventy-five degrees."

Dean closes my car door for me, and he walks with me. I

unlock the padlock, and we make our way inside. "How is everything going with the crew out here?"

Dean scratches the back of his head, "Do you want the good news or the bad news?"

My face falls. "Only good. I don't want bad news at all."

"We are ahead of schedule. Should be done at the end of this week instead of next. With the single exception of sealing the deck. Technically, we can't do that until it has weathered a bit, so I can take care of that right before it gets too cold out."

"Oh my god! That is great news!" Then I remember the "bad news" he mentioned. "And the bad news?" I ask, peeking up from below my lashes.

Dean closes the distance between us, placing a finger under my chin and lifting my eyes to his. "The bad news is, I won't get to see you on the job site." Then he lowers his head, fusing his lips to mine. I tip my head and grab his shirt at his sides, pulling him closer.

He groans as he deepens the kiss, walking me back until my back is flush with the wall. He tangles his fingers in the pieces of hair that have fallen at the nape of my neck. His other hand is snaking down my side and wrapping around to my lower back, pulling me closer to him. I can feel his hard length pressing against my stomach, and I can't get close enough to him.

I haven't struggled with the physical aspect of having a love life, but the emotional connection is where I always stutter and fail. If he is always going to make me feel like my body is on fire like this when he kisses me, I'm going to have to learn how to let him in and trust that the universe won't deal me yet another shit hand. And with the way my body is reacting to him, I'm starting to rethink my need to take the physical aspect slow.

I lean into the kiss, pressing as much of myself as I can against him, trying to fuse myself to him. I groan into the kiss as Dean tightens his grip on my neck. My brain is short-circuiting the longer the kiss goes on. I can't think about anything but the feel of him against my body and his lips and the way he tastes—like cinnamon and coffee. Considering my favorite coffee is this cinnamon bun-flavored coffee, I'm so here for this.

Dean starts to pull away, and I whimper at the loss of him. Chuckling, he places a small kiss on the corner of my mouth.

"Fuck, Rosebud, you will be the death of me. I could do that all day."

"I might let you," I smirk up at him.

Groaning, Dean takes a step back, putting distance between us. I can't help myself as I lower my eyes and take in the situation he has going on in his pants.

Damn.... I have never been happier about fitted jeans in my life than I am when they don't leave much to the imagination, the way they do on him.

Dean taps my forehead with a finger, "My eyes are up here, darlin'."

I can feel the flush creeping up my neck as I try to stammer out an apology. Which completely catches in my throat when he sucks in a deep breath before shoving his hand down his pants and adjusting himself. *Right. In. Front. Of. Me.*

"I guess I'll allow it this time," he laughs. "I'm gonna get back to work before I decide to lock us in here the rest of the day." He presses a kiss to my hair before turning and striding out of the shed.

I stand there for what feels like an hour, catching my breath and replaying his kiss. I drop my head into my hands with a groan. "Get it together, Cordelia. You are going to break your very expensive toys if you don't," I scold myself. I shake my head and walk over to the AC unit, turning it on. Once it gets running and I can feel the cool air blowing, I turn to my craft table. I pick up the epoxy sign that I worked on yesterday to inspect it and see if it needs any additional work before I finish it today. I decide that it really doesn't need anything else, so I grab some gloves and get to mixing up the last layer.

An hour later, after answering a few emails while I was here, I gather up my stuff, deciding that nothing else needs to be done here today, and I can answer emails from home. I freeze as I start to put my laptop back in my bag and turn to look out the window. I see Dean off by where they are working on the stairs for the second-story deck addition.

Deciding that the view here is going to be much better, I move my chair around so I can see out the window while I work.

A few hours later, I'm so focused on my work that I don't hear the door open.

"You really shouldn't sit with your back to the door," Dean says as I scream and jump.

Clutching my chest, I face him, "You could have knocked!"

He shrugs and laughs, handing me a bag, "I wasn't sure if you brought anything for lunch, so I asked Graham to grab an extra sandwich."

"Oh. Thank you. You didn't have to do that."

"You're welcome." He adds with a shrug, "I just wanted to make sure you are taken care of."

"Here," I start moving my chair so we can use my desk as a table, and gesture to the extra chair.

"So, why did you move your chair to the other side of your desk?" he asks as he takes a seat.

"Oh, ummm, the view outside was better," I answer truthfully.

"Oh, Rosebud, were you checking me out while I was working?"

"Maybe." I can feel my face getting warm. *Does this man live to make me blush?*

"Mmm, I like knowing you are checking me out," he winks as our eyes meet.

Deciding to try to change the subject from something less likely to keep me blushing, I ask, "Are the guys sad about finishing early and losing their three-day weekends?"

Dean pulls out the sandwiches and holds them up; one is chicken salad, and the other is a turkey sandwich. I opt for turkey. "I told them that if we get this done and spotless by noon on

Friday, I'd give them Monday off before I move them to the next job site. Essentially, they get a four-day weekend this weekend. They didn't seem to mind too much."

We settle in and open our sandwiches, and Dean hands me a bag of chips.

"So how about a little game of twenty questions while we eat?" Dean asks.

I finish the bite I took of my sandwich, nodding my head. "Maybe a shorter version? Like five questions each?"

"Alright," Dean says before wiping his face with his napkin. "Favorite color? Mine is blue."

"Mine is green, but I have been loving rose gold a lot lately, too. Do you have any tattoos? I have a few, just haven't been able to see them much. Although with the weather warming up, I'm sure you will see them more." I offer a smile.

"I can think of another way to get you to show me those tattoos." He gives me a sly smirk and lifts one eyebrow. "But as for me, I have a couple, shoulder and thigh. Nothing overly exciting. I copied Graham, and we both have honeybees tattooed for Madison. My thigh is just a cool-looking skull-type design. No meaning or anything really behind it."

"Hmm, I can't wait to see them," I return his smile.

"I like how you think. Okay, next question. Cat or dog person? I think I would be more of a dog person if I had the time."

"Cat person. I used to have a couple of them, but they passed before Harper and I moved here. With starting this place, I haven't had time to get another one." I take a bite of my sandwich while I think about my next question. "Do you like to travel? I love traveling, but again, I haven't had a chance after moving here, unless you count a yearly trip to the Outer Banks. But I love traveling and experiencing new places."

Dean makes a noise in the back of his throat, and I watch his throat work as he swallows his bite. "I haven't traveled, but I have my passport, which sits in a drawer collecting dust, waiting for the chance to use it. I want to see a lot of the world. When Bast came back from the Marines and told us all about the places he saw, the good parts, anyway, it lit a fire for me, wanting to see the world." I can feel my smile slipping thinking about the places Brian wanted to see while he was in the Marines. "What's your favorite place you have been so far? Murph and I took a weekend trip to Nashville once, so I guess I would have to say that by default." Dean shrugs, "Not the most fantastic place, but at least I got out of this state once in my life so far."

Hearing him talk about Nashville brings me back to when I took Brian two weeks before he left for boot camp. He was mesmerized by it all. The people, the buildings, all there was to see and do.

"Oh, I did enjoy Nashville. I went once a few years ago. It was very people-y for me, though. I guess my favorite place that I have seen so far would be a toss between St. Lucia and Alaska. They are so different, but both just stunning in their own unique ways."

Before I can ask my next question, Dean interjects, "Those are pretty far apart. I have always wanted to go to Alaska."

I gasp, saying, "You would love it. The air is so fresh and clean, and everywhere you look, there is something different to see. So, what's your favorite food? Mine is pasta, pizza, or potatoes."

"Probably steak and potatoes for me. I can't help it, I think it's hardwired in us men to love that." Dean laughs as he throws his empty sandwich container back in the bag. "Movie night out, or movie night in? I think I prefer in, better snack options, and usually more comfortable."

"I would agree with that for the same reasons," I answer. "Favorite childhood memory? Mine is when my mom and I lived in Texas, and we would go to Corpus Cristi for Easter breaks. I loved being on the ocean, I guess that's where I got the travel bug from."

"Mine is when my mom used to always make us cupcakes when we got home from the last day of school before summer vacation. She would have cupcakes, lemonade, and ice cream for

Graham and me. Then she would help us set up the sprinkler in the backyard to kick it off. Dad would come home, and we would help grill hamburgers, hot dogs, and corn on the cob. Those were good times." I don't have to look at him to know he is smiling as he talks, you can hear it in his voice. But when I look up I can see the glimmer of sadness that comes from missing people you love that are no longer with us.

I reach over and place my hand on top of his, "You miss them, don't you?"

"Every day. But I know they are still with me, proud of everything Graham and I have done with our lives." Dean sits up a little straighter. "On that note, what's your favorite memory? Mine just might be the day that I met you. Something about the way you looked when you opened that door and stepped out into the sun." Dean twists his hand under mine, wrapping his fingers around my hand and squeezing it.

I look down at our hands, but all I can see is the way Brian was crying, standing there in formation at his graduation. They couldn't move until a family member touched them. That was the single best hug I have ever had in my life. Nothing will top that. That was my proudest moment, seeing him become what he had always wanted to be. His dreams fulfilled. I can feel my eyes start burning with tears as I try to blink and will them away.

Chapter Thirteen

DEAN

"On that note, what's your favorite memory? Mine just might be the day I met you." I adjust my hand so that my fingers wrap around hers and squeeze. "You took my breath away when you walked out those doors. It was like my whole world froze in that moment." My eyes linger on the ring on her right hand that I'm holding, a blue diamond set in a thick rose gold band that twists like vines. Cordelia lets out a small exhale, one that, if you weren't paying attention, you would have missed. I bring my gaze back to her face. Her eyes are closed, and I can tell that she is lost in some memory. And I can't tell if it is a good memory or not.

Running my thumb across the back of her hand, I say, "Hey, it's ok. I'm not sure if it's what I said or the question, but you don't have to say anything."

Cordelia slowly opens her eyes and brings them up to meet mine. Those green eyes are full of tears, and the second she blinks, a tear rolls down her cheek. I wipe it away with my thumb, letting my fingers linger against the soft skin. "You're too damn pretty to be so damn sad." I offer a small smile in the hopes of easing the tension.

"I'm sorry," Cordelia starts, and she pulls her hand out of my grasp and wipes at her eyes. She opens her mouth to say more, but I cut her off before she can.

"You never have to apologize for anything that you feel with me, Cordelia. I know you have something in your past that ripped a hole through you, and I can tell that it is still very much affecting you." I move out of my chair and take a knee next to her. " I'm not going to push you to tell me all your secrets, but I will keep reminding you that you can."

She lets out a shaky breath before responding, "Thank you, Dean."

Not wanting to keep her on the spot, I start to stand, pressing a kiss to her hair as I do. "I'm gonna get back out there and make sure no one has staged a mutiny."

Nodding, she gives me a small smile, "Thank you for lunch."

"You are very welcome. Thank you for being far better company than those guys." I give her a wink before I turn and head out.

Whatever she thought of in that moment was something that was probably equal parts happy and sad, based on her reaction. I keep thinking that if she did lose someone who was in the Marines, it could be so easy to just Google her name, but for some reason, that seems like an invasion of her privacy. So, that is off the table, no matter how much I want to know. I can't betray the trust she has placed in me, not if I want us to be endgame. I keep thinking about that ring on her right hand. She doesn't have a tan line or anything on her left hand, so it has me questioning if it was a husband or a fiancé, and she still wears the ring? Or maybe it isn't even that kind of ring. I know Bast would be a vault on this, so I can't even attempt to get a little bit of information out of him.

I throw myself into my work for the rest of the day to try to distract myself from the puzzle that is Cordelia Rivers.

A few hours later, we are wrapping up the work for the day, and I see Cordelia walking to her car, phone pressed to her ear. I make my way over so that I can at least say goodbye for the day.

"Yes, Mom, I'm fine.... As fine as can be, yeah..." She glances skyward as if she is praying for patience. When she brings her chin back down, her eyes lock on mine. "Look, Mom, I gotta go. The contractor needs to talk to me about the work being done before he leaves for the day... Ok, I know, I know. I love you too, ok, bye." She throws her phone onto her seat through the open door. "Thank you for the save." Then her eyes widen. "Fuck, I'm sorry, Dean. You would probably love to have your mom talking your ear off."

I smile at her, "I would, but I also remember how mothers are. But they mean well."

"She does, but sometimes she can be too much. I thought it would be better once she moved to Alaska three years ago to live out her retirement years, but now she calls every other day to tell me about the moose or bear she saw, and I wake up to texts or pictures of bald eagles almost every day. Especially in the summer when she has twenty-four hours of daylight."

"Wow. Alaska? That is a big move. Impressive."

"Yeah, she's retired, and in the summer months, when it's the tourist season, she works at one of the spots the buses stop at in Fairbanks. Offering directions or answering questions." She lifts a shoulder in a shrug, "She went years ago on a vacation for a couple of weeks, fell in love with the people and the state as a whole, and decided to move a year after she retired."

"I take it sometimes the distance isn't always far enough?"

She lets out a small chuckle, "You said it."

"Well, I'm not going to keep you. I just wanted to say bye before you left. Are you going to be here tomorrow?"

"Tomorrow, no. I'm placing some decoration orders with Gwen at her boutique. She has some good connections for getting me better prices for some stuff, not to mention she has a fantastic eye for this kind of thing."

"Gwen? Would she happen to be the owner of something Sage? I can't remember the name now."

"Yeah, Scarlett Sage. Have you met her?"

"No, but I think Graham has met her before," I say, doing everything I can to mask my amusement over this development, while inside I'm crying with laughter.

Cordelia narrows her eyes at me, letting me know I might not be doing such a good job at hiding it as I think I am. "I feel like there is more to that story."

I let out a bark of laughter, "I will tell you the whole story tomorrow at dinner, if that works for you?"

"Sounds good to me." Cordelia raises on her toes to press a quick kiss to my cheek, but that just won't keep me for the next twenty-four hours. I bring both of my hands up, cupping either side of her face, and dip my head, capturing her lips with mine. When her hands grip my forearms and she lets out a little moan, parting her lips to allow me entry, I step closer to her. I need her body to be closer to mine.

"Sorry," I say when I break the kiss, "I couldn't go until tomorrow night without giving myself something to get me through the rest of today and tomorrow."

Her cheeks have a slight tinge of pink to them when she smiles at me, "You don't have to apologize for kissing me. Ever. I thoroughly enjoy it."

Once I get her in her car and she starts to drive away, I reach down to adjust myself before I turn around. Just as I am pulling my hand back out, I hear the wolf whistles start up.

"Yeah!"

"About time!"

"Fucking finally, brother!" Graham yells.

I hang my head and let out a long sigh. I turn and find Graham and a couple of the guys standing there, tools at their feet, applauding. "Graham, you're in charge. I'm leaving. Get this place cleaned up." I turn and stalk to my truck to head home. I don't even make it out of the parking lot before my phone goes off.

Graham: Dean and Cordelia sitting in a tree....

> Me: What did I ever do to deserve your shitass for my brother?

> Graham: You would be lost without me.

> Graham: Also, don't use my words against me. Get your own lines.

> Me: * middle finger emoji *

I drop my phone into the cup holder before continuing my drive home.

The rest of my evening and the next day passed quickly, thankfully.

All I want is to see Cordelia again.

"Hey, Graham!" I yell making my way across the parking lot to my truck and open the door at the end of the day.

Graham jogs over. "What's up?"

"Just wanted to make sure you are on top of everything tomorrow morning. I might be late."

"Got your second date tonight, don't you?"

"Yeah."

"Not a problem. I got everything under control. You could take the day if you wanted to."

I shake my head, "No, I want to be here to make sure everything gets done this week, like I promised I would."

Graham crosses his arms, "And you don't think I'm capable of doing that?"

"I didn't say that, I'm just going to be a control freak with this until it's done. I don't want to screw anything up for her."

Graham assesses me, "I get it, I do. But you can trust me. If you're here, you're here. If not, then I got it. Don't stress about it."

"Thank you, little bro." I close the door and wave as I take off.

Once I get home, I see that a package is by my front door, so I swipe it up before I head inside through the garage. Once I get in the kitchen, I take the knife out of my pocket and slice open the package, finding it's the cologne I ordered. I went to use it before our first date and realized that Graham must have never given it back when he borrowed it for parent-teacher conference night a couple of months ago. My house was on his way from a site where we got stuck late, and he didn't want to smell awful, so he changed his shirt and grabbed the bottle. I hardly ever use it, so I never noticed. I take the bottle with me, speed through a quick shower, and get dressed so that I won't be late picking up Cordelia. I opt to keep it casual with nice jeans, boots, and a light green Under Armour collared shirt. I put one spray of my cologne on before walking out the door.

When I get to Cordelia's, she once again comes out the front door and locks it behind her when I pull in the driveway. I'm starting to wonder if she doesn't want me in her house.

I leave the truck running, opening my door to get out because she won't open a car door when I'm around if I have anything to do with it. Once I'm out of my truck, I get my first full look at her. She's got on another dress, but this one is a little shorter than the last one, and every step she takes, it flutters, and I can see glimpses of a tattoo wrapping around her thigh. My eyes travel up, and the black dress is cinched at her waist with a deep V neckline, showing me the valley between her breasts that I want to run my tongue up. I force my eyes up to her lips that are a siren red with her eyes done in that impressive eyeliner trick that Madison calls 'winged' and caused a meltdown when she couldn't get it right two months ago. And her hair is done in loose, glossy waves that fall over her shoulders.

My heart stops. It physically stops. I bring my hand to my chest because I think I might have a heart attack. I have never seen a more gorgeous sight in my life than how she looks coming down the stairs right now. My eyes travel down to her gold strappy heels and back up to her red lips again before I can form words.

"Cordelia," I manage to get out breathlessly. I rub my hand over the spot on my chest, trying to calm my body down. "You look absolutely stunning."

"Thank you," she says as a blush creeps up her neck. "You don't think it's too much?"

"Not at all," I say as I take her hands to pull her into me. Raising an eyebrow, I continue, "But if I kiss you the way I want to right now, how bad will that be for you?"

"Not as bad as it will be for you. It's a lip stain with a gloss over it. So as long as you don't mind some shi—"

I cut her off by pressing my lips to hers, pulling her body into mine, claiming her, demanding entry that she allows as she molds her body to mine. She whimpers as I deepen the kiss even further, and my hand lowers to her perfect ass to press her into my growing erection so she can feel what she does to me.

"Dean," she says on a sigh, and fuck if I can't let her go yet. Now I'm imagining her saying that while she's under me, in my bed. I keep my hand on her ass, pressing her into me, and my other hand grips the back of her neck, pulling her into me. I finally pull back after what feels like barely a moment, and it is not nearly long enough.

"Fuck, Rosebud, you drive me crazy."

She smiles up at me, lips still red, but they shine with my kiss and not the gloss that was over them. She's flushed, and I messed up her hair a bit from the way I was gripping her. And somehow it makes her look even sexier.

Suddenly, something changes in her eyes. She pulls back a little bit. "Dean, are you wearing cologne?" She immediately backpedals, "Not that it's bad, you just don't smell like you. You usually have a woody pine scent about you."

"Yeah, I normally only wear it for special occasions. Graham stole my last bottle, and I never realized it until I didn't have it for our last date and had to order another bottle of it. Do you not like it?"

She closes her eyes for a long second and softly smiles before she opens them. "I do like it... umm.. Is that Sauvage by Dior?"

I chuckle, "I think so? I'm not sure. I just know that it is in a blue bottle."

She laughs further, asking, "Is it the one that Johnny Depp did the commercials for?"

"Yeah, I think so actually."

"I thought so." She offers me a small smile.

"Why do you ask?"

"Oh, just a favorite of mine." She waves it off, but I can see that something is going on in her head over this.

I walk her over to the passenger side of my truck and open the door, helping her inside. Once she's seated, I close the door and get in the driver's seat.

"So, I was thinking we could grab a quick pre-dinner drink at Music and then I have a special surprise for dinner."

"That sounds like a great plan to me." Cordelia smiles, and I grab her hand, lacing our fingers together on the center console.

We fall into easy conversation, mostly about how our days went, on the drive into town. Once we arrive at Music and Margaritas, I notice the quietest table, which sits on its own in a corner, is open. Wanting to have Cordelia all to myself, I lead us over to it. Pulling her chair out, I ask, "Do you want a glass of wine or something else?"

"I would love a glass of the rosè. If Rita or Max are at the bar, they will know which one, thank you."

"I'll be right back," I say as I place a kiss on her lips.

Making my way up to the bar, I see Max behind the bar, thankful that they are here so I can ensure I get the right wine for her.

"Hey, Max! How's it going?"

"Dean, son, good to see you. Can't complain. I don't have to ask how you are." Max raises an eyebrow and gestures toward Cordelia.

"Yeah, having that woman with me is making life so much better lately," I smile.

"You treat her right, or you're gonna have to answer to Rita. And you know that means she will probably ban you from here for a very long time. She loves that girl something fierce." He gives me a stern look before smiling and adding, "But I know you will, so there's nothing to worry about. What do you two want to drink?"

"I will take a beer, and Cordelia said to tell you she wanted a rosè, and that you would know which one?" I say with a question mark at the end.

"You got it." Max reaches into the cooler, pulls out a Modelo, and pops the cap before sliding it across the bar. He turns to the wine fridge and grabs a bottle, pouring it into a glass and sliding that to me as well. "You want to start a tab?"

"Nah, just these. We have dinner plans after this," I say as I throw a twenty onto the bar top. I don't wait for the change, grab the drinks, and head back to the table.

I place the wine glass in front of Cordelia and take my seat across from her.

Holding up her glass, she says, "Ziveli!"

I chuckle and clink my bottle to her glass, repeating the phrase. After taking a sip, I say, "I see Max and Rita taught you the proper Croatian way to cheers."

"Yeah, I think Rita taught Harper and me our first time here. Those two are great, kind of like the cool aunt and uncle you always wanted."

I can't help but agree with her. If they take you in, they do it with their whole hearts. Some of the best people I have ever known.

"So, I have to ask since you promised to tell me tonight. What's the story with Graham and Gwen? I know there is a story there, and I want the outsider's story before I ask Gwen about it."

Cordelia gives me a mischievous smile before taking a sip of her wine.

I take a deep breath followed by a drink before I answer her. "Well, it's actually not too much to tell. But I always wondered... We had a job for the store next door to her shop. We needed to cut into the original brickwork, and Graham, being the nice guy he is, went next door to let the store owner know and maybe prevent any damage the vibrations would cause. He never told me exactly what happened, but all I know is he was over there for longer than it would take to just deliver a message, and he came back flushed from his neck to the tips of his ears. He wouldn't say anything either. Just ignored me and got back to work. So I know something happened between them, but I don't know what. In case you haven't noticed, Graham doesn't really shut up." I laugh before taking another drink.

"When did this happen?"

"About a year ago, why?"

Cordelia taps her finger to her lips, thinking, "I don't remember her saying anything about that. I'm going to have to ask her tomorrow."

We chat a little more while we finish our drinks before I take her hand and lead her back out to the truck. I picked up some items last night and threw together a picnic dinner, complete with wine. I have two blankets in the backseat and a couple of pillows. I'm thankful for the clear sky, as we are going to enjoy dinner under the stars.

I'm a hopeless romantic, and typically, I keep it on lockdown because the guys would never let me hear the end of it. No one was ever enough to make me want to be this way with them before, either, not until her. The second I met her, it was a lightning strike to my system, and I only want to do whatever it takes to make her happy and keep her. There's something about her that makes me want to throw her over my shoulder, lock her in my house, and tell her she's mine. Yet I know that if I want to earn all her trust, that won't be the right way to go about it. I'm really hoping that I can start to crack those walls she has up tonight.

Once we are back on the road, Cordelia asks, "So what is the plan for dinner?"

"Well, that would ruin the surprise if I told you instead of showing you."

She sits back with an oomph.

I laugh, "No pouting. I promise you will like it. At least I hope you will."

Once again, I intertwine our fingers together, and we make the rest of the drive. We are actually not far from her venue when I pull off onto a dirt road that, unless you know about it, you would drive by and miss. I slow the truck and switch it over to Four Wheel Drive, knowing we had some rain recently.

"So, is this the part where you tell me you're really an axe murderer or something?"

"I'm not taking you out into the woods to do anything you don't want me to do. I just thought a nice quiet evening under the stars might be... romantic. Just wait till you see the spot up here. I think you will agree with me." I raise her hand to my lips and press a kiss to her skin.

We bounce along the road a little way further until we reach the meadow. I park in the center, hopping out and telling her to give me a moment before she gets out. I don't want her ruining her shoes. I grab the blankets and pillows from the back and lay them out in the bed of the truck. I open her door and pull her out bridal-style, carrying her to the tailgate and setting her down, telling her to get comfortable. Then I grab the basket and hop into the bed of the truck with her.

"Dean, this is gorgeous." Her head is tilted back and she's looking at the stars. All I can see is her.

"It really is." I never take my eyes from her, and when she looks at me, I can see a blush across her face as she realizes I was talking about her and not the sky. I grab the basket and pull out the bottle of wine, the cheese, crackers, and grapes to start. I pour us each a glass before I pull out the rest of the deconstructed charcuterie board that I made.

"Dean, did you make a charcuterie board for dinner?" she asks with a smile in her voice.

"I might have had a little bird suggest this." I shrug.

"Is that little birdie maybe barely five feet tall with blonde hair?"

"Nope, that little birdie would be over six feet and with dark hair."

"You mean Sebastian?" she asks, her eyes wide in shock.

"Yeah, he may have mentioned something." The truth is, I grilled him about what would be a good idea for tonight that wasn't actually going out in public. I wanted her all for myself tonight.

We stay in a comfortable silence for a little while, eating and sipping our wine. I start pointing out the few constellations that I know, and when Cordelia shifts closer to me to lean against me while looking where I'm pointing in the sky, I know I made the right choice coming out here.

" I found this place one day when I missed a client's driveway and had to turn around. The road was too narrow, so I had to follow it all the way to here. I knew I was going to be back out here after that, and I have been. Quite a lot, actually. I usually come out here when I need a break from everything or when I want the world to fall away for a little while." I adjust my seat so I'm leaning against the back of the truck bed, against the back glass, and pull her in between my legs with her head on my shoulder. "I knew I needed to bring the most gorgeous woman I've ever met out here."

I look down and meet her eyes. Her eyes bounce between mine and my lips. I tip my head down and press my lips into hers. She reaches her hand up to grip the back of my neck, pulling me in closer. I don't ever want to let her go. I love the way she feels in my arms. The feel of her lips against mine. The way her hair feels as the wind causes it to tickle against my neck. There isn't a single thing that I don't like about her. And every time I kiss her, I can feel myself slipping more and more. I'm so gone for her. I would give her anything she asked of me.

She breaks the kiss before I would have liked, but she sits up and turns to straddle my legs in that short dress, causing the bottom to settle high on her legs, revealing more of her tattoo that wraps around her upper thigh. A dragon tail, maybe? With no one out here but us, I don't care at all; in fact, it might be the sexiest thing I have ever witnessed. She brings her lips back down to mine, and I wrap an arm around her waist and my other hand up the back of her neck into her hair, gripping it to pull her closer to me. She lets out a moan into my mouth, and it goes straight to my dick. I can feel it starting to strain against my zipper, and against her. I know when she feels it, too, because she rocks ever so slightly against me, pulling another moan from her and a sharp inhale from me. I can feel the heat from her pussy against my dick with every little movement she makes against it.

"Fuck, Rosebud, I don't know what you are doing to me, but if you grind down on me again, you're gonna make me come in my pants."

She gets an evil glint in her eye and does it again, slower. Painfully slower. Without breaking eye contact. I put my head into the space between her neck and her shoulder, biting down and pressing her into me.

"You are a naughty little thing," I say. "It is taking every ounce of control that I have not to lay you down right here, strip this dress from your perfect body, and make you come on my cock until you forget your own name."

"Oh, if that's your idea of a threat, I might have to do it again," she purrs as she starts to lift herself to grind down on me again. Before she can complete her movement, I twist us until I have her on her back underneath me.

"I won't make our first time be in the bed of my truck in the middle of a field where anyone could walk up on us." I press her hands above her head, holding her in place below me. "The first time I take you, it will be in a bed where I can spend hours upon hours worshiping every inch of your body." I press kisses from the hollow of her neck and lower until I know I could easily nudge the neckline of her dress to the side and it would reveal everything to me.

But I don't. Not here. I want the first one to be perfect, to leave no room for doubt in my feelings for her. I press a kiss to each of her breasts, right where her dress covers her. I can feel her body tremble.

"Dean," she moans my name, and I have to pull away because I am less than a second from coming in my pants. Before I can pull away any further, she adds, "Take me home, Dean."

"Are you sure? I don't want you to do anything you aren't ready for."

"If you wanted to put your hand under my dress and see how ready and willing and needy I am for you, you wouldn't question me. Dean, please take me home and make me forget everything but your name."

Fuck. Me.

How can I say no to that?

Chapter Fourteen

CORDELIA

The second the words leave my mouth, I know I'm making the right choice. I know I wanted to go slow, but it has been so goddamn long, and the fact that I have a man who looks at me like he does, and makes me feel things again, *fuck*. He makes me feel. I have closed so much of myself off over the years; this is almost a new feeling. I forgot how good it feels just to feel again. I keep pushing the lingering thoughts of second-guessing myself out of my head, and instead, I focus on how my body is reacting to him.

Dean makes quick work of sitting me up and carrying me back to the passenger seat of the truck. Once he sets me down, he reaches over me, buckling me into the seat. I turn to watch him grab the basket and blankets from the back of the truck, and he tosses them into the backseat before he climbs back in.

The silence over the first few minutes is almost too much. I keep trying to slow my heart down, but I can't. Butterflies in my stomach are threatening to riot the closer we get to town. I'm questioning my decision, not because I don't want this, because I really, really do, but with him driving, I know this means going back to my house, and I'm trying to remember if I closed my office door. I'm in no way ready to delve into my past with him.

Which means he cannot see into it. I usually keep it closed when people are over, and I cannot for the life of me remember if I closed it earlier today. Thankfully, my bedroom is the opposite way and upstairs, so there shouldn't be any reason for him to be in the hallway to my office.

Despite the constant worry in my head, my body isn't letting me forget about my current state either. I can't stop pressing my thighs together, and honestly, I don't know how long I can last sitting here without him touching me. Deciding to try to distract myself from the heat that is pooling low in my core and the way I can't stop clenching on nothing, I break the silence. "Are we going to your house or mine?"

Dean glances at me, and at the same time, I shift my thighs together. He smirks as he answers, "Well, your house is a little closer, and judging by the way you keep fidgeting in your seat, I would guess that I need to get you out of that dress sooner than later, am I right?"

I tilt my head back against the seat, "Well, you're not wrong." I turn my head toward him and add, "Does this truck go any faster?"

"We are only about five minutes away," Dean answers as he reaches over the console and grabs my thigh. The heat from his hand sears into me, amplifying the way my body is reacting to him.

I let out a groan as his hand inches up higher on my leg, reaching the hem of my skirt. But he doesn't go higher, he just tightens his grip. As he slows to a stop at the one light we have to sit through between where we are and my house, his hand slides between my thighs, not going higher, just forcing his hand between my legs and gripping me tightly.

"Almost there, Rosebud. And then I plan to slowly strip that dress off of you and take my time learning and memorizing every inch of your perfect body. All night long." His voice is deeper, rougher, and drips with sexual tension that I now know he is feeling too. I glance at him as the light changes, and his gaze drifts back to the road and away from me, letting my gaze fall lower. The bulge in his jeans looks like it wants to break his zipper, given the way the fabric is stretched, and I swear that when he goes under the streetlight, I can see a wet spot. I tear my eyes away before he notices and squeeze his wrist that I'm holding.

Was that wet spot from him or me?

A couple of minutes and two turns later, he's pulling into my driveway, and I reach for the door handle, opening the door and hopping out of the truck. I'm rounding the front of his truck when Dean blocks my path. "I should punish you for opening the door without me." His eyes are dark, and he crowds into me.

"Punish me?" I ask a little hesitantly.

"Yes." That's all he says as he throws me over his shoulder, causing my dress to rise dangerously high on the backs of my legs and ass. Carrying me to the door, he demands, "Keys," as he holds out his other hand to his side. I fumble with my purse and drop the keys into his hand.

"It's the rose key," I say as I try to wiggle out of his grasp.

I hear the keys go in the lock and then the click, and when the door opens, he smacks my ass, making me go still. He strides inside, slams the door, and locks it.

"Bedroom?" he asks as he starts making his way through my living room to the hallway.

"Upstairs."

He walks straight up the stairs inside the door into my bedroom, where he tosses me onto the bed.

He stares at me like he wants to devour all of me and he's deciding where to start. I toss my purse from my hand onto the floor next to the bed, never breaking my gaze from his smoldering stare.

"Fuck, Cordelia, you are the most beautiful woman I have ever seen. I don't want to rush this. I want to take my time, explore every inch of you."

I shift nervously. The last person to see all of me was Jason, and he knew all the details that went into this body. All I can think about is what Dean is going to think. He doesn't know that I have stretch marks, and gravity has taken a toll on my breasts. What if he doesn't like what he sees? He's easily the most handsome man I have ever been with, and the thought of not living up to his standards or expectations is terrifying.

"Hey," he says as he crawls over me on the bed, "where did you just go in your head?"

I lower my eyes from his, trying to find the words and go for the easiest explanation. "It's been a little while since I've done this. I think I'm just nervous about..." I trail off, hoping he understands without me having to say it.

He pinches my chin, bringing my eyes up to his. "We don't have to do this tonight. I don't want you to think that all I care about is getting the chance to fuck this perfect body. If you're worried that I may not like something, I can assure you that there is not a single part of your body that I won't like. You have the most amazing curves." His fingers drop from my chin and trail down my neck, over my collar bone, down between my breasts, pausing when he says, "I haven't stopped fantasizing about what these would feel like in my hands." His eyes flick up to mine, asking a silent question. I arch my back, pushing my chest out in a silent answer. His hand slowly pushes the fabric back, and when he realizes that I didn't wear a bra, his eyes land on my fully exposed breast, and he lets out a groan. I've always been a little self-conscious about the size of my areolas, but the way he licks his lips before he cups my breast and brings it to his mouth tells me he likes what he sees. When his tongue licks over my nipple and he starts to suck the peak into his mouth, I could almost come right on the spot.

I let out a moan, and my hand goes to his hair, pulling him closer. Demanding more. More suction, more bites, more everything. When he notices my reaction, he gives me exactly what I want. "Fuck, Dean, oh my god." I'm whimpering with need. I need him everywhere. I can't remember the last time I felt this way. He is awakening a side of myself that I thought died a long time ago. It was never like this with Jason. That was more about strictly scratching an itch for us. This is so much more. It feels like so much more.

It feels like the start of something that mere words won't define, but actions and emotions.

He releases my nipple with a pop, and his hand slides into my hair, pulling my mouth to his. Our kiss is full of desperation, and suddenly, there are too many clothes between us. I reach for the bottom of his shirt and start to lift it. He pulls away and rips his shirt off, throwing it to the floor, and all I can see is muscle. They're not defined, ripped muscles, but he's hard everywhere. He has the body of a man who works hard and gets his muscles from his work. You can see the muscles moving under his skin, and given the way he was able to throw me over his shoulder like I weigh nothing, it tells me that he uses his muscles every day, and they aren't for show.

I run my hand down his chest, stopping just above his belt. I look up at him, and he's watching me, taking in all my movements. I start to fiddle with his belt, trying to unhook it when he places my hand over his, stopping my attempt. I look at him, questioning why he stopped me.

"Tell me you want this, tell me you want me. I don't want you to do something you aren't comfortable with."

"Dean, please fuck me. I need you. If you don't give me what I want, I will probably break my vibrator tonight trying to imagine what this would have been like." I take a breath, lick my lips, and whisper, "I want *you*."

Dean growls as he stands up and rips his belt off, popping the button and then lowering his zipper. He steps out of his pants and grips the bottom of my dress. "Lift your ass, Rosebud, I need to see all of you right now."

Bracing myself on my hands, I lift myself as he drags the material up and over me, dropping back down. I raise up on my hands, and he pulls the dress over my head. He sucks in a breath and stares at me as I recline back on my elbows. I start to bring my foot up to remove my heels, and Dean places a hand over my ankle. "Leave these on. I want these wrapped around my waist." I nod and slowly lean back as he cages me in. Scooting up the bed, he moves with me and presses a kiss to my neck, then lower to my collarbone. He starts trailing kisses between my breasts to my stomach and lower. When he reaches the black lace of my panties, his eyes lock with mine before he hooks his fingers into the fabric. He doesn't move, waiting for my consent. I lift again, and he slowly drags the lace down my legs, carefully removing it over my heels. When he stands back up, he removes his boxers, and when I see his cock bob free, it's my turn to suck in a breath. He's big. He's gotta be eight, maybe nine inches long, and I'm wondering if my fingers will even close around his girth.

I want to lick him, to taste him. I can see the precum glistening on his tip, and I want to know how he tastes. I sit up more and reach for him. Once I have my hands wrapping around his velvety, warm skin, I stroke him a couple of times before I look up to meet his eyes. His eyes are so dark and filled with lust when he looks at me. I stroke him again, and he bucks his hips with my movement. I lower my head and lick the tip.

"Fuck, Cordelia," Dean groans as he places his hands in my hair. I take him into my mouth, and he barely fits. I slowly lick and suck, twirling my tongue around his tip. I slowly take him as far as I can before my gag reflex kicks in. I slide him back out. Dean grips my hair and pulls me off of him, saying, "If you keep doing that, I'm not going to last, and I want to be inside you when I come."

Fuck. I want that. I scoot back up the bed and recline on my elbows. Dean crawls up the bed, surrounding me with his body. "I want to feel all of you. I don't want anything between us. I'm clean and um, on birth control." I hate that it isn't exactly the truth, but that's not a conversation to have right now, at this moment.

"Fuck, I haven't ever not used a condom. I'm clean too. But I want to make you come on my tongue and my fingers the first time, and then I want you to come on my cock."

Dean starts peppering open-mouth kisses down my stomach, going lower with each kiss. Right as he kisses my belly button, I feel his fingers slide through my folds, and I throw my head back, and he groans out, "Fuck, you are so wet. Is this all for me?"

"Yes," I answer breathlessly as he slides his finger inside me, and then I feel his tongue on my clit, swirling before he sucks it into his mouth. I arch my back and try to press closer to him.

He lets out a small chuckle, "So needy for my touch, aren't you? Do you want to come already?"

"I've needed to come since you kissed me in the bed of your truck, Dean. Please. Please let me come, make me come for you."

He growls against my flesh and presses his tongue into me and keeps pumping into me with his finger. I can feel the heat rushing to my core, my orgasm building, and when he returns to my clit and sucks it into his mouth, using his teeth to apply just the right amount of pressure, I combust. "Dean! Oh my god, yes!" I scream as my orgasm tears through me. He keeps going, sucking my clit into his mouth, and then he goes lower, his tongue spearing into me, drawing out my orgasm as long as he can.

"Fuck, Rosebud, you taste like heaven." He goes back to licking and sucking until I can't take it anymore.

"Please, oh my god, please, I can't," I whimper as he licks and sucks my overly sensitive flesh again.

Finally releasing me, he pulls himself back up and over me, kissing me, and I can taste myself on his tongue, his lips. When he breaks the kiss, I plead, "Dean, I need you inside me."

I can feel his hot tip pushing against my pussy, and I try to adjust myself to get him inside me. Dean reaches between us and lines up his cock with my entrance.

"Once I do this, I won't be able to stop. You can still say no if you don't want this."

"Dean, if you don't fuck me right now, I will never speak to you again," I spit out.

He smiles and presses a kiss to my lips before he starts to press inside of me. Once he's fully seated, we both release a groan.

I feel so full. He fills me so perfectly, hitting spots that haven't been hit before. I need him to move, though. I need to feel him everywhere.

Sensing what I want, Dean starts to pull back before he slams back into me. I arch my back and squeeze my eyes shut. "Oh fuck. Please don't stop," I pant.

"Eyes on me, Rosebud. You're going to look me in the eye when you come on my cock like a good girl."

My gaze is locked on his as he starts moving, setting a punishing pace before his fingers start circling my clit again. I wrap my legs around him, the heels of my shoes pressing into his back. I try to meet his thrusts with my hips, but he's setting such a hard pace, I can't keep up with him. I clench his cock as he pinches my clit, making me convulse around him.

"Dean! Fuck!" I scream through a second orgasm as he slams into me four more times before I feel him pulsing his release into me.

"Cordelia," he breathes out, dropping his head between my shoulder and my neck and pressing kisses into my neck.

The only thoughts going through my head are that this was the most amazing night I have had with a man in my entire life. It also makes me realize that my walls are starting to crack where this man is concerned. And if I let them crumble down, I have more than just him to let inside at this point. I push those thoughts out of my head and force myself to focus on this feeling of serenity that is floating around me.

Chapter Fifteen

DEAN

I can't believe I only lasted a few minutes, but my God, does she feel so good wrapped around my length. I lift my head and capture her mouth in a kiss, trying to convey how much this moment, this night, has meant. She moans into my mouth before I break the kiss.

Slowly pulling my softening dick from her, I suddenly have the overwhelming urge to push my cum back inside her, so I do. I take my fingers and slide them up from her ass, gathering my cum and pushing it back inside.

Fuck. I might have a breeding kink, which is new to me. I've never wanted to have kids and have always been so careful, always using condoms before, never going without one, and I know that I will never be able to use one with her after this. I will always need to feel her soaking wet pussy wrapped completely around me.

"I love seeing my cum inside you and dripping out. I want to keep you this way, filled to the brim with my cum."

Cordelia pushes up on her elbows, raising a perfectly arched eyebrow at me, "Do you have a breeding kink, Dean?"

"Never did before this moment. I've *always* used a condom before," I say as I look back to where I'm slowly pumping my fingers into her. "I should probably clean you up, but I won't lie, thinking of you filled with me all night is more sexy than it should be."

I slide my fingers from her, and she grips my wrist, sucking our combined wetness from them.

"Fuck, if you keep doing that while looking at me with those eyes, I'm going to need to take you again."

She smiles around my fingers before she slides them from between her lips.

I stand and head into the joining bathroom, getting a towel and wetting it before coming back to clean her up. She hasn't moved, just lying there propped up with her legs propped up, my cum slowly leaking from her. My eyes travel over the tail of the dragon as it wraps around her left thigh. She is the sexiest thing I have ever laid eyes on, like this. I so badly want to flip her and see the rest of the tattoo, but I stop myself. I clean her up and then myself in the bathroom.

"Can you stay? I understand if you can't, since you probably have to be at work tomorrow." There's a vulnerability in her tone telling me that leaving is probably not the right option. Not that I was planning to. I want to hold her against me all night.

Stepping out of the connected bathroom, I say, "Rosebud, I can be late if it means I get to hold you in my arms all night. That's the perk of being the owner."

She stands and heads into the bathroom. "I have an extra toothbrush, and I also need to wash my face. I hate sleeping with makeup on."

I follow her into the bathroom, and I can't get over how much I love this domestic feeling of brushing our teeth together and seeing her go through her nightly routine. I stand in the doorway watching her while she washes her face. Studying the dragon that wraps from her hip to her back. Its green scales are almost too realistic just to be a tattoo. Its nose and eyes are raised and turned toward a smaller dragon in flight. There's so much emotion in the eyes of the bigger dragon, a longing as it watches the smaller one. I wonder if that was intentional or just the result of the artist's technique.

Once she's done, we climb into bed. Cordelia curls into my side with her head on my chest. Neither of us put anything on before climbing into bed. I press a kiss into her hair and draw slow circles over her back with my hand, while the other is covering her hand on my chest.

"I just want to check in and make sure you are ok. I know you said you wanted to go slow, and I don't want you to feel like I expected anything after our couple of dates."

She lifts her head and looks at me. She opens her mouth to respond and then promptly closes it. Her brows furrow before she says, "There's too much, so I will sum up. This," she gestures her hand up and down between us, "is not my issue. It's my heart, Dean. I haven't been good at letting people in. The easiest way to describe it would be abandonment issues, but that's not entirely accurate. I don't know how to tell you exactly what it is, not without telling you a very long story. I need time to get there." She lets out a small, barely audible scoff. If she wasn't pressed against me, I wouldn't have caught it. "I will tell you, a Google search of my name will give you a lot of hits, resulting in the highlights. But I'm asking you not to do that, please. If you do that, you will have far more questions than you will answers. And those are questions I'm not yet ready to answer. I know that asking you to trust me and let me do this in my own time might be too much. I wouldn't hold it against you if you were to run a search. I know that curiosity can be... a consuming feeling. But I'm still asking you to let me do this in my own time."

I start sliding my fingers through her hair, mulling over her words. I know I'll respect her decision; I've already been doing that without being asked. I know whatever happened is not pretty, and it's probably left a lot of scars on her heart.

"I've put some things together so far, and I had a feeling I could have tossed your name into Google and gotten a hit, but I haven't done it. I won't do it. I will be as patient as I can possibly be. But it's important that you know I'm not going anywhere. I know this is so new, and we are still getting to know each other. But, Rosebud, believe me when I tell you, I want this. I want you. I've never felt this way about a person before in my life, and I have no intentions of giving you up."

I can feel her smile against my chest before she responds. "Sounds like you might be contemplating some light kidnapping there, Dean. I'm not sure if that should worry me or turn me on."

I laugh, a full belly laugh, jostling her head on my shoulder. "For you, I would handcuff you to my bed if I thought you were going to leave me... if you're into that anyway."

"Guess you will have to wait and see."

"If waiting means you plan to stick with me, I will wait for as long as you need me to."

Cordelia lifts her head and searches my face for something, but I know she won't find anything besides sincerity. Whatever she sees seems to appease her, and she puts her head back down, snuggling in closer.

"Thank you for tonight, Dean. And thank you for staying."

I press another kiss to her hair, telling her, "There's nowhere else I would rather be."

After a few minutes, her breathing evens out, and I know she's fallen asleep. I watch her sleep on my chest for a little while until I can feel sleep drag me under as well.

It takes a few seconds to remember where I am when I wake up to a warm body pressed against my chest and recall the night with Cordelia. I know I fell asleep with her on my chest, but we must have shifted in the night, with her back to my front now, but it doesn't appear that I ever let go of her. I have my arms wrapped tightly around her, and she's tucked into my chest. When she adjusts herself in her sleep, my erection prods between her thighs.

Fuck.

When she lets out a small moan and she shifts back a little

more turning her head and locking eyes with me over her shoulder, I know I'm not leaving this bed without filling her with my cock and making sure I'm leaking out of her. I pull my hips back just enough to thrust forward again, and the tip of my cock runs through her wet folds. I have to bite back the groan that comes from knowing she's wet for me already this morning. I pull back a little more, adjusting before thrusting forward again. This time, the tip catches her opening, and I slowly ease into her. This time, she moans and arches her back into me, spurring me on. I start thrusting into her, slowly picking up the pace.

Fuck, I have never felt something as good as her pussy wrapped around my dick. I know I won't last long like this, not when I can feel how wet she's getting, and when her arm reaches around to grab the back of my neck, pulling me in closer, I know she's just as affected as I am. I reach up and pinch her nipple and grab a handful of her tits. I love how they overflow my hands.

"Fuck, Dean, please don't stop. I'm so close," she breathes around a moan.

I renew my efforts, thrusting into her harder. I let go of her nipple with my top arm and slide it down her body, making circles on her clit with feather-light touches. Just enough to drive her wild. When she lets out another moan, I pinch her clit, and her pussy starts fluttering and spasming around my dick, milking my orgasm out of me. "Fuck," I groan into her neck as I bite down, making her arch into me even more. "I love knowing you are filled with my cum. I think this whole new kink you unlocked is going to be a problem," I chuckle out.

"Mmm... I'm not complaining at all." Cordelia stretches like a cat, and I bring my hand down to push my cum back inside her as I pull my softening dick out of her wet and messy pussy. She lets out a little whimper as I thrust my fingers a couple of times before pulling them out.

"As much as I would love to spend all day in this bed, I should probably get up and go make sure that Graham is doing what he's supposed to be doing over at Glass." I press a kiss to her shoulder and roll out of her bed.

I'm pulling up my boxers when I turn and see the morning light filtering through directly across her exposed breasts. I groan out, "I'm not going to be able to control myself if you keep flashing those at me."

She giggles before pulling up the sheet to cover her. "Better?" she asks.

"No," I grit out. The only way she should be is naked and bouncing on my dick at all times. I cringe internally at how fucked up that sounds, and yet it's making my dick hard already. This woman is bringing out a whole new side of me that I never even knew existed.

I finally drag myself away and step into her bathroom to brush my teeth and relieve myself. I venture back out to find my shirt and give her a kiss before I leave.

"When can I see you again?" I ask as I lean down, pressing a kiss to her lips.

"I will be at Glass tomorrow for most of the day, if you're planning to be there. If I cancel on the girls tonight, they will probably use the Find My app and track me down," she answers and kisses me again, this time pulling me down to her.

I have to forcibly push myself away when every fiber of my being is telling me not to. "Well, I will see you tomorrow. But I'm going to call you later and text you all day." I flash her a smile at the top of the stairs.

"Have a good day at work, handsome," she says as she rolls over and the sheet dips low, exposing a nipple. I run my hand down my face and turn, stomping down the stairs with her laughter drifting after me.

Chapter Sixteen

CORDELIA

After Dean leaves, I lie in bed replaying the whole night. Jason was the last person I was with, and that was almost two years ago now. He ended up being shipped off to California the week after our trip to the Outer Banks that year. They had wanted him to report the week before, but given the reasoning, he wanted to be here, so they agreed to delay his transfer.

I never loved Jason, not in the way I thought I did Evan. We were actually good together for the almost six years we were together, until that knock on the door.

A part of me died along with Brian. He was the best and greatest thing I ever did.

I've been wearing a mask ever since. Playing the parts I need to play when I need to play them. When I tried to explain my feelings, Evan dismissed me. Granted, not in those first couple of months, but after the holidays were over, that was a different story. It was like he felt that I should have bounced back to my old self after that.

When someone you thought not only you loved, but loved you, tells you that you need to get over losing the single most important person in your life and move on, it leaves you wondering if there is something fundamentally broken inside you. Especially when that person tells you as much.

Thankfully, with therapy, I learned that it is not the case.

I was, hell, I still am, grieving a life I thought I would have, battling through things, and craving a future that no longer exists. But it did leave me with some very deep-seated trust issues. My head is screaming at me not to trust Dean, not to let him in, yet my heart, the cold, black, shriveled thing I thought was long dead, feels like it is starting to thaw out.

Dean is making me feel things I never thought I wanted to again. It's not that I would say I'm falling in love with him, but he's just making me *feel*. And it's scaring the fuck out of me, because I am starting to be able to see a new future. One that includes him and involves putting weight into something that can change in the blink of an eye. More than being terrifying, it's incredibly hard to have faith in that.

I toss my head back into the pillow and throw the blanket over my face. I feel bad about lying to him last night. I have NEVER felt bad about that lie before. Not once. But telling him I'm on birth control when really I had a hysterectomy, it feels wrong. But telling him the truth about that means telling him the rest of the story. I can't tell him that I had that done, not without explaining the reason behind it. Which will lead to me having to tell him everything. I'm not ready for that.

I hear my phone vibrating on the nightstand next to my bed, pulling me out of my spiraling thoughts. I grab my phone to find Harper's smiling face on my screen. Hitting accept and then the speaker button, I leave it on the nightstand.

"Morning, Harp."

"Oh, you're awfully chipper for someone who was supposed to be here fifteen minutes ago for morning yoga," Harper snips.

"Oops?" I say, laughing.

"What the fuck, Cordy?! That's all you got for me? Oops?! You better have gotten some last night, and you better be ready to share all, and I do mean ALL the details when you get here."

"Dean only left a couple of minutes ago. If you wanna walk over, I'll be ready by the time you get here."

Harper squeals, "He slept over?!" I can hear her clapping through the phone.

"I will see you in a few minutes," I say, and I hit the end button. I jump out of bed and make it really quick. I toss my hair into a messy bun on the top of my head and take the world's fastest shower because I am NOT about to do yoga with my bestie with Dean's cum dripping out of me.

Once I'm done in the shower, dry off, and get dressed, I head to the kitchen and grab a Celsius from the fridge. I've never been one who can do any workout after coffee, but I need the caffeine within half an hour of getting up to keep the caffeine withdrawal migraines at bay. I know it would be easier just to start slowly weaning myself off caffeine, but let's be honest, I know that will never happen.

I'm such a hot mess some days.

Last night was the first night in years that I didn't have to be medicated to sleep. I don't know if that was because Dean was there or because of all the orgasms, or both.

Who am I kidding? It was Dean. Jason never got me so sated before that I didn't still need a Xanax to sleep. I don't know what's worse, the possibility of becoming addicted to controlled substances or Dean.

It's definitely Dean, the little voice in my head says.

Because you never know what curveball life is going to throw at you. And putting so much stock into a person in your life, well, that doesn't always go the way you think it will. Sometimes they just go away. For no reason.

I shake myself out of my dark, swirling thoughts again. I cannot keep going down this path. It's not healthy, and worrying about things outside of my control will drive me insane. I've played the 'What If' game far too much over the last five years, and I know how bad that can actually be for me.

I take my second round of box breathing when I hear Harper try to open the front door.

"Open the door right fucking now, Cordelia!" Harper yells through the door, and I twist the lock on the handle and pull it open.

"Sorry, I forgot to unlock it." I step back, letting her pass me and close the door.

Now, Harper is a tiny thing. She's just barely over five feet, and she probably weighs ninety-five pounds soaking wet. You know that thing where you see the taller, bigger guy just put his hand on the smaller girl's forehead and just hold her back while she swings?

Yeah, I can do that with Harper. And I'm thinking I might have to. She looks absolutely feral.

"What. The. Fuck. You have some serious explaining to do!" She wags her finger at me before she throws her yoga mat at my head.

I deflect her mat, step over it, and head toward the back door, knowing she loves to do yoga outside until I draw the line when North Carolina gets too hot. "What do you want to know? That Dean planned a perfect night, and I gave in to my baser needs and invited him over, and then asked him to stay the night after he gave me two mind-blowing orgasms? Or how I didn't take medication for the first time in, what, four years, to sleep, AND I slept all night with no nightmares? Or how he woke me up this morning with another round before he left?" My tirade is met with silence, causing me to turn around. Harper is staring at me like I have two heads, her mouth open, and I think she's about to cry.

"Ohmygodohmygod! Cordy!" She runs at me and throws her arms around me. "I'm so fucking happy for you right now." She sniffles while her hug is strangling me. "I love you so much, and you are my sister from another mister and my best friend in the whole world. I know I'm jumping ahead of myself here, but it is about goddamn time you found someone who could love you. All of you."

She finally lets me go and steps back, wiping her eyes. "It is a little early to be throwing the 'L' word around. And the 'all of me' you mention, well, that will remain to be seen." I walk into my kitchen and grab my drink from the counter but end up putting my head in my hands. "Harper, I'm terrified. I'm always terrified. I always feel like I am waiting for the other shoe to drop. And I really want to believe that Dean could be someone that I would want to open up to. But..." I let the rest of my sentence hang in the air.

Harper gives me a sympathetic look before she responds, "You won't know until you give him the chance. I won't push it, but you do need to decide when you should tell him. And I think it needs to be before the Outer Banks this year. Especially if Jason really will be back in town." Harper grabs her mat before continuing, "Maybe you should consider inviting Dean out this year. With the way the week breaks down, I could come out a day late with the girls, maybe let everyone hear the whole thing? You can take your time with Dean the first night, and I can help fill things in the next day. If Jason comes out, he could, too. That way, you aren't repeating the whole story multiple times. Obviously, you don't need to decide now, but if you really think this could go somewhere, it could be a good idea."

I grab my mat, and we head out to my back deck and throw the mats down. All the while, I'm turning her words over in my head. She has a point. It would be easier to explain everything on the anniversary. Considering I had the same thought, maybe that is the way I should go with it. We already have heightened emotions around that time of the year. I can get it all out, have some time to decompress from sharing all the heartbreaking details, and then come back to reality. If things progress with Dean, maybe it would be a good idea to invite out his friends and his brother. I know Sebastian knows more than he has let on, but I don't believe he knows some of the more personal details. As I lay out my mat, I say to Harper, "You might be onto something. Maybe Graham and Sebastian could come out as well. Obviously, you can stay the whole week, but the house won't fit all of us unless we double up."

"I like this plan. Let's talk to the girls tonight; they will need the heads up with the shop and hotel to make sure they have it covered."

We leave the conversation there and go through our morning yoga routine. Once we wrap up, Harper heads home, and I get myself ready for the day. I spend a little more time on my appearance since I know I will be meeting the girls for our weekly night out. I'll have to go directly from Glass, as we have a micro wedding be held there tonight. I need to get out there and help with decorations and make sure the construction guys have everything cleaned up.

I finish diffusing my hair and do a little more makeup than usual for my weekday look. I stop in my office on the way out to grab my iPad for setup today. As I turn to close the door behind me, my eyes linger on the shelf with the folded flag in its wooden case. I inhale a breath through the pain in my chest and close the door.

Once I get to Glass, I see Dean walking toward my car before I turn to grab all of my things off the passenger seat. Before I can open my door, Dean does and offers me a hand. Smiling, I take it, and he helps me out.

"Wasn't sure when you were going to be here," he says before pressing a kiss to my lips.

"Yeah, Harper and I had a little yoga session this morning. Now, I gotta get the bride and groom's sign out of my shed and go do some setup inside. The rest of the team should be here or almost here. How's the work going today?"

"Nothing too crazy today; they're just finishing up the top of the lanai. I know I told you, but we can't stain any of the fresh wood until next year, probably early spring. But we will want to do that around your weddings, let it set for a good two days."

I smile up at him, "Can I see the lanai?"

He chuckles and takes my iPad and bag from my arm and tosses them back into my car before taking my hand and leading me down to the river.

The roses aren't in yet, obviously, but it looks gorgeous. The structure has a cement pad, with the posts just outside the concrete. They are currently adding the last couple of pieces to the roof. I can picture the roses climbing the pillars and flowing fabric draping over the top. He's really done all he could to bring my vision to life. And I cannot wait to see the roses once they finish the top and everything is done and together.

"Dean," I breathe out, "this is perfect. I love it so much, and I can picture the rest once it's done." Turning toward him with tears threatening to spill over, I pull him down for a kiss. Pulling back just a little, I murmur against his lips, "Thank you for making my dreams for this place real." I press another quick kiss to his lips before dropping down from my toes.

"You are so welcome, Rosebud. We should have the rose bushes in before we all break for lunch, worst case, after. But either way, those will be in before we wrap up today. This was our big one to get done as much as possible for you. We are planning to wrap up early so we can have everything out of the way for that wedding tonight."

"That's perfect," I say, taking a small step backwards. "I have to go help with setting up inside." Before I can take another step, Dean pulls me into him again. He brushes a loose curl behind my ear before kissing the breath out of me.

"Now, you can get back to work. I needed a proper kiss." I can feel myself blushing, knowing all his guys are around us, witnessing our kiss.

I turn, heading back up to the barn, stopping to grab my iPad and purse from my car on the way.

The next few hours pass in a blur of tablecloths, floral arrangements, and decor. Once we have all the setup done in the reception area, I go to check on the team working on the ceremony area, happy to see they have it all under control and are putting the finishing touches up. I decide that they can handle the rest without me. Telling them to call me if they need anything, I head out.

I check my watch and see I have a few minutes, just enough time to go see if the roses are in yet. I head down toward the river, and when I get there, I freeze, letting out a gasp. Dean is on his knees, steadying the last rose bush as he uses his hands to press the dirt back into the hole around the base. They are still smaller, only reaching about a quarter of the way up the posts, but tall enough for us to start twisting and securing them so they can grow up and around. But I can see that the picture he created of these is exactly how it is going to look.

I take a couple of breaths to compose myself. "You've really outdone yourself with this," I say, causing Dean to turn to me over his shoulder. He winks before he pushes the last of the dirt and stands up, tossing his gloves to the ground.

"I was hoping to show you this before you left."

"I finished up inside and wanted to go home and change before I meet the girls tonight, but saw I had enough time to run down here for a quick peek. I really love this." I add the last bit in a whisper.

"I'm glad you do. I know your reaction was pretty strong when I showed you the photos of this one, so getting it right was really important for me."

"And it is flawless." I offer him a genuine smile. "Anyways, I should get going. The wedding party is starting to show up, and I need to go change."

Dean grabs my wrist and pulls me into him, his hand snaking from my wrist to my lower back while the other tangles in my hair at the base of my neck. He grips my hair and tilts my head back before saying against my lips, "If you think you can walk away from me without kissing me, especially since I won't see you tonight, you are sorely mistaken." Then his lips are mine, his tongue demanding entry, and I open to him. He grips me tighter to him, and his kiss is consuming, searing itself to my lips. When we break apart, I'm breathless and so incredibly turned on. My body is still sore from the night before and this morning. But I don't care. I would let him do things to me right here in the open. I shake myself out of the haze of lust and put an inch of space between us.

"You are a terrible influence on me. I'm almost tempted to cancel on the girls right now, but if I do that, they will literally hunt me down." I laugh out the last part.

"You should hang out with your girls. I have Graham and Madison stopping over for dinner tonight. Which is happening more and more often lately. I think having a teenage daughter is wearing on him."

"Yes, teenagers will do that to a parent." I smile, my thoughts threatening to drift. Before I let them go too far, I shake myself out of them. I press a quick kiss to Dean's cheek and tell him I will talk to him later, when we can set up another date night.

At home, I head into my room to find what I plan to wear tonight. I settle on a flowy teal top and jeans, pairing them with rose gold sandals to dress it up a little bit. Once I get to Rita's and head inside, I find Faye is the first to arrive and already has a bottle of wine at the table. I see Rita at the bar and wave before I make my way over to Faye and grab a seat.

"Hey," I say, taking a seat and turning the wine bottle. "Moscato?" I say with a slight pout.

Faye rolls her eyes at me before saying, "I like what I like."

"Don't I know it. I'm gonna go grab a bottle of the rosè," I say, standing up just as Rita walks up with a bottle in her hands.

"Sit down. You act like I don't know that you prefer this one to the Moscato," Rita scolds me as she sets the open bottle on the table. "Oh, be sure to tell Harper to see Max when she gets here." Rita sends us a wink and turns to leave.

"Um, why is Rita sending Harper to Max? What's going on?" Faye asks.

I raise my eyebrows and answer, "Girl, your guess is as good as mine on this one." I pour a glass and take a sip. "Where are they anyway? It's not like Harper to be late, especially today."

"I don't know. Why? You got some updates for us?" she adds with a lift of one perfectly sculpted eyebrow.

"Yes, but I can wait on that. I have something else I need to tell you guys before anything else."

"Everything ok?" Faye's tone switched from her usual bubbly tone to one full of concern.

I let out a breath and wave my hand, "Yeah, no, I don't know. Just something I need to say before the wine hits me and it becomes more of a thing than I want or need it to be."

I can feel Faye's eyes on me, and I know she wants to pry more, but she doesn't. It's crazy how someone I haven't known for long has become so important in my life. When we first met, I just felt something click into place with her. Kindred spirits, or maybe we really were sisters in another life, but either way, Faye has become incredibly important and pivotal in my life. I say that, and yet I haven't told her all the details. I know I have her on social media, so she knows the basics, but there is a lot that is not public knowledge.

I can recognize that it took Dean to start cracking my carefully constructed walls to realize putting so much on Harper these last years isn't fair to her or me. I can't expect her to always be here to pick up the pieces with me. I know it's only been a couple of weeks since I've gotten to know Dean, but I know that in that short time, I can trust him. I do trust him. It's not him that's the problem, I know that.

It's me. I'm the problem.

I can still hear Evan's words in my head, telling me I'm too broken, a shell of the person I used to be. And ya know what? *Fuck him.* What was I supposed to do? Be happy and act like my life was totally fine, and it wasn't in ruins all around me? That was never going to happen.

Here we are five years later, and I know I'm not where I was prior, and I never will be. But I've started to be able to live with the pain and grief. It's not going to go away, and I finally made peace with that in the last year. Choosing to walk with grief as an old friend, not trying to run and hide. Once I made that choice about two years ago, I think that was the first full breath I took. I knew it would take time to accept that it would always be part of me and would never go away, and over time, I embraced the pain that comes with that. It has made things easier to deal with. I meet with my therapist once a year, usually a couple of weeks after the anniversary. I drive back up to Ohio, make a few stops to say hi to friends, and meet with her in person. She only does virtual sessions but makes an exception for me. We grab a coffee, sit in a park, and talk. Catch up. Reflect on how the past year went and set goals for the next year. I couldn't imagine seeing any other therapist, so going back to the old stomping grounds is easier for me. There's too much to unpack to find a new one.

Harper comes in and brings my thoughts out of my head when she hops onto her stool across from me. "Sorry I'm late. I couldn't find the shirt I wanted to wear. I don't know what is going on with my clothes lately. I think I need to do a full inventory."

"First your bikini and now a shirt? That is really weird, Harper," I say.

"Tell me about it," she sighs. "It's also starting to piss me off."

"You are always so meticulous with your clothes. I thought you had, like, a full photo inventory in the cloud." Faye laughs before adding, "Before I forget, Rita was very clear when she said the second you got here, you needed to find Max."

"Um, okay," Harper drags out the last word before asking, "Why?"

"She didn't say," I offer.

Harper lets out a groan, slides back off the chair, and goes in search of Max.

Gwen steps inside a moment later, sitting next to me. "Please tell me you have that rosè."

Laughing, I grab the bottle and pour some into her glass. She takes a sip and groans.

"Fuck I needed this. I also really need Sunday to get here," Gwen states.

"Oh yeah, Sunday is spa day, isn't it?" I ask. Every six weeks or so, we girls make a day out of coloring our hair together and doing hair removal with hot wax. Harper and I started this a long time ago when we realized that our wonderful Italian heritage, which we both share, was much easier to manage on our bikini lines when we just waxed. We realized very quickly how much easier it is to do when we would do each other over ourselves. After ten years, Harper and I have made it so incredibly manageable that we barely need to torture ourselves much anymore, but the other two girls have a way to go to catch up to us.

"Fuck me, I'm gonna need to get a couple bottles of wine." Faye groans into her glass.

"Why the urgency for having pain inflicted on you?" I ask.

"Yeah, you got a hot date?" Faye asks.

"No, but is it weird that I just like having a day with no responsibilities outside of helping put hair color on, ripping off hot wax, and drinking wine?"

"Not weird at all."

Just then, Harper comes bouncing up to the table holding two cans. "Oh man, Max is the literal best ever!" she squeals.

"What are those?" I ask.

"These are MY kind of drinks. You know I'm not a huge wine or any alcohol type person. I just do it on these nights and only ever have one glass with you ladies. But these? These are THC drinks. I'm so excited. I didn't even know it was a thing!" She cracks it open and takes a drink. "Oh, this is good. It tastes just like an Orange Crush!" She takes another sip before adding, "This is so much better than wine. No offense, ladies."

I laugh, "I was always surprised you would partake in wine with us, so I'm more than ok with this. But maybe see how the first one hits you before you do the second one."

"Max said to take the second one home with me, unless the first one doesn't hit me at all within an hour. He knows my tolerance is a little higher than his, but he suggested one at a time. I'll listen, since I've never had these before. I don't know how it will affect me."

I shake my head and take another sip of my wine.

"Well, we are all here. What did you want to tell us?" Faye asks.

"Bitch," I mumble into my wine glass.

She flashes me a smile and says, "Jerk."

"Alright, I'm just gonna go ahead and say this, get it out. I'm inviting Dean to the Outer Banks this year. And, if things don't go horribly off the rails, I think when we get back, I would like to actually lay it all out there for you." I stop and add a pointed look at all three of the girls before continuing, "I will obviously be inviting his brother and Sheriff Murphy, as well as Sebastian. I know he's more privy to what happened than anyone else, but he doesn't know the small details, the ones y'all don't know either." I let out a breath.

Gwen chimes in immediately, "I will be there."

"I will be there as well," Faye adds, setting her glass down.

Harper casts me a look that says she's proud of me across the table.

"Well, now that we got that out of the way," I say before smirking and taking a sip of my wine. "Gwen, I have to ask you about something that happened about a year ago. A construction guy in your store? Ringing any bells?" I ask, raising my eyebrows at her. I hope no one catches how quickly I change the subject, as I want to take the focus off of me for as long as I can.

She drains her wine glass with an exasperated expression

before saying, "He started moving stuff off my wall that I had just finished. It's not like it's easy for me to do that ever since my diagnosis." Gwen was having some health issues, and right after we met, she finally saw a doctor, who was able to tell her what was wrong with her. He diagnosed her with POTS. Doing anything physical can knock her down for the day, and she can scare us pretty bad when she gets so lightheaded that she faints. Thankfully, that has only happened a small number of times and hasn't happened in the last year. "He just started taking things off the shelf and moving them. I ripped him a new one before he could explain. I did apologize, though. But it probably came out a *little* snarky and bitchy." She shrugs, and then Gwen changes the subject, much to my dismay, demanding to know about Dean. I spend the rest of the evening filling them in on the details, leaving a few to their imaginations, which they were not happy about in the least bit.

Chapter Seventeen

DEAN

The rest of my week flies by, with me working hard during the day to ensure we meet our Friday deadline for Cordelia and Glass and spending my evenings talking to her on the phone. She had a lot on her plate after her night out with the girls. I would be lying if I said I wasn't worried that she's pulling away and second-guessing us. But she always answers my texts and calls. So maybe I'm over-reacting.

Sunday afternoon, I decide to swing by her place and see if she wants to make dinner and watch a movie to end the weekend together. I pull down her street, and I can see a couple of cars in her driveway. When I park and make my way up to the door, I can hear music and laughter before knocking on the door.

Cordelia opens the door with a flushed face and what looks like hair color on her hair, wrapped in a plastic cap on top of her head.

"Fuck, Dean, hi," she smiles. I love that she makes no move to cover the plastic cap. "Um, I'd invite you in, but I have the girls over. Doing some uh, self-care." She points to the cap as she finishes speaking.

I hear someone yell, "Cocksucker!" from somewhere in her house. My eyebrows shoot up. "What is going on?" I chuckle out.

"That's why we keep the music up when it's Faye's turn. She has a low pain tolerance. I would invite you in, but we have half-naked girls in here, and it involves hot wax. That's all I'm going to say." Cordelia's eyes sparkle with humor, and her cheeks are flushed.

"I just wanted to see if you wanted to have dinner and maybe watch a movie?"

She visibly relaxes against the door. "I would love that, but we have another two or so hours before we are done here."

"I could go pick up some stuff to make, and come back when you are done? And you can tell me no if you want to." I try to give her a sad look, hoping she will take pity on me and say yes.

"Ok, fine, we should be completely done and cleaned up by six if that works?"

I lean in, kissing her before I smile against her lips, "Six is perfect. I'll take my time picking up some stuff."

She smiles, and as she goes to close the door, I hear another yell from inside. I laugh, turning back toward my truck.

I head to the grocery store in town, deciding to grill up some chicken for salads, opting for something a little lighter with the summer heat starting to make itself known. Once I get everything I need, I head back to my house and get the chicken marinating. I decided instead of asking if she has a grill, I would just grill everything up here and head over there once it's all done.

While the chicken is marinating in the fridge for about an hour, I try to find something to busy myself with. My house is already pretty spotless. I did laundry earlier, so I decide to just open a beer and relax by the pool.

My mind wanders over these last weeks, ever since meeting Cordelia. I know she is starting to relax her guard with me, but knowing she is still holding back from fully letting me in rattles me. I keep wondering what is so bad in her past that she would be this scared to tell me. Is she afraid that it will make me see her differently? Or is she afraid to speak about her past, afraid to relive it? If it's the latter, it worries me even more. I could so easily search her name and find it all out.

Fuck!

I can't do that. I can't betray the fragile trust she might have in me. I know without a doubt that if I were to do this and she ever found out, it would damage our relationship, possibly more than just that. I can tell trust is not something she gives easily. And I refuse to ruin what we have started. I know it all happened so fast, but I remember what my parents used to say. They used to say that when we meet the right person, we would know. Dad was always so insistent that when he met Mom, it was like his heart stopped. He never looked at another woman again. He knew right away that there would never be anyone else for him.

After meeting Cordelia, I feel like this could be true for me as well. I will do whatever it takes to make sure that my future includes her. And if I have any say, it will be with her as my wife, because there is no other way I want her in my life. I know I sound crazy to think that so quickly, yet I can't bring myself to care.

My mind starts wandering over honeymoon destinations. That passport in my safe is just yearning to finally be used. My vote will be anywhere she can be in a bikini the whole time, so I can see all of her tattoos. Maybe one of those places with a swim-out hotel room, or an over-the-water bungalow. Yeah, I like that idea. I go to take another drink and realize my beer is empty. Pulling my phone out of my pocket, I check the time, five o'clock. Perfect. I'll open another beer and grill up the chicken, and then I can get packed up with dinner and head over.

It takes me about twenty minutes to grill the chicken and cut it up. I put the container into the bag from the grocery store with the rest of the items we will need. Then I load up my truck, heading over to Cordelia's.

She's sitting on her front step when I pull into her thankfully empty driveway. I kill the engine and hop out of my truck. Before

I grab the stuff from the back seat, I stride over to the woman who is turning my world upside down.

"Hey," she says as she stands from her steps.

"Hello, beautiful," I respond before I pull her into me and kiss her. I don't need to make it a deep, all-consuming kiss, but I needed to feel her. When I pull away, she's smiling, and her cheeks are pink. "Your hair looks good, almost looks blue in the light," I say, giving a little tug on one of the still slightly damp midnight ends. I wink and turn to grab the bags out of the back of my truck.

"Thank you, and yeah, the blue always fades kinda quickly. So what's the plan for dinner?" she asks.

"I grilled up some chicken and got stuff to make some salads. It's starting to get warm out, and I thought a nice light dinner would be perfect. Maybe some popcorn and a movie after?"

"What movie did you have in mind?"

"Whatever you want."

"Oh, it's incredibly tempting to pick a chick flick, but," she lets out a sigh, "I'm not in the mood for that. I've kind of been itching to do a rewatch of the Marvel movies."

I freeze on the top step, "You're a Marvel fan?" *Please say yes, please say yes.*

"Yep, not the comics, just the movies. RDJ is just," she brings her fingers to her lips and kisses them, "chef's kiss."

"Robert Downey Jr.? But he's so short!"

"I mean, a solid argument could be made for Loki as well," she teases. "I always tend to prefer the villains anyway."

I growl at the thought of her looking at any other man, yet I still follow her inside, set the bags down, and grab her around the waist, picking her up and setting her on the counter. I nudge her legs apart and step in between them, holding the back of her neck in one hand while the other is gripping her thigh. "Rosebud, you are playing a dangerous game. I don't want to hear another man's name on those pretty lips, fictional or not." I pull her lips to mine and kiss her before I back up and let her down. I turn to grab the bags and start pulling out all the items. Cordelia smiles as she watches me before grabbing large salad bowls and utensils.

We work in comfortable silence while we add the toppings we like, and she pours us each a glass of iced tea. I can't help but picture this, in my kitchen, with traces of her all over. I noticed that she has silk flowers in a vase on a table, with some framed photos behind her couch, creating a divide between the open concept eat-in kitchen and living room. She has pictures on the walls and decorations to make her house feel like a home and like it's lived in. I've always wanted that feeling back in my home. It hasn't felt like a lived-in home since Graham and Madison moved out almost ten years ago, and before that, it was when Mom was still with us. Cordelia's home smells like she does; there's a lingering scent of roses in the air, which is probably from her perfume. But more than that, the scents of vanilla and lavender—calm and beautiful.

Her home is in an area of Green Haven that was built during the 1950s; are all two story bungalow-style homes. I have done a couple of renovations on these, but not this one. I know the upstairs on this one is renovated as well, since the en suite on the upper level is not typical of these houses. Most only have one bathroom on the main level. Shockingly enough, they made all the garages attached when they were initially built, which started the trend of additions over the garage to expand the square footage. Those are my favorite things to do, creating a whole new space and helping the owners have their vision realized.

Cordelia hands me a napkin and a fork, pulling me out of my thoughts. "Thank you."

"You're welcome. Do you want to sit outside or in the living room and start the movie?"

"How do you feel about outside? Then we can get the popcorn made before we start the movie?"

I follow Cordelia to her patio, and we take seats around her little table and umbrella set. Cordelia takes a bite and hums, "This is really good. Thank you for making dinner."

"It was my pleasure."

She drops her eyes after a second, and little creases form in her forehead. I can tell she's thinking about something, and I debate whether I want to push her or not. But before I can say anything, she does.

"I know everything is still pretty new, but I wanted to ask you about something. More to give you a heads up so you can plan accordingly. You can totally say no, I would understand. Like I said, this is still very new—"

I cut her off by pressing a finger to her lips. "You're rambling, babe. And just because this is new, doesn't change a thing about how I feel about you."

Cordelia's eyes widen slightly before they soften. She pulls back from my finger, and I drop my hand. She sits up a little straighter and asks, "I go to the Outer Banks every year for a week in September. I know it's a couple of months out, but I wanted to see if you would be interested in going? Ya know, if you haven't realized what a complete basket case I am by then and stick around." She smiles, but it doesn't quite reach her eyes. It's almost as if she's trying to make a joke about how she might actually feel about herself, or what she thinks I will think about her.

I grab her hand, squeezing. "Unless you are secretly an axe murderer—actually, no, not even then would I not want you. So, count me in for the Outer Banks. Just let me know the exact dates, and I'll have Graham cover the company." She pulls her hand back to take a drink of her iced tea. "I think I would enjoy seeing the ocean. I never have, ya know."

"What?!" she sputters out. "You are only a couple of hours from the coast."

"I know. I just never took the time to go. Our parents never did vacations, and then I was taking care of Graham and starting my company. I never had time. I want to change that, though. I want to slow down. Hand some of the reins to Graham and actually have the life I want. Life is too short not to enjoy it."

I glance at Cordelia, and her eyes look glazed over like she's lost in her thoughts. "I know all too well exactly how short life can be and how important it is to live it to its fullest." There's sadness in her tone. It breaks my heart to think of her having to go through something that would cause this. I notice she's spinning that blue diamond ring on her finger. Which just further solidifies my guess that the ring was an engagement ring. And now I feel a level of jealousy toward a guy that I've never met and who, quite possibly, isn't even alive. I'm not a jealous person, but I've also never felt this way about someone before.

I try to push down my emotions. "Cordelia, I've said this before, but I feel like I need to say it again. Whenever you want to share with me what happened in your past, I will listen, and I won't judge, and I honestly don't think anything could change how I feel about you."

She meets my gaze and smiles, still not quite meeting her eyes, but it doesn't seem forced either. "I will tell you, but it will take time for me to be able to tell you this story, and," she takes a deep breath before continuing, "If I don't tell you before the Outer Banks, I will tell you there," she picks up her drink, taking a sip. I can't help but linger on her lips and her tongue peeks out, followed by the flash of her teeth dragging over her lower lip. She gives a subtle shake of her head, like she's forcing herself back to the present. "Harper is the only one who knows everything. Although, I've always suspected that Sebastian knows more than he has ever said.

"The point is, Dean, I'm starting to come to terms with the fact that I can tell this story. I *should* tell this story. But it will not be easy for me. I'm just asking for your patience with this."

"You will have it. You *do* have it. I'm gonna change the subject now, okay?"

She nods, "Okay."

"So, which Marvel movie do you want to watch? I personally love Thor, so that would be my pick."

"I love the full ensemble ones; there is so much going on, and it's always fun watching them all interact with each other. So maybe we can do *Age of Ultron?*"

"Sounds good to me," I reply.

We finish our dinner, and I help her clean up the kitchen and make some popcorn. The cool air inside the house feels comfortable, but when I glance at the thermostat, I subtly turn it down a couple of degrees. I want her to cuddle up with me on the couch, and if it's just a little bit colder in here... I smile at myself and take our drinks to the table, placing them on the coasters she has. I see a mix of Alaska and Caribbean-themed ones. Noticing that she likes to use her souvenirs from traveling for everyday use, I glance around to see if I notice anything else from places she has been. The blanket on the back of the couch is folded so you can read 'Outer Banks, NC' on it. She has a small shelf with a bunch of mini Yeti-style tumblers, all in bright colors from different places. I'm reading all the names on them when she comes out.

"Oh, yeah, those are new things I started noticing when I took my last couple of trips. I feel like I need to go back to all the other places to get ones for all the places I've been. But I guess that's what all the magnets are for. I started running out of room for those, saw these, and realized I would need a way to display them. Br—" She clears her throat and continues, "I just kinda built that out of some old pallets. I know it's probably not really to your standards," she adds a little sheepishly.

"Nah, I think you did pretty good for it being pallet wood. That's not always the easiest to work with. But if you want me to build you one so that each little cup has its own little cubby hole with room for more, I would gladly do it."

"Dean, you don't have to do that, but I would LOVE that." This time her smile is full, and her eyes sparkle.

"Then it's settled. I'm going to make you one."

She gives me a curious look before asking, "Can I help? I like building and making stuff and getting to be creative. It's an outlet for me."

"So, you're telling me I can put safety glasses and a tool belt on you?"

Her smile takes up her whole face as she answers, "Yep."

"Oh, Rosebud, you just want me to lock you away somewhere so you can never leave me, don't you? Because now I can't stop picturing how incredibly sexy you would look like that."

She smacks my arm and laughs as she settles on the couch, and we start to pull up the movie. Once the opening credits begin, she puts the bowl of popcorn in her lap and leans into my side, already cuddling up with me. I know if she turned around right now, she would see the sly smirk that is plastered all over my face. I'm feeling pretty proud of myself.

About halfway through the movie, she pulls the blanket off the back of the couch, covering her legs as she cuddles closer to me. I can't get over how well she fits into my side. We fit together so perfectly, like little puzzle pieces. Glancing down at her, my heart gives a little pang in my chest. It's at this moment that I realize that I am in love with this woman. I've never been in love with anyone, not even a high school girlfriend. This is such new territory for me, and I know that I can't tell her. Not yet. She's letting me into her heart, I know she is. But she's still guarding it. I know she feels more for me, even if she won't admit it. I just can't believe that she would have let me stay over and given me her body if she didn't feel more for me. I can be patient and wait for her to catch up. I just worry that I will slip up and say those three words at the wrong moment, and she will pull back from me. Which is the last thing I want, so I have to shove the feelings down for now and let her come to me in her own time.

I force myself to refocus on the movie.

When Wanda's brother, Pietro, is killed in the movie and Wanda unleashes her grief on Ultron's army, Cordelia lets out a shuddering breath, and I look down to check on her, and she's rubbing her chest over her heart.

"I've always been on her side, through all the things she did.

And I always say to myself that if she knew the full extent of her powers, she would have taken care of Thanos without breaking a sweat in Infinity War. She would—is—unstoppable," she says.

"What would you do if you had her powers?" I ask, hoping to get a little more insight into what has shaped her.

She lets out a laugh, "I wouldn't even know where to start, but I feel like I would have my own private island in the middle of the Caribbean."

I know that she gave me a generic answer, but I let it slide and don't push for more. "I think I could get on board with that."

She lifts her head to meet my eyes, "I would let you stay on the island with me."

I lift her chin and press a quick kiss to her lips. I pull back and rub my thumb over her bottom lip. "I'd never want to be anywhere else except with you," I say, trying to put all that I feel for her into those words. To let her know that she's not alone anymore, that she has someone willing to be in her corner for whatever she needs.

Her eyes bounce between mine, searching for something before she tucks her head back down and goes back to watching the movie.

Once the movie is over, I help clean up the popcorn and the bowls from dinner. I don't want to assume she will let me stay the night again, but I'm hoping she does. When I finish drying the knife I used to chop up the chicken and place it back on the magnetic strip, I turn to find her watching me with a small smile on her face.

"There's something incredibly sexy about watching a man do dishes."

I lean against the counter, crossing my arms over my chest. Raising an eyebrow, I tease her, "I'm not a piece of meat for you to objectify."

I can tell that she knows that I'm just teasing her when she lets out a shocked gasp and puts her hand to the base of her neck, like she's clutching a string of pearls. "I would never do such a thing!" Her eyes have a mischievous glint to them. "But if you ever wanted to clean dishes naked, I would not be one to stop you."

I let out a bark of laughter and grab her, pulling her into my arms. "Rosebud, I will gladly do anything you want me to, wearing just my birthday suit if it would make you happy. Maybe not anything that involves a chainsaw, though."

"No chainsaws while naked, got it."

She tucks her head under my chin and wraps her arms around my torso. I wrap my arms around her back and press a kiss to her hair. When she presses into me tighter, I can't help the shift in my hips, pushing my hard cock into her stomach. When she feels it, one of her hands shifts from my back and slides lower, palming me through my jeans. When she gives it a little squeeze, I groan into her hair. "Fuck, babe. You see what just having you in my arms does to me?"

Cordelia giggles and looks up at me, "Can you stay again?"

I scoop her up bridal style and say, "I thought you would never ask." I stride toward her stairs, making sure the front door is locked on the way.

As I start up the stairs, she says, "You don't have to carry me. I can walk, ya know. And I know I'm not that light."

I let out a growl and stop on the stairs, "I will carry you everywhere if you would let me, and, Rosebud, you practically weigh nothing to me. I could carry you around like a little spider monkey all day and never get tired of it. I don't ever want to hear you talk about yourself like that again. You are beautiful and sexy and incredibly perfect to me in every way." I start back up the stairs when she ducks her chin down. Once I have her in the bedroom and I turn, sitting on the edge of the bed, and keep her in my lap, tilting her chin up to make her look at me. "Do I need to punish you for speaking about yourself like that?" I quirk an eyebrow up at her.

"I just know that I don't have the perfect body. I have stretch marks, and my stomach isn't flat. I have extra curves," she says as she tries to look down. I don't let her. Instead, I keep my fingers on her chin until she brings her eyes back to mine.

"No one ever had as much fun on a straight road as they do on roads with curves. And, baby, you have the perfect curves for me to have a lot of fun handling." I adjust my grip on her and flip her over so that she's lying across my lap. "Now, I think you are going to take a couple of spankings for talking about yourself like that." I rub my hand over her perfect ass, and she moans and grinds herself into my lap harder. "Oh, does my girl like that idea?"

She nods, but I demand, "Use your words."

"Yes," she breathes out, "I like that."

I chuckle, bringing my hand down on her ass.

TWACK!

I massage her ass, saying, "Tell me that you are beautiful."

She whispers it so meekly that I barely hear her.

TWACK! A little harder this time.

"I didn't hear you," I say, rubbing over the spot.

"I'm beautiful," she says. But it lacks conviction.

TWACK!

"Like you mean it."

She puts a little more steel into her voice. "I'm beautiful!"

"There ya go," I say, shifting her up and off my lap. I stand from the bed and pull her up to me. My hands go to the bottom of her shirt, my eyes meeting hers in a silent question. When she gives me a small nod, I lift her shirt over her head and throw it to the ground. Her nipples are little peaks in her bra, and I pinch one through the fabric as she groans. "I think my girl really liked being spanked. Are you wet for me, Rosebud?"

"Yes," she breathes out.

I unhook her bra and pull it down, letting her tits bounce. When I squeeze one and it overflows my hand, my cock twitches in my pants. I just know that precum is already dripping from the tip from when I spanked her, and seeing how turned on she is from it makes me harder than I have ever been. I rip my shirt off, throwing it to join hers on the floor. Moving to her shorts, I flick open the button and drag the zipper down before pushing her shorts and her underwear to the floor in one swipe. As she steps out of them, I toss them over to the pile of clothes before doing the same with mine. When I stand back up, her eyes are cast downward, and her hand comes up to wrap around my length.

Groaning, I cup her tit with one hand, and the other comes up to her throat. Her eyes meet mine before I say, "I'm going to fuck you hard and fast, Rosebud. Get on the bed on your hands and knees."

Her eyes widen at my command, and her lips part on a slight gasp. She turns, slipping from my grasp, and when she crawls up on the bed, I get the perfect look at her ass, and I can see her pussy is already glistening and wet.

"Fuck, baby, you are really wet for me already, aren't you?" I swipe a finger through her folds and gather some of her wetness before I plunge a finger inside her. She gasps and whimpers, moving her hips to try to get some relief. "You don't get to come until I tell you to," I say, using my other hand to give her a light swat on her ass and slide another finger into her. When her pussy clenches around my fingers, I suck in a breath. "Such a needy pussy."

I pull my fingers from inside her as I crawl up the bed behind her. Using her juices, I stroke myself a couple of times, from root to tip, before I line up at her entrance.

She tries to push back, causing me to grip her hips and still her. "Patience."

She drops her head to the bed in a low moan of frustration, which makes me chuckle.

"You know I'm going to take care of you," I say as I start to slide into her. Once I'm fully seated, we both moan, and I bend over her and press kisses down her spine.

As I straighten, I take in the dragons on her back up close. It's the first time I've truly seen them and been able to fully take them in. The details in the scales and eyes are incredibly lifelike. The sadness I saw before in the larger one's eyes is definitely directed at the smaller one that is in flight. Something I will have to ask her about at another time, as I don't think this moment, with me inside her and her pulsing around me, is the best time.

I start sliding in and out so slowly, torturing us both, before I slam into her hard, causing her to whip her head up as her walls squeeze my cock.

"Fuck, Dean, you feel so good. Please don't stop."

"Never. If I could live inside you, I would." I start truly fucking her, and when I reach around to stroke soft circles around her clit, she comes undone. Her walls are spasming around me as she lets out a scream.

Splaying my fingers around her opening and coating them in her come, I bring them to her ass, and I start to rub, putting pressure on her tight little hole.

"Have you ever been taken here?" I ask.

Her pussy feels like a vise around my cock as she answers, "Yes, but it's been a really long time."

"Mmm," I say as I slide my thumb lower and push inside her cunt alongside my dick, making us both suck in a breath. Once I'm satisfied with the wetness, I slide out and start to push into her ass. As I break the barrier and slide to my knuckle, I pick up the pace of my thrusts. I pump my thumb a few more times before I pull out completely, intent on using her juices. I start sliding my finger in and out of her ass before I add another finger, scissoring them and getting her to relax so she can take all of me.

"I'm going to fuck this ass of yours and make you come again," I growl out.

Cordelia starts meeting my thrusts and whimpering. "Please, Dean. Anything you want, just please fill me."

Her words nearly cause me to come; I have to grip the base of my dick to keep myself from completely losing control. "Fuck, you almost made me lose control, and I'm not ready to come yet."

I slide back into her pussy, giving her three hard thrusts before

I pull back out, pulling my fingers from her ass. I line up and start to push inside of her slowly.

Her back arches and she's breathing heavily, panting around her words, "Oh fuck, please..." Her words trail off as the head of my dick is finally fully enveloped in her. I've never seen anything sexier than the way she takes my dick.

Chapter Eighteen

CORDELIA

Oh dear Lord. His cock is huge, and he's barely inside me. It feels like he's splitting me in two, and yet I can't help it as I start to push back, wanting to take him further.

Dean gives my ass a light smack again, causing me to clench around him. "Needy and impatient girls don't get to come," he growls as he slowly slides further inside.

I feel so full like this. I can't believe how good this feels and how much I need this. It's been so long; I've almost forgotten how good this feels. It's overwhelming, but at the same time, I can't get enough.

"Please, Dean," I whine. I don't know if I'm asking for another orgasm or if I'm asking him to start fucking me. Maybe both.

I just know I need more, and I need him to give me everything.

When I feel his thighs flush to the backs of my legs, I let out a low groan. I thought I was full before, but taking all of Dean inside my ass has me on a whole new level of fullness.

He hisses out, "I'm not gonna last long inside your ass, but I need you to give me one more before I fill up your ass with my cum. Play with your clit, Cordelia. Right now. I want you coming and milking my cum from my cock."

My hand flies to my clit, and I drop my head to the bed. I start moving my fingers in a circle in light touches as Dean starts to move out and back in. Going deliciously slowly, ensuring that I feel every last inch and vein of this cock.

As I feel my orgasm start to rise and peak, I scream out, "Fuck, Dean, I'm gonna come."

"Yes, fuck, you are squeezing me so tight. Come for me, come for me right fucking now." He grunts out as he thrusts into me hard and fast. I break apart around him, whimpering into the bed from the intensity of my orgasm, when I feel his fingers tighten on my hips. I know I'm going to have bruises from his grip, and it just turns me on more than I already am for this man.

When Dean lets out a curse and pushes his dick to the hilt inside me, I can feel it jerking with his release as he fills me.

Dean collapses onto my back, his breath coming out fast and hot against my skin.

I realize my heart is racing as well, but it's not from the way he just played my body. It's something else.

Oh my god. I think I'm falling for him.

This really shouldn't be a surprise. The man has done everything perfectly. He's been far kinder and understanding than I deserve. He has done everything that I have asked. He's being patient with me and doesn't push me to explain my past or why I need him to go slow—emotionally—with me. I can't imagine what he must be feeling; he's so aware of himself and his emotions. I lock mine into pretty little boxes in my head and heart and shove them to the corner to collect dust because that's easier than admitting the truth that I'm terrified every day.

I'm so afraid of losing those I love. Harper, Gwen, Faye, Sebastian, and oh my god, now Dean? Just the mere thought of losing him is causing my anxiety to spike.

I can feel my heart picking up the pace and not slowing down. I try taking a couple of small breaths; I don't want to alarm him with my panicked thoughts. I try to focus on his heartbeat that I can feel on my back. Trying to count the beats.

I only make it to twenty when he starts to lift off me, slowly pulling his dick out of me. I give a little whimper at the loss of him.

"Don't move, I'm going to clean you up," he says as he pushes off the bed and goes into the bathroom.

I can feel my heart slowing, but I'm sure my eyes are expressing everything going on in my head.

When I hear the water running, I let out the shaky breath I was holding, and it comes out as an almost choked sob. I bury my face into the sage green comforter and breathe in the clean smell of the detergent that is still lingering from the last time I washed it.

I'm just getting my breathing under control the rest of the way when I feel the warmth of the washcloth on my skin. I let out a little whimper into the blanket, and when the touch disappears, I collapse onto the bed. I hear Dean walking back to the laundry basket, and then he joins me a moment later, cuddling in behind me and pulling me into him. I wrap my arms around his arms that are around my front.

"That was by far the sexiest thing I have ever done. You look so good when you're wrapped around my cock." He presses a kiss onto my neck.

I know I need to say something before he starts assuming the worst. I go for the closest to the truth that I can. Clearing my throat, I whisper, "I think you might have broken me."

I can feel him silently laughing behind me and the smile in his voice when he says, "As long as it was the good kind of broken and not the bad kind."

"No, that was—I don't think I even have words for what we just did," I say, "It was good. Maybe too good."

"Nothing is ever going to be too good where you are concerned." Dean pulls me into him more, and I can feel his breath on the back of my neck. We stay that way for a while, soaking in the afterglow and just holding onto each other. My mind is still racing with thoughts of 'what if'. What if the same thing happens with Dean, and I lose him too? What if, after he finds out my story, he decides I'm too broken, like Evan did? What if, what if, what if. It's a slippery slope to go down, I know that. I also know it won't do any good. Yet, I can't stop myself sometimes.

I ask myself these questions all of the time over the last five years. What if I had called him when I thought about it that night? Could I have stopped it just by calling him? Or would I have been on the phone with him when it happened? I know that I *never* would have recovered from that. And maybe that's why something told me not to. Because while losing Brian was the single most destructive thing that has ever happened to me, I know that if I had been on the phone and heard it all, it would have been so much worse. I honestly don't think I would have been anywhere but a padded room, or worse, a coffin.

I wouldn't be here with this man.

That thought causes me to tense my whole body. I can never believe in the words "everything happens for a reason" because there was no reason for it. But maybe I'm supposed to be here. Maybe it would have taken a little longer to get here, and maybe it would have been too late. Maybe Dean would have found someone else.

"What is going on in that head of yours? I can feel you thinking," Dean mumbles. He sounds as if he is on the verge of sleep.

I let the tear fall from my eye into the pillow. I don't answer. Instead, I burrow into the pillow and his arms more. Hoping that I can shut down the thoughts, worries, and anxiety.

"Stop thinking, just relax and get some sleep." He lets out an exhale before continuing, "I care for you deeply. I don't want to send you running for the hills with a declaration of love. However, you should know that I don't see this going any other way for me. I will admit that my first impression of you was that you were the most gorgeous creature I have ever seen. When you spoke, your voice was like music to me.

"I know this has been bordering on a whirlwind for you, but I can't begin to tell you how right this feels to me. I'm going to lean into this with you. With all of me, my head, my heart, and my soul. I just ask that you try to do the same. I know you might be a little slower to give in to what this is between us. I'm okay with that. I can be patient. Just don't pull away or second-guess us. Can you do that for me?"

I know that I should be terrified of his words, and I am. But there's a conviction in his voice that tells me how much he believes every word he says. I wipe the tears and turn in his arms so that we are chest to chest, wrapping my arms around him. I take a steadying breath. "I can try. I don't know if I can promise that I won't pull away at any given time, but I can promise to try not to."

"That's all I ask. To try."

I can feel his growing length pressing into my stomach as we both shift closer. "You can ignore him; he doesn't know how to read a room aside from you being in it." Dean chuckles.

I smile into his chest and snuggle in closer, just breathing him in. After a couple of minutes, I can feel the tension leaking out of my muscles. Dean is becoming a calming presence in my world, one I desperately need. One I needed more than I ever thought that I did. The more I relax into him, the sleepier I get. Instead of fighting it, I let it pull me under.

The next morning, I wake up alone, much to my dismay. I check my bedside clock and see that it is almost nine in the morning. I realize I must have never set my alarm last night, which isn't an issue, as Mondays are typically just computer work for me, and yoga with Harper.

When I see the folded piece of paper next to my phone, I reach for it, finding my name scrawled across the front. I open it and read;

Good Morning Rosebud,
I couldn't bear to wake you up as you were sleeping so
soundly.
I have to get the team set up on a new site this
morning.
Text or call me later if you want to do dinner at my
place.
X,
Dean

I smile at the thought of him cooking dinner again. Maybe I could even go over early and enjoy the pool in his backyard since today is supposed to be another hot one. I grab my phone to text Harper that I will be a little late for yoga this morning, and I see a text from her with a timestamp of two this morning.

Harper: I'm cancelling yoga tomorrow because I went down the rabbit hole trying to find my missing clothes. And now I've downloaded an app that you upload photos of what is in boxes and then you print off QR codes that go with the boxes. That way I can see exactly what I put in each box. I'm going to lose my mind over this.

Harper: *photo of clothes all over the room*

Me: If you need any help, let me know.

I know she won't see it for a little while, since she's probably asleep, so I send another text off to Dean.

Me: Good morning, Dean. Thank you for letting me sleep this morning. I think I needed it after all the things you did to me *winky face emoji*. As for dinner, I would love to come over. But I have two questions; the first question is, should I bring a bag and assume that you will be kidnapping me for the night? And second, would you mind if I went over early and tried out the pool?

I hover over the send button., second-guessing myself over sort of inviting myself to use his pool, but then I think about how it's incredibly clear that all he wants is to make me happy. I click send as I realize how true that is.

As I kick the blankets off and stretch, I can feel where Dean gripped my hips, and I'm fairly certain there will be bruises that will look suspiciously like his fingers. The tinges through my body remind me of what we did last night. I can feel the blush creeping up my neck as the memory dances through my head. Getting up, I take a quick shower, and while my hair is still wet, I braid it over my shoulder and start getting dressed. Once I'm dressed, I check my phone and see that Dean responded, but not Harper, which I figured.

Dean: I think I wore you out pretty good last night. I wouldn't complain if you brought a bag to stay the night, either. And if this means I get to see you lounging poolside or in the pool like you belong in my home when I get home, by all means. Please use my pool. I have a key under the blue rock next to the back door that goes into the garage. Let yourself in and make yourself at home. XX

Me: Thank you *kiss emoji*

I pocket my phone as I head downstairs to make coffee and some breakfast. Then I get my work done that I need to do.

As I am finishing up the last thing on my to-do list, which is placing an order for more epoxy, my phone goes off with a text from Harper. I realize that it's almost noon as I open up her message.

Harper: I never found my bikini *crying face* or that shirt I was looking for.

Me: Do you have a mouse with some incredible fashion sense?

Harper: This isn't a joking matter. I know that bikini was in here. I remember the last time I wore it. And now it's gone. I have two more bins to catalog, then I'm done. I'm taking the day off today. Fuck being an adult.

Me: Well, you are running on only a few hours of sleep. I think that's understandable.

Harper: Wanna be lazy with me later?

I get an idea, and text Dean before I text Harper back.

Me: Would you mind terribly if Harper joined me? Something weird is going on, and she's frazzled.

His response is almost immediate.

Dean: That actually works, since Graham just informed me that Madison wanted to come over tonight. I was about to ask if you minded, but it looks like we are gonna have a little party on a Monday night LOL

Me: Do you need me to pick up anything on my way over?

Dean: Not unless there's anything specific you want.

Me: *light blue heart emoji*

I back out of our thread and go back to Harper's.

Me: How about you hang out with me at Dean's pool and be lazy?

Harper: I'm so fucking in!!

Me: I'll text you the address and let you know when I'm on my way, and you can meet me there.

Harper: Little sleep over on a school night for you two? *devil emoji*

. . .

I laugh and roll my eyes at her as I find a bag to use for tonight and stuff two changes of clothes, some pajamas—not that I ever seem to wear them around Dean—and my bathing suit into my bag. I grab my favorite beach and pool towel from the linen closet and toss it over my shoulder as I head out the door.

I head into town to stop by the grocery store and pick up some ingredients to make brownies and grab a couple of containers of pasta salads. As I get in the checkout line, I shoot a quick text to Harper to see if she's ready yet.

As I'm putting the bags in my car, Harper replies.

> Harper: I just finished the last box. I can deal with the cleanup and putting it all away tomorrow. I'm gonna change and I'll be ready in 5 minutes.

> Me: Ok, I'm on my way from the store. I should be at Dean's in 20.

I toss my phone into my purse and head over to Dean's.

Harper pulls in seconds behind me, parking behind me and leaving one side of the driveway open.

"Hey, hot stuff! Ready for some pool fun?" I ask as she gets out of her car.

"Fuck yes, I am." Harper laughs.

"So, no luck on finding your clothes? Was anything else missing?" I inquire as we walk around the garage.

"Nothing that I noticed, but if I'm not looking for something specific, it makes it harder to know." She lets out a heavy sigh. "I'm just so confused as to where they went."

"It is weird. But maybe they will turn up. Maybe they got mixed with something. I'm sure you will find them." I offer her a smile as I look down and spot the blue rock. I find the key under it and unlock the door to the garage.

"Yeah, maybe," she sighs. "Anyways, how is it going with Dean?" She wiggles her eyebrows at me and smiles.

"It's going extremely well. If I could only get out of my own way. But, fuck, Harper, it's so hard to take the last five years of unhealthy coping mechanisms and lock them away and stop waiting for the other shoe to drop."

Harper is silent for a beat before she gently says, "But I don't think you would have realized how much damage you were doing to yourself if this hadn't happened."

I send a questioning glance her way as we step into the garage.

"I just mean, I could see how much of yourself you were locking away. Not even after the funeral, but after Evan and the bullshit he spewed. You are NOT broken. You might have been for a minute, but that's allowed, given the situation. No one really expected you to bounce back after three months. Evan is the worst kind of human. He and Brady are probably best friends right now. Living it up and enjoying being complete assholes to women."

I scoff out a laugh as Harper follows me into the garage, because she's not wrong. Brady, her ex, is possibly worse than Evan. He tried to control so many aspects of her life, and even tried to tell her that being a social media manager wasn't good enough. Even though she makes more than he does, which is probably why he didn't like it. We both suspect that was part of his issue. I was so happy when she left him. He didn't make it easy, though. We kept bouncing her around our friends for the first month, just so he couldn't find her. Once he stopped showing up at everyone's houses, she moved in with me, and then a few months later, we started looking into our move south.

"I know I shouldn't let his words get to me, but in those moments, hearing them, it really messed with me. It still does." I pause with my hand on the door knob to go in the house. "Especially since I feel like I'm closing myself off to Dean. I feel this sense of peace when I'm with him, and then I feel guilty all over again because I don't know if I will ever be able to be the same for him. I might actually be broken, Harp." I take a deep breath before continuing, "I just don't know how to let the walls down and let someone back into my heart. It's scary to think about losing them, and I really don't think I can handle going through that again." I twist the knob, pushing the door open and add, "No, I know I can't." I step into the house with Harper following.

"I don't think you will ever go through that again. That was such a unique situation. You can't keep living your life with the expectation that this is what happens to those you love. I mean, hello? I'm right here. Totally fine." Harper raises her arms out from her sides, "I never even get sick. I know that letting go is not an option; what happened with Brian is not a wound that ever heals. But you can't keep living in the past and letting the past control your present and your future. *You* are the one who has to keep living in this world, and, Cordy, I think it's time you started again."

I know she's right. Objectivity, I know that. But it's so much harder to actually do. Maybe I can share some small pieces with Dean, but I'm in no way ready to share the whole story. Everything is still so new and fresh, and the last thing I want to do is blow it all to hell and back with this story. I also don't want him sticking by my side because of some sense of male need to fix everything. It's not like he can fix it anyway. Not without a flux capacitor. I know I need to get to the point where I stop hiding from this. But there's such a fine line between letting something traumatic define everything about you and letting it shape you and just be something you had to go through. But when I think of it that way, it doesn't do it justice. I can tell myself that I won't let this define me, but once it starts getting out there, it becomes what others define me as. So, by not talking about it, I've allowed it to be something that happened, which makes it that much harder to admit to it. It's a double-edged sword that keeps cutting me no matter how I try to handle it.

Harper lets out a whistle as she walks into the kitchen. "Wow, this house is so nice! I thought the outside was gorgeous, but wow, it's even better inside!"

He really did a beautiful job with it. The whole house is white on the outside, but all the trim around the doors and windows, as well as the doors and shutters, is black. The roof is a black metal roof as well. It's a ranch, but with a basement off the dining room.

"He even has Carrera marble," I say, setting the grocery bags on the counter.

Harper lets out an exaggerated gasp, "Carrera marble?! Your favorite!"

I laugh and head down the hallway with my overnight bag.

Harper calls out, "Does he have any pool floats?"

I turn, "I can check and see or text him. I'm gonna change first."

I head past the open staircase that goes downstairs, into a hallway, and see that it has a bedroom set up as an office to the left, a Jack and Jill bathroom, and a guest bedroom. Then I turn to the right and see his room. I head in, and you guessed it. Black furniture, but his duvet is a soft gray. So he added a little variety to this room. I laugh to myself and shake my head before setting my bag on his bed and starting to change into my bathing suit.

A couple of minutes later, I hear Harper yell something as I come out of Dean's bedroom. I find her in the garage, trying to carry out three floats that are already blown up.

"I will be out in a couple of minutes. I'm gonna mix up the brownie batter and put the pasta salad in the fridge. Dibs on the green float!"

I make my way back into the kitchen, where I start going

through his cabinets and the pantry before I find a gorgeous, brand-new, and possibly never-used KitchenAid stand mixer in mint green. I have always wanted one of these, in this exact color. I grab it, hefting it up to carry it out to the kitchen. I spot an open plug and set it on the counter near it.

Once I put the pasta salads in the fridge, I pull out the eggs and rummage around until I find the rest of what I need.

I start pouring the brownie mix into the mixing bowl and the rest of the ingredients into the mixing bowl while I search for a baking dish. Once I find one, I spray the dish and pour the batter into it Covering it with tin foil, I pop it into the fridge.

I quickly clean up, knowing I'll put everything away once it dries when I come in to put the brownies into the oven.

I wander out of the kitchen into the open living room. He has the necessities: a couch, a TV, a table, but there's a cold and detached feeling to the space. He doesn't have anything on the walls, and there's no color. His walls are white, and his couches are black leather. He certainly carried the theme from the outside to the inside. I laugh and decide the next time I'm over here, I'm going to bring one of the paintings I did and hang it up to add a little color to his house. I just have to get into my attic and find a couple of the canvases that I ran out of room for in my house with its limited wall space.

Once I stop snooping and get back outside, Harper is already on the pink lounge float, soaking up the sun.

"Enjoying yourself?"

"Girl, I needed this after tearing apart and then cataloging my entire summer wardrobe," Harper quips back. "Oh, I found the fridge in the garage, fully stocked, and tossed in a couple of my new favorite drinks, and I grabbed you a hard cider. I set it on the table over there." She points toward the table in the sunroom.

"Thanks," I respond as I go grab the drink, and then, before I get into the pool, I send off a text to Dean asking him what time he thinks he will be home. While I wait for his answer, I slide open all the glass walls. When he responds, I set an alarm on my phone for forty-five minutes before then so I can get the brownies in the oven. We have a little over four hours before that even needs to happen, and I know if I don't put sunscreen on, I will be a tomato by then. "Harper, help me do my back, please?"

She slowly paddles over to the steps and then carefully gets out of the float, so she doesn't tip over into the water.

"You should probably put some on too," I say.

"I did that before I left. I was prepared."

We spend the rest of the afternoon back and forth between the pool and the sunroom for some shade. Once I have the brownies in the oven, Harper and I are back to lounging in the pool. I set a timer for half an hour so that I can be mostly dry when it's time to pull the brownies out and not track water all through the house.

I never heard Dean's truck over our music, but when I open my eyes to paddle over to where I left my phone to check the time, I find Dean smirking at me from the edge of the sunroom.

"Hey," I offer with a wave.

"Hi, ladies," he smiles as he strides over. He squats down so he can be low enough to give me a kiss.

"Aw, you two are disgustingly adorable," Harper laughs.

I smile against Dean's lips and pull back, using my foot to splash water toward Harper. "Don't be jealous."

"Only a little bit. But I'm also perfectly fine not having to worry about having any crazy in my life right now," she quips.

"It smells amazing in the house," Dean tells me.

"I thought I would whip up some brownies for tonight," I tell him as the alarm on my phone goes off. "That's my alarm to get out and dry off so I can pull the brownies out in a few."

"I can take them out," Dean offers as I try to gracefully get off the lounger and fail horribly. Thankfully, I didn't go under.

"No, I will get them. You are already making dinner for all of us. I can handle these while you shower or just jump in the pool."

He smirks down at me as I take the last step out of the pool. His eyes are sparkling with mischief. I take a step back because that look can only mean one thing when there's a pool involved. "Dean, no. Don't you dare." I hold up my hands to try to ward him off and take another step back. Before I can take another step, though, he grabs me around the middle, pulling me flush to him.

Dipping his head so his lips brush my ear, he says, "But you look so good dripping wet." The husk in his voice makes the innuendo clear, and I have to clench my thighs together as I feel my skin start to heat.

His grip loosens, and I ease back, looking down at the water that transferred from me to him. "Well, now you're wet too," I smirk.

"It's the only way I want to be. Covered in your wetness," he whispers the last part.

Before I can open my mouth to respond, we both get hit with a splash of water. "Break it up, you two. Fuck. I think I might be pregnant from having to witness that!" Harper exclaims with a shudder.

Laughing, I offer Dean my towel to dry off a little, and he takes it and wraps it around my waist instead. "I'm just going to shower, I don't need a towel. You ladies keep enjoying the pool," he calls as he walks back in the house.

Chapter Nineteen

DEAN

Once I make it into my bedroom, I pause mid-step because Cordelia has a bag and her stuff across the bed. When I step closer, I can faintly smell her rose scent from the clothes on the bed.

Fuck.

If seeing her in that bikini wasn't bad enough, now to smell her in my bedroom, my dick is painfully hard, as it always seems to be around her, and I think I'm about to take the coldest shower I've ever had.

I strip out of my clothes, then turn the water on as I get into the shower. The cold water actually feels good after being in the heat today.

I hate making my guys work in the summer months when it's this hot if I'm not out there helping them. I spent the morning getting the office work done, and then after lunch, I went out and helped the boys work. Thankfully, we were able to wrap a little early today.

Once the water turns from frigid to lukewarm, I grab the soap and get to work washing the sweat and dirt off of me. I move quickly, since I want to get back out there to Cordelia. Coming home today to my house smelling like warm chocolate and hearing the laughter in the backyard, it hit me like a truck, how much I have been wanting and wishing for this.

Fuck, this is everything to me.

This is what I have been wanting for so long. The first time she's in my house alone for a little bit, and she bakes. Yeah. I'm going to need to make sure that she understands we are doing this. That she is *my girl*. Girlfriend doesn't seem like the most accurate of words, but calling her just a lover doesn't work either. No, the only word that really works is *mine or wife*. Maybe I can just call her wife in my head until I can make it a reality.

Once I'm done showering, I throw on some swim shorts and grab a shirt, opting not to put it on since I plan on jumping in that pool. I can't wait to grab Cordelia and take her into that pool with me.

When I come out of the hallway after leaving the bedroom, I'm met with something that, until this very moment, has only been a wet dream that I didn't even know I had. Cordelia, in just her bikini, bent over pulling the brownies out of the oven.

So much for that cold shower.

I let out a groan as I walk up behind her as she sets the brownies down on the stove top. Once her hands are clear and the oven is closed, I grab her around her waist, turning her to face me, and set her on the counter.

"Cordelia," I growl out, "I just had to take a cold shower when I came home to this." I wave my hand at her, indicating I mean *all* of her. "And now I have to see you bend over in that same thing, which barely covers anything, knowing that I can't rip them off you right now and bury myself in you until your screams echo through this house. Once again, I find myself with a problem that is probably not going to go away any time soon." I raise my eyebrow before finishing, "What do you think I should do about this situation?"

I watch as her eyes flick to the window that looks out to the back, and when she sees Harper still in the pool, her eyes bounce back to mine. "Well, I can move these to the side, or I can get on my knees. And given my age and these floors, I'm not so sure the latter is the best option." When her hand travels to the apex of her thighs and she starts to move the scrap of fabric to the side, showing me exactly where I want to be, my dick twitches in my pants. "You gonna fuck me quick and then make me get on my knees to swallow you down?" She mirrors my earlier movement with a raise of her eyebrow in a questioning challenge.

"Fucking hell, woman, you are going to be the death of me," I ground out as I push my shorts just low enough to free my cock. I pull her closer to the edge of the counter and line up and push into her in one fast motion. We both let out a shuddering moan, trying to keep quiet at the same time.

"Fuck, Dean, you feel so good like this," she purrs before she pulls me to her, and her mouth meets mine.

I start pistoning into her, and my hand reaches for that sensitive bud, drawing circles before I flick and pinch. When I feel her pussy start to flutter around me, I know she's close, and I do it again.

"You gonna come for me? You gonna be a good girl and come on my cock before I fill your mouth?"

"Fuck! Yes, Dean, yes!" She arches her back as her pussy squeezes around me like a vice. I barely have the control to pull out and pull her off the counter. When she drops to her knees and takes the tip into her mouth, and her eyes move to mine, I know I'm not going to last. She sucks my cock halfway in, her cheeks hollowing out, and the second time she does it, I feel my orgasm tingling at the base of my spine. The third time has me falling apart.

"Fuck, Rosebud," I gasp out as I feel my cum shooting out, and she keeps sucking. When I'm spent and sensitive, she keeps sucking, causing my whole body to convulse before she pulls off with an audible pop and pulls my shorts back up to cover my spent cock.

I pull her up to me, putting her bikini bottoms back to rights before crashing my lips to hers, my tongue immediately demanding entry. I can taste myself on hers when she opens. It's incredibly sexy knowing that she lets me fill all of her with me. Pulling back, I take her face in my hands, "You are the sexiest thing that has ever dared to walk this earth, you know that?"

I can see the embarrassment flash across her face. "That's just the orgasm talking," she tries to play it off.

"Oh, Cordelia, if you think that's all, I haven't been doing a very good job showing you just how important you are to me." I drop one hand to her ass and squeeze it, *hard*, pushing her against my still hard length. "You see what you do to me? Now, be a good girl and tell me you understand that it is not the orgasm talking."

When she doesn't answer right away, I tighten the grip on her ass, causing her to jerk in my hold. "I understand, it's not the orgasm talking," she mumbles, barely audible.

"That's my good girl." I grab her hand and drag her toward the door to the garage, and once I have her through the doorway that leads outside, I throw her over my shoulder and cannonball into the pool before she has a moment to protest.

I hear Harper laughing when I break the surface and turn to see Cordelia scowling at me. "You can't just go around throwing girls into pools, Dean! I almost lost my contact lenses!" she yells.

"Then I guess I would have had to drive you home in the morning and be late to work."

She narrows her eyes at me before she pushes water at me. "Oh, you wanna play? You're gonna lose," my voice drops low.

"No! No splashing! I'm gonna end up in the crossfire and I don't want to wash my hair tonight!" Harper starts screeching from her lounger as she tries to grab the handle of the stairs to help her off the inflatable. She really is a tiny thing, so watching her try to maneuver herself off the float and not go into the water is something worth laughing over. It reminds me of a little sea turtle that's stuck on their back and their little flippers can't get them flipped over.

"Alright, alright. I won't splash. You're gonna hurt yourself trying to get off that damn thing! Just stay there," I say to her.

"Oh sure, you'll be nice to her but not me?" Cordelia tries to sound hurt, but I can hear the humor in her voice.

"It's only because watching her try to get off that reminded me of a baby sea turtle, and I felt bad."

Cordelia starts laughing so hard that her eyes are watering. Between breaths, she tries to say, "I can – totally – see that!"

"You two are jerks," Harper pouts from her float.

"You didn't have to get off the thing, and you didn't get splashed, and we are the jerks?" Cordelia giggles.

"I said what I said."

Cordelia starts making her way to Harper, and when she grabs the float, she smirks at her. "What was that?"

"You're a beautiful and wonderful friend that I would never say a mean or bad thing about. You are my favorite person that I did not birth." Harper's white knuckle grip on the float is the only indication that she's a little nervous that Cordelia might actually flip her.

"Aww, there's my bestie," Cordelia coos. "Thought I lost you for a minute there."

"Just no splashing or flipping. We literally just did my hair. I do NOT want to wash it yet," Harper pouts.

"Should have just said that. You know I don't cross the hair gods." Cordelia backs away and holds her hands up in mock surrender before she turns to me. "You, however, have angered the hair gods. If the chlorine screws up my hair, I'm gonna have a bone to pick with you."

On one side, my mouth lifts as I say, "Rosebud, I got a bone you can have all day, any day."

"Gross! I do NOT need to hear that!"

"What do we not need to hear?" Graham questions as he steps out of the open sunroom.

"Their sex life, in detail," Harper quips.

"Yeah, we don't need Madison to hear that," Graham laughs and then leans over to fist-bump me. "Good job, bro."

I laugh and tap my knuckles to his.

Madison joins us in the pool a few minutes later, and we all take a little time to enjoy the cool water after the heat of the day. Eventually, I get out, get the grill fired up, and get some burgers going. At least always assuming that Graham and Madison will stop over any given day means I always have enough burgers and buns should the situation arise that I need them.

Turning on the large ceiling fan in the sunroom, I decide that we will eat outside. With everyone still in semi-wet bathing suits, it makes more sense, since we can all dry off a little bit more.

Before I can start setting out plates, Cordelia comes out with paper plates, napkins, pasta salad, and some silverware. "I couldn't find the plasticware, but these are easy enough to toss in the dishwasher after." Her eyes meet mine, and I'm once again blown away at how effortlessly she fits into my space, my life. She lifts the paper plates up, asking, "Are these ok? Did you want real plates?"

"Perfectly fine. I was actually going to get them. You just beat me to it. I usually just use regular silverware unless it's an actual party. Like you said, it's easy to toss into the dishwasher."

She tucks a stray hair behind her ear and smiles. "Great minds think alike, huh?"

"They certainly do."

Once we all get settled around the table, Cordelia across from me, Harper next to her, Madison at an end, and Graham next to me, everyone digs in, and no one talks much except to say how good the food is.

"Dean, you are a grill master. Please feel free to invite me over anytime you feel like cooking," Harper says after her first bite.

"Ya know, speaking of that. Fourth of July is two weeks away. Are you setting off fireworks again?" Graham asks.

"Please say yes, Uncle Dean!" Madison chimes in.

"I already got the fireworks for it, like I would ever let you down, Mads," I say, pointing at her with my fork.

Madison claps her hands a couple of times, "Yay! Uncle Dean puts on an even better display than the town does. A couple of years ago, they asked him to stop doing them on the same day because more people were coming out to see his and not theirs."

Harper laughs, "It must be a damn good display. Do you do it all yourself?"

"No, all the guys help out, Graham, Bast, and Lach. And for the record, they didn't ask me to change it so much as they said they would deny my permit for the Fourth."

"You have to get a permit?" Cordelia asks.

"Yeah. I mean, technically, yes, but I could probably get away without it. It's gotten to the point where they pretty much have it ready to go when I get there, and I just have to sign it," I chuckle. "But they do like having it so they can let the fire department know. There's usually a truck sitting down on one of the roads, depending on which way the wind is blowing. Just in case. There's not a lot of houses out this way, but it's better to have them close in case one spark lands on something it shouldn't."

Graham adds, "What Dean isn't saying is that you ladies are invited. Obviously. And if you have any other single girlfriends, you should bring them too."

I almost choke on my drink, and Cordelia's eyes catch mine and wink.

"You good man?" Graham asks.

I cough and wheeze out, "Yeah, just went down wrong." If he knew that one of their single friends was the shop owner he had his run-in with last year, he wouldn't have asked that. I meet Cordelia's eyes again, and they seem to say something along the lines of what I'm thinking.

"Yeah, we have two, actually. I mean, Harper is also, so technically that's three for ya," Cordelia offers in a matter-of-fact tone.

Harper punches Cordelia in the arm, "We don't need to flaunt it. Besides, I JUST told you that I was happy right now being on my own."

"I didn't mean anything by it, I was just saying."

"Besides, no offense, Graham, but you're a little on the young side for me."

Graham points his fork between the two ladies and says, "Y'all aren't the same age?"

They laugh, and Harper says, "Nah, I'm three years older. I'll be forty-five in October. And she will be forty-two in December."

"Well, I'm only two years younger," Graham says, flashing a grin at Harper.

"Save it, you man-child. Any guy who is not six months older than I am at the *minimum* falls into the too young category. Sorry about your luck." She shrugs and goes back to her food.

"Harper, you said something earlier. Do you have kids?" I ask after swallowing a bite of pasta salad.

Harper's eyes soften, "Yeah, I have two. A boy and a girl." She laughs and adds, "That makes them sound like little kids, but they are grown. My daughter, Lilith, is twenty-four and lives in Orlando. She took after me with the social media thing. Except she managed to get in with NASA. Blows my mind sometimes how far she's come." Harper's eyes dart to Cordelia quickly and then away again. If I weren't watching her, I would have missed it. "And my son, Dante, he's twenty, is in California getting his PhD., he loves school. It's crazy, he wants to be a professor and teach psychology."

My eyebrows shoot up, and Graham's eyes widen, "Whoa. Those are some impressive career choices."

Graham chimes in, "You must be one proud mama."

Harper smiles and nods around a mouthful of food. "All the time."

Cordelia slips inside with a handful of plates to toss and comes back out with the brownies a few minutes later. I grab one and take a bite, mumbling out how good they are. Once I swallow the first bite, I tell her, "Ya know, coming home to the house smelling like chocolate, I haven't experienced that since my mom made cupcakes that last summer break she was here for." She grabs my hand across the table, giving it a squeeze.

Graham lets out a groan, "Man, I miss those cupcakes. Fu-

fudge," he corrects himself since Madison is here. "I miss summer breaks." Pointing at Madison, he adds, "Must be nice!"

She just smirks and sticks her tongue out and goes back to her brownies.

When everyone has had their fill and is starting to gather their things to head out, I take a moment to enjoy the feeling of things finally falling into place. Feminine laughter starts to tinkle through the sweet summer air as Cordelia and Harper gather up the floats from the pool, refusing to let us do it since they are the ones who pulled them out. I catch Cordelia saying something about a baby turtle between laughs, and I know what she's laughing about. The whole scene brings a contented smile to my face.

Once everyone leaves, I pull Cordelia into my arms, with her back flush to my chest.

"I gotta ask if you talked to Gwen about Graham."

"I sure did. She claims it was just a misunderstanding." Cordelia turns in my arms, "It's not really my place to say this, but Gwen has POTS, and it makes doing certain things hard for her because it wipes her out. That's the easy explanation, anyway. So, when she had just finished that display the day before, and she was still exhausted the next day, and here comes Graham taking it all down without asking because she was tossing the trash out the back of the store when he came in, she kinda lost it."

"I guess that makes sense. I could see how that would be upsetting. Did Graham help put it all back? I honestly don't know because I had to leave early that day."

"Nah, she left it down once she knew why he did it. The next day, she had Faye run over from the hotel across the street, and she helped her get it all back up. Thankfully, she got pictures of it, so they were able to make it look the same." Cordelia shrugs and adds, "She did also say she apologized once she knew why he was doing it."

"Well, it would be interesting to see those two interact again,"

I say before pressing a kiss to her forehead. "Think you will invite them over for the party? I'm doing it on the third."

"Yeah, I will let them know. I'm sure Faye will be here. Gwen is a maybe, just because of her health issues. It's always a day-to-day thing." Before I can comment further, she asks, "So you can shoot off fireworks, huh?"

"Yes."

"What if I wanted to add it as a service for weddings? Could I hire you?"

"You're not gonna pay me to blow stuff up, it's too fun."

"Ok, well, not me, but the bride and groom would technically hire you. Come up with a cost package, like maybe three options? I'd love to add that to the list of services we can make happen for them. I know it would be a huge hit."

"I can do that. I enjoy setting those things off."

"Thank you," she says before she rises on her toes to press a kiss to my lips.

We take our time getting ready for bed, and she emerges from the bathroom in one of my shirts. The thought of ripping it off her is overwhelming, but I also love seeing her in my clothes. I wish I weren't as tired as I was from being in the sun and heat all day. Nothing would make me happier than to sink inside her body again and show her how much I love having her here in my bed.

Although the way she climbs into bed next to me and cuddles up, resting her head on my chest, tells me she might be just as tired.

"There isn't much more I would love to do than worship this body tonight, but I am beat after today. Summer heat always takes a lot out of me."

"Such an old man," she giggles. "But I'm pretty tired too. This was the most I have spent in the sun in a while, and it kicked my ass as well." She yawns and curls into me more.

I brush some hair back so I can see her face and tip her chin up with a finger so I can kiss her. It turns heated, tongues tangling, until we are both breathless.

"We can just sleep," she says softly, brushing her fingers down my cheek.

I take in her face. Her eyes are truly a remarkable shade of green, and she's got a smattering of freckles across her nose. Her lips are perfectly plump and pink. "You really are just beautiful," I tell her softly.

"Thank you," she whispers as a blush spreads across her face and she ducks her head back down to my chest.

I know she's still healing from whatever loss she had to endure, and before I know what I'm doing, the words are spilling out.

"I know you lost someone. You don't need to tell me details, but I really need to say this," I start as my fingers draw lazy circles across her back. "Losing someone that is a defining part of your life can destroy and break you, it can also shatter your world, and it really comes down to who is there to help pick up those pieces and put them together. I won't tell you it will make you stronger, and you will be better for it. That's not always the case, but just because something is broken, it doesn't mean it can't be beautiful. There's this ancient Chinese technique where they use gold to fix broken vases. It's not as strong as it was, but it's still beautiful. You are still beautiful. I will do anything I can to help put the pieces back. Even if we are missing some, I will try to help fill them in and make things whole for you."

I can feel the tears falling onto my bare chest by the time I'm done.

"I don't want to tell you everything right now, but what I will tell you is that it is a huge part of me now. When everything happened, the guy I was with after a few months was pushing back and telling me that he couldn't understand why I was still such a broken mess. He had never lost someone aside from a couple of grandparents, and that's not easy, but it's easier to process when someone has had a full life and passes away. When someone is taken when they are younger, it's just... different. I struggled a lot during that time. But I had to put a brave face on because it was what was expected of me; I had things that I needed to do. I never took the appropriate—" she lets out a little scoffing laugh and continues. "There is no appropriate amount of time for healing from that. Hearing that he was expecting me to bounce back after a few months just made me push it all down. I felt like I wasn't allowed to grieve for what I had lost.

"And then a month or two later, where I was working, they started making comments as well. I left there as soon as I could. But that took longer. I packed my stuff at the end of my shift one night, left my badge on my desk, and walked out. I ended it with Evan far sooner than that. It was shortly after he said that to me. I had a therapy session a week later, and I broke down, telling her what happened. She helped put things in perspective, and I realized that he would never understand. I went from that session to telling him he needed to pack his things and get out of my house.

"You know the worst part? He didn't seem like he cared. He didn't fight me or anything. Just packed up and walked out."

By the time she's done, I want to go find these assholes and punch their lights out. I'm shaking with anger. I can't even begin to fathom telling someone who has lost someone important to them, and that they loved, that they need to get over it. To imply that they are not allowed to grieve has me fuming. I adjust us so that I'm facing her.

"Cordelia, I'm telling you right now, I've seen firsthand what happens to people who don't work through their grief and become shells of the person they were before. You have such a light inside of you, and I need you to know, to understand, to believe me when I tell you that there is no set timeline for grief and how you process it. But you do have to go through it. You are gorgeous inside and out, and there is nothing that I won't do to remind you of that. You are not broken. You went through something, something difficult, and anyone who can't give you grace and understanding during a time like that is not worthy to even breathe the same air as you."

She's got tears streaming down her face, but her eyes are full of light. I take her face in my hands and kiss her again.

"Thank you, Dean. I needed to hear that." She puts her head back on my chest and snuggles in.

My head is spinning, filled with thoughts of how to exact revenge for this girl. I want to rip that Evan guy to pieces. I don't even know the guy, but he's a real piece of work. But I keep coming back to the fact that, given she was with someone, whoever she lost wasn't a husband or a fiancé. Maybe a brother? Maybe a—I cut the thought off. Because that simply cannot be an option.

Chapter Twenty

DEAN

I spent these last two weeks running around and getting things together and ready for the Fourth of July party. The last time I saw Cordelia was when I woke her up with my tongue on her sweet pussy that Tuesday morning. She's been busy, and my days have been long between work and all the errands for the holiday. We texted and I called her every night. Thankfully, with the holiday falling on a Friday this year, I ended up calling the crew off before noon today, giving them an extra bit of a holiday break. Not to mention, I always give them the day before the Fourth off as well, since most of them like to come to my show, and well, to be honest, I need the day for setup.

Cordelia and I were supposed to spend last weekend together, but she had to help with a wedding where the bride was being, what she called, a bridezilla. By the time the wedding was over and everyone had left, she stayed to clean up and apologized about twenty times the next day for bailing. I know how it is when you own a business that deals with customers and relies so heavily on making them happy. Sometimes, our social lives take a hit to ensure that our livelihood is intact. She was very happy that, this holiday weekend, the two weddings both happened to hire actual wedding planners, which means she doesn't need to be there as much. She knows both of the planners well, and they know their way around the venue and where everything is. She was just going to get the signs she made and drop them off, as she is the only one with a key to her craft shed.

I cannot wait to have her back in my bed tonight. It's been too many days without her in my arms, in my bed, without her wrapped around my dick. I scrub a hand down my face as I finish locking up the office trailer. I haven't thought about my dick this much since I first realized what it was good for.

I shake my head and take a deep inhale. The air has that sweet mountain smell with a hint of wildflowers out here. Thankfully, it's not as humid as it has been. The storm last night seemed to break some of that. And it looks like it will be clear the rest of the weekend as well.

I have to drive over to Asheville today to pick up the steaks for the cookout prior to the fireworks. I like to splurge on the good steaks for this weekend. It's the one holiday I go all out for. Something about grilling up a bunch of good food and then blowing stuff up later... Yeah, I'm probably a child on this holiday, but it really is fun. I've been going back and forth in my head all day about asking if Cordelia wants to go with me, just to spend some time together.

Fuck it.

After I climb into my truck and start it up, I call her.

"Hey, handsome," she says after the first ring.

"Were you waiting by the phone for my call?"

"Ha-ha, no, I actually just picked it up to send you a text."

"What's up?" I ask.

"Just wanted to see how your day was going and when you would be done."

"Funny enough, that's why I called you. I kicked everyone off the site and sent them home early for the holiday. I'm about thirty minutes from my house, and I need to take a quick shower yet, but..." I trail off.

"What?"

"Want to take a trip into Asheville with me? There's this fantastic butcher I always place a special order of steaks with for the Fourth, and I need to go pick them up."

She lets out a little squeak of excitement, and I laugh. "Yes! I love Asheville! Fuck—wait, no, it's fine. I can just bring everything to your house and finish up the cupcakes for tomorrow when we get back. I was just about to start frosting them," she rushes everything out in one breath.

"You made cupcakes?"

"Yup! And honestly, your kitchen is almost twice the size of mine, so frosting these there the way I want to will be much easier."

"I love cupcakes. What flavor?"

Cordelia's laugh filters into my ear from the phone, making my heart skip. I love making her laugh. It's like this little mini reward, to know I'm responsible for bringing her joy.

"Dean! You'll see when you get home. I'm gonna get all this packed and cleaned up and head your way. We should get there about the same time."

I let out a groan and put my truck into gear. "Fine," I pout, "But I get to taste the first one when they are ready."

"Deal, but you get the first one tomorrow, or you will ruin my whole design. Now, be careful driving. I'll see you in a few."

We hang up, and the thought that once again, I get to go *home* and see her makes these last days without her seem worth it.

Once I pull into my driveway and see her getting out of her car, it confirms everything. Coming home to her is what makes coming home worth it. It solidifies what I have been missing in my life these last forty-some years.

Her.

She looks gorgeous, with her hair braided over her shoulder, and she has on these short shorts that hug her ass and a tank top that's just low enough. My dick is suddenly paying attention and starts hardening behind my zipper.

We really need to have a talk about when it's ok to do this to me,
I think while glancing at my groin.

I park my truck in the overflow spot that is reserved for the
work truck so that I don't have to move vehicles around. Once I
park, I adjust myself and jump out of the truck.

Cordelia saunters over, and she either is putting an extra sway
in her hips or I just haven't seen her or been able to put my hands
on her that's the reason I'm picking up on everything she does.

She wraps her arms around my neck and presses flush to my
chest, "I missed you."

"I missed you too, Rosebud," I press my lips to hers and let
my hands travel up her sides, one gripping her waist and the other
the back of her neck.

She pulls away too soon, saying, "It's already hot out here, we
don't need to make it worse."

"Yeah, that didn't help my situation either," I flick my eyes
down, and her eyes follow. When they land on my straining erection, she lets out a giggling, "Oops."

"I don't think you're actually sorry. Not even a little bit."

"A little bit, since we don't have time for a proper reunion." She
backs away, going to grab her bag and the container of cupcakes.

I quickly grab the container, and when I see the other bag in
the back, I grab that too before I head into the house through the
garage. I place my items down on the kitchen counter, press a
quick kiss to her cheek, and jog off to take a quick shower.

When I come back out, pulling a shirt over my head, Cordelia
is leaning against the counter. "You ready yet? Let's go. I'm tired
of waiting on you."

"Oh, it's like that today? Gonna be a brat?" I say as I place a
hand on the counter on each side of her, caging her in.

"Maaybee," she drags out the word and bites her bottom lip.

"You are not helping here, Rosebud. We got a schedule to
keep."

"Says the one who came down the hall without a shirt on,

looking mouthwatering with your wet hair and that freshly showered scent."

I press a kiss to her collarbone and push off the counter, grabbing her hand and forcing her in front of me and back out the door to the garage. I give her a little slap on the ass, "Mmm, you're gonna have to walk in front of me the whole day. I don't want other guys looking at this perfect ass." I can feel the eye roll she gives me as she makes her way out to the garage. I grab one of my hats from the rack next to the door before I step through, closing it behind me. I open the passenger door and help her into my truck before I get in, and we pull out.

Once she adjusts in her seat until she's sitting almost sideways with her back against the door, she breaks the silence. "I hate that I haven't gotten to see you at all in almost two weeks. Work swamped me."

"Me too, Rosebud, me too. I was happy you agreed to join me today."

"I'm glad you asked me. I'm also really excited to use your kitchen, too. I don't think I ever told you, but the way you have that kitchen set up, darker lowers and white uppers, and the Carrera marble, it's almost exactly how I would have done it. It's my dream kitchen."

I raise my eyebrows, "You knew that was Carrera?"

Cordelia laughs, "Yeah, a little too much HGTV back in the day. But I love how no matter if I wanted to change the colors ever, everything would go with it. It's classic."

"That it is."

"I did bring something over for your living room. You don't have a lot in the way of personality in your house; it's very minimalist. I thought it could use some color." She shrugs and bites her bottom lip.

"Cordelia, you can decorate anything in my house however you want. Bring some of you into it. Make it colorful. Fill it with photos, flowers, and whatever girlie shit you want. I can build them and design them, but when it comes to personality," I shake my head, "That's where I fail."

"Dean, I don't think you realize how much stuff I have stacked in my attic that I don't have room on my walls for. I could easily put something on every wall in that house."

"I'm telling you right now, once you decide that your feelings mirror mine, I will be moving you into my house so fast, so please. Decorate until your heart is content."

She doesn't say anything, and when I glance over at her, she's staring at me with her mouth in a little *O* shape. "What? What did I say?"

She blinks a couple of times before she says, "You want me to move in with you? Already?"

"Well, if you wanted to, I wouldn't say no. Although the appeal to not go two weeks without seeing you again certainly has its perks. But I know you probably aren't quite ready for that."

She sputters, closes her mouth, takes a breath, and tries again, "I mean, it is a little soon for me to be moving in. But I can agree that going two weeks without seeing you was a little too long for my taste as well."

"Well, at least we agree on that point." She huffs out a laugh and shakes her head. "I know you said you needed to go slow with these kinds of heavy emotional things. Moving in is a big step. I'm not rushing you. But I wanted you to know that I would be ok with it when you are ready."

"Yeah, there's a lot of conversations we need to have before that happens," she readjusts her seat and looks out the window.

"Hey," I say, reaching for her hand. "I didn't mean now. I just wanted to let you know that you can use the kitchen of your dreams any time you want, the pool, all of it. Anytime. You know where I keep the spare key, and honestly, I would just get you your own if you wanted one. No more two weeks between seeing each other." She eyes my hand and then places hers in mine, intertwining our fingers together. I give it a squeeze before I pull it up to my lips and place a kiss on her knuckles.

"What if I show up at ten at night and just need a hug?"

"Use the key, get a hug." I smile.

"And if you are asleep?"

"Rosebud, I would gladly be woken up by you just for a hug."

Her eyes drop to our hands, and I can see a hint of a smile tugging at the corner of her lips. "Ok."

We settle into a comfortable silence for a little while. Once we get into Asheville, her eyes bounce around at everything.

"I'll never get tired of coming into this town. There's so much to see and do here. I feel like I never get to see everything there is, though."

"Might have to make a weekend of it. Come up and stay at the Biltmore?"

She whips her head over to me. "That place is the reason I was inspired to start a wedding venue down here. Obviously, mine isn't nearly as grand and magnificent, but there's a natural beauty to Glass where Biltmore is all manicured gardens and lawns. I just don't have the green thumb I like to think I have to be able to do that. That's why I have just roses that I deal with. Harper is trying to talk me into doing a sunflower field."

"You know, we could do that. I'm fairly certain that Murph has a big tractor I can trailer out there to make planting easy."

"Guess we have a project for next spring, then, don't we?" She smiles at me.

I pull into a parking spot on the street a block away from the butcher and turn to her, "We'd better find the right spot on your property for it then."

Cordelia and I walk hand in hand to pick up what I need. We walk back to the truck, and when I open her door, my gaze lands on the coffee and ice cream shop across the street from us. "Hey, you wanna grab an ice cream before we head out?"

"Why does ice cream always taste better when it comes from a shop?" she asks as she takes my hand and steps out of the way of the truck door so I can close it. "I'm not even talking about the difference in soft-serve vs traditional hand scooped. Even when they make it and sell it in stores, it still always tastes better at an ice cream shop."

I'm smiling as she keeps talking; the little glimpses into who she is, like this, are my favorite moments. She tells me so much about herself when she does this. I know she has a carefree nature underneath it all. I can see that her default setting is to be this way. To be happy and enjoy the little things in life. But I also notice that a moment after speaking, her eyes dim a little bit, almost like she remembers something that makes her sad. Wanting to bring the joy back to her eyes, I pull her back and pin her against the tailgate of my truck. I lean down and put my lips next to her ear, "Tell me, Rosebud, have you been a good girl for me these last two weeks? I need to make sure you earn those sprinkles I know you want."

When I pull back and see her smile reaching her eyes, I know I did my job. She nods, and her words come out in a breath, "Yes. But how did you know I was going to get sprinkles?"

"Because you deserve all the pretty things, and sprinkles make ice cream pretty, at least according to Madison." I shrug.

She laughs and shakes her head, "I like that your niece has made sure that you are such a smart man."

I laugh and take her hand and lead her up the street. The butcher shop is only a few storefronts away, and since they have my order ready to go, it took us longer to walk up to them than it did to get my order.

Once we finish that, I unlock the truck, put the steaks in the truck, and grab Cordelia's hand, leading her across the street to get our ice cream. I order a double scoop of cookies and cream in a waffle cone with sprinkles, naturally. Cordelia has to sample a couple of different flavors before she settles on the raspberry cheesecake in a bowl with the unicorn sprinkles that they offer. I chuckle when I hear her ask for those specifically. While she waits, I pay, and then we head back across the street to the truck. There's just enough room between the car behind us that I can put the tailgate down, making us a spot to sit. We eat our ice cream side by side, and I smile as I watch Cordelia swing her feet back and forth. The simple joy that she exudes from just getting ice cream is making my heart swell. I would do anything to have a lifetime of these moments with her. The heat is almost too much as it forces all my attention back to the ice cream before it melts all over my hands.

"That's why I got a cup. It's way too hot out to try to make sure your hands don't get all sticky," she giggles, watching me try to keep up with all sides of the ice cream cone.

I give her a glare, and she leans over and licks up my cone. My eyes track every movement. Her pink tongue flattens against the cone, and then the little flick when she gets to the top of the scoop. All of it sends a jolt down my spine right to my dick, which is rapidly lengthening behind my zipper. "Mmmm, that's good too."

"Well," I say and try to glance around quickly before I pull at my pants to give myself a little more room. "You're going to be paying for that little show when we get home." She smirks and puts a spoonful into her mouth.

We finish our ice cream, and I end up having to pour a little of Cordelia's water over my hands to rinse the stickiness off.

"I'll have to remember to get a cup next time if we are going to be sitting outside for ice cream," I say as I start my truck and put my seat belt on.

"I'll remind you."

"You better," I say before I ease out of the parking spot and we make our way back home.

We chat about anything and everything. She explains the Jeep Poke game that she and Harper always play when they go anywhere together. Essentially, if you see a Jeep Wrangler, you call out the color and poke the other in the car. She's kicking my ass, which I have to say is to be expected. When I go to poke her as we pass a dealership, she explains that dealerships are not allowed, but the car transport trucks are.

When we get home, I stalk over to her side of the truck, rip her door open, and throw her over my shoulder. "Dean! What are you doing?!" She squeals as she tries to keep herself from flopping around and puts her hands at the top of my ass to push up on.

"You wanna play a poking game? I'll show you a poking game." I grab the bag of steaks from the door behind her seat and shut the door. I toss the bag into the garage fridge and then carry Cordelia into the house and straight to my bed. Tossing her into the middle, she gives a little bounce before I command her, "Strip. All of it. Off. Now." She rips her shirt over her head, and when she reaches behind her to unclasp her bra, her hooded gaze meets mine. Her eyes never leave mine as she unclasps and lets her bra fall to the floor. I open and close my hand to keep from grabbing her.

"That's not all of it," I growl as I remove and toss my shirt to the floor.

As she stands, I can feel her nipples brush against my chest from how close she is standing. When she unbuttons and lowers the zipper, she starts to wiggle out of the shorts, and it makes me groan from the way it feels against my bare chest. Once the shorts drop to the floor, I grab her waist and lift her back to lay her on the bed, before I spread her out.

"Fuck, Cordelia, you're soaking for me already." I slide a finger through her bare folds and sink it inside. Her back arches, and she mumbles out something that sounds like my name. I pump a few times before I add a second finger and hook them just right to hit her g-spot. It takes barely a flick and her pussy is fluttering and squeezing my fingers as she cries out, "Fuck, Dean, I'm coming!" The second the words leave her lips, I latch and suck on her clit, drawing out her pleasure as long as I can.

"Fuck, you taste like heaven," I rasp as I keep pumping through her aftershocks. "Fuck, you are squeezing my fingers so tight, I think you're gonna cut off circulation." I press kisses along her thigh, and once her body relaxes around me, I slowly pull my fingers from inside her. I use my other hand to pop the button on my shorts and drag the zipper down so I can shove them along with my underwear to the floor. I use my fingers, still wet from her release, to coat the head of my cock. Kneeling on the bed, I notch the head at her opening and shove in without any warning.

Cordelia's back arches up, and I take one nipple into my mouth. I set a punishing rhythm. I piston in and out of her, and the bed is groaning under us. I've never been so happy that I built this bed frame and know just how solid it is, until this very moment. If anyone else had made this, I would be worried that we would end up on the floor before we are done.

"Oh, Dean, I'm going to come again. Don't stop," her words come out in a rush. I smile because I have no intention of stopping, and when I feel her convulse around my cock, it's even tighter than it was on my fingers. I don't know if I'm going to be able to keep moving.

"Fuck, yes, that's right. Come on my cock like my good girl," I grit out as I manage to a couple more thrusts before my own orgasm starts building. "Fuck, Cordelia, fuck," I hiss out as my orgasm rips through me and I unload inside her pussy.

I brace myself on my arms, caging her in under me. When she opens her eyes and locks onto my gaze, I drop my head and kiss her.

This kiss doesn't feel like any of our other kisses. There's something special about this one. Maybe it's how quickly she meets me, tongues tangling, as we pull each other closer. Like we can't get enough of each other, can't get close enough to each other, despite the fact that I am still inside her.

I know in this moment, when I pull back and take in her flushed skin and sated expression, that I will move mountains for this woman. I knew I loved her, but this is different. This is like she has completely taken my soul and my heart; they are entirely hers.

I suddenly and fully understand why the whole town said my dad died of a broken heart.

If something were to ever happen to Cordelia, I wouldn't last in this world without her.

Chapter Twenty-One

CORDELIA

When I finally come back down to my body after that mindbending orgasm—actually two, there were two of them—my eyes meet Dean's, and there's a softness in them. I watch as it morphs into something else. I can't place it, but it almost feels like he is realizing something.

I place a hand on his jaw, my thumb brushing the corner of his mouth, "Are you ok? Because that was on a whole new level."

He doesn't move off of me but adjusts his weight so that he takes the bulk of his weight off my chest. "Everything is perfect. That was pretty amazing," he chuckles.

But his eyes don't match his tone and words. He's trying to lighten the mood when his eyes are saying something else entirely.

My eyes bounce back and forth between his, and I think he realizes that I suspect something more.

He lets out a sigh and brushes his fingers along my neck and collarbone. His hand slowly wraps around my neck, just resting there. Not squeezing. He uses his large hand to force my chin up so that I can't look at anything but him. "I love you, Cordelia."

I don't know what to say. This is such a shock to my system. I haven't allowed feelings like this into my life, and I'm overwhelmed. I can feel my head warring with my body that just wants to stay in this spot and bask in his love, but my head is spinning. It's conjuring the worst-case scenarios. I can feel my heart rate pick up, and my breathing hitches as the panic attack tries to get its claws into me.

The second Dean realizes what's happening, which doesn't take long with his hand on my throat, he immediately lifts off of me and helps me sit up.

"Breathe, Cordelia, just breathe for me." There is so much concern in his voice. I focus on his words and his hand on my back, rubbing circles.

It takes a couple of minutes, which is longer than they typically last anymore. I can usually get these under control quickly. But I think when the force of his words hit me, they sent me sideways.

I take a deep breath and whisper, "I'm so sorry. I haven't had that happen in a long time."

"Rosebud, there isn't anything you need to apologize for. I should be saying that. I'm the one who caused this." He drops his head, and I realize just how scary that must have been for him. To say those words and then to see my reaction.

I turn and force him to lie back down with me, since I don't think my legs are still fully working after the orgasms and the panic attack.

I place my hands under my chin and rest them in the middle of his chest.

"Dean, I need you to understand that this is in no way a reflection of what you said and how I feel about it. I know it seems like that. And I guess, in a way, it is, but it really isn't. This is because of me. I did all of this to myself. I haven't quite figured out how to not feel like the things Evan said about me being broken aren't true. Realistically, I know they aren't. But there's *a lot* to unpack for me to believe that fully." I close my eyes for a second and gather my thoughts.

"I am the problem. And before you tell me that I'm not, please believe me when I tell you that I am. I closed myself off and didn't allow any of this in again. I'm trying, I really am. I enjoy being with you. You bring a sense of calmness when you are around. The best way I can describe it is like coming home.

"I love so much about you, and the fact that you are comfortable enough to say those words to me means more than you realize." I let out a sigh and close my eyes for a moment. "I just need to get past some things before I think I will be at the same point as you. I know I've asked for your patience, and I ask you again for a little grace on this." I cup his face with one hand and lift myself up, pressing a kiss to his lips. "I may not be able to say the words as freely as you can, or even be able to let my walls down enough right now, but I think you know that I don't want to go a day without talking to you. And right now, I need that to be enough."

Dean closes his eyes and leans into my hand. "It's enough, Rosebud." He opens his eyes and pulls my lips back to his before murmuring against them, "*You* are enough."

Dean puts everything into the kiss as his lips take mine. Consuming me in a way I have never felt before. It's like he said the words, and now there's all this extra emotion in his touch. I'm doing everything I can to go against the self-preservation instincts I have used to keep my heart safe as well as my mental stability. Harper is right, and the closer Dean and I get, the more I see how right she is. Living to survive is not living. I have to actually live and trust that the universe won't take someone from me again.

I give myself over to the kiss, allowing him entry, and when I wrap my arms around the back of his head, using my nails to comb through his hair, I can't ignore how right this feels anymore.

Once we're able to tear ourselves apart, we clean up and get dressed. Dean is out back working on setting up everything for tomorrow. I have the cupcakes just about done; I just have to add the stars to the blue frosting to finish off the flag. I line up all the cupcakes into a rectangle and frost over them to make them appear like a sheet cake, frosting them into the American flag.

Dean walks in, sliding his sunglasses to the top of his head, just as I am starting the stars. "Hey, can you—wow! That looks so good! I get why you wanted to use my kitchen for this," he gestures to the three bowls of frosting that I have on the counter and the piping bags of the blue and red frosting. The blue one is trying to leak out a little drop onto the counter.

"Yeah," my voice trails off as I cast a glance at his kitchen, "I know it's a mess. But I will clean this up when I'm done."

"I'm not worried about it. I was actually going to ask for your help when you're done. I need a second set of hands for something."

"Ok, I can do that. I just need to finish off these stars."

"No rush, a little break from the heat is a wonderful thing." He walks past me and opens the fridge. I hear the twist of a cap and glance over my shoulder to see him drinking down a bottle of water. His head is tilted back, and his Adam's apple bobs as his throat works.

It's not fair how good he looks all the time. I shake myself out of it and go back to the cupcakes. I add the last couple of stars, which are more like spiky dots, and set the frosting bag on the counter. "Well, that finishes off that portion." I turn around to face Dean, "What did you need help with?"

Grabbing my sunglasses, I follow him outside past the pool, going a little further than I have ventured before. When we get around the side of the shed, I see an ATV with a tarp tied to the rear bumper.

"So, I can't hold this piece of concrete up while I put the tarp under it to move it out to its spot. I use this to set off the fireworks. I can't have them on the ground, or they could cause a very large fire."

"Makes sense. But why don't you leave the concrete out there?"

"I had to get a new one after last year. Graham was helping with cleaning up the next day, and it turned into a water gun fight. The next thing I know, he tripped, and in an attempt to save himself, he grabbed the wheelbarrow, and it hit the pad just right and cracked it. So this one is twice as thick. We should be good for a while. I just never took it out there when I got it last fall because it was too wet. Totally forgot about it until yesterday." Dean shrugs and squats down to lift the giant round piece of concrete.

"Wait, so I just need to hold it up? That's all? I mean, I have some muscle, but that has got to weigh a couple of hundred pounds. How are you going to even pick that up?"

Dean sighs and straightens back up. He takes the three steps until he closes all the distance between us and says, "Rosebud, do I need to carry it to prove a point? Cuz I will." He raises an eyebrow and continues, "Besides, I already lifted it twice trying to do this without asking for your help."

"Well, I'm glad you asked for help before you hurt yourself. Ok, so just hold it up, right?"

"Yep." He steps back from me and bends his knees. I can see his muscles rippling under his shirt across the span of his back. It's mouthwatering. I knew he had muscles—I could feel them—but watching them in action is a new experience.

Damn. Watching this man be all manly-man has me all types of hot and bothered.

I'm watching his ass flex as he stands, tilting my head to get a better look. I pull my bottom lip into my mouth, catching it with my teeth, before I hear a deep chuckle. My eyes snap up and meet Dean's gaze behind his sunglasses.

"Enjoying the show, darlin'?"

Fuck it, I've been caught red-handed. Might as well own it.

"I was, actually." I walk over and place my hands against the slab that comes up just past my waist now that it's standing upright.

"At least you can admit it." I can hear the smirk that I know is on his face in his tone. "Now, I'm not gonna let go until you tell me to, and even then, I'm gonna hand the weight over to you slowly. You ready?"

"Yep." I brace myself, and when Dean starts to let some of the weight transfer to me, I realize that this might be easier than I thought. I just keep reminding myself to keep a slight lean on it so that I don't send it toppling to the ground in the opposite direction.

"Ok, it's all you now. I'm gonna do this part as quickly as I can. You ok?"

"So far so good."

I hear the tarp moving, and then Dean is back, taking the weight from me. I step back as he lowers it down to the tarp. Then he lifts the other side to pull the tarp out, so the whole thing is firmly in place.

"Wanna hop on the back and ride with me?" Dean asks as he steps over to the ATV.

"I haven't been on one of these in years." I chuckle as I remember that time at Brian's grandfather's house when I was out in the woods and got stuck because I forgot to put the thing into four-wheel drive, and it was still in two-wheel drive. I brush past Dean and throw a leg over the seat. "Ready," I say as I grab the rack on the back of the quad to hold on to.

"Yeah, you are," Dean laughs as he swings his leg over, settling between my legs. I can't help the tingle that travels straight to my core.

Fuck, at my age, I should be having less of a sex drive, not having it ramp up every time the man touches me.

He starts it up and slowly begins to move. We both keep glancing back at the slab and the tarp when I finally tell him that he can just drive, and I can watch the tarp and concrete. It takes us about five minutes to get it out a good two hundred yards. We do the same thing but in reverse to get the disc off the tarp and place it over the cracked one.

"Well, that was the last thing I needed to do for tomorrow. What do you say I whip us up some grilled cheese sandwiches and we can watch a movie?"

"I still have the kitchen to clean up, but I can do that while you make those, which sound amazing by the way. I do have one condition, though," I say.

"Hit me with it," Dean says as we climb back onto the ATV.

"You have to cut it into a diagonal."

He gasps, "Is there any other way that's acceptable to cut a grilled cheese sandwich?"

"There is not," I laugh. Then he fires up the ATV, and it takes us about thirty seconds to get back to the house, as he fully opened it up. He shuts it off and leaves it by the shed, not putting it away, and takes the key into the house. He hangs it up on the hook by the sliding door from the sunroom into the dining room.

"I'm gonna take a quick rinse off shower, then I'll be back out to make us some dinner."

"Ok, I'm gonna get this mess cleaned up while you do all of that."

Dean walks down the hallway, and I get to work cleaning up my mess of frosting. Just as I finish loading up the dishwasher and turn the water on to start washing out the decorating tips from the frosting, I hear Dean's footsteps.

"Mmm, I could get used to this, seeing you in my house, in my kitchen, like it's all yours," he says as he wraps his arms around my middle and presses his lips into my neck.

I moan and tilt my head to the side to give him better access. He nips the skin lightly before running his tongue over it and then kissing me again.

"Don't start something you can't finish, Mister. You promised me a grilled cheese," I try to put more authority into my voice, but it still comes out too breathy and needy.

"My queen requires sustenance, and she shall get it." He gives my ass a playful smack, and a moment later, he opens the fridge.

We work in silence like that for a little while, him cooking and me cleaning.

"Dean, this is so good," I groan around a bite of the sandwich before I even sit down. "I didn't realize how hungry I was until right now."

"Come sit down and eat," Dean chuckles. "What do we want to watch?"

"*Independence Day*, obviously. Can you even celebrate the Fourth of July without watching that?"

Dean finds the movie and queues it up, and we sit back and eat our sandwiches. Once we both finish, I take our plates into the kitchen, rinse them, and put them in the dishwasher. I find the detergent packs under the sink, toss one in, and turn it on.

I snuggle back into his side just in time for Will Smith to complain about dragging an alien through the desert.

I start falling asleep on him shortly after that and tell him to let it keep playing while I run to the bathroom. I know I'm going to pass out on him, so I quickly toss my contacts, wash my face, and brush my teeth. When I come back out, Dean has adjusted from sitting to almost lying down. I lay down in front of him and snuggle in. Accepting my fate, I get comfortable.

I wake up the next morning to something hard pressing into my lower back. I try to move away, and Dean's arms tighten around me. That's when it clicks that I never even woke up when he moved me from the couch to the bed. I press back into him and wiggle around a little bit.

"You keep doing that wiggle and you're gonna end up impaled on my cock," a sleepy mumble comes from behind me.

"Maybe I want you to impale me." I turn in his arms and say, "Oh, look. I've been impaled." I stifle the giggle that tries to work itself past my lips.

"Ok, Olaf, do you like warm hugs too?"

"Yup," I say, popping the p. "And some people are worth melting for, too."

Dean cracks open one eye and smiles at me. Before I can blink, he rolls us and has me pinned under him. "Now, I'm going to spend a little bit of time kissing every inch of this gorgeous body, showing you how much I love you, then I'm going to fuck you like I hate you. Hard and fast." His eyes are on mine waiting for my answer, and all I can do is nod.

Yes, please.

Dean spends the next hour doing exactly as he promised. I can still feel him everywhere on and in my body. He didn't downplay any of it; he had me coming on his tongue, then his fingers. When he finally slid into me, I was a crying, begging mess. He fucked me hard and fast before making me come on his dick, and then he went back to lick and suck my clit until I was begging him to stop. I literally didn't think I could move. Dean went and started a shower for us and carried me into it. He washed my hair and the rest of my body, and when he was done with me, I started on him.

Before we could get out, he had me pressed against the cold tile, while he fucked me again. Before he finished, he pulled out and pressed the head of his cock into my ass and stroked himself until he filled me again, telling me, "I love watching my cum drip out of both your holes," and playing with my clit until I came apart again.

It's been over four hours. Everyone will start getting here in the next half an hour, and every step I take, I can still feel everything he did to me. My clit has never had that much attention in one week, let alone from one morning. Every step is causing friction to the sensitive little spot, and I'm starting to think the only relief I will get is in the pool with the cool water.

I so badly want to go do that, but instead, I play the good hostess and am ready to greet everyone when they get here. I finish setting up the table with the snacks, plates, cups, plasticware, and napkins when I hear Harper's voice.

I turn as I see her come in the sunroom, and she's got this ridiculous headband on that no one but her could pull off. It's got three fireworks floating above her head on clear stands to hold them up. Her hair is in two bubble braids with the bands alternating in red, white, and blue. She has dangly earrings with about ten stars on each. Her eyes are done in red and blue with a dusting of stars across her nose like little patriotic freckles. She has on this cute red tank top with stars all over it and a tiny little blue-and-white skirt. I just know without a doubt she has a flag bikini on under that as well.

"Well, look at you! You look like the Fourth of July."

"Makes me want a hot dog real bad!" we say at the same time and dissolve into a fit of laughter and hugs.

"You look adorable in your little flag tennis skirt! I love this!" Harper says as she makes me do a little spin. The front of my skirt is smooth and blue with white stars, while the back is pleated, alternating red and white strips. My tank top is black, with a deep V-neck, and a waving flag is printed across it.

When Graham and Lachlan follow a second later, I quip out, "Happy Treason Day, boys!"

Harper snorts out a laugh, and the guys chuckle.

"Treason day, huh?" Lachlan says, "That is actually clever and oddly accurate. Where did you get that one from?"

"A friend's wife is British, she always sends me a text today," my phone buzzes on the table, and I glance down at it, "Speak of the devil."

Carmella: Happy Treason Day, you ungrateful colonialist.

I show Lachlan, and he laughs before I respond with red, white, and blue heart emojis.

"I tried to tell her that my grandparents immigrated from Italy in the early 1900s and that technically I'm not a colonialist, but she always waves me off."

"What is this about being a colonialist?" I turn to see Sebastian walk in the front door.

"Just Carmella's yearly reminder text." I walk over and give him a hug, "Happy Fourth, Marine." I give his arm a squeeze as I step back.

"Playing the hostess in Dean's house looks good on you, Cordy," he says before he greets his friends.

I introduce Harper to Graham and Lachlan; she's met Sebastian a couple of times before. It's not long before I hear Faye and Gwen coming up the front steps, and I greet them at the door.

"I shouldn't be here. I really don't want to see him again," Gwen hisses to Faye as I come into view.

"Gwen," I start with my mom voice, "don't worry about it. His daughter is here, so he's going to be on his best behavior. If he isn't, I'll tell Sebastian to handle him."

"Ugh, fine, I guess. I'm also a little on the tired side today, so I'm just kinda bitchy."

"No worries, I know how it is, just relax in the pool and take it easy. You literally don't have to do anything today."

The boys have headed outside, so I give them a quick tour to show them where everything is in the house, and we follow everyone else outside.

Chapter Twenty-Two

DEAN

I'm chatting with the guys, standing in the shade of the umbrella, when Cordelia leads her friends out. She's got a smile on her face, and she looks happy. More than that, she looks like she belongs here. The first time I had that thought, I was falling for her, but having that thought now, after I told her that I loved her, I have to rub at my chest at the swell of emotion that goes through me.

"Hey, this is Faye and Gwen, and we have Lachlan, Graham, and Sebastian," Cordelia says, gesturing to everyone. "There, you all know each other, so have fun!"

I walk up and wrap an arm around her waist and pull her to me, "You look happy. Are you?"

Her eyes meet mine, and her smile doesn't falter at all, "I am." I press a quick kiss to her lips. "You need anything? I'm gonna grab a drink and get in the pool. Everything is set up inside, and I'm ready to be done with responsibilities today."

"I'm good, you go relax with your friends. Let me know when anyone gets hungry; otherwise, I plan to get the grill going in about an hour." She gives me a quick kiss before disappearing into the house and returning a few seconds later with a drink in her hand.

I can't even hear anything the guys are saying when she starts to shimmy out of her skirt. You'd think after seeing her completely naked, the sight of her covered ass in a bikini wouldn't affect me like this, but it still steals my breath and makes my cock thicken in my pants.

"Yo, earth to Dean!" Graham snaps his fingers in front of me. "Get your head out of the gutter and stop staring like a creeper at your woman."

I slap his hand down, "Don't be jealous."

"I am not jealous!" All three of us raise our eyebrows at him. "Ok, a little, but that's not the point. I asked you a question."

I sigh, waiting for him to tell me what he asked when I tuned them all out.

"I asked you how it's going with her."

"Oh, geez, that's a lot to get into," I say, cutting my eyes over to the girls. They seem to be immersed in their own conversation, and even Madison seems to be enjoying being around them. "It's going really well. On my end. I mean, hers too...it's complicated." I sigh and run a hand down my face and adjust my hat. "She's taking longer to get where I am, and I want to be clear here," my eyes cut to Bast, "I am okay with that. I don't know what happened to her before, but I know she had a pretty shitty ex who said some things that have stayed with her. I know she invited me to the Outer Banks, and she said that if she hasn't told me by then, she will when we're there. I think she needs some time to realize that she can trust me at my word and believe that someone can be back in her corner."

"Well, shit," Graham says as he runs a hand through his hair.

"Nah, man, it's ok. You didn't know. This one, however," I make a fist and jerk my thumb at Bast, "he knows. Has known. Whatever. And we aren't going to pressure him to tell us anything because he will kick our ass, right, little bro?"

"That's a ten-four on that. I do NOT need to get my ass kicked by him, again."

"Might be the smartest thing you have ever said in your life," Bast says as he claps him on the shoulder. Graham winces a little bit, and his face says he's bracing for something worse. I can see the knuckles on Bast turn white as he applies added pressure before Graham twists and dances out from under him.

"I am a delicate flower, Bast! That's gonna bruise!"

We all fall into laughter.

Graham wanders off to check on Madison, I assume, while Lach and Bast stay in the shade with me.

"So, is there anything you can tell us, Bast?" Lachlan asks.

"Sorry, Lach, there isn't. I've told Dean, it's not my story to tell. One I don't even know all the details to." His lips purse ever so slightly as he says the words. It's a subtle tell he has. Which means, he knows a lot more than he is willing to admit, even to us. "We don't talk about it. I know enough, though."

"Yeah, I'm slowly piecing things together, little comments that have been said. I can make assumptions and speculate, and she was clear on the front that it's public knowledge. I could Google her and find it, which I will not be telling Graham about because he will go do it." Both guys nod their heads in agreement before I continue. "I'm not going to do that. I feel like that would be a violation of her trust, and with how sparingly she gives it out, I'm not going to hurt that."

"You care about her more than that, though," Lachlan says in a questioning tone, but not actually asking. He's appraising me with those two different colored eyes that tell me he already knows the answer. I do the only thing I can do; I nod in agreement. I may have already told Cordelia the depth of my feelings, but I don't need to actually voice it to these guys just yet. There's a part of me that wants to keep us in this little bubble of ours for a while longer.

After a couple of hours, all the food has been made, everyone has eaten, and I have a fire in the firepit going for s'mores while we wait for the sun to set. The guys helped me set up all the fireworks, so there is nothing left to do but wait.

I take a seat with a bottle of water. I have about an hour before the sun sets enough, and something about playing with explosives around my niece mixed with alcohol just doesn't sit well with me. This last hour when I sit with my water and wait for the sun is always my favorite hour of this day. For the most part, the guys leave me alone, and Madison is usually making s'mores. I can just take it all in and enjoy another successful holiday with friends and family.

I catch movement out of the corner of my eye and see Cordelia walking over. I adjust around and open my arms, indicating she should sit in my lap. When she does, she nestles in and presses a kiss to my cheek.

"This was a good day. Thank you, Dean," she whispers against my skin.

"Nothing you need to thank me for. Having you here made it that much better than previous years."

She leans her head on my shoulder, her gaze going to the sky that is just beginning to take on the orange of the setting sun. I wrap my arms around her, pulling her into me. She smells like summer—a mix of coconut sunscreen, chlorine, and the faintest hint of roses. We sit like that, in silence, enjoying just being together as the sky continues to dance in colors, slowly darkening.

"I have to say, next to the views from Glass, this might be one of the best in the county," she says, breaking the silence. "Starting and ending the day out here would be a dream. How many acres do you have?"

My breath catches at her words. There isn't much I wouldn't give this woman, and if she wanted to move in to make that happen, I'd start packing for her right now. I know she's not ready for that, so instead, I make a mental note to look into adding a bay window off the master bedroom so she can have a reading nook with this view. Maybe I should just build out a little, add an office for her, so she has a dedicated spot to work in the future. I start making a list in my head to get the permits, figure out exactly what she would like, and make it happen for her.

"All you have to do is say the word, Rosebud, and you can have that. It's ready for you when you are," I murmur against her hair. "I have three acres. The house was always on one acre, but about ten years ago, I purchased the additional two acres from the guy who owns all that land."

Turning, she meets my eyes before she says, "I love how much space you have back here." Letting out a sigh, she continues, "I know. And when I'm ready for that, you will be the first to know."

I tangle my hand into her hair, and I take in her eyes. I've always loved the emerald green of her eyes, but out here in the setting sunlight, you can see small gold flakes sprinkled in the green. So subtle that I don't think it would be visible if not for the golden-hour lighting, which makes the gold really pop. I pull her closer, pressing a kiss to her full, pink lips. She melts into my chest and the kiss as she allows me to deepen it. When her tongue tangles with mine, bringing notes of chocolate and marshmallow, she moans into my mouth, making me tighten my grip on her hair.

I have to break the kiss sooner than I would like, before I take it a little too far with all the extra eyes around.

"I'm gonna need you to stay here for a couple of minutes and talk about something that will stop all the blood rushing south," I say with a half laugh.

Cordelia laughs and taps her blue nail to her lips with a "Hmm" before she says, "Gwen is trying to avoid Graham, and Graham keeps casting glances at her. If you really watch those two, like I did for a solid fifteen minutes from behind my sunglasses, they keep gravitating toward each other, and once they realize they are within six feet of each other, they split apart. I think there's far more to the story than we know. Gwen isn't going to admit to anything until she has to, so I'm going to bide my time for now."

"Really? I didn't notice." I turn my head and see Madison chattering away to Gwen as they both slowly spin their marshmallows over the fire. "Those two seem to get along at least."

"Yeah, I overheard Madison ask Gwen if she would consider

hiring her to help out in her store. I didn't catch Gwen's response, but if they are still chatting..." She trails off, letting the sentence hang between us.

"Well, this could certainly be interesting if it happens," I chuckle. My dick has deflated enough that I think it's safe to get up, gather the guys, and set off a couple of practice shots before we lose all of the light.

Cordelia gets up, and I follow, taking her hand and walking back to the party.

"Ready?" I ask when we get close enough.

The guys nod. We grab a couple of those long candlelighters and head out to the back of the property, where we have everything set up.

We fire off a couple of testers, adjusting things in between until we have everything set up the way we want it. Once we are happy, we start setting up for the real show and put our headlamps on so we can see more easily. We still have about fifteen minutes before it's truly dark enough, and that's when I hear it. The faint cheers in the distance. I glance out across the field and see a few headlights on the far end near the road. Usually, half the town is out there in their trucks waiting, but I never really know how many are actually there until the following day, when people start posting on social media about it.

It's funny how this started as just a thing we did on this day ten years ago, and it slowly became part of the town's traditions. It makes me smile, being a part of this town and its people, who have been there for Graham and me when we needed them. It's a small way for me to repay that.

"Just think, if Madison hadn't disappeared when she was two, watching fireworks in town, we never would have started this," Graham says, nodding toward the headlights.

"She didn't disappear; she was on the other side of the truck, but I get your point. We've come a long way."

A moment later, Lachlan starts the countdown, and we all take our spots to set off the start of the show.

An hour and a half later, as the booms are finishing echoing around us from the finale, we all high-five each other, double-checking that no one lost any fingers, congratulating each other on another year of a good show. We turn on the light bar on the ATV I left parked out here from earlier today. Once we have the area lit up, we start tossing the rest of the trash and debris into the tub that I will tow back to the house.

When I pull up to the house, all the girls congratulate us on our show.

"That was one of the best fireworks displays I have ever seen. I'm really impressed!" Harper squeals as she bounces up to us.

"I haven't been out here to see one of your displays in a few years. I forgot how good they are," Faye offers.

"Thank you, ladies," Graham laughs. "It's just fun getting to blow stuff up."

"Boys," Gwen says with an eye roll.

My eyes bounce over the girls before I settle on Cordelia. Madison is lying in her lap on a blanket, and she looks like she's sleeping, which is unusual. She typically stays up far later than this. I turn off the ATV and hop off, striding over to them.

"She fell asleep?" I ask as I take a seat on the blanket with them.

"Yeah, she's had a bit of an eventful night. Nothing major. I think it was just being around so many girls. She was trying to keep up with everything we were talking about and trying so hard to fit in with the big girls. Once I realized that Faye and Gwen started talking about," she sucks her teeth and gives a slight cringe, "well, things that young ears don't need to hear, I distracted her and asked if she could find a blanket for us to watch the fireworks on. We sat down just as you guys started the show."

"When did she fall asleep?" Graham asks, walking up.

"Maybe ten minutes before the finale. I told her that Harper was recording the whole thing. She likes using videos like that for content purposes. Once I told her that, I could feel her head get heavier, and she started drifting."

I lean down and slide my arms under my niece, carefully lifting her so she doesn't wake up. Graham stands to get the door for me as Cordelia says, "Graham, can I talk to you for a second?"

He nods, and after he closes the door, I watch him walk over to Cordelia. I turn and walk into the living room to put Madison on the couch. As I'm setting her down, she whispers sleepily, "I really like Cordelia, Uncle Dean. You should marry her."

I smile and press a kiss to her head, and as her breathing evens out, I say, "That's the plan." I stand and make my way back outside, and I see that Cordelia is helping the other girls clean up the table.

"What did you need Graham for?" I ask, coming up behind her.

She jumps and smacks my chest as she turns. "Don't scare me like that!"

"Sorry," I chuckle.

Cordelia glances around, "Just girl stuff. Madison told us that she's worried about her first period, apparently her dad gets a little —what was the word she used?"

"Banana balls," Harper interjects.

"Yep, that was it," Cordelia says.

"Well, she's not wrong about that. He does get a little freaked out every time he realizes that she is growing up."

"We all had her save our numbers, and we started a group chat with her, so when she needs some girl advice, she can just ask us all. I also told her that if she was more comfortable talking to me when it happens, I would help her out. I can't imagine that would be a fun call for a dad to deal with."

"You just filled him in on that all, I take it?"

"Yeah, gave him my number too. Told him I would obviously let him know if she comes to me first and encourage her to talk to him, but that I won't turn her away either."

I wrap a hand around the back of her neck and pull her into me, wrapping my arms around her and nuzzling my face into her neck. I whisper, "Thank you for being in her corner and for respecting Graham at the same time. We haven't had a lot of female energy, and I know she needs it."

My mind is spinning with thoughts as we finish cleaning up and saying goodbye to everyone. I can't stop thinking about how much Madison seems to care about and trust Cordelia and her friends as well. It warms my heart to know that I'm not the only one who sees how special she is and how well she fits in with us. She's like this little puzzle piece that has been missing from our lives, and now, with her here, everything is starting to click into place.

Chapter Twenty-Three

CORDELIA

The next month passes quickly. I spend most of my nights at Dean's house. I have too many things around mine that would lead to questions. And since I haven't spoken to him about, well, everything, I'm trying to avoid it altogether. I'm not entirely lying when I tell him I just really like his kitchen and prefer to use his. I'm just omitting some of the truth that goes with that. Like today, for example, I'm making spaghetti and homemade garlic bread.

I'm just putting the appetizer in the oven when my phone pings.

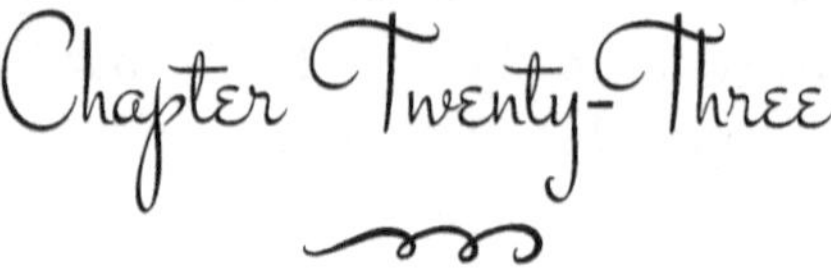

Well, fuck me. I take a deep breath and exhale as I think of what to say to him.

I don't text him back. I hit the call button instead, putting him on speaker.

"Hey, Mama."

"Hey, Jason," I reply. "Sorry, I'm in the middle of making dinner, and it was easier to call."

"No worries," his deep voice filters through the speaker.

"I also thought that it was better to talk about it over the phone and not via text message."

"Well, this sounds ominous," he says with a chuckle.

"I, um," I stumble over my words. "Fuck, why is this so hard to say?" I laugh nervously.

There's silence for a second before he sighs. "Seems like you have one of two things to tell me. Either I'm not invited, or you're seeing someone, and it might be serious. Which would cause me to ask if I'm still invited."

I freeze, mid-stir of the sauce in the pot, and stare at my phone. *How the fuck did he even guess any of that?!*

"Your silence is very loud, Mama."

"Fuck, sorry. Obviously, you are always invited. You are the reason we even do this every year. But yes, I am seeing someone. I did invite him as well." I say the last part with hesitation.

"It's about time, Cordy. You deserve someone in your life," he says, clearing his throat. "Have you told him about Brian?"

"Um, yeah, about that. I have not. And before you get all high and mighty on me, Marine, I told him I would tell him at the beach house if I don't before." I sigh, "I just don't want to see that look of pity on his face when he looks at me. He doesn't do that. He doesn't treat me differently. And I *know* when I tell him, he will. It will change everything, Jason. I'm just not ready for that."

"Oh, Cordy, what am I gonna do with you? But I get it. I do." He pauses and asks quietly, "Do you love him?"

I huff out a laugh and open my mouth to respond. Then close it. *Fuck.* I know I'm falling for him, have been. But I have been ignoring and tamping down the actual feelings beyond that.

Do I love him?

No one has asked me that, and Dean tells me he loves me every morning when he leaves for work when I stay over. I think he does it so I don't feel the pressure to say it back. When he says those words, it always leaves me with this feeling of contentment, even if it does cause my heart to give a little squeeze.

Romantic love is so different to me. I haven't had it in a very long time, and I don't even think I could say I did with Evan. But Dean? It's such a natural feeling. It's almost like gravity. The way he seems to always just say the thing I need to hear, even when he has no idea how accurate his words are sometimes. Then there's the way he commands my body unlike anything I have ever known.

It feels like I'm holding onto the last tether of my sanity with Jason's question. All I have to do is let go, then it's as easy as falling. *Right?*

"Cordy?" Jason's voice snaps me out of my thoughts.

"Um, fuck, Jason, I think I do." My voice comes out shaky, and I feel like I can't breathe. It wasn't a matter of letting myself fall as much as realizing that I already did, and now I just need to trust him to catch me. And if there is anyone who can do that, it would be Dean.

Jason lets out a breath on the other end of the phone, "Cordy, I'm really happy for you. I'm assuming you have some talks that need to happen before we are all in a house together? And you know, maybe tell him how you feel since I'm thinking you've only told me at this point."

"Well, you're not wrong. Guess I have some work to get done before he gets home in about thirty minutes."

"Well, keep me posted if you need anything before we get to *Nautical Comfort*. And, Cordy, don't wait till the last minute to tell him everything. Might be good for him to know what he is walking into, sooner rather than later. I'm not just talking about us, but all of it." I can feel the pointed look he's giving me through the phone.

"Sir, yes, sir," I say in a mocking tone.

"Smartass. I'll see you in a little over a month."

"Bye, Jason, and thank you." I hit the end button on my

phone, open the oven, and see that the cheese needs to melt a little longer.

Double-checking the time, I see that I have a few minutes, so I can call Harper while the sauce keeps simmering and the mozzarella finishes melting.

"Hey, pretty lady, what's up?" Harper says before the first ring even finishes.

"Were you waiting by your phone, or did you sense I was calling you?" I laugh.

"I actually just hung up with a client. So my phone was in my hand."

"I gotta talk to you. I only have a couple of minutes, so I'm gonna just throw it all out there really fast, ok?" I tell her.

"Oooh, this sounds juicy. Hit me."

"I just talked to Jason, and he confirmed he will be at the beach house this year. But that's not all of it. I told him about Dean, and he, uh, asked me if I love him." I take a breath before continuing. "I kinda realized that I did—do—and now I'm kinda freaking out, and I don't really know what to do. Obviously, Jason, being a guy, is all 'tell him the truth,' but I can't just dump everything on him in one go. That would be too much and a lot to take in." I clamp my mouth shut when it hits me that I'm starting to ramble.

Harper blows out a breath and says, "First off, it's about fucking time you realized that you love him, you idiot. Second, maybe just start with that? Worry about the rest later. I do agree with Jason, though. I think you need to tell him before you get there. At least about Jason, which I know kinda leads into everything else. But it's your call, your story, your past, your trauma that, at some point, you have to share with him. I know you don't spend a lot of time talking about everything that happened with Brian, but I also know that's ALL you talk about when you're there. Maybe that would be easier for you?"

"I can agree that waiting until the house is easier for me. It's like I save it all up for a year and let the floodgates open. I also agree that telling Dean about the intimate details between Jason and me might be best to talk about beforehand. Maybe on the car ride, if we ride together? Then he can't run away?" I try to make it sound light-hearted.

"Jesus Christ, Cordelia! You have a past, you have past *lovers*," she puts emphasis on the word lovers, dragging out the syllables, "He's not going to leave you because you slept with some guy and remained close, unless you're still sleeping with him. That might be an issue at that point."

"Harper! Fuck! Obviously, I'm not still sleeping with him. It's been two freaking years. Besides, the way Dean is, I don't think my body could handle a second one, as tempting and intriguing as the idea for a little MFM action would be"

"Ew, gross, do not need those details. Also, I think all your books are starting to warp your brain."

"Yet you always ask for them," I laugh.

"Yeah, but that's when I ask, not randomly told to me in the middle of an almost existential crisis."

I laugh, "Fair enough." I open the oven again, and the cheese is about thirty seconds from being golden on the edges. "Look, I gotta finish this dinner. Yoga tomorrow as usual?"

"Yep, see you then. And Cordy, I love you, bestie. Anything you need, I'm here for you."

"Love you too, Harp."

She ends the call, and I slide my phone to the back of the counter while I grab a trivet to set the pan on. I grab the oven mitt and pull the pan out of the oven. Just as I'm setting it down, I feel arms wrap around me from behind, and I stiffen.

Fuck. How long has he been in the house, and what did he hear?

"Hmmm, it smells so good in here," Dean whispers against my ear before peppering kisses down my neck, sliding my tank top strap down to kiss my shoulder as well.

I hide the worry on my face as I turn and wrap my arms around his neck. "Hi, handsome," I smile before pressing a kiss to his lips. "How was your day?" I keep studying his face, trying to see if he heard any of that conversation. Not that there was anything wrong with it, but if he walked in at the wrong moment, it could be bad.

"Oh, I really love domestic Cordelia, making dinner and asking about my day. I could get used to this." He takes a step to the side and leans against the counter, away from the stove. "It was long and hot. I need to shower before we eat. Do I have time?"

"Yep, I haven't even started the pasta yet. I was waiting till you got home." He loosens his grip, and I take a step back so I can turn the burner on for the pot of water I already had prepped on the stove.

Dean is grabbing one of the little baguette pieces when I turn back to him, "Careful, those just came out of the oven. The tomato can be a little hot, so don't burn your mouth."

Dean groans, "These are amazing; what are they?"

I laugh, "Ya know, I never named them. Just a baguette with tomato, pepperoni, and fresh mozzarella. One of my favorite things to make. I have literally just made these for dinner more than once."

"So good." He says as he pops the second bite into his mouth.

"Go shower and stop eating before dinner is ready." I snap a towel at him, and his gaze turns dark. He stalks toward me, his eyes glinting. Once he has me backed to the wall, he cages me in. I watch his throat work as he swallows. "Don't start something you won't be able to finish, Rosebud." His voice is quiet, slow, and deliciously tinged with a dark warning.

I have to clench my thighs from the way his voice affects me. I smile sweetly and say, "I wouldn't dream of it. I don't start anything, but I sure finish it."

Dean chuckles low, the sound coming from his chest, "Mmmm, we will just have to see about that." Then he pushes off the wall, grabs another slice of baguette, and heads out of the kitchen.

I stand here mentally fanning myself for a full two minutes before I remember I need to set the table yet and get moving.

The whole time I'm setting the table, all I can think about is that I love Dean. I love him. I don't even know when it happened, but I know I shouldn't be surprised. He's incredibly generous and kind and listens to me. He respects the boundaries and walls that I have put up, and I know that he wants them to come down, but he isn't hammering away at them. He's more like a steady river that is running along them and slowly eroding them. You don't notice that anything is even happening until it's almost too late. Until they start to crack and crumble under the gentle pressure.

As I'm lighting the candle I brought over a couple of weeks ago, the finishing touch on the now set table, Dean walks down the hallway into the dining room.

He stops in his tracks, taking in the table, the candle, and the low lighting.

"Wow, what's the special occasion?"

"Do I need to have one?" I ask, even though the low lighting and candle *are* for a special occasion. I don't know if the words will come out while we're having dinner or later. But all I know is that ever since Jason asked me that question, I have to get these words out. They are just flitting around in my head and my chest like little trapped birds, trying to get out.

It would be so easy just to say it right now, but that doesn't feel right. Not with how this man has been with me for months now. He's got the patience of a saint, or he just knew that I would eventually get here. Either way, he deserves to have some sparkle on this, to make it worth the wait.

"No, there doesn't need to be a reason. Any night where I get to come home to you is a special enough reason for me," he says as he closes the distance between us, backing me into the breakfast bar. "Although I could go for laying you out on that table and starting with dessert first." His eyes are dark, his pupils blown wide.

My cheeks heat, and my thighs rub together as I shift under

his lust-filled gaze. I clear my throat and say, "Dinner first. Then you can have whatever you want for dessert, wherever you want it." I raise my eyebrow in challenge.

He drops his head and, blowing out a breath, he backs up and pulls the chair out for me. Once I'm seated, he takes his seat next to me at the head of the table. "Thank you for cooking, I know it's not your favorite thing to do."

"I may not like cooking and only have a handful of things I can make that are edible, but I do like being able to have dinner ready for you when you get home. If I didn't fully love owning my own venue and being my own boss, I would think I was born in the wrong decade." I twirl my fork against the spoon as I gather up some strands of spaghetti. "I would have made a great 1950s housewife. The dresses, the hair," I let out a contented, dreamy sigh at the thought.

"Mmm, I like the idea of you in one of those dresses. But I wonder, would you be more Sandy or more Rizzo?" I look up to see him doing the same thing with his spoon and fork. I smile to myself that he didn't ask about the spoon, and either knew or watched me and didn't belittle me about it.

"Well, you don't know *Wicked*, but you know *Grease*. That counts for something in my book. But to answer your question, why not a bit of both?"

"Oh, I like that answer." He takes a bite of his food before he lets out a moan. "Oh, this might be the best spaghetti sauce I have ever had."

"I'm glad you like it," I say after swallowing my bite.

"So, tell me something. What made you decide to start Glass anyway? Were you in the wedding business before?"

Thankful for just having taken a bite, I can consider my words carefully with this explanation.

"I guess, I've always loved love, watching people fall in love, the start of their lives together. The happily ever after. I haven't exactly found that myself before, but there's something about watching it happen. It's uplifting and full of hope." I pick up my glass of wine, taking a sip before I continue. "I was just working in an office setting before," I cast a quick glance at Dean, "When someone goes through the things I did, you start to consider what's truly important to you. Is working for someone else, in a mindless job that does nothing but cause you added anxiety and more depression over the ceaselessness day in and day out, really good for your soul? I kept coming back to the answer being no. I hated it. I hated the feelings and the way it just felt like I was slowly drowning in that world. I needed to get out, to do something that mattered to me." I blink and realize I have tears in my eyes. I lean my head back, blinking to try to clear them and take a breath. "Sorry, I don't know what's wrong with me." I try to laugh it off, but Dean sees right through me.

He grabs my hand, squeezing, "I didn't mean to make you upset."

"It's not your fault. I don't even know why I'm crying. Now, I didn't slave all afternoon in your kitchen to make you a lovely meal for you not to eat it while it's still hot." He smiles, giving my hand another squeeze.

"Alright, but no more crying," he says quietly.

"Deal." I offer a smile.

After he takes another bite, he says, "Ya know, I get that. I think that's why I never hated my job. I never had to work for someone else. I always worked for myself. That's a luxury not many people get in this life. Honestly, I didn't even think of it as a luxury until now."

"It's not something I take for granted now. It wasn't easy in the beginning, but all the work we put into it was actually really fun. Harper's brother, Gabriel, came down with us, showed us how to do a few things, and was our muscle during the demo days at the beginning." I shrug and take another bite.

"If only you had found me sooner," he winks.

"Yeah, that would have made things a lot easier for sure. We got lucky with this being a small town, though. I kept going into the hardware store—"

"Frank's?" Dean interrupts.

I laugh, "Yeah, I think he was ready to come out himself. He was starting to get worried about what we were doing and how we were doing it." I chuckle at the memory. "Thankfully, the day I asked if he knew where I could get those windows, his son, Leo, just happened to be there. He helped measure and install them. I wanted to do giant panes of glass, but when we saw the cost for those versus doing just a wall of framed-out windows, it was no comparison."

"Well, I could help you make that change if you wanted. I'm sure we could work something out for the labor costs." He licks his bottom lip, his eyes never leaving mine.

"Maybe we will have to talk about that in a year or so," I try to keep my voice even, but this man can affect me so easily. "With these renovations you just finished, I don't want to spend money before I make it."

"Fair enough, you will always want to plan that out far enough in advance that we can have," he pauses while he thinks for a moment, "at least two weeks, with no weddings booked."

"Maybe we can plan for spring in a couple of years, before the weather gets too hot to do a full wedding and reception outside."

He hums his agreement as I go quiet. I realize that I only just came to the realization that I love this man today, and I'm already discussing making plans with him a few years out. The last hour has made my world shift on its axis, and I'm doing all I can to not completely freak out. As I'm turning over all these thoughts, the dream from last night pops into the forefront of my mind.

I'm sitting on the sand. I know it's St. Marteen. I don't know how I know, but I know. I'm watching the turquoise waves breaking against the white sandy beach.

It's so peaceful.

I'm lost to the unrelenting ocean, so I don't notice when someone sits next to me on the blanket until they speak.

"Hey, Mom. I miss you."

I turn my head, and I see Brian sitting next to me. I stop breathing, forgetting for just a moment.

It's so real.

"Brian?" I can feel the tears falling. "I miss you so much, kid."

I wrap my arms around his neck and hug him like my life depends on it. He squeezes me back, and the way he hangs on so tightly reminds me of the hug that day at Parris Island.

"I miss you every day, so much it hurts to breathe."

"I know," he says simply. "I'll never leave you. I'm always with you." His arms tighten around me more. "But I need you to keep living for me, Mom."

I sob into his shoulder, "I just love you so much."

"I love you, too."

I jerked awake after that from the sounds of the sobs leaving me. Thankfully, Dean had already left for the day, so I didn't need to explain to him why I woke sobbing hysterically.

I look down and see I have been twirling the same spot on my plate for more than a second. I can feel Dean's eyes on me, and I don't dare meet his gaze until I know that my eyes aren't going to betray me.

Chapter Twenty-Four

DEAN

I'm not sure what happened in the middle of dinner. We were joking around and making plans, and suddenly the air shifted. Cordelia barely met my eyes through the rest of dinner. It wasn't until she got up to get a cheesecake out of the fridge that she started to return to herself.

I let her have her moment, but I can't take it anymore. I stalk up behind her in the kitchen as she is closing the dishwasher, and before she can do anything else, I grip her waist and spin her around.

"What happened during dinner? You checked out and you haven't come back," I grind out.

She looks shocked at my reaction. Her eyes are wide and glassy, like she's fighting back tears. Her mouth opens and closes twice. After the second one, she closes her eyes and takes a breath.

"I'm sorry. Just had a very vivid dream last night, and I can't shake the feelings." She says it so quietly that I have to concentrate to get what she said.

"Do you want to talk about it?" I ask, my voice softening.

"No, not really. I'm just holding onto it with both hands, because I don't want to forget it. It was just a lot. Emotionally."

I blow out an exhale before I ask, "Was it about the person you lost?"

Her eyes fly to mine, and after a beat, she dips her head once.

I wrap my arms around her and just hold her, trying to let her know that she is safe with me. That I'm right here and I'm not going anywhere.

"You can talk to me if you want to. I'm not going anywhere," I murmur against the top of her head. She clutches my shirt into her fists and holds on while she shudders and silently cries.

Seeing her in this state is eating me alive. I don't know how to help her other than be there for her, like this, and hope that she will open up to me.

We stay like that for a few minutes, until her cries become quieter and she stops shaking. She takes a step back from me, wiping her eyes and face. I hate that she's hurting. I hate that I can't do anything about it but hold her and be there for her. I don't think she realizes the level of depravity I would sink to take care of her. To fix this, however I can.

"I'm sorry, I—"

"There is nothing to apologize for. You're allowed to feel whatever you feel, and you shouldn't be apologizing for it."

She nods before she turns back to the sink and starts cleaning the last of the pots she used. I already packaged up the leftovers. I nudge her out of the way. "Go take your glass of wine and relax. I will finish this."

She dries her hands and nods. I watch as she pads into the dining room, grabs her glass, and tucks her legs under her in a corner of the couch.

I turn back to the dishes. I let my mind wander over the last hour. I can't pinpoint anything that was said to trigger her. But then again, it could have been that conversation I overheard the tail end of. Something about someone she used to know and had some kind of relationship with, and it sounded like she was going to be seeing him, and I can't say that I like that. But I also don't want her to know that I heard that conversation. It seems like an invasion of privacy since I purposely stopped and listened instead of making my presence known. Which also means that I only got half the conversation. Maybe I missed something that was said earlier, and I'm taking the whole thing out of context.

I finish drying the last pan, and I put everything away and sit next to her. Before I can say a word, she says, "I realized something today. It wasn't some grand moment; it was a quiet question. I think it's partly why I'm such a basket case right now." She twirls her wine glass in her fingers before she continues. "I'm sorry it took me so long to realize it, or rather voice the words, because I think I've known deep down for a while." Her eyes snap up to mine before she says the only words that I have longed to hear from her. "I love you, Dean."

When I tell you that the world stopped spinning, I mean that I felt everything around me come to a screeching halt. There was no sound except for the blood rushing through my veins. I was completely frozen.

I never in a million years would have expected to hear those words from her tonight.

I've been praying and hoping to hear them for over a month. I've never wanted anything more than for her to love me. I don't even care that I might have been consoling her while she cried for another man she loved and lost. All I care about is that this woman in front of me *loves me*.

Me.

"Say it again," I breathe out as I close my eyes.

"I love you," she says, and I feel her hand on the scruff on my cheek. I open my eyes as she says, "I love you, and it's terrifying. I don't think I can survive another loss in my life, Dean."

I wrap my fingers around the back of her neck and the base of her skull, pulling her into me. "I will never leave you. I know that it can be so scary to let love into your heart after a great loss, but sometimes, you come across something worth taking the risk for. But more to the point, it would take the end of the world to pry me away from you, and even then, I would tell the fates and all the gods to fuck off, because they can't have me. I never want to be apart from you in this life and any that come after, Cordelia. You are the reason the world seems so much brighter, so much better. My life and my world have actual color in them now. I love you so very much, Rosebud." I press my lips to hers, sealing everything I said to her with that kiss.

Never breaking the kiss, I take the wine glass from her hands and set it on the table behind her. Then I pull her to straddle my lap. My need to touch her and feel her is so great. I can't think straight. As I deepen the kiss, I tug her hair in my fist, and she whimpers against me.

The sound is what it takes to break me out of my lust-filled haze. I pull back, resting my forehead against hers. It feels like everything I have wanted and asked for in my life is coming true in this moment, with those words falling from her lips and her in my lap.

I breathe in her rose scent, trying to make sure I remember every detail of this moment, to sear it into my mind, so that I will forever have this.

"Is that what the candle and low lighting were for?" I ask.

"Partly. I mean the candle, yes. The lighting, I was just trying to make it romantic, is all."

I want to just carry her to bed and make love to her all night. But I have some apprehension over it. I don't know if that is the right thing to do, given the rest of the things she has going through her head right now.

Deciding to put the ball into her court, I carry her into the bedroom, turning off lights as I go. I sit her on the bed, kneeling in front of her. "Tell me what you want, Cordelia. Anything you want," I tell her.

Her eyes meet mine, she straightens her shoulders, and says, "You. I just want you."

I plan to take my time with her tonight. I want to show her exactly how much having her heart means to me.

I stand and peel her shirt off and over her head. Then I reach behind her, unhooking her bra before I drag the straps down her arms and throw it across the room. I press a hand between her perfectly full tits and press her back onto the bed. I slowly strip her shorts and panties off at the same time.

I place a knee on the bed between her legs and lean over her body, taking her lips with mine.

There's no hurry or desperation in our kisses and movements.

Now that I have her completely bared to me, I slide down her body and lick once up her slit, groaning around her taste and how wet she is.

Cordelia whimpers and grips the sheets above her head. Her back arches with every lick and stroke, and when I push two fingers into her without any warning, she arches almost completely off the bed. I take my time. I want her to build up to that release instead of crashing into it. I want to draw it out of her slowly.

I keep slowly sliding my fingers in and out of her while alternating between sucking and licking her sensitive clit. Once I graze it with my teeth, she sucks in a sharp breath, making me do it again, adding pressure. It's all she needs as unintelligible words fall from her lips as she comes.

I don't stop lapping at her wetness until she's practically squirming out of my grasp. I stand, toss my shirt to the floor, and push my shorts down to step out of them as I crawl over her.

I can feel the head of my dick right at her entrance, but before I push inside of her, I take one breast in my hand and latch on to her nipple, sucking hard. That's when I push into her.

I let out a groan around her nipple. She's so fucking wet, and she's still clenching around me, coming down from that first orgasm. Instead of rutting into her hard and quick to fuck her through the rest of the orgasm, I go slow.

I need to make love to her. I need to show her that I will care for her when she needs me, and I can be hard and rough when she wants me to be.

As I pop my mouth off her nipple, I latch onto the other one. My hand trails down to her sensitive bud, drawing soft circles.

Just then, I feel her hands on the sides of my face. I let her nipple drop, and she pulls me to her lips. But before she brings me all the way down to her, she whispers against my lips, "I love you, Dean."

The words hit me right in my chest and take my breath away.

Maybe that's just her. I don't know. It doesn't matter either way.

The only thing that matters is that she loves me.

I kiss her back, my tongue tangling with hers.

I flip us, putting her on top of me, never letting my lips leave hers. When she pulls back, I tell her, "Ride me, Rosebud. I want to watch you come while you bounce on my dick."

She leans down and places a kiss over my heart. She pushes herself up, and when she starts to lift herself up my length, it sends my eyes to the back of my head. I grip her hips in my hands, trying to control her movements because if she keeps going like she is, I'm not going to last long enough, and I need to feel her come again.

Just as I pull her down on me hard, she changes the angle, sucking in a breath. I do it again, and I can feel the fluttering of her pussy around me. Her eyes flutter closed when I do it a third time.

"Eyes on me," I grind out as I pull her down a fourth time. Her eyes fly open, meeting mine, just as she tips over the edge. "Fuck," I growl from how tightly her pussy is gripping me, and it's what I need to send myself falling over the precipice with her. The orgasm is so strong, it causes me to jackknife up, my arms wrapping around her, and I bury my face in the valley between her breasts, directly over her heart.

She's panting and her heart is racing. I can feel her fingers stroking through my hair. She's not making any movements to pull away, thankfully. I don't think I could withstand her even moving an inch right now. Her pussy is still convulsing around me, and my dick is so sensitive that I fear the moment she tries to lift off of me, it will send me into full-body convulsions.

"Dean, that was_"

"Perfect? Amazing? Life changing?" I finish for her, smiling against her skin.

"Yes, all of that." I can hear the smile in her voice.

"I love you so much, Cordelia," I say as I pull back to look at her. "I didn't know that any of this could feel this way. Everything is so much more with you." I slide a hand up her back to her neck, pulling her lips down to mine. The movement causes her to lift a fraction of an inch, and I suck in a breath as her lips meet mine. I don't release my hold when she tries to pull away. Only after I fully kiss her do I let her pull back.

"Are you ok?" she asks.

"Just a little sensitive, is all. Don't move yet. I don't know if I can handle it."

She laughs but doesn't make a move, keeping my dick and my cum as far inside of her as she can. I can feel our releases dripping down over my balls.

Once I've recovered and helped Cordelia move off of me, I drag her into my shower with me. She pulls her hair up into a messy bun on the top of her head as the water warms. I take my time lathering up every inch of her body before she does the same with me. Once we rinse off, I grab a towel, securing it around my waist, and then wrap her in another.

After we are dry and back in bed, with her head on my chest and her slow and even breathing the only sound in the room, I let my mind wander back over the whole evening. What started as it has so many nights before, turned into exactly what I have been waiting for.

She's admitted that I have her heart.

I can understand her reluctance and the time it has taken to get here, but it's a huge step for her, for us. Now I need to get her to give me her trust as well. To trust me with her past. To open up to me and let me into the last piece of her she's keeping locked away.

I know she mentioned that she would tell me when we got to the Outer Banks if she hadn't told me by then. I'm starting to think she's decided, perhaps unconsciously, to just wait till then. And maybe that would be easier for her. There's something special about the trip and the place. I know that much even if she hasn't explicitly said it.

I also remember listening to her side of a conversation when I got home. I know I walked in and probably missed some important pieces of the conversation, but I heard her say she's not still sleeping with someone else and that it had been two years since she saw him or slept with him. Both? I don't really know. I'm not going to press for those details; I have more than my fair share of past partners, and holding that against her wouldn't be fair to either of us.

Hearing her mention a second guy into the mix was intriguing to say the least. Not that I would ever share her, but it does give me some ideas for another day. I know she has some toys, and as Bast likes to always remind us, "a woman's toys are not your enemy, they are your friends and partners." I smile, thinking about the ways I could use her toys on her one day to give her that experience.

I brush a strand of hair off her forehead and study her as she sleeps. Her pink lips are slightly parted, her face relaxed in a way that only comes in a deep sleep. Her long lashes are splayed across her cheeks, and freckles dot her button nose and cheekbones. I can tell she has gotten some sun since we first met, as her freckles are more pronounced and her skin has that golden glow. Just a subtle tan since she uses sunscreen on her face like it's her job. She told me one morning, when I asked why she was using her fancy face stuff on a day we planned to stay in and lounge around, that the sun on her face is not her friend if she wants to keep looking almost ten years younger than she actually is. I won't complain, because she does look like she's still in her early thirties.

As I'm studying her face, her body tenses up and her breathing gets a little faster as her eyes start darting under her eyelids. She lets out a sound, something between a gasp and a sob. I draw my arms around her tighter, whispering, "It's ok, Cordelia, I've got you. I'm not going to let you go." I repeat it a few more times, hugging her to my chest as tightly as I can without cutting off her airflow. After a minute or two, she calms down and relaxes back into my touch.

I stay awake a while after that, holding her tight until sleep finally claims me as well.

I wake the next morning to my alarm going off. I grab my phone and turn off the alarm. Cordelia is still curled into my side, her fingers gripping into my chest hair. She's got a grip on them, like she was trying to anchor herself to me while she slept. I try to move, but the sharp bite of pain that only having your hair pulled can cause forces me to stop. I start lightly drawing circles on the back of her hand, hoping the sensation will begin to relax her, but my plan backfires when she grips tighter, forcing a yelp out of my mouth. Cordelia sits up with a start, the blanket falling to her waist, leaving her perfect tits level with my eyes.

"What happened? Are you ok?" she asks as she looks around.

I rub my chest before I answer her, "Everything is fine now." I haven't taken my eyes from her chest, and she must realize because suddenly she pulls the sheet back up to cover them. "Hey!" I say as I reach to pull the sheet from her hand, but she smacks me with her other hand.

"You woke me up! I'm not giving you a show before the sun comes up," she huffs out.

"To be fair, you wouldn't have been woken up if you hadn't been trying to pull out a handful of my chest hairs." I'm still rubbing the spot. "I'm not sure what you were dreaming about, but you did not want to let go of me."

Cordelia's eyes cast to where my hand is, and hers was, before her eyes flick back up to mine. "I'm sorry. I don't even know what I was dreaming about." Then she lets the sheet drop and lowers down to place a kiss on my chest.

"Cordelia," I growl out. "You're gonna make me late for work."

She flops back down next to me, leaving the sheet around her waist, and stretches her arms above her head. "My apologies, please don't let me get in your way."

I have to force myself out of bed, even though the last thing I want to do is leave her today. I want to stay home and bury myself in her all day, not leaving the bed unless we need to. But I can't. Graham took the morning off since Madison has a doctor's appointment before school starts back up, and I can't leave the guys to figure things out for themselves without any warning.

I head into the bathroom, brushing my teeth and relieving myself. When I come back out, I find Cordelia lying on her side, in the middle of the bed. One leg on top of the blankets, her perfect peach of an ass sticking out, the sheet pulled just below her breasts, and she's wrapped around the pillow I was using. She's got her Kindle in her hand, and she looks over at me as I step to the dresser.

"You realize the whole 'going to make you late for work' thing is about to be your own fault when you walk around without anything on, right?" She smirks.

I pull open the drawer and yank out a pair of boxers before stepping into them. "Says the one lying in my bed looking like sin personified."

She rolls her eyes at me, but I can tell she loves it from the blush that paints her chest and face. I turn to grab the rest of my clothes and finish getting dressed before I lean over the bed and place a kiss on her lips.

"I love you, and I can't wait to see you when I get home later."

"I love you, too," she says just above a whisper. "Be careful driving."

I let out a satisfied hum at her words, "For you, always." I walk out of the bedroom, casting one last longing look at her from the doorway, and taking a moment to memorize the way she looks in my bed like this.

I groan as I sit down in the mudroom and lace up my work boots.

I can't wait to hand this company over to Graham someday and take a step back. My body is increasingly feeling the effects of years of manual labor.

I need a vacation.

The thought sends my mind to the beach trip that is coming up.

But something tells me it's not going to be the kind of vacation that I need.

Chapter Twenty-Five

CORDELIA

The last couple of weeks, I have been so wrapped up in spending time with Dean after confessing my feelings that I feel as though I have been neglecting my friends.

No, scratch that, I *know* I have been a shitty friend. I have been to all our girls' nights every week, but I haven't done the little things I used to do before this whole thing with Dean started. Not to mention the anniversary is rapidly approaching, which always adds to my withdrawal from everyone around me.

So I got up early and took care of the couple of pieces of work I needed to get done. Then I start making my way out to drop in on Gwen and Faye, like I usually do a couple of times a month.

I grab a couple of coffees before heading over to The Rosewood.

When I walk in, carrying the two cups and enjoying the way it always smells like cinnamon in the hotel, Faye lets out a squeal of excitement from behind the desk.

I will never get over what a gorgeous little hotel she built out of this place. She has plush rose red carpet in the two sitting areas by the big windows, and white tile with gold veins running through all the main walkways and hallways. The sitting areas have antique pink and red wingback chairs in one window and a plush black matching sofa in the other. The huge antique mahogany desk is the only thing she kept from when this was her grandmother's. The walls are a forest green below the chair rails and a crisp white above. I always teased her about the green and red, saying it's just missing a Christmas tree. With Christmas being Faye's favorite holiday, she just smiles and nods, since that's what she was going for.

"Oh, you are a goddess, Cordy," Faye says as she takes her drink from my offered hand. "What's the special occasion?"

"Since when do I need a reason to bring my self-proclaimed little sister a coffee? I'm truly offended." My tone drips with mock offense.

Faye eyes me suspiciously before saying, "It's just been a while since you randomly dropped by with a morning coffee for a chat. Too busy gettin' some to spend a morning with me, I know."

"I have been a little absent in some regards lately, I know. I'm sorry." I pull up a chair and sit behind the counter with her.

"You brought me coffee, so I can forgive you for letting me fall to the wayside," she says before taking a sip. "This is so much better than the coffee I make here, but don't tell anyone I said that."

We spend the next hour catching each other up, and I fill her in on how I admitted my feelings, not just to myself but to Dean as well, which is received with a shriek, followed by her jumping up and down and pulling me into a hug.

"I'm so fucking happy for you. Brian would be too, you know," she says when she pulls back from her hug.

I offer her a small smile, saying, "I know he would. He would just be happy that I was close enough for him to come home on long weekends when he got leave." I take the last sip of my coffee, tossing the cup into the trash under the desk before adding, "So, really? Nothing new going on with you? I thought you had some date lined up a couple of weeks ago?"

She waves me off, "I did. It was a disaster. I'm over it. I'm not going to let anyone but myself set me up anymore. It never works out. I swear, people see a thirty-six-year-old single woman, and it's all about the biological clock. One that I smashed, thank you very much. I don't want kids. I want a house with some land and a bunch of dogs. My grandma used to have a retired greyhound when I was a kid, and I want to just go save them all and keep them on a big plot of land where they can just be dogs. I don't need to add kids to that."

"You would make a wonderful fur-mama to a pack of dogs. But I gotta ask, does the whole 'not letting anyone else set you up' include me? Cuz I was gonna try to see what I can do with a certain mechanic that *seriously* needs a woman in his life."

Faye narrows her eyes at me, "What did you do?"

"Me?! I haven't done anything," I pause before muttering, "Yet."

"Yeah, see that right there. The 'yet', you're up to something."

I put my hands up and laugh, "I wanted to talk to you first about it. But I also wasn't going to even attempt that conversation with him until I get back from the Outer Banks."

Faye is quiet for a moment before she says, "I don't really know. I mean, he's incredibly hot and all those tattoos, he's like a walking fantasy for me. But I also know he's got some PTSD from his time in the Marines. I think the whole town knows that.

I remember the first time he came home after his time in, and he was at Dean's for his usual firework display. Rumor was, and I've never asked to confirm this, but I guess he kinda lost his shit. It took Dean and Sheriff Murphy to restrain him. It was the only year that Dean didn't do a whole big display." Faye shrugs and continues, "It never felt right to ask about something so personal before. I've thought about mentioning it to you a few times, since y'all are so close. But after seeing him at Dean's, and he was ok, I'm wondering how much of it was true. I do remember his show not happening that year, but I heard him setting them off, one here and there, for a while. I always wondered if they did some kind of immersion therapy."

I absorb everything she's telling me. I never pushed for background on Sebastian before; he never pushed for mine, so it never felt right to do. But hearing this puts a lot into perspective, and I feel like, knowing Dean like I do now, he one hundred percent was letting Sebastian set off one firework at a time to get him through it.

"That sounds like something Dean would do for someone he cares about."

"I'm not saying that those issues are a dealbreaker for me, I just wanted you to know that I knew some stuff. I'm not hanging my hopes on him. As far as I know, I don't think he really hooks up or dates anyone that I have ever seen or heard of. And you know I hear all the gossip around here," Faye explains. "Sometimes being the granddaughter of Lucy Banks is a curse more than a blessing."

I laugh, asking, "The little biddies still coming in here and having coffee and gossip hour?"

Faye's grandmother used to host morning coffee and gossip for all her friends back when the hotel was a bed-and-breakfast. They started calling it a book club as it got bigger to keep their husbands out, and eventually it turned into the gossip hotspot for the whole town. Everyone knew everything every week with those ladies. Apparently, there are a few that still try to keep the tradition alive.

"Thankfully, they have toned it down. I have them down to once a month. Which was yesterday."

"Well, that's a start," I smile.

"So, how are you feeling about the trip? Nervous?" Faye questions.

I exhale before replying, "We're going out that Saturday morning. Jason is gonna meet us out there, and we're going to fill Dean in on everything. And I need to tell him about Jason before then, which is almost scarier at this point than the rest of it," I let out a humorless chuckle.

"Which means you are going to procrastinate until the last

possible second." Faye arches a perfect eyebrow at me, daring me to say anything to prove her wrong.

God, she really is exactly like the annoying little sister I never had.

I decide to ignore that comment and say, "I was gonna pick up lunch and go bother Gwen after this. I've missed you girls these last couple of months. I just wanted to stop, check in, and chat. I need to get back into the habit of doing this again."

Faye narrows her eyes at my avoidance but allows it with a wave of her hand, "It's ok. It's the honeymoon phase right now. Enjoy it. Besides, if you haven't been there - spending all this time with Dean - like you have been, maybe you wouldn't be in a good place emotionally that allows you to admit to yourself that you *can* feel love again."

"I really hate how intuitive and smart you are sometimes, you know that?" I say, standing up and putting the chair back in the corner I got it from.

"Yes, but despite that, you still love me," Faye says as she wraps me in a hug. "Now, go tell Gwenny I said hi!"

I wave goodbye as I push open the doors, stepping outside.

I go a couple of doors down to the diner and order two grilled cheese sandwiches and fries. While I wait, I take a seat on the red, cracked plastic counter-height stool. The diner was built in the 1950s, and it still looks like it. Black-and-white checkered tile, red booths and stools, and white tables with metal trim. The smell of decades of grease lingers in the air along with the memories of milkshakes with Harper when we first got here. You can't even drink their milkshakes; they are too thick. You either have to let them melt for a few minutes or use a spoon. But they are the best.

I pull out my phone and text Dean.

> Me: Hey, I don't know if I will be back in time to make dinner. So if you want me to pick up something, let me know.

. . .

A few minutes of mindless social media scrolling pass, and I see a text come through.

> Dean: I can make us something if I get home before you do.

> Dean: BTW, I really like saying home, like it's yours too.

> Dean: Fuck, I didn't mean I wanted you to move in. I mean, I do, but I'm not trying to pressure you into it.

> Dean: ... I'm gonna go back to work before I say something else that could get me in trouble.

I'm trying so hard not to burst out laughing at his messages. This is one of those moments where you really see the similarities between Dean and Graham.

> Me: Patience is a virtue, but that was adorable. *heart emoji*

> Me: I will see you when I get home.

I add that in just to let him know that I'm not mad or upset over what he said. I'm old enough to realize that if we continue the way we are, that would be a logical next step in our relationship.

And trying to at least be honest with myself, I don't think that it's too incredibly far off, *if* everything goes well next month.

"Cordelia?" I turn at the sound of my name to see Rita walking up to the counter next to me. "Oh, it is you. How are you?" she asks as she wraps me in a hug. The smell of sugar clings to her, as always.

"I'm ok, picking up some lunch for Gwen and me. How are you?"

"Oh, living the good life. Tell me about how you and Dean are. Because I know that 'okay' is not a good enough answer." She takes a seat next to me and waits for me to respond.

I smile. "We are good. I've practically moved in with him at this point. I guess you could say it's serious."

Rita grabs my hand, giving it a squeeze, "That's good, dear, really good. You deserve a little happiness after everything you have been through." She cuts me off before I can get a word out, "I've never mentioned this since you never brought it up either, but Max was Navy. He tends to follow the stories that make national-level news when the military is involved. He recognized you."

I blink rapidly a few times, trying to absorb this information.

Rita and Max have always been like this amazingly fun aunt and uncle; they are people I would consider family. They are both in their early sixties and just genuinely care about the people they have in their circle. I'm trying to process what she told me, and at the same time, I'm trying to recall moments when they ever treated me differently. I can't recall so much as a single look, or touch, or word that would have ever told me that they knew about Brian. I don't know what to do with this information, and the thought of the rest of the town knowing has me casting a nervous glance around the diner.

"Oh, stop it, we never told a soul. I can't say that no one knows of the story; it was a big deal for a minute. But I don't think anyone else committed your face to memory like Max did. He had to pull up an old news article with a photo to show me. I don't know how the man remembers the things he does when he can't remember where he put his glasses or keys most of the time."

Before either of us can say anything, the waitress comes out of the kitchen with two to-go bags, "Here ya go, ladies," she says as she sets them down in front of us.

We take our bags, and Rita leads me out of the diner. "Just remember that we are always here if you need us. We have been through something similar ourselves. Car accident," she clears her throat of emotion. "Well, don't let me keep you from your friend; tell Gwen I said hello." And with that, she turns and walks off down the street.

What the fuck just happened?

CORDELIA

I stand on the sidewalk, staring at the last spot I saw Rita before she turned the corner.

They knew? All this time, they knew and never said anything?

I don't know how long I stand here before someone bumps into my bag and shakes me out of my thoughts.

I turn, walking over to Gwen's shop in a daze and on autopilot. I don't even remember crossing the street or opening the door. Suddenly, I'm standing at her checkout counter.

I set the bag on the counter, still trying to wrap my head around this. I don't even notice Gwen come out of the back room until she's standing across from me.

"Hello? Cordy?" Gwen snaps her fingers in my face, and I shake my head. "Are you okay? You look like you saw a ghost."

My eyes take a second to focus on Gwen's bright blue eyes. "Um, yeah. Actually, no. Not even a little bit. But I brought you lunch," I say as a gesture to the bag. "Grilled cheese and fries."

"Thanks for lunch. It's been a while since we did this." Gwen studies my face as she takes the to-go containers out of the bag. "You wanna talk about it?"

I let out a breath and lick my lips, trying to make up my mind, even though I know what the answer should be. "Rita and Max know. Have known? Always knew? Whatever the right wording is. She just told me as I was picking these up. I guess Max was in the Navy, and he keeps up on the happenings in the military? I don't know," I rush out.

Gwen is frozen in place. A single French fry halfway to her mouth, just staring at me. She blinks a couple of times, sets the fry back into the container before saying, "I'm sorry. What?"

"Yeah, that's where I kinda am right now."

"How did they know it was you? It's not like you lived here when it happened."

"Rita said Max kept saying he recognized me from the news segments, possibly my name, I guess. Once he put two and two together, he told Rita." I tilt my head to the side and continue, "Rita said they had been through something similar? A car accident?"

"Oh," Gwen draws out the word, "Yeah, that was sad. It was their nephew. We got hit with a bad ice storm. I guess he was already on the road and thought he could beat it. He was only ten minutes from their house. Hit a patch of ice, and his car went off the bridge into the river. It's why Rita and Max give everyone they care about those little window-breaker keychains. Not that it would have helped in that situation. They were told he was knocked out from his head hitting the steering wheel before he even went into the water. There's no telling if he regained consciousness or not." Gwen sighs, "It shook up the whole town. They put up improved barriers on all the bridges that go over the river after that. Rita and Max were really close with him, too."

I go quiet while I absorb her words. I know a nephew isn't the same, but given the type of people they are, they would have thought of him like a son of their own.

"It does make sense why I've always felt a pull toward her. I just assumed it was because she's just one of those few people who genuinely care about people, ya know?"

"Yeah, I get that. She and Max have always been that cool older couple for as long as I can remember. When I was in Raleigh for college, they would always check in with my parents, and if they mentioned I was coming home, Rita would always text me the day before, asking to let her know when I left and when I got home." Gwen picks up her container, walking away from the counter, and says, "Did I ever tell you that Rita is a big part of the reason I opened this shop?"

I grab my container and follow her over to the little dusky teal couch and table by the changing rooms. "No, I don't think you ever told me that." I take a seat while Gwen settles in. I glance around the shop and realize that it has been far too long since I was in here. I think the last time was when we came to pick out a dress for that first date.

Not much has changed, except it looks like all the new summer clothes are out, and a small rack with some fall outfits. It's a small shop, nothing overly fancy. But the details that went into designing the space make the whole shop feel like you stepped into a high-class boutique in New York City. Which is fitting, since Gwen did an internship there after college.

She left some of the brick walls exposed, while the rest is painted in jewel tones, teal and purple and green and ruby reds. All her lighting and accents are done in gold; none of the lights are the same. Yet they all work together since they all have a vintage feel to them. Her point-of-sale desk looks like someone took half the back off one of those old roll-up desks.

My favorite spot in this whole shop is right where we are sitting. This vintage teal wing-back couch looks like it would be uncomfortable, but I could nap on this thing. It just hugs you when you sit down on it. She wanted to have a comfortable spot for anyone sitting, waiting to use the changing room, or waiting for someone in the changing room, which is next to us, back in the corner, with luxurious fabric draped from the ceiling as the door.

Her shop always smells like vanilla and fresh cookies. She says it makes people happier, and happy people will spend more money. She's not wrong about it making you happier. It feels like stepping into grandma's kitchen and getting a warm hug.

"Yeah, I was in the city and I was really thinking about staying, for good. My last night in Raleigh was," she trails off as she shakes her head and scoffs. "Well, it messed with my head a bit. That's a story for another time. Anyway, I guess my parents mentioned it to Max and Rita. A couple of days later, Rita sent me a picture of this storefront. It used to be a tailor shop. The only thing I kept was the desk; it's perfect and fits my vibes." She clears her throat before continuing, "The guy was retiring, and it was going to be for sale, not rent. He owned it. It was the opportunity of a lifetime. To be able to make it everything I want and not have to answer to a landlord? I mean, yeah, you know how it goes, it sucks when things break, but I couldn't pass it up. Took some doing and about eight months of emails and phone calls, but I got it done. I think she knew that this was the only way I was going to come back home. She knew my parents and the twins missed me." I smile at the thought of her younger siblings, who love to cause her as much trouble as they can with their antics. "But she also knew how important it was that I was independent at that point. And since there is a full apartment upstairs, well, she knew what she was doing," she shrugs, taking a bite of her sandwich.

My stomach is still in knots after Rita, but I take a fry and pop it into my mouth.

"So, you gonna tell me why, after a few months, you suddenly show up in my shop with lunch? You used to do this almost every other week." Gwen gives me a smug smirk, and I narrow my eyes at her.

"Can't I just miss my friends?"

She just raises her eyebrows at me and takes another bite. I throw the fry I was holding down and lean back against the couch.

"Either Harper can't keep her mouth shut, or you and Faye

know me all too well. I don't know which is better or worse, to be honest."

"Actually, it was when Dean picked up donuts a couple of mornings ago. He was whistling while he was carrying a couple of boxes back to his truck, which was parked a couple of spots up from here."

"Oh," I say, and I can feel my cheeks heat up.

Gwen giggles out, "I fucking knew it. You told him you love him, didn't you? That's why you practically dropped off the face of the earth and have been so vague with us on Wednesday nights." She points at me with a fry, "And don't deny that you love him, everyone can see it."

I pick up a fry and throw it at her; she catches it and pops it into her mouth. "Yeah, I did. It was a whole thing that day. It's funny that it took Jason asking me if I loved him for me to realize it. Once I said it aloud to him, it was like I couldn't stop it from coming out to Dean. I thought feeling it would be scary, but saying it to him turned out to be scarier than I thought it would have." I sigh and lean back into the couch.

"Cordy, I'm gonna stop you right there." Gwen leans over and grabs my hand in one hand and uses a finger from her other hand to rub a circle around my ring. "Just nod or shake your head as I go, alright?"

Nod.

"Good. You've been desperately trying to fill a void in your life for the last five years, whether you realized it or not."

I drop my eyes, but I nod, because she's right.

"There is nothing wrong with that. It's to be expected in all honesty. You closed yourself off as much as you possibly could, never wanting to leave yourself open to finding something that could be ripped away from you again." She keeps one hand holding mine and pops another fry into her mouth with the other while she waits.

Nod.

"Maybe Brian got tired of seeing you miserable? And before

you deny it, remember, I've seen you completely fall apart before. And I know that what I saw that day wasn't a one-time thing." I cringe internally at the thought of the time Gwen saw me at one of my lower points. It was a couple of days before Brian's birthday. I don't even remember now what set me off, but I lost it. I couldn't stop crying. Gwen just wrapped me in a hug and let me cry it out on her shoulder. "I know you wear a mask every single day to try to prove to yourself or the world that you aren't a shell of the person you were before. But you were never a shell of that person, Cordy; you were just heartbroken and grief-stricken. You needed someone to pull you out of that, and if you ask me, Brian decided it was about time as well."

When did Gwen and Faye become so intuitive? I don't like it. I don't like that they can read me so easily. That my mask doesn't work like I thought it did. She's not wrong, though. I have been trying to hide that so much of me died along with Brian with that knock on the door.

Sure, I can smile and laugh and joke around and have fun. But under all of that is this feeling of dread, that something so vital to this world is gone. Because it is. My reason for striving to be the best I could is gone.

I blink to try to clear the tears that are blurring my vision before I meet her bright blue eyes.

I nod. I lick my lips and slowly swallow. "You might be right. But it still feels like I shouldn't have this, this happiness. Sometimes," my voice drops to a whisper, "I still feel like it's my fault."

Gwen blows out a breath before she says, "I'm not going to try to unpack that right now, but it wasn't your fault. There was nothing you could have done to stop it or prevent it. Nothing, do you hear me?"

"Rationally, I know that, but it doesn't change what it feels like." I exhale and drop my head into my hands. "How the fuck am I supposed to tell all of this to Dean? How am I supposed to tell all of you the details in a couple of weeks? I'm a fucking hot mess."

"Emphasis on the hot part," Gwen smirks. I know what she's trying to do, and damn it. It's working. I can feel the corner of my mouth tip up in response. "Ok, but in all seriousness, Cordy, you have been in survival mode ever since I met you. I've watched you run yourself into the ground when you and Harper were building up Glass. I've seen how every time you go into Corner Coffee, you gravitate toward Rachel because she reminds you of Brian. I've watched as you flinch when people use certain words around you. And yes, I never use them because I can understand why you don't like them. I also know that you refuse to tell anyone how those words affect you because you don't want to be an inconvenience to others. You don't want to be labeled as the 'broken woman with a warning label'.

"But, fuck, Cordy, you have earned your peace. You may not feel like you earned a damn thing, but you did. You earned it and you deserve it. You deserve laughter around a table with all your friends. You deserve to be loved and made to feel safe and supported. You deserve to be able to exhale a full breath after so many years of holding it all in."

I keep wiping the tears away. She's right; I don't feel like I deserve a fucking thing, but maybe she is right about the rest, too. I had to do all the hard things; I was the one fighting, the one who refused to leave a room at the hardest moments. I couldn't. I was physically unable to walk away from that room. I force the memory of that away; just thinking of it for a second is all it ever takes to break me.

Gwen reaches over, handing me a napkin. I wipe my face and glance up. "You're not wrong, but I can't say that I believe you are fully right either." I raise my hand to stop her from arguing with me, "I just don't see it. And that will come in time." I scoff a laugh, twisting the tissue in my hands. "I hate time. I hate that there was nothing I could do to stop the world from spinning. That everyone was just going about their lives around me, the world rushing by, and I still feel like I'm stuck in those moments. I hate the whole construct of time and how Brian feels further and further away every day. It was a huge part of the reason I flung myself into building Glass. The day-to-day grind in an office, *needing* the weekends and counting down to them, always came with the feeling of dread because it meant I was further and further away. I couldn't handle it anymore. I needed to stop counting the days, to stop thinking about it. I can say that now, the only times I feel time flying by me are around the holidays, the anniversary, and his birthday.

"Coming here has been good for my soul, my heart, my sanity. I know I have made strides in places, yet I still struggle in others, and I probably always will. So as much as I hate the saying, I need time." I exhale a harsh breath.

Gwen stays silent, letting the words hang in the air around us for a moment. "I can't say that I fully understand how you were feeling in those moments, but at the same time, I get it. I don't think I could ever do the nine-to-five grind. I'm fairly certain it would kill my spirit," she smiles. "Now, I'm going to finish this sandwich and so are you, and you are going to fill me in on all the details around you and Dean that you haven't been sharing the last few weeks." She takes her container with her as she curls her legs under her and leans back into the sofa.

Laughing, I do the same before I start the process of filling her in on how it has been going, living in the little bubble I didn't realize I had put Dean and myself into. Thinking back on it, I realize he must have done the same because even Graham and Madison haven't been over in at least three weeks now. Seems like we both needed some time just for us after putting so much out there and sharing.

Now if only I could share everything else.

There is just so much to go through, and I don't really know where to start.

Chapter Twenty-Seven

DEAN

I grab the string and pull, hearing the click before the light in the attic comes on. I turn and glance around from the ladder, trying to see where I put that suitcase up here. I spot it in the far corner behind me. I carefully make my way over to it. "Really need to do something up here," I mumble to myself as I step slowly onto each support beam so as not to fall through the ceiling.

Just as I take the first step back down the ladder with the suitcase, I hear Cordelia's voice. "Dean?"

"I'm up here. Can you come over here so I can hand you this suitcase?" I yell as I take the second step down.

"Yeah, I'm right under you, on your left," Cordelia says below me.

I lower the suitcase, and when I feel the weight lighten, I let go, pulling the string to turn the light off before I come down the ladder.

I hook an arm around her and pull her in for a quick kiss. I step back, fold the stairs up, and close up the attic.

"Gonna get started on packing?" she asks.

"Yeah, figured we got a week, so I should probably get started," I shrug. I wanted to get started on this yesterday so that I had a full day today to get this done. Then Graham and Madison showed up for a little impromptu Saturday night hangout.

Cordelia's expression is vacant, and her green eyes look like they are seeing something a thousand miles away. I slide my hand over hers, which is resting on the handle of the suitcase. I reach up with my other hand and slide a finger down her cheek to her chin, tilting her head up. "Come back to me, beautiful," I say gently.

She blinks rapidly as her eyes focus back on me. "I'm sorry," she breathes.

I cup her face, and she leans into my touch. "Should I assume that you have officially decided that you'll tell me all the details next week?"

Her green eyes are suddenly filling with unshed tears, and she nods. I pull her into my arms, resting my chin on the top of her head. "I've got you. If you need to cry and let it out, I have you. Whatever you need." She just lets me hold her, her arms wrapping around me.

I've noticed over the last week that she's been pulling away and distancing herself. I don't think it has anything to do with me and everything to do with the trip.

She's also been working a bit later this last week and more than likely will be this week as well. I understand that, and I would probably be in the same position if I didn't have Graham to lean on to step up. She handles everything herself, so she doesn't have that luxury.

When she finally pulls back, she has dried tear tracks on her face, and her eyes are a little puffy and red. But seeing her like this? Knowing she trusts me enough to let me see her like this makes my heart squeeze in my chest.

"What do you need?" My voice is thick with emotion and need.

Her eyes bounce between mine before she says, "Make me forget for a little while."

I don't usually need to be told twice, yet I hesitate. "Dean, I just want to shut my head off. Please." Seeing the sadness in her eyes, I bring my lips to hers and pick her up, cradling her ass in my hands. When her legs lock around my waist, I delve into the kiss further.

Fuck.

She tastes like mine. I will never get enough of her lips, her eyes, her smell, the way she tastes when she's coming apart on my tongue.

I turn and spread her out on the dining room table. I pull away just long enough to pull her shorts down, pulling her to the edge of the table so I can feast. I don't wait or tease her. I don't ease into it. I just lock my mouth over her clit and spear her on two fingers. When her back arches up off the table, I flick my eyes to hers. I want to see those beautiful pools of emeralds.

But she has them closed.

I pull back and growl, "Eyes on me, Rosebud."

When her eyes meet mine, and I hold them as I go back to licking and sucking.

I've learned her body over the last few months, the little things that make her fall faster than others.

It takes all of them to get her to peak for me. Adding a third finger, rubbing her asshole, and finally biting, lightly at first, then harder on her clit is what finally pushes her over the edge.

She shatters on my fingers, soaking the table under her as she calls my name.

As I stand, I say, "Fuck, Cordelia, that was the best meal I have ever had at this table."

The basketball shorts I'm wearing are doing nothing to hide how hard my dick is. I shove them down and slide my dick through her release, soaking my dick. I stroke my length, spreading her wetness all over me.

"Fuck, Dean," Cordelia whimpers. Her body is still lightly convulsing from the aftershocks.

I groan as I slide into her, and her pussy keeps pulsing around me. "I'm going to fuck you hard and fast, because the way your needy little pussy is gripping me, I'm not going to last long."

It's the only warning she gets before I pull back, leaving just the very tip inside her and slam in all the way to the hilt. I don't stop, I don't ease up. I hold her legs wide and keep her at the edge of the table. Her fingers slide down, finding the edge of the table, and her knuckles go white with her grip. She holds on with everything she has as I give her everything I have, setting a punishing pace as I slam in and out of her.

"Fuck, Cordelia," I grind out as I feel the tingles at the base of my spine starting.

Three more thrusts and I unload inside her. I push so hard into her that I couldn't tell you where I ended and she began.

I drop my head to her stomach, resting there to catch my breath.

My heart is racing, but so are my thoughts. I can understand needing to forget the things that take over your head. But I also know I don't want to be just a distraction for her.

But if that is what she needs sometimes, in certain moments, I will gladly do anything she needs.

As I come back to myself, I plant my hands on either side of her waist and push myself up, staring down into her eyes.

The green is brighter, more vivid, and they don't look as sad and empty as they did. I smirk to myself as I take her in.

"You look awfully smug and proud of yourself right now," Cordelia quips playfully.

I give her a smile and pull her up to a sitting position. I tuck strands of her hair behind her ear. "Rosebud, seeing the light back in your eyes is the only reason I'm proud of myself."

"I'm sorry. I know I have been retreating into myself this last week." She plays with the hem of her shirt, twisting it between her fingers. "I just wish... I guess wishing doesn't matter. It won't change anything."

Fuck. I'm losing her. Just had *to say something.*

I pinch her chin, tilting her eyes to mine, "Stop. Yeah, you can't change the past, and it fucking sucks. But I will do anything to make you smile. I will always be proud of myself for accomplishing that. Even more so when you're feeling sad."

She leans in and presses her lips to mine.

"Your table is a mess," she breathes against my lips.

"But it was a delicious mess." I press another quick kiss to her lips.

After we have cleaned up ourselves and the table, I order a couple of pizzas and start packing. Cordelia lazes around on the bed with her Kindle.

"When are you going to start packing?" I ask her as I fold up another shirt.

"I'm half packed already. It's really just the last-minute stuff that I need to pack the morning we leave. Shower stuff, things like that." She looks up over the top of her Kindle and continues, "I will probably bring my bag over here; it's easier to leave from here together that morning. Assuming you still want to go out together?" Her tone is laced with apprehension.

"Yeah, Cordelia, I do. Something about having you next to me, enjoying whatever music you decide to turn on and singing along with it, makes me smile just thinking about it."

She gives me a little smile and goes back to her book. I watch her for a moment as I keep folding up clothes. Her nervousness over this trip, probably more over my going, is starting to worry me. But I've waited this long to find out, I can wait a little longer. But I can't help feeling like there is more that she isn't telling me. And I would bet anything it has to do with that phone call I overheard between her and Harper months ago.

I don't know why, but her comment about not sleeping with someone has been this annoying little itch I can't quite reach. I don't want to ask her about it directly; she seemed so on edge, though, like she was worried I had overheard.

If there's one thing I have realized over these months, when I push a little too much when she's like that, she shuts down. Now, I can be a patient man, but that only goes so far. If I don't get an answer about this week, I'm going to ask after. If she weren't here more often than not, I would question if something was going on behind my back that I don't know about. Thankfully, my logical side has won this round. But it doesn't mean I don't still need, or rather, *deserve* answers on that.

Which I will get.

One way or another.

I finish up packing just as there's a knock at the door. Cordelia glances up, "I'll get that."

"It should be the pizza," I call after her as she heads out of the room.

Following behind her a minute later, I find her plating up some slices for us.

"Wanna sit in the sunroom? Or is it still too hot out there for you?" I pose the question since I know she gets migraines when the humidity gets too high.

She thinks about it for a second before responding, "Sunroom sounds good. It didn't seem too bad anymore when I opened the door for the pizza."

I grab her plate from her and head out the door. I open up the folding doors on both sides as she flicks the switch for the ceiling fan with her elbow.

"I grabbed you an iced tea," she says as she sets the glass down on the table.

"Thank you," I say as I push the last of the panels into place and take a seat across from her.

"I'm going to have a really crazy week, between prepping everything I need to at Glass and packing. I just want to relax with you tonight," she states as she takes a bite.

"If you need any help with anything, you know you just have to ask. Thankfully, Graham is picking up the slack for the most part, and I've talked to Ray a bit as well and made sure he was aware of everything that is expected to be done in my absence." I pause to take a bite of pizza before swallowing and continuing. "He actually seems really excited for the extra responsibility. If he does well and keeps the guys in line, he might be a good one to take over for the hands-on stuff a bit more. Gives me a chance to take some vacations and spend time with you."

Cordelia nods, "That would be good. You deserve a little bit of a break every now and then. I know it seems like this should count as one, but I don't. This trip isn't a vacation. It's an escape from reality, and at the same time, it's like being thrust into my worst nightmares all over again. But it's also cathartic," she shrugs, and her voice is more subdued than usual.

I start to respond, but she cuts me off. "I'm sorry. I didn't mean to bring down the mood for you. I've been really short with everyone but you and the girls the last few weeks. Everyone at Glass is scared of me right now and is doing everything they can to avoid being the one I take it out on." She huffs out a breath and whispers, "I hate that I'm this way, but I don't know how to change it."

I reach across the table, brushing my fingers over hers. I don't offer any words because what is there even to say when I don't know all the details? I don't know how to comfort her. I don't want to say the wrong thing and set her off. She's so fragile right now, and the last thing I want to do is crack her defenses or make her angry with me. Especially since she just stated that I'm one of four people that has not been on the receiving end of her wrath.

I would very much like to stay that way.

The rest of the night is quiet, and we settle into just being with each other. I turn on the TV, but I'm not really paying attention to what's on. Cordelia curls up next to me, lost in her book. I've noticed that she's been more absorbed in reading this last month than she has been before. It seems to be something that brings her peace, and as much as I want to be the reason for that, I can't expect her to be dependent on me for everything. And I wouldn't want that anyway. She has a lot in her life that keeps her busy and makes her happy.

Fuck, am I seriously jealous over books?!

"What are you reading?" I question when she lets out a little giggle.

Her eyes flick up to mine from where she's lying with her head in my lap. I've been mindlessly playing with her hair for the last twenty or so minutes.

"Just a book."

I raise my eyebrow. "Is it a funny book?"

Her face flames red at my question, and she looks away. "Oh, so it's *that* kind of book," I chuckle.

She doesn't take her eyes from her Kindle as she says, "Yeah, we can go with that."

I pluck the device from her fingers and do a quick scan of the page. "What in the actual *fuck* is he doing with a pineapple, Cordelia?!" That image will be burned into my brain for the rest of my life.

She snatches the book back, "We aren't going to kink shame Bennett, Dean. He just," she trails off, choosing her words, "Well, he just likes food a little bit."

"I'm never grabbing a book from you again." I shake my head.

"That's probably smart. I tend to read her books when nothing else is holding my interest. This one has been out for a little while, but I'm just now getting to it. I don't want to read all of her stuff and then have nothing when I need it later."

"So, fucking pineapples are a pallet cleaner for you?" I ask.

"Just the fun yet slightly fucked up brain children of Lauren Biel."

I wipe a hand down my face and grumble, "I'm going to regret asking this, but what are you planning to read next?"

She makes a humming sound, setting down her Kindle and grabbing her phone. "Let me see what I have in my library." She scans through a few book covers before she answers, "Oh! *The Wrong Player* is the next one. It's a football-themed one. If he's half as unhinged as Lincoln and Ari in the previous series she wrote, it's going to be a really good book."

"Unhinged is an interesting word choice."

"Well, those red flags look really pretty waving in the wind."

She's picked her Kindle back up and her attention is back on her book.

"I'm hoping you mean they are pretty for your books and not real life, because I'm not above having Lachlan come over here in full Sheriff Murphy mode and give you a good talking to."

The laugh that falls from her lips is full and real, and it's been far too long since I heard it. It makes my heart clench knowing I did that for her. "Yes, just in my books. I technically had real red flags before, and they aren't nearly as fun. But in a book, when the guy decides that he loves her too much to lose her when she's trying to walk out on him, so he chains her to his bed, then it's hot."

"Yeah, I regret asking about your books now," I grumble.

That night, when she cuddles up to me in bed, she presses a kiss to my cheek, letting out a contented noise and whispers, "I love you, Dean."

"I love you, too."

I fall asleep replaying how those three words sounded like she wanted to say so much more with them. It felt like there was more wanting to slip from her tongue.

The next few days pass in a flurry of trying to make sure Graham and Ray are both on the same page with what needs to happen next week.

"Boss, seriously, I got it. I know we have to finish the remodel over on Forest and be ready to start the addition on the church off Main *no later* than Wednesday." I don't miss how he emphasizes the words, proving he was actually listening to me. "I'm well aware that we must have the demo done *and* cleaned up before the weekend for Sunday services. I got this. Besides, that's my mother's church. I will get my ass handed to me if I don't get it done."

Graham and I laugh and nod; he's not wrong. His mom absolutely would kick his ass if it's not done.

"I have to go meet a potential client and get a quote worked up for them. I shouldn't be more than an hour or so. I expect you guys to handle the end-of-day tasks because I'm just going to go home after that," I explain. I glance at my watch, noting that I have roughly a twenty-minute drive from this site, putting me there right about four o'clock as agreed upon.

* * *

Almost three hours later, I'm finally leaving the potential client's house. They kept adding quotes they wanted while I was there. First, it was just to add a roof over their back deck. Then they asked about a deck around their pool, followed by a privacy fence. When they started talking about a kitchen remodel, I drew the line. Told them we would need to schedule a separate appointment for that.

One I will NOT be coming to.

I can't figure out if this couple is actually even going to go through with anything. They were all over the place.

I get in my truck and exhale all the frustration from that appointment out. I grab my phone from the cup holder and see I have twelve missed calls from Cordelia and a handful of texts from her and Graham.

I hit call right away, a sense of dread fills me as my stomach sinks.

"Dean?" Cordelia's voice cracks. She sounds like she's been crying or on the verge of it.

"Yeah, baby, sorry. I had to deal with some difficult potential clients. Is everything ok?"

"I was so worried something happened to you. I couldn't get a hold of you, and Graham said you had to meet with some clients, and he hadn't heard from you either. You were supposed to be home over two hours ago." She sounds frantic. The tremors in her voice are scaring the hell out of me.

"I'm not far from home, I will be there in ten minutes."

"Ok," she sniffles and hangs up.

I drive like a bat out of hell and make it home in seven minutes. Cordelia is on the front steps waiting for me and runs to me as I get out of the truck, jumping up and wrapping her arms and legs around me so tightly I can't breathe. I close my arms around her and hug her tightly to me, pressing kisses to her neck.

Her whole body is trembling. "Cordelia, what's wrong? You're scaring me."

"I thought something bad happened to you. Graham didn't know the address you were at, and you weren't answering your phone. I was so scared." Her arms tighten around my neck.

I hold on to her and walk into the house. I drop us onto the couch, keeping her in my lap. "I'm sorry. I left my phone in the car because I thought it was going to be quick. I'm sorry I worried you and Graham."

"I called him after I talked to you. Told him you were ok." Her words are muffled from her face being burrowed into my shoulder. I draw circles on her back with my hands, trying to calm her down.

"I'm never going to leave you, Rosebud."

If she weren't so close to my ear, I don't think I would have heard her whisper, "You can't promise that."

Once she has calmed down, she demands my phone and uses the Find My Friends app to share my location with her, and then she shares hers back. I don't question it, I just let her do what she needs to do to feel better.

I don't ever want to be the cause of her pain and suffering like that. Not ever again. I'm already mentally preparing to tell that couple, should they call, that we won't be able to accommodate them. I won't risk getting stuck there ever again.

Chapter Twenty-Eight

CORDELIA

I have spent the last three hours, out of the eight hours so far, of this drive in the passenger seat of Dean's truck with my anxiety over this entire week at an all-time high. Between my absolute meltdown last week when I thought something had happened to Dean and all of my other emotions, I have been an emotional wreck. I haven't needed a Xanax in a while, and I needed one that night. I also have yet to tell him about tonight's additional guest.

I keep telling myself, the next song, I will tell him about Jason and prepare him for what he is walking into this week. And then I chicken out at the last second and tell myself, after this song, I will tell him, and thus it has gone for three fucking hours. We just started to drive the Virginia Dare Memorial Bridge, and I know I'm running out of time to have this talk with him. Deciding to test my luck, I fire off a text to Jason.

> Me: Hey. We are roughly an hour out from the house. Give or take. What is your eta?

I'm staring at my screen like I can will a response to come faster. Relief floods me when the little bubbles start bouncing within seconds.

Jason: I opted for the ferries today. We are almost unloading on Ocracoke right now. I have the drive to the north end, and then the ferry to Hatteras, and then the drive to the house. If I get the first ferry, maybe an hour and a half?

Me: Sounds good. We will see you when you get there!

Jason: Cordy… you haven't told him everything yet have you?

Me: ….

Jason: I'm getting tequila on my way to the house

Me: Probably a smart plan

Jason: Fucking hell Cordelia. This is going to be a long ass fucking night.

Me: I will tell him when we get to the house. Being trapped in a car and nowhere to get space if we needed it didn't seem like a great plan, ok?!

Jason: I will give you that… But Cordy, you gotta tell him. I also know you well enough to know you are looking for any excuse right now.

I narrow my eyes at my screen.
Fucker.

Me: I know. I will. I promise. Just take your time driving once you hit Hatteras.

Jason: *facepalm emoji*

I tuck my phone into my purse as we start to come into Manteo before we make our way across the Washington Baum Bridge.

I roll down my window and breathe in the salty air. "I've always thought all the little hotels and houses right on this bridge were so cool. There's a part of me that wants to stay in one, but I can't bring myself to book something so close yet so far from the ocean," I say as I lean my head against the window frame, letting the ocean wind wash over me.

"Yeah, I can understand that. I can tell we are close, but I gotta be honest here, Rosebud, I don't know how close we really are to the ocean right now." Dean lets out an embarrassed laugh.

"From here? A couple of football fields, maybe." I laugh.

"At least you know where we are."

"Yeah, and be ready to take the next right. Follow the signs for the Hatteras Seashore."

"Aye aye, Captain," Dean says as he reaches over the center console of his truck and takes my hand, interlacing our fingers together.

I know he knows that he's getting hit with a bomb while he is here.

But he doesn't know he is getting two bombs dropped on him.

He will find out the entire story of Brian and what it really means to be with me.

How broken I really am.

And he will find out that he's about to spend the next week with the last man who has seen me naked, and I won't lie and say that idea isn't tempting, because what woman wouldn't want two extremely handsome men to worship her? But I somehow don't think Dean is the sharing type. I hope he can understand and move past this. I have Harper and Jason. I don't plan on cutting either of them out, and Dean is going to have to be okay with that. This is just how it is, and Jason is a part of my past.

It's time to lay all the cards on the table.

"If you keep watching out your side, you will see the ocean over the dunes," I tell Dean as he takes the right turn, taking us south on Highway 12.

A few minutes of searching over the dunes go by before Dean gets his first glimpse of the Atlantic. He pulls my hand to his lips, placing a kiss on the back of it. "It's almost as beautiful as you." I smile and give a small shake of my head.

Since Dean let me play DJ the whole drive, I change the music to my OBX playlist. I hit shuffle and, as always, send up a silent prayer to Brian, "Put the songs in the order you want them in." I do this every time, and while I know it's technology that does it, I can't help but feel like the first song is almost always perfectly picked. Today is no different. *God, Your Mama, and Me* by Florida Georgia Line and Backstreet Boys starts filtering through the speakers.

"Did you change up the playlist?" Dean asks.

"Yeah," I try to clear the emotion from my voice, "this is the playlist I always queue up when I hit Highway 12."

"I always thought it was funny that a country band teamed up with a boy band for this one."

I whip my head to glare at Dean, "You take that back. Right. Now. We don't talk down on BSB. If this is going to be a problem for you, we might have to rethink this whole relationship thing we have going." I raise an eyebrow in challenge.

"Alright, alright. I take it back."

We continue down the highway, over the Oregon Inlet, onto Hatteras Island, and into Rodanthe. Once we make our way out of Salvo and it's nothing but ocean, road, and the sound again, Dean asks, "Since you are the GPS, how much further?"

"Not much longer. Honestly, driving through Buxton and Frisco always feels like the longest part. We usually hit up Conner's for groceries the next day and just order pizza tonight.

Just like to get to the house and unpack and chill out a little bit."

"And you are sure I can't chip in for the house at all? It doesn't feel right not helping out."

I let out a loud sigh, "Dean, there isn't anything to help out with. It's a long story, and it kind of all ties together, and I'd really rather get it all out in one go because if I start now, you're gonna have questions. Let's get there, and get the pizza ordered, and then I will start at the beginning, ok?"

Dean meets my eyes for a few seconds, and he must see how much I need him to give me this because he relents. "Ok, but I'm buying the pizza, and I think I wanna stop and grab some drinks."

Already starting to feel nauseous, I turn up the music and lean my head out the window, keeping a grip on his hand like it's my only lifeline when I can feel that I'm on the verge of drowning. It's then that *Dress Blues* by Zac Brown Band comes on. Changing the song will bring more attention to it, so I let it play. I close my eyes and inhale slowly when the line about the high school gymnasium starts to filter through the speakers. I try to will the tears away, but all I can see is the picture the song paints—the picture I witnessed.

We stop off for some drinks at a liquor store, and I make sure to grab a few limes just in case Jason forgets, which works out in my favor since Dean grabs two cases of Coronas.

Once we pull up to the aqua-colored house, which is both sound-side and oceanfront, and one of the few houses like this, we get our bags, I enter the code into the door, and we head up to the top floor. I knew we were taking the master, which I usually take. Typically, Jason would stay with me if I asked him to, but he never just assumed. I start tossing my stuff where I usually put it like I live here.

Which, I guess, when this is your seventh time in the same house in five years, you kind of do.

"You seem to know your way around here pretty well." Dean is smiling, watching me.

"Oh, sorry. It's a habit. I'm on autopilot. I'm gonna stop. I can do this later. Let's get pizza ordered and then we can crack open a drink and…" I trail off, letting the rest of the sentence hang between us. Dean follows me out of the bedroom and into the kitchen, where I point to the magnet with the pizza place's phone number on it and tell him to get a pepperoni and whatever he wants. I pull up the address of the house on my phone and wait for him to signal that he's ready for it, then read it off for him to relay. Once that's done, I slice up a lime while Dean opens up a couple of beers. I glance at the time, and I know I have minutes at the very most left to get some of this out before all hell could break loose.

"Dean, I gotta tell you something real quick about all of this, something I probably should have told you on the drive out here, but I don't know, I just chickened out, I guess. Um, fuck, alright. It isn't going to be just you and me here tonight."

"Who else is going to be here?" Dean asks, taking a pull of his beer. He doesn't seem upset or anything. He seems overly calm, and honestly, that is freaking me out more.

I can feel my heart beating in my throat, and I grab my beer and down half of it, and when I open my mouth to answer him, I hear the loud footsteps running up the stairs. "Fuck."

"Hey, Mama," Jason says as he comes up the last step.

"Hey, Jason. Great timing," I deadpan.

"Oh fuck. Should I?" he asks as he points down the stairs, his eyes ping ponging between Dean and me.

"If you have the tequila, hand it over and let's get this over with."

Jason offers the tequila. "Got your favorite. The Blanco."

"That's because you don't want a repeat of the first time we came out here. You learned that lesson." I raise my hands and bring them together in front of my chest, "God, sorry, I am so bad at this. Jason, this is Dean. Dean, this is Jason."

Dean is clenching his jaw so tightly I think he might break a tooth, and then I remember that I always suspected he overheard that conversation with Harper about Jason, and that right there confirms it.

Fuck. My. Life. This just got far more complicated.

"Dean, Cordy has told me so much about you. It's great to meet you." Jason offers his hand.

Dean eyes it for just a second before taking it and saying, "Nice to meet you, but I can't say the same thing." Then both of them turn their eyes toward me.

I divert my eyes quickly and grab some glasses since I already know the shot glasses are in the bar area on the bottom level and not in the kitchen. I pour a couple of shots and grab a lime wedge. I do my shot, biting into my lime. "Yeah, I was thirty seconds away from telling you, Dean, before Jason walked in. I'm sorry."

"I told you to tell him sooner, Mama," Jason says pointedly while grabbing a glass and throwing back the shot.

"I'm sorry, why do you keep calling her 'Mama'? And tell me what? What should she have told me sooner? What the fuck is going on?" Dean booms, causing me to flinch. I have never heard him raise his voice before, and it catches me off guard.

Jason notices the flinch, and I'm pretty sure he misinterprets from the fact that I have never heard Dean raise his voice like that, to I hear him do it too often, because he goes into defense mode immediately.

Jason turns to Dean, standing to his full height. "You don't talk to her that way. I don't give a fuck who you are to her." Jason's voice is so calm, but there's a deadly edge to his tone. And knowing what I know about him, I know exactly how scary that actually is. Jason is a couple of inches shorter than Dean, but he has been trained for twenty years to be a lethal weapon of the US Marine Corps. He's about as scary as they come when he needs to be. Where I'm concerned, he's a teddy bear. He looks like everything a career military man would: the tattoos, the build, the mustache, and the intimidating stance.

Dean doesn't back down; he takes one step to get even closer to Jason. "I don't know who the fuck you think you are to talk to me that way, but it will be the last time you ever do it."

Jason laughs, and it's the scariest laugh I have ever heard. It's so unhinged, and I just know that whatever is about to happen or come out of his mouth is not gonna be good. I slam both my hands on the counter as hard as I can and yell, "MASTER SERGEANT!"

Both of them turn and take a step back from each other. "Enough. Fuck. Sit the fuck down. Or put your bags in your room. But do NOT say another word for the next ten minutes unless you are telling me the pizza is here." Jason opens his mouth to say something, "What the fuck did I say, Marine?!" He shuts his mouth, pours a double shot, grabs a beer and two lime wedges, and goes back down the stairs.

I take a breath and let out a long exhale. "I'm going to do another shot and then I'm gonna try this again," I say to Dean.

"I think I might need one of those."

"I think you might as well." I pour us each a shot, and after we throw them back, I pour us each another one and point toward the deck. Dean nods and grabs the glasses and a couple of limes, while I grab our beers and open the doors. I take a seat on one of the tall chairs so I can see the ocean over the railing, and Dean follows my lead, taking a seat next to me. I take a pull from the bottle before setting it down. I know I can't drag this out for so many reasons; I need to just get it over with. I take a deep breath, steeling myself for the onslaught of literally everything that is about to rain down.

"I'm just going to get out as much as I can, and I'm going to ask that you say as little as possible until I'm done. Can you do that for me, please?"

"I can do that, but I need to know one thing. Did you love that guy?"

I laugh, a real and genuine laugh, "No. Not in the way that you are asking. I do and will always love him the same way that I love Sebastian. They are protectors of sorts that have stepped up when I needed someone."

"But you," Dean swallows and continues, "You slept with him? And why does he keep calling you 'Mama'?"

I let out a sigh and turn my gaze from the ocean to look at Dean. "I told him to stop calling me ma'am, so he just rearranged the letters, and I hate that it works, but..." I trail off before taking a deep breath, turning to look at him, and continuing. "Yes, I did sleep with him. But, Dean, what you have to understand is when that happened, it didn't happen from the same place that it does with you." Harper's words come flaring back to life from all those months ago, and I realize in this moment just how right she really was. "With Jason, it wasn't love; that was solace, and I haven't even seen him in two years."

Dean lowers his head, absorbing my words, before he sits back and downs half his beer.

I turn back to the ocean and let the memories wash over me like the waves...

"I told you that I was on birth control, but that was a lie, kind of. I can't get pregnant. I did once. I had a son. Brian. When he was born, it was the scariest and happiest day of my life. Not only was I a single mom about to do this on my own, but then I started hemorrhaging.

"In order to save my life and stop the bleeding, they had to perform an emergency hysterectomy. One and done for me." I shrug and go on, "I mean, it had its perks, I suppose—no more periods to deal with, unlike all my girlfriends. I also never really wanted kids, but life doesn't always give us what we want.

"I was young, barely eighteen, and made some stupid choices. His dad wasn't in the picture. So it was just us; he was the happiest kid, always smiling, always cracking jokes. He loved rocking out to Backstreet Boys and Lady Gaga with me in my Jeep. I actually got his name from Brian of the Backstreet Boys." I smile at the memory of when I told him that. By the time he was a teenager, he hated it when I publicly said that. Which always made me say it more.

"When he was about seven, he came home one day and told me, 'Mom, when I grow up, I'm gonna be a Marine' and he never stopped saying it. Except for about six months. When he turned fifteen, I had saved for a few years and booked us a cruise. I wanted to take him on a trip and get him out to see the world—a real vacation. After being on the water for a week on a ship, he wanted to join the Navy. But he ended up changing his mind at the last second, and in the middle of his junior year of high school, he started the delayed entry program into the Marine Corps.

"One month after he graduated high school, he went to Parris Island, South Carolina, for boot camp. I still have all the letters he wrote me, and the ones I wrote to him. I have an aunt and uncle in South Carolina, about an hour from Parris Island. When his graduation rolled around, I went down a couple of days early and stayed with them. We all drove down to see him graduate together." I take a breath, knowing this memory will start the tears.

"You asked me a few months ago about my favorite memory." My eyes meet Dean's, "When these kids graduate, before their main ceremony, they have a family day celebration. They have to stand in formation and at attention until a family member touches them. I sprinted across that parade deck to give him a hug —the first hug in three months. When I saw his face and the tears streaming down from his eyes, I lost it. He hugged me so tightly he was cutting off my oxygen, but it didn't matter. I got to hug my kid. It was the single best hug of my entire life." I stop to wipe away the tears that are falling. It's at that moment that Jason opens the door.

We both turn to look at him.

"Sorry, the pizza is here. I put it on the counter. I also brought you this, Cordy," Jason says as he hands me a small box of tissues over my shoulder. He doesn't say anything else, turns, and closes the door behind him.

I turn to Dean, "Did you want to take a minute before we keep going?"

"Only if you do," he says as he brings his eyes up to meet mine. Eyes that are filled with the one emotion in the world I never wanted to see reflected from him back at me.

Pity.

"Dean, please don't look at me like that," I say, looking at my fingers twisting a tissue in my lap. I can't bear to see that look in his eyes.

"Cordelia, I can't—I don't even know what to say. I don't have all the details, but I know enough to know where this is going. I know he isn't here. And I'm so fucking sor—"

"Dean. No. Please, don't." My voice breaks on the words. I grab the other shot and throw it back. "I think I need to eat a slice and pour a couple more of these, and before we finish this story, I think I'm gonna grab Jason for the rest of it. He can help when it starts to get to be too much." I grab the glasses and open the door to head inside, but before I get the door open more than an inch, Dean forces it closed.

"Cordelia, Rosebud, look at me." My eyes slowly rise, and I meet Jason's gaze through the glass door for a brief second before turning to look at Dean. He grips my chin and forces my gaze up the rest of the way. "I've said this to you before, and I think you need to hear it again. I love you. This, your past, will not change that. If anything, it will only deepen what I feel for you. I don't want you to think that pity is all I feel for you and that I love you out of pity. I don't. I can't help that I feel what I feel with everything you are telling me; you have to give me a little grace here, babe. Please. I'm not perfect. I will make mistakes. But I will be here for you, and more importantly, I WANT to be here for you. Let's grab a slice, I'll try not to throw the jarhead off the balcony, we can have a shot, and you can tell me more about Brian, alright?"

My eyes bounce between his, searching for a hint of something, anything to tell me that he doesn't mean what he's saying. His eyes never waver, never leave mine. His gaze is steady, albeit a little glassy, but... "Okay," I answer.

"Okay," Dean smiles, places a kiss on my cheek, and opens the door.

"Please tell me you are going to eat something before you keep downing shots?" Jason asks as I reach for the tequila bottle.

"Did you really only bring one bottle?" I ask, ignoring his question as I see Dean opening cabinets, looking for plates.

Jason glances at Dean, then back at me. "I'm not really sure I want to answer that. This doesn't feel like the safest place to be standing between the two of you, no matter *how* I answer that question."

I scoff and reach for the knife to slice up another lime, pointing it at Jason, "Says the Marine with how many tours under his belt?"

"Yeah, and you have a knife. This might be the most unsafe I have felt in the last ten years."

"Chickenshit," I say, and I throw a lime at his head, which he catches.

Dean lets out a little chuckle, "You two sound like Graham and me."

"Brother," I add for Jason, glancing at him and going back to slicing the limes.

"Hey, man, I know we kinda got a little heated for a second there. As you hear the rest of this story, you will understand why my reaction is to jump to her defense. It's just my default setting with her." Jason offers his hand, "No hard feelings." He says it as a statement, but I know he's asking for Dean's acceptance at the same time. I hold my breath and wait to see what Dean does.

Dean's eyes bounce from Jason's offered hand to my eyes and back to Jason. "Yeah, man, we're good. I get it. It's also my natural reaction with her, too." As Dean takes his offered hand, I let out the breath I was holding, feeling some of the tension melt out of my body. I'm thankful that I know I can count on Dean being ok with Jason being there for the rest of the story. I know there are parts that will be easier for everyone if he can tell them from his perspective instead of me telling them.

CORDELIA

After we eat, Jason brings the shots I poured earlier over.

"To Brian. And to new beginnings." Jason says, holding up his glass.

"To Brian," Dean and I say together, before we clink our glasses and throw back another round of tequila.

"I'm going to grab us another beer each if you wanna bring the glasses, Jason, and Cordelia, if you want to just bring the bottle and the rest of the limes outside with us?" Dean asks.

"Works for me. I'm gonna put these outside and grab something from downstairs. Meet you guys out there in a minute," Jason says before turning toward the deck.

I follow Dean into the kitchen and help him open the beers and shove limes into the bottles as Jason makes his way back inside and downstairs. Before I can make a move to swipe the bottle of tequila off the counter, Dean grabs my arm and turns me to face him, pressing my back to the counter while he presses into me from the front. He presses a kiss to my forehead before pulling back to look me in my eyes. "You don't have to finish this now if you don't want to. If you need a break, or..." He trails off.

"No, I need to do this. I've been putting this off for too long now, Dean. You deserve to know the whole truth." *You deserve to know how broken the woman you love really is, and you need to decide if that is something you can live with.* But I don't tell him that part. I'm hoping that I don't have to ask this of him, that he tells me.

Searching my eyes for what I'm not saying, he finally relents. "Ok, let's go." He takes a step back, giving me room to pass as he grabs the beer bottles, and I grab the tequila. Just as we are getting settled, Jason comes out to the deck.

"Here ya go, Mama," Jason says as he tosses me something. I catch it and let out a half-hearted laugh.

"I know you don't smoke, so I'm assuming this is a stress-related thing?" Dean asks, eyeing the pack of cigarettes that I'm holding.

"Yeah, I also don't really drink much except out here either, these kinda go well with shots." I fiddle with the pack in my hands, flipping it over before adding, "We had both just quit before, but..." Letting the sentence hang, I open the pack, and Jason tosses me a lighter.

"So where did we leave off?" Jason asks, pulling one of the cushioned chairs over closer.

"Bootcamp graduation," Dean answers.

Jason flicks the lighter a couple of times, getting lost in his own thoughts for a moment before he opens his own pack and we both look at each other. The silent "fuck it" passes between us as we both pull a cigarette out and light it almost in unison.

"So, he got to show us around Parris Island. His barracks, some of the training areas. Made all of us buy him ice cream and pizza and candy and so much junk food, my god." I'm laughing, remembering the way he was holding two ice cream wrappers in the line to check out because he ate them before we could even check out. "He was so excited to show us everything and have food that wasn't an MRE or from the chow hall.

"He told me about when they got a little liberty for a few hours before family day, and they were allowed to do some shopping. His friend questioned why he would spend so much money on cologne. Brian told him, 'Because I want to smell good for my mom.'" I look at Dean, adding, "It's the same cologne you have."

Dean nods in response and smiles, understanding why I recognized it so quickly the first time he wore it.

I continue, "His grandpa had him pick out a K-Bar knife, his grandpa on his dad's side. His dad wasn't really in the picture, like I mentioned, and we were okay with that, but he had such a great relationship with his grandpa. Those two were peas in a pod. They used to go on hunting and ATV trips all the time. We didn't get too long that day, as it was only family day, and it meant just a few hours. So we all left and came back bright and early the next day for the formal graduation ceremony, and he would be allowed to leave with me after that. We got to watch him walk in his dress blue deltas, the dress blues pants with a tan shirt, and the white cover. Not the full-dress blues that are iconic of the Marines, but a less formal version.

"After graduation, he wanted to go to this place on the water near Charleston, where we had gone before, after the cruise I took him on. Brian had asked in one of his letters if we could have lunch after graduation, where we saw the dolphins. So we went, and he was still in uniform, too. Then we all went back to my aunt and uncle's. Brian got to play with my aunt's horses, and the next day, we had a cookout with some other family in the area. It was nice to have the family back together for a short while." I smile, thinking about how my cousin and I became close again because of Brian. I clear my throat of the emotion building before I continue.

"When we got back to Ohio, I had planned a big welcome home party, and we had everyone over, and a week later, he got on a plane to go back to North Carolina for more training, and then he went to his MOS schooling. From there, he received orders that he would be stationed at Camp Lejeune. Working in the armory where he was, as he liked to word it, 'you know the parts that tell the missiles where to go? Yeah, I fix those.' He was so excited to get to his first duty station and get started.

"Right after he got those orders was the same time that my mom decided the Mustang she had for twenty plus years, she wanted to put it in my name. It was getting to be too hard to have two vehicles and drive a manual. Brian didn't talk to me for a week. He was so mad. That was his car, or so he thought. She had promised it to him at one point, and now she was putting it in my name. I had to explain to him that he would have nowhere to keep it. North Carolina gets ice storms; that car has never seen a winter, it cannot be a daily driver." I fiddle with the beer bottle, remembering how mad he was at me for something I didn't even do. "I wasn't going to get rid of it; it would be here for him when he got to the point he had somewhere for it.

"Fuck. Hindsight really is 20/20. I couldn't have imagined having to add that to everything else that was going on at that time." I scoff and reach for another shot. "Anyways, he got there in early May, and I remember in July I got this call, 'Mom, Gunny told me I have to use leave or I have to stay and help clean the armory. I know you can't get me, but Grandpa can. BUT I can't have someone pick me up, on paper. Gunny said I have to show a flight itinerary, and then he doesn't care what I do from there, but just to prove I'm taking leave.' So I booked him a flight, but we didn't officially pay for it. I got the email confirmation, and then he printed it, and we canceled it."

Jason starts laughing. "So *that's* how that went down. I never did ask about that. I just knew his grandpa picked him up, and I never looked close enough to it even to know it wasn't paid for. Nicely done, Mama." Jason clinks his beer bottle with mine. I offer him a watery smile.

"His grandpa picked him up, they did a little mountain boys' trip, and then came up to Ohio for about twenty-four hours. Just long enough to say hi, and then they headed back down to base." I ease out of the chair and finish off my beer, but before I can turn to get another one, Jason is heading inside to grab more, and Dean's eyes are following me.

I discard the end of the cigarette into my beer bottle now

that's its empty and set it down on the table. I walk to the railing and take in the ocean on the other side of the dunes.

When Jason returns, Dean pours us each a shot, and I turn to face them both.

"Two months later, the world as I knew it crumbled around me. It's really weird, the things you remember in the most traumatic moments. I remember being woken up to a knock on the door in the middle of the night. I had one of those doorbell cameras, and I tapped the thumbnail on my phone, and my first thought was, 'Why is Brian home, and why is he in uniform? And why is he knocking and not using his key?' I think my brain was trying to protect me in the moment, enough to get me moving, anyway."

I absently mindlessly pick at my cuticles before I force my hands down. "As a Marine Mom, you know there's always a chance of this moment happening to you. Of having to face the greatest fear you have in your life when your child tells you they want to join the military. It's something that you have to accept that could come to pass. You hope it never does," I cast my eyes toward the sky, "*Fuck,* do you hope it never comes to pass. And when it happens when they aren't deployed but are stateside, in their barracks room... Nothing prepares you for that." I take a breath and wipe the tears away. "The Marines who came to my house didn't know anything outside of the facts that he was gone and a gun was involved. I had just spoken to him earlier that day, and he had asked me to find something that he thought he had left at my house. When I found it, he asked me to mail it to him. So I couldn't comprehend that he would have done this to himself. I needed that to be made clear. So one of the Marines made a phone call and was able to at least tell me that it wasn't self-inflicted, but he didn't have any other details to share at the time. We made arrangements for him to come back later the following day, or rather the same day, and he said he would set it all up so that when he came back, we would have a phone call with NCIS and I would find out more details at that time." I shift from the railing and take my seat again.

"Then I had to be the one to make the rest of the notifications." I close my eyes and take a deep breath. "The phone calls I had to make at three in the morning that day. The number of people who were showing up at my house, when people would normally be leaving, and instead they were all showing up." I glance at Dean, and his eyes are locked on me, his face expressionless as he listens to everything I tell him. "I remember I called my mom, and you can imagine how that went. After her, I called Harper. She didn't answer and then called me back within seconds. I will never forget that call. She had said, 'I was in the bathroom, what's wrong?' and all I said was 'two marines just knocked on my door', and she said she was on her way and hung up on me. She lived almost thirty minutes from me at the time, and she made it to me in fifteen, and you figure she had to get dressed first. I didn't realize it, but I guess her brother had shown up the night before and was crashing for a few days, so he drove, and he's a little speed demon.

"I was seeing this guy, Evan." Jason scoffs and takes a drink of his beer. "At the time this happened and the best thing he did, since he didn't do much after, was offer to go pick up my mom so she didn't have to drive and be alone. By the time they got back, Harper and her brother, Gabriel, were there too. I was just sitting on the garage couch, since Elfie, my Jeep, was too tall to fit in it, and the garage was just a hangout. We all just had questions and no answers." I take a drink and lean back in my chair—the memories washing over me as I wipe the tears that keep falling away.

"I had to pull out so many stops to get connected with the right channels because Brian's grandpa was on a cruise with his wife and didn't get the internet package. I didn't know which exact ship they were on and started using Facebook to try to figure it out, seeing where they had checked in, and what day they left. When we finally figured it out, we were able to make an emergency call to the ship, explain the situation, and get a hold of them. I felt so bad having to tell them about this while they were on that ship. His wife, Carmela, ended up having to call the medical bay to have them administer a sedative to Mike."

"There was nothing to feel bad about, making that call and letting them know, Cordy. I have told you this so many times. Mike and Carmela have told you this. You know this," Jason says, putting his hand on my knee. Logically, I know he's right, but it doesn't change how I felt and still feel about doing that to them. The helplessness they felt, we were all feeling it, but they only had each other in those first days.

"I know, but still. I was the one who had to tell everyone. I had to deliver that news. It was bad enough that my world was crashing and burning, and yet I had to hold it together and deliver the blows to everyone else. And then to top it all off, knowing that the media would release his name within twenty-four hours and having to go public with it." I close my eyes and shake my head. "So not only do I have to make these important calls before dawn, but then I had to start making calls to others after the sun was up, and then twelve hours later, I had to figure out how to post and tell everyone else that he was gone publicly." My voice breaks, and I stand from my chair, leaning over the railing again. I try to take calming breaths and steady myself when I hear Jason start speaking.

"He was shot in his barracks room by another marine who worked in the armory with us. I don't know if Cordy touched on it, but I was Brian's CO. The kid had so much potential and was already on the right track to make a name for himself in the Corps. He was determined to be the best at everything. But he wasn't cocky about it; he knew he was smart, he knew he was capable, but he also helped others. Those are rare qualities to find in people these days. I tried to take him under my wing without making it obvious. My telling him to use leave was one of the small ways I tried to cut him a break. He already did more than he needed to, and he didn't need to stay and clean when others who worked under me didn't pull their weight nearly as much.

"The Marine who shot him was drunk; he brought his own personal weapon on base, which is prohibited in the barracks. Before Brian even got to Lejeune, this particular Marine had tried to start an investigation into me, the way I operated as a CO. He claimed that I played favorites, and that I punished him more harshly because I disliked him." I set the bottle down and Jason lets out a sigh. "I never disliked him, I just saw someone who was ready to be done with the Corps and looking for an easy end to his enlistment. So, I was already on the command's radar, and I explained to Brian that I would deny telling him about taking leave if someone were to ask. I couldn't risk essentially proving this kid right at that point. From what I have gathered, when Brian was approached numerous times to side with the other Marine, he denied him every time. I don't think he handled it well. I think he saw this young and impressionable kid and thought it would be easy to sway his opinion. That Marine was only a couple of months from getting out. He made one final attempt to get Brian to side with him. Brian told me about it the next morning. He wasn't comfortable being around this guy anymore and was asking what he needed to do or if I could help. We were going to sit and discuss options the next day."

No one speaks for a moment. It's just the wind and sound of the waves breaking. I know Dean is absorbing what exactly all of these words mean. What Jason and I are trying to tell him without either of us having to say the word. It's an odd thing to go your whole life never having to deal with triggers. To one day not be able to say such innocuous phrases, simple terms, or flinch when someone else says them. Having to call what happened to Brian what it is, it's a word that I struggle to say. I raised a child with a knowledge of gun safety, as did his grandfather. I always did and still do own and keep a handgun. I haven't fired it since the day I found out what happened. I won't even keep a round chambered in the barrel. I know that guns don't kill people; people kill people. But it's really hard to have a trusting relationship with something that aided in destroying your world.

"Was this premeditated? Obviously, he was charged with murder, because what else would there be to charge him with?" Dean asks, his voice barely audible.

Jason and I both scoff out a laugh, and I turn around to meet both sets of eyes.

"Jesus fuck. You have to be fucking kidding me." Dean's tone is full of unbridled rage. I can feel it dripping from every word. I hear his chair scrape the wooden deck as he pushes out of it. I've had five years to process this, and it doesn't by any means make me less sad, heartbroken, angry, or downright pissed off; I just control it better. I let Dean take the time he needs right now before I even think about turning around and continuing.

"I'll be right back," I murmur, slipping past them and into the house, heading for the bathroom. As I'm washing my hands, I glance into the mirror. I look like an absolute wreck. Mascara in little black dried rivers down both sides of my face. My hair is windblown, and I just look so tired and broken. I close my eyes for a second and use my wet hands to try to clean up my face, which makes things worse, as my skin is now all red and puffy.

I'm almost out of the bedroom door when my eyes fall on my duffel bag. I walk over to it, easing open the zipper, to see the brass urn. I grab the white gloves and, using them to avoid leaving fingerprints, pull the urn out. I set it on the dresser, deciding that I will bring it outside for the sunset after we finish this.

Dean is still pacing the deck when I come back out. When he sees me, he finally stops next to me. He wraps his arms around me, pulling me into his chest. His arms are constricting and suffocating around me as he places a kiss on my hair. "I'm so fucking sorry you had to go through this. No parent should ever have to go through this. It isn't fucking fair." His voice breaks at the end, and I can feel his body shaking as he tries to bottle his emotions.

Whispering, I add, "We haven't even told you the rest of what happened." My words are thick with emotion, because while all of this story has been incredibly sad, we haven't even gotten to the part that will bring nothing but anger.

Dean releases me just enough to pull back and place a kiss on my forehead before tightening his arms around me again. We stay that way for a few heartbeats before we break apart and take our seats.

"It took weeks to get any answer. We were given false information at first, which was quickly corrected, but for the sake of getting through this, Jason just told you what happened without all of that. Once the medical examiner was done, Jason and Brian's roommate brought him home. We created such a cluster for the five o'clock rush hour traffic in Cleveland. Roadways were shut down for the procession to and from the airport. The first time I met Jason, I didn't know who he was beyond a Marine tasked with bringing Brian home to me. I had seen this movie years before called *Taking Chance* starring Kevin Bacon, and I gotta say, they got it pretty much right down to the last details. But in this special case, instead of a random volunteer to bring him home, those two got to do it." I offer Jason a small smile.

"I will never forget seeing the flag-draped coffin coming off the plane. Or once we got to the funeral home and all the Marines who helped carry him, those are some of the images I don't need pictures to remember with vivid detail. I will remember those moments long after I have forgotten my own name." I let out a heavy sigh before continuing. "It took a couple of days once he came home before I could see him. I was terrified of that image being imprinted in my mind for the rest of my life, so I told the funeral home director to make the choice for me. I hadn't seen any photos to know what I was walking into beyond the wound being to his head. There is no chance on this earth I would have been able to see him if they didn't tell me that I would never know where the wounds were. They upheld their end. I didn't know, and I honestly, in that moment, couldn't have told you where the entry and exit points were. The day before the calling hours is the day I got to see him for the last time. I had a few precious minutes with just him, and then the next day, I had to greet hundreds of people who came out to pay their respects. And the following day, we held the memorial at his high school. There were so many people in the field house that day. It was filled. I didn't realize how many until I got up in front of everyone to speak.

"After that, I had about two weeks to just sit with everything. Then the report from the medical examiner came. Apparently, it's standard operating procedure to send the full report to the family once it is completed."

"Wait, are you telling me the *medical examiner* sent you the report and the photos…" Dean trails off to take what seems to be a calming breath before he continues. "They sent you the full autopsy report?"

I nod once. Then I hand Dean the tequila, not a glass, the whole bottle. He takes it and pulls the cork out of the top and drinks it straight from the bottle. "What in the actual fuck, Jason? How is the military allowed to do this?" Dean is barely holding back his rage at this point, and I'm honestly scared to tell him the rest of the story right now. I know that it gets worse.

Jason puts his hands up in a show of surrender. "Man, I don't have any control over that. I didn't know until Cordy said something to me about it after one of the hearings. That she had the report and saw the photos. That pissed me off, too. I get it."

"You said you were seeing someone when all this happened, Cordelia? Where the fuck was he with all this?" Dean asks through clenched teeth.

"He is so not important, and really a non-issue that I don't want to talk about right now. That's a different conversation. For the sake of your own sanity right now, let's just pretend that you never heard any of that and I was doing this on my own. Which I was, essentially." I glance at Dean, and I can see the calculations in his head. I already know he's going to pull out the stops and do whatever he can to fuck with Evan, and knowing that his best friend is a sheriff, one that is about to hear all of this as well? Yeah, Evan is gonna finally get his karma served to him on a silver platter, and honestly, I am more than okay with that. I might ask them to record so I can watch with popcorn. I don't know how they would do it, but I have a feeling having a sheriff for a best friend would come in handy.

Before Dean can say anything else, I decide to keep going. If he needs to get up and pace again, I'm done, I will make us wrap this up for the night and continue in the morning. He hasn't left his chair, so I'm counting this as calm at the moment. "After the memorial ceremony, we attended with his battalion on base; that's when the constant travel for the court-martial started. I was down there almost every six to eight weeks. Jason went to all the hearings with me. Not just so I wouldn't be there alone, but because he wanted to be there. After the first hearing, he started making recommendations for places to grab some food, and then we just agreed to meet there." I knew I was going to get into uncomfortable territory, so I was trying to choose my words carefully, which was becoming increasingly difficult with the tequila. "It was after the second hearing I was there for, and that was when they started talking about plea deals. I did everything in my power to keep myself under control in that room."

"The start of the tequila tradition." Jason smiles. He's leaning forward in his chair, with his elbows resting on his knees, head down. And I know without even looking at Dean that he knows what it means. He's figured out that was the start of Jason and me sleeping together.

Fuck.

"There were a LOT of shots that night," I try to add humor to my voice to keep it light, "and I flew home the next day. Then once it was clear that the commanding general wasn't in the mind to entertain a plea deal, I think we all breathed a little easier. Everything was moving forward to a trial as we wanted. We didn't want him getting off easy; we wanted to have a fighting chance. Then, almost a year to the day after we lost Brian, when we thought we had hit the point where we were good to go, it all changed. There was a command change, and the new CG wanted to clear the docket and just accepted the plea deal. I was there for about a week. I had witness prep with the prosecution on the

Friday before, and the sentencing was starting the following Monday. I always get asked why the need for witness prep if a plea was accepted, so let me explain." I shift in my seat, tucking a leg under me. "They do character witnesses to help ensure the results they want in the sentencing. We didn't get those results. We got twelve short years, with time served counting."

Jason shifts in his seat, leaning forward, his eyes lock with mine for just a moment. But it's enough to know that whatever he is about to say is going to hurt.

"I never pushed to testify, I was concerned that it would give the defense more shit to pry into, and I did not want to be the reason that the sentence was less. I also think that the prosecution had the same thoughts, as they never called me to be a witness at any point." His voice turns hard, his eyes darkening as his emotions get the best of him. "I wanted him to be in prison for as long as he fucking lives. I regret, to an extent, not making sure that my voice was heard. But the last thing I wanted was to do anything to jeopardize the legacy of Brian. Whose character, I know, could stand on its own."

He leans back in his seat, closing his eyes, almost as if he is resetting himself. He opens them, smiles, and says, "And now we come to spend the week here on the anniversary. This house is actually owned by a retired Marine that I served with in my earlier days. He had reached out about what happened when he heard, wanting to check on me. When he found out how close I was to Brian, he wanted me to extend an offer to use this place as a retreat. He blocks off the week of the anniversary every year for us and refuses to let us pay him to use the house. I wasn't able to make it last year; I shipped out to Camp Pendleton right after the third anniversary. I got back to this coast a month ago. I know Cordy was here with Harper, though. I took the day, and we basically sat on FaceTime the whole day with tequila from coast to coast." Jason's eyes meeting mine, "It's much better being here to do this instead of through a phone screen."

"Yeah. It also felt weird being in this house without you since you're the one with the contact to let us stay here," I add, pointing my beer bottle toward him.

"Oh, whatever. He didn't even text me the code this year. I had to text him, and you know what that old man had to say? 'I sent it to Cordelia, she's the mom.' So, yeah, I'm fairly certain he's your contact now." Jason laughs.

"Touche," I grin.

I hear Dean's chair scrape again as he throws himself out of the seat and stalks into the house without a word. I set my drink down and scramble to get up. By the time I make it inside, I see him halfway down the first flight of stairs.

"Dean!" I call after him. But he doesn't stop.

Fuck. I hope he doesn't think I was flirting with Jason. *Fuck fuck fuck.* I start down the stairs after him, and he's already cleared the landing to the middle level, and I can't see him. Just as I begin to take the second step, Jason grabs my arm.

"Let him go, Cordy."

I look between the stairs and Jason and try to rip my arm out of his grasp and go after him. "No, he can't leave, Jason. He can't." It comes out as a strangled sob. My fears are being realized; he wouldn't be able to handle my past and my trauma. But for him to walk away? This is so out of character, but I can't fault him. I can't say that this amount of baggage is something I would ever expect anyone to deal with willingly. I let out a sob just as my legs give out on me. Jason wraps his other arms around me and hauls me into him. I'm sobbing into his shirt as he leads us away from the stairs. He doesn't take us outside; he keeps us in the kitchen.

"Cordy," he says, softly petting my hair, "take a deep breath. Just breathe. It's okay. He isn't leaving." He takes my face in his hands and forces my eyes to his. "He never had the privilege of knowing Brian, but he knows you, fuck, he loves you." I look at him with a question in my eyes. "Don't give me that look. Any idiot can see it." Jason takes a breath before continuing, "It stands to reason he is going through all the emotions and turmoil we have. We have been going through it for five plus years now. He has had five fucking minutes. The only thing he wants to do right now is make this right *for you*. That man looks ready to burn the world to the ground for you, and he knows he can't. He can't touch Rogers while he's in a military prison, and he knows it. We've had years to deal with our feelings over this. Give him a minute, Mama." His eyes drift, focusing on something next to me, "Besides, his keys are on the counter. He won't get far without those."

I pull back from his embrace and look down, seeing his keys there.

"Come on, let's go sit you back down and I'll grab us another beer and maybe a water for your lightweight ass, and we can watch the waves and wait for him to come back up, because he will. The man looks at you like his whole world starts and ends with you."

I look up at Jason, a small smile tugging at my lips, "Yeah? And how would you know what that looks like?"

He doesn't say anything, just shrugs. I get back to the deck, and I can see Dean walking just before he clears the dunes and drops from sight on the other side of the road, making his way to the ocean. I take my seat, and Jason returns a few moments later with a glass of water for me and a beer for each of us. He sits next to me in the tall chair that Dean was using.

"You know, when I tell him the rest of the details about that sentencing hearing, he's really going to lose it," I whisper under my breath. A prayer to the wind and sea, and with any luck, Brian will hear it too.

Chapter Thirty

DEAN

I couldn't stand to listen to another word or see the hurt on Cordelia's face for another second. I want to find this mother-fucker and rip him to pieces, but knowing that I can't get to him while he sits in a military prison makes me feel so incredibly help-less. I want to present his head to her like I just slayed her demons and lay it at her feet.

I know walking out of that house and away from Cordelia as she called for me wasn't the right or smart move by a long shot. But this rage and overwhelming need to break something, to do *something*, to make this right, when I know I can't, is consuming me. I have never thought of myself as a violent man, but in this moment, I know without a doubt that if I were by her side when this happened, I couldn't say that I would have restrained myself in those moments of being in the same building, let alone the same room with him.

I may not be a father, but I did help raise Madison, and I can't even begin to imagine how losing her would feel for me or how that would completely destroy Graham. My heart is in pieces for her and everything she had to shoulder on her own. I already know I'm going to get her ex's last name, and then I'm going to enlist a little help from Lachlan to track down an address and take some petty revenge on him. I may not be able to get my hands on the bastard that took her son away from her, but I can do something about the person who was supposed to be there for her. I know it's petty, but I can't bring myself to give a fuck.

As I make my way over the dunes and really take in the breaking waves, I can't help but notice the calming feeling that immediately comes over me. I can feel the tension leaving my muscles as I roll my shoulders. I realize in this exact moment why she comes here every year.

I make my way down to the edge where the sand is just shy of getting hit with the waves and sit down. I watch the waves and try to breathe and calm myself. As the feeling of wanting to watch the world burn just to be able to get her justice starts to lessen its hold, and I can take a deep breath again. I realize just how my leaving probably made Cordelia feel. After her reaction when she thought something had happened to me a few days ago, I probably scared the hell out of her.

I swipe my hand down my face, "Fuck!"

I pull my phone out of my pocket and send off a text.

> Me: I'm sorry I walked away. I was just so angry at the situation and knowing I couldn't do anything to fix it for you… I just need a minute. I will head back soon.

I watch as she reads it right away, and then the bubbles start dancing.

> Cordelia: I understand. Don't rush. I know it's a lot to take in. I was scared you were leaving leaving, not just taking a walk.

. . .

Me: I'm sorry. I didn't think. I let my emotions get the better of me, thinking about if this was Madison, and I just lost it. I know that isn't fair to you.

Cordelia: You're allowed your feelings, Dean. I'll be here when you come back. Take your time.

I stare at her text, wondering what I ever did to deserve someone like this woman. She has been through the most awful thing a parent could ever go through, and she survived. And to make it worse, after she just had to relive the whole thing, she's comforting *me*.

She's probably so used to doing this all on her own, pushing and fighting through the grief, that she doesn't know any other way at this point. I don't want that for her. I want to be the one she can lean on and count on, and if she wanted me to, I would take care of the problem for her once and for all. I have no idea how I would even do that, but...

Glancing down, I realize that my phone is still in my hand.

Finding the contact I want, I hit the call button.

One ring is all it takes. "How are you holding up right now?" Sebastian asks.

"Like I want to commit so many crimes and rip that fucking piece of shit to pieces," I answer truthfully.

Sebastian lets out a humorless chuckle. "You're gonna have to get in line for that, sorry to say. I already have a friend keeping me notified on when and if he's moved, as well as when he actually gets out. And I don't think I'm going to tell you where he is right now. We can talk about that at a later time. But I have details. You really think I wouldn't?"

I exhale loudly, so incredibly thankful for the friends that I have. "No, I guess I wouldn't expect anything different from you."

"Is there something you specifically needed, or do you just need to make sure that you're not the only one who wants to deliver their own brand of justice?"

"I guess, both."

Sebastian chuckles through the phone, "Yeah, it's a heavy story. I know more than most probably do. But there are things that I don't know, and I've never asked, so I don't even know if Cordelia knows them all. I'm sure I will find out when y'all get back, though." He goes quiet for a moment, but the way his voice trailed off has me keeping my mouth shut. Waiting for what he is going to say next. "I'm really happy she's doing this. She's kept it bottled up for years, Dean. I really don't think she would have told any of us if it wasn't for you. I just want you to know that, and I thank you for it."

I swallow around the lump in my throat, "I don't know that I feel I should be thanked for anything. All I did was fall in love with her."

"You gave her a reason to be open about her past. To talk to us. To let us in. Don't discount that."

Sebastian is right, keeping it all bottled up and refusing to talk about it with people isn't healthy for anyone, especially her.

"Thanks, man. And we need to have a conversation with Lachlan once he is up to speed on everything, because her ex, he's going to get what's coming to him." There's steel in my voice. This is the one thing I can actually do something about.

"Anytime, brother. It sounds like I need the rest of that story, but you know I will be in for whatever. I'll see you soon." With that, he hangs up, and I shove my phone into my pocket.

I pull my knees up and rest my forearms across them, taking

in the sunset and the waves breaking against the sand. About twenty feet away from me are a couple of little sandpipers running back and forth through the surf, trying to find dinner. I zone out, watching them for a few minutes.

Just as the sky is darkening over the water, I decide to head back to the house. I stand and brush the sand from the back of my shorts. That's when I see a perfect conch shell, rotating in the waves and then catching on the sand. I quickly jog to the water before the next wave breaks, grabbing the shell to take it back to Cordelia. I don't know if she would even want it, but there's something about no one else being on this beach, and it showing up as it did. It's like something—*or someone*—wanted me to find it.

As I start up the walkway between the dunes, I take in the three-story beach house. It's a bright teal color, with white trim and stained decks and railings. I can see the hot tub on the second-story deck, directly under the one portion of the third-story deck that has a roof over it.

Smart. Can still use it even if it's raining out that way.

They have an outdoor shower under the house and a pool around the back. I stop at the outdoor shower to rinse the sand off my feet and legs so as not to track it through the house. I decide to take my time heading all the way up, so I go inside and head up the stairs. I take a quick walk through the game room level, finding a pool table and a mini fridge. I open the cabinets and find an array of shot glasses. There's a full bathroom on this level, and I would bet that the couch pulls out as well.

On the second level, I find a bunkbed room and two master bedrooms. It looks like Jason claimed the bigger master. This is also the level with the hot tub and a door in the hallway leading out to that front deck. I notice a back deck that faces the sound and that has access from the two bedrooms as well. The bunkbed room just seems to have windows and no doors outside.

When I get to the third and top level of the house, I walk into the main living room with the dining room and kitchen. The master that Cordelia set us up in is also on this level, with doors out to the back deck.

I glance out the doors from the dining area, where I see Cordelia and Jason still outside in their chairs. I'm sure they saw me walk back from the beach since they are facing the ocean. I take a moment to get my thoughts together before I set the shell down on the dining room table and walk to slide the door open, stepping outside.

Jason greets me with a head nod, not getting up from his chair. I walk in front of Cordelia and pull her up from the chair and into my arms. I don't think she's been crying in a while, she was earlier, and her eyes are still red, but the tears seem to have dried.

"I am so incredibly sorry that you had to go through this and that you had to do it without me. I don't even know what to say." I squeeze her to me so tightly, dipping my head down to rest on top of her head. "Tell me what I can do," I whisper.

After a couple of heartbeats, she pulls back, her eyes reflecting the moonlight, "Just love me, even though I'm cracked and broken in places."

"Always, I will always love you."

I wrap her back up in my arms, pulling her tight against my chest. I breathe her in, contemplating what I can even say right now. But it's Jason who breaks the silence.

"I would imagine that there are still questions that you have. There are a few more pieces of the story to tell you as well." Cordelia doesn't move away, instead tightening her grip on me. I can feel her hands fisting my shirt at my back. "I don't know what your preference would be, but you might want to hear them sooner rather than later. We can always do it after we get back from Conner's with the groceries in the morning, too."

I think about the options, and I'm leaning toward waiting until tomorrow. I'm afraid of what hearing more right now could do to me. I just want to take Cordelia into another room and check in with her. I know reliving this hasn't been easy. But I also know it might be easier for her to get it all out now.

Pulling back half a step, Cordelia offers, "I think we might want to finish this after Conner's. We should also get a list together."

"You mean you don't have a grocery list already written out? Usually, you have that done before we even get here," Jason smirks.

"I was a little preoccupied this time," Cordelia blushes.

Jason makes a humming noise in his throat before finishing off his beer, "Is that what the kids are calling it these days?"

I chuckle as Cordelia flips Jason off. "I'm going to find some paper and a pen, get this list written up, drink some more water, then I think I want to shower and just go to bed. Call it an early night." She raises up on her toes to press a kiss to my cheek and turns, heading inside.

The door is barely shut behind her when Jason says, "You are in love her; any idiot can see it every time she's near you."

I turn to meet his eyes, "I am. And I'm fairly certain you are too."

Jason leans back into his chair, resting his arms on the armrests. "Can you blame me? But it's always been one-sided, and I've never said anything to her. I wasn't what she needed. I'm a reminder of the worst pain she has ever had to endure. I'm sure there's a part of this that's rooted in what happened." He raises his hand closest to me in a waving-off gesture. "I'll get over it and move on. I always knew I would need to someday. She's too good to be alone forever."

I absorb his words; he's being honest, and I can tell from the way Cordelia is around him that there are no romantic feelings on her side. When she's not looking, though, I see the way Jason looks at her. It's like she hung the moon. I can't exactly blame the guy. I fell for her so hard and so quickly. Before I can respond, Cordelia comes back out. I nod my head toward Jason, making sure he knows that I understand and that there are no hard feelings.

After we get the list together, we clean up our glasses and put the pizza away. Cordelia gives Jason a hug before he heads downstairs.

"Oh, I found this on the beach, it washed up just as I was leaving to come back," I say as I pick up the shell.

"Dean, this is such a perfect conch shell, I love it. Thank you." She takes it from me, turning it around before putting it up to her ear. I smile at the sight. "They say you can hear the ocean in them."

I grab her free hand, pulling her into our room, closing the door with a soft click.

"I don't know what the rules are here, so tell me if you want me to stop." I take the bottom of her shirt and pull it over her head. I throw it on the floor as I start backing her into the bathroom. Thankfully, the shower is similar in size to mine, so I know we will both fit easily.

She doesn't stop me; instead, she grips my shirt and raises it over my head, letting it fall to the ground somewhere behind me.

I turn the shower on, letting the water warm as I strip her out of the rest of her clothes, then do the same with mine. I guide her into the shower and under the spray, wetting her hair. I grab the shampoo she already unpacked and put in here, squeezing some into my hands and slowly massaging it into her scalp. She moans as I work up a lather before rinsing.

She squeezes water out of her hair as I put the conditioner into my hands. She turns and lets me work the conditioner through her hair, letting out a light sigh as I work. Once I'm done, I turn her again and grip her chin with my fingers, tilting her head back so she looks me in the eyes.

"I don't know what to do or say for you. I just know I want to fix it. I wish I could go back and change things for you. I wish I had been there for you. I wish..." I trail off, letting the sentence hang in the air.

"I know, it's not something you probably ever expected to hear, either. I'm sorry it took me so long to tell you. But at first, it was too new, then we were in this little bubble, and by then it was easier to wait until excuses couldn't be made anymore. I know how that sounds, and I'm sorry. I should have trusted you with this sooner."

"Baby, stop. You did what was best for you. It's ok to be a little selfish when it comes to protecting yourself. I'm not mad about it. I'm only upset that I wasn't there for you when you needed me."

"But you're here now, and that's all that matters."

I take her face in my hands and kiss her deeply, letting my tongue tangle with hers, tilting her head back for more access.

I break the kiss, help her rinse her hair, and give my own hair a quick wash and a rinse before we get out. I wrap a towel around my waist and pull one around Cordelia, drying her off as I go. I dry myself off as I watch her in the mirror, rubbing lotion into her skin, her hair wrapped in a towel on top of her head. After we brush our teeth, she puts her hair into a braid and pulls a shirt of mine over her head.

I pull her into my arms when I get into bed. "I don't want you going to sleep thinking about everything you've told me and haven't told me. I want you to go to sleep thinking about something good. Tell me something about Brian. Anything."

She sighs as she settles her head on my chest, "When he came home from boot camp, he placed an order for some items, and they came after he had already left for military combat training before going to his MOS schooling. Which is military occupational specialty, essentially teaching him how to do his job. So his package came right before he was set to leave MCT, and I asked him if he wanted me to open it and repackage whatever it was to mail it to him. He told me to hang on to it, and he would grab it when he came home at Christmas, but he wanted me to open it and send him pictures." Cordelia starts giggling as she remembers. "So, I open this box, and I find a box with a figure of some anime character, and then a poster as well. And then there was this mouse pad." She's laughing harder now. I can feel her body shaking against me. I'm smiling because this memory is making her happy, and therefore it makes me happy. "I pull this mouse pad out, and it's this anime girl's face, but the wrist fatigue pad is her very large and squishy boobs. So, being the mother I am, I take the plastic off this thing and proceed to take a video and send it to him. Just poking and squishing the boobs. Laughing the whole time." Now I'm laughing with her. I can picture this as she's telling me. "He went and posted the video on some Discord chat or something and had to tell me that all of his friends said to tell me how cool of a mom I was because I didn't tell him he couldn't get it, and because I sent him a video of my poking it. He would randomly tell me that here and there when the video was brought up in his friend group. One of his friends told me about it after he got back after Christmas, saying he's never seen anyone so excited about a mousepad in their life."

"He sounds like he would have reminded me of Graham. Little more energy than a person should actually have, laughs often, loves too much, and always wants to smile and make others smile."

"That was him in a nutshell. The number of people that reached out, the lives he touched, just because he didn't want people to feel alone." Her voice breaks and turns to lie on my arm, looking up at the ceiling. "I'm sorry. You were trying to make me smile, and now I'm trying not to cry." I barely make out her eyes sparkling in the dark. "Can you just hold me until I fall asleep, Dean?"

"Of course," I concede easily. I roll her to her side, pulling her back to my chest, wrapping myself around her. "Just sleep, Cordelia. I got you."

Chapter Thirty-One

CORDELIA

The next morning starts off with breakfast at Orange Blossom Bakery for Apple Uglies. These giant, as big as my head, apple fritters that are my favorite thing on this island.

We stop at Conner's after to grab groceries for the rest of the week.

As we finish putting everything away when we get back to the house, Jason pipes up from the dining room, where he is folding up all the paper bags. "Did you ever tell Dean about your ring?"

I freeze in the middle of putting the coffee creamer in the fridge, my ring catching the light and sparkling. I stare at it for a moment before I let go of the creamer and close the fridge. "No, I haven't," the words fall from my lips, my eyes never leaving the diamond on my finger.

Dean takes my hand, pulling it closer to him. "For a while, I thought this ring was an old engagement ring, and maybe that was who you lost." He shakes his head, "I hated how much jealousy I felt for someone whom I had never met, didn't know if they were even real, and who was probably not among us anymore."

I smile at him, "Nope, it's a bit more than that, actually. This diamond was made using carbon from Brian's ashes."

Dean's eyes bounce between the ring and my face. I think he's stopped breathing for a moment as well. "You mean, this diamond *IS* Brian?"

I nod my head.

"Cordelia, this has to be the most beautiful thing I have ever heard of. I had no idea that you could do something like this." He twists my hand, letting the light catch on the diamond.

"I was able to pick the color I wanted, but they couldn't say what exact shade of blue it would be. I just knew it had to be blue; he loved the ocean just like me. He picked the perfect shade; it's almost exactly that London blue color I have always loved for a diamond. But I love that some days it's so clear and light, like the shallow waters in the Bahamas, and other days it can look so dark, like the deepest parts of the Atlantic. The company told me that the carbon decides the color; effectively, Brian picked it. When it changes color, it's like I have this little piece of not only him, but the ocean with me too."

Dean's eyes meet mine. The blues and greens swirl together like the Northern Lights in his eyes. "I love that you have this, that you knew about this company and were able to do this."

"I found out about it back when we lost our dog, which was years and years ago. I looked into the pricing, and as much as we loved that dog, I couldn't justify spending that much for her. It was a no-brainer for Brian. He was worth every single cent it cost to make. They offer a personalized engraving option as well. Only fifteen characters. It says, 'I love you 3000' on the side, only visible with a jeweler's microscope."

"Tony Stark," Dean breathes.

I nod, saying, "We both cried so hard together in the theater over that movie; it was the last one we ever saw in a theater together."

* * *

After Dean grills up some steaks and potatoes for a late lunch or early dinner, we all take up our spots on the deck again.

"No tequila?" Jason jokes.

"I was thinking of relaxing in the hot tub after this. I don't want to pass out and drown," I laugh.

Dean is antsy and can't seem to sit still in his seat. He knows we have the last little bit to tell him, and he knows he won't like it.

"Dean," I start, "Let me get through this last bit. Tomorrow is the anniversary, and I really don't want to spend it talking about this stuff. I want to try to remember the good things. So, let me know when you are ready to hear it."

Dean finally settles a minute later, "I'm not ready, but I feel like there is no being ready for anything that has been said this whole time."

I purse my lips and close my eyes as I shake my head a little, because he's not wrong at all.

"At the sentencing, they played the 911 call. You think you know, because of all these action movies, but you really don't. It's so much worse. For months after hearing this call, every time a phone rang at work, I was right back in that courtroom. I pored over that autopsy report for months, because I needed to know. A nurse friend even read through it, telling me that it was instant. But what she didn't tell me, what all my research didn't tell me, is that movies get it so incredibly wrong."

I can feel my shoulder muscles tensing as I prepare to tell this to him. I try to roll them out a little, and it does nothing to help.

"I don't remember a whole lot at the beginning of the call. I just remember hearing another Marine in the background, and I think he ended up putting the phone on speaker; they were trying to stop the blood loss. But I don't know what he said other than hearing him say to Brian, 'Come on, Rivers. Fight. Don't do this.'" My voice breaks, and my eyes are welling up. But I keep going. "The only thing I can remember from that call was the gasps for breath, the choking sounds. Jason kept trying to get me to leave the room. But I couldn't do that to him, I couldn't leave Brian alone in those moments. I know the recording was over a year old by then, but Dean, it didn't feel like it to me. If I left that room, it was like I was abandoning him. I couldn't do that." I'm fighting back sobs, and I don't know when Dean moved, but he's crouched in front of me, hands on my thighs. Not saying anything, just providing the comfort that I need.

I take a deep breath, trying to calm down to finish. "After that, they had the medical examiner on the stand. I asked my victim's legal advocate if I could talk to her after. She asked me specifically what I needed to ask. I told her, and she let me. I caught her just as she was leaving the building. I only got out a little bit, but she knew what I was asking. She said it was just what the body does, but that he didn't know. He wasn't in there anymore."

I'm full-on sobbing by the time I'm done.

When I finally calm the sobs and pull my hands from my face, I find Dean and Jason both in front of me.

"That was the worst I had seen you through it all. You held yourself together so well, from the airport to the eight hours of greeting people and listening to their condolences, to all of the hearings. That was the one time—" Jason sucks in a breath, his muscles shaking. "Fuck, Cordelia, that was the one time when I didn't want to jump over that half wall for myself, but for you. Because you had to hear that. I don't think anyone would have stopped me; those escorts would have let it happen. His family wouldn't have been able to stop me. The only thing that stopped me was thinking that it would cost you another person."

Dean mumbles, "You could have pleaded temporary insanity."

That makes my lips turn up on the edges.

"Fuck, I need a shot after that. Do you want a shot?" Jason asks, standing from his chair. "I'm getting us each a shot, and then we can go relax."

We spend the rest of the early evening hours soaking in the hot tub. The warm water does wonders for all my sore and tense muscles. The three of us decide to dry off, and the guys go to the game room to play a couple of games of pool.

. . .

When I wake up in the morning, it hits me all over again. It's always my first thought when I wake on this day. How at 4:47 pm, it will officially mark five years since I last spoke with Brian.

But for me, it's always the day after that hits me the hardest. I think it's because I talked to Brian only a few hours before, and I was woken up at two in the morning the next day.

I know to expect a nice phone call from some of his friends today. Some of them try to get together and FaceTime me as a group. They like to check in and remember the fun stories. I swear I hear at least one new story every year. For those brief seconds, it feels like he's still here, still with me.

I roll over and find Dean's eyes on me. And that's all it takes for tears to well up in my eyes. I throw my hands over my face, sobbing, as Dean pulls me into his arms.

He doesn't say a word, he doesn't make a sound. He just holds me. I don't know how long I cry for. But I have a headache, and my eyes are swollen when I finally calm down.

Dean presses a kiss to my forehead when I pull back and roll over to stare at the ceiling. He gets up and comes back a moment later with a cool washcloth to place over my eyes.

"Madison always does this after she has a good cry. Says it makes them feel better. I don't know how true it is, but I thought it couldn't hurt," he explains as he sits next to me in the bed. "Can I get you anything? Coffee? French toast?"

"Coffee and aspirin, my head hurts so much right now," I whimper.

"You got it," he says. He squeezes my leg, and I feel his weight leave the bed. A few minutes later, I can make out the hushed murmurs of Dean and Jason talking. I can't make out what they are saying, but I'm sure I could guess.

Dean brings me coffee and a couple of aspirin, and I ask if I can just stay here for a while until my headache goes away. He gets me a fresh, cool washcloth and places a soft kiss on my lips.

Once my headache breaks, I take a shower and throw my hair into a loose braid. It's my go-to style on the beach like this, too much wind, and it keeps it tangle-free.

I find the guys on the deck. The sun is shining so brightly, and there's barely a cloud in the sky. I know we are supposed to have some weather move in later with that possible nor'easter, so I want to get an early start with our day.

"Hey," I say as I open the doors.

"You look like you feel a little better," Dean smiles as he reaches for my hand from his seat.

I nod, "Yeah, a bit." I turn to look at Jason, "I want to get moving before that weather moves in." I know he knows what I mean.

"You got it. My truck or Dean's? he questions as he stands up.

"I did have him get a permit for his truck, so unless you got one too..." I shrug. I'm not really in the mood to make any decisions. I just want to get to Ocracoke and get as close as we can to Teach's Hole.

"I can drive. I don't think my truck has ever been on a ferry before, and it hasn't driven on a beach," Dean says.

I nod, and we grab the things we need and pile into his truck.

It's a short drive to the ferry terminal, and since it's the off-season, we get on the first ferry. It takes just under an hour to get from Hatteras to Ocracoke and another twenty minutes to get into the town of Ocracoke. I opted to ride in the back of the truck, letting Jason direct us to the spot we park at. I don't feel like talking right now. I just want to get to our spot and talk to Brian.

Jason explains that it will be tight if any other cars are down there, as it's not a big spot to park, let alone turn around with a full-size truck. Thankfully, no one else is there, so Dean is able to get turned around and parked. The truck barely stops before I jump out. I start walking down the little trail and bridge, making my way to the edge of the island.

Teach's Hole is a spot where Blackbeard the pirate used to

always anchor his ship, *Queen Anne's Revenge*. Brian always loved pirates. So when I had a little bit of his ashes returned to me along with my finished ring, I came out here, spreading a little bit of him with the pirates. I always come out here now, it's a spot where I can talk to him, and it's quiet.

I hear Dean's voice as I clear the bridge before it's cut off. I figure Jason is explaining, and I don't stop, I don't turn around. I don't acknowledge anything, I just keep going.

Once I'm at the edge of the water, I leave my water shoes on and take a couple of steps into the small waves.

The nice part about this being on the sound side is that the waves are gentle. They don't crash over the sand, they ripple. I spot a white egret wading through the water, looking for food, and I smile at the pretty bird. I couldn't have picked a more beautiful spot to be able to come out and spend some time with Brian.

He's never even been here. We were planning a trip to Hatteras when he was ripped away from me. He always wanted to see this place. He's heard me talk about it before, since I'd been here a few times before. I used to come with a girlfriend and her family back in grade school. I fell in love with this place. I used to talk to Brian about all the pirates that used to frequent these waters, and all he wanted to do was come here and see this place. One of his favorite movies has always been the *Pirates of the Caribbean* series.

I lift my hand, moving my finger as the sun dances on the diamond, making it sparkle. A little piece of him that I will forever carry with me.

I stand in the water for a while, letting the waves ebb and flow, taking deep breaths of the salty air, listening to the quiet that is anything but quiet when you are on the ocean. The sounds of the waves, the birds, the occasional fish jumping and breaking the surface in the sound. I take it all in. This place, the ocean, has always been my happy place.

Taking a breath, I close my eyes and think of this past year, and I let the words pour out of me.

"Hey, kid, I miss you every day, and I love you more than I can put into words. But you know that. It probably seems silly that I do this here, where such a small part of you is, maybe more like *was*. I'm sure the tides have carried you further to other places by now. But it's always easier to talk to the sea than it is to talk to a bronze urn.

"I'm sure you've checked in, and I'm fairly certain you have had quite a hand in the way the last few months have played out, haven't you? Tired of seeing me going through the motions? Had to give me a reason to keep going, didn't you?" I smile, closing my eyes as the tears well up and begin to fall.

"Dean's a good man. That was obvious from the moment I met him. It took me a while to be able to let him in, but he finally knows now. I told him everything. Well, almost everything. I'm sure I missed a few things. But I think you know how much I struggle with feeling like I even deserve this life, when I couldn't save you. I will never forgive myself for that. I know I couldn't have done anything, but I always ask myself, what if I called you? Could that simple act have prevented it? Or would it have put me on the phone with you when it happened? Would you have looked up from your video game and seen what was happening and been able to move? I will never stop asking myself these questions. I don't think any mother could be in my position. It still gets to me that I didn't have this feeling, and Reese did. Reese was a friend, a neighbor, and a personal trainer of ours. And that's why she texted me. Asking if I was ever worried about you with the state of this world, but I didn't, that wasn't my direct worry. I never worried about you being stateside. I knew you were supposed to go to Japan the following year, but not into a combat zone. I guess I should have been worried about you playing video games in your barracks room. I never in a million years would have guessed that I needed to worry about you there.

"I hope you know that I'm thinking beyond what I can see, beyond just what Glass needs. I'm thinking of new places to go and see, and I'm thinking about it with Dean by my side. You know he's never left his corner of the world? Aside from a trip to Nashville once. He's never even been to see the ocean, and he's lived in North Carolina his whole life. I mean, it's not a short trip by any means to get here, but it's closer than Ohio was. You've given me the gift of myself and helped to bring some joy and happiness to my life again. I don't know if Dean is going to take part in this little tradition that Jason and I do. But if he does, I hope you listen to him. I hope you get to know him, while I do all I can to make sure he feels like he knows you too."

I'm trying to keep the tears at bay as much as possible, just so I can get the words out.

"If you could help me out with the weather, give me at least one day where the sound is like glass again so I can take your paddleboard out, that would be amazing. Maybe one of these days, I will learn how to stand up on it and not worry about falling. But if I lose your paddle, I know it would break me. I love you 3000."

I hang my head as the last words leave my lips.

When I turn around, I see Dean and Jason picking their way toward me. I look down into the water before I take a step, and less than two inches from my foot is a stingray sitting on the sand in the water. He wasn't there when I came down here. I'm always so careful to make sure I don't step on anything. He must have come up while I was talking. "Hey, little guy. I'm gonna move really slowly and carefully, don't panic." I lift the foot further from him, taking a slow side step to my left, slowly shifting my weight, and moving the foot close to him.

"Careful, there's a stingray over here. So watch your steps," I call to the guys.

Jason gives me a thumbs up as he finishes winding his way through the grass and steps into the water.

I take a couple of steps back, joining Dean in the grass, while we give Jason a couple of minutes. "Did he explain this? Sorry, I kinda dipped out. I didn't even think. I just needed to get here."

"You don't have to apologize. And yes, he did. He said you

come out here, you each get a couple of minutes to talk to him, update him on your lives. He didn't tell me why here, though?"

I point out over the water, "A little way out there is a spot they call Teach's Hole. It was where Blackbeard the pirate used to anchor his ship. Brian loved pirates." A watery chuckle escapes me. "One year at Halloween, he dressed as a pirate, and we saw a police officer patrolling the streets and handing out candy to the kids, and Brian," I laugh at the memory, "Brian goes up to him and asks him if he has any rum. The cop laughed it off and told him he was fresh out."

Dean laughs. It's deep, and his whole body is shaking with his laughter. "I guess that makes sense as to why you come out here."

"I also left some of his ashes out here. Not much, but a little bit." I fiddle with my ring at the words.

Dean takes hold of my hand and pulls me to him, pressing a soft kiss to my lips. When he pulls back, his eyes flick toward the water, and we see Jason carefully picking his way back out of the water. I meet Dean's eyes again, "Are you...?" He nods. He slowly lets go of my hand as he makes his way out to the water. Jason and I stand in the grass with each other, him wiping his tears away and me watching Dean have his first conversation with my son.

I can feel the tears sliding down my face, and I let them. There's no reason to stop them when I know they won't stop. Jason and I don't talk. We just wait. We never talk about what we say out here. It stays between Brian and us and the sea.

A few more minutes pass by before we see Dean turn and head back to us.

Falling into our routine, we wordlessly head back to the truck, grab the big jug of water, take our water shoes off, and line up on the tailgate. We rinse the mud and sand away before we slide on fresh shoes and head to 1718 Brewing Company.

After we have some food and a drink or two, we head back to the house, just pulling into the driveway when the clouds start rolling in.

By the time we make it inside and up to the top floor, the rain has started falling, and there's thunder and lightning in the distance. I change out of the clothes I was in since the air is a little chilly, grab my big beach blanket towel, and head out to the covered portion of the deck.

Jason and Dean join me a little while later, bringing with them drinks and the leftover pizza.

We watch the storm move over us, accepting the silence that we all seem to need.

Chapter Thirty-Two

DEAN

I will admit watching Cordelia jump out of my truck yesterday about scared me to death. Jason stopped me from going after her, explaining the whole situation. I didn't know what I was going to say, if I was even allowed to. Jason told me that I should. And when Cordelia asked me, I knew I would too.

I hold her in my arms while she sleeps as the sun is coming through the windows, and I think about what I said to him yesterday.

"Hey, Brian. I know we haven't met, but I think I know your mom pretty well by now. I know there's still so much to learn about her, and I know that a lot of that will have to do with you as well. I wish this had never happened to you. Nineteen is far too young for a life to be cut short like it was for you. And the way it happened, fuck, it's incredibly fucked up. There's no other way to say it.

I'm going to keep this short this time, since I have so much to learn about you yet, but please rest easy knowing I'm going to be looking after your mom. I will do everything in my power to make her happy and give her the life she deserves.' I glance over my shoulder back at Cordelia.

"She told me about the ring she wears. I hope you don't mind, and I really hope Harper agrees to help me, and then I really, really *hope it doesn't make your mom angry with me, but I already know I want to marry her, and I hope you are okay with that as well.' I let my head hang for a moment before I tilt it back up, looking over the water, tears filling my eyes again. "I want the ring I propose to her with to be part of you as well. I should be asking for your permission to marry her. She should have you to walk her down the aisle to me, but I think this might be the best compromise I can make, given the situation.'*

I don't really know how to finish the conversation, so I leave it at that, and when I glance up again, I see a pod of dolphins out in the distance. Dorsal fins cutting through the water and their water spouts. I take that as Brian's approval of my plans.

Cordelia starts to stir, shaking me out of the memory.

She rolls over, her green eyes already sparkling with the tears welling up in them. I wrap my arms around her and pull her into me while she silently cries.

* * *

That night after dinner, Cordelia's phone goes off with the sound of a FaceTime call coming through. She runs into the bedroom to grab her iPad, and when she comes out, she connects the call to it.

"Hey, Mama Rivers!" I hear a couple of voices say through the speaker.

"Hello, boys. It's good to see your faces."

When Jason enters the frame, all the young faces on the screen yell "Gunny!"

"Not a Gunny anymore," he mumbles.

"Nah, but you will always be our Gunny!"

There's a lot of laughter down the line, and I smile as Cordelia joins in with them. I watch from where I'm standing at the kitchen island as her and Jason sit shoulder to shoulder so they are both in the camera frame.

"Dean, come meet some of the guys that Brian was friends

with," Cordelia calls to me. I pull a chair up next to her and slide down into it.

I spend the next hour listening to stories and learning a lot more about Brian. I think my favorite story that was shared by his friends was when Lew, whose name I only committed to memory when it was added that he is also Sebastian's nephew, started and stopped his story because he couldn't tell it to Brian's mother. Which naturally caused everyone to goad him into sharing it.

"I cannot believe I have to share this story with Brian's mom! But fine, don't say I didn't warn you. He told us when he lost his virginity that he didn't know what to do and just," Lew pauses and winces before rushing out, *"stuck it in like a thermometer."*

Cordelia's eyes were so wide, and then she started laughing so hard. You could see the instant relief flood his face when she started laughing.

There were so many stories shared back and forth: some volunteer adventures they did at a NASCAR race, a game of chicken at the beach, which was also his last time at the beach. That story seemed to hit Cordelia hard. I think it's because we are just north of that beach right now.

* * *

Our last full day at the beach house turns out to be the day Cordelia has been waiting for. Jason and I are sitting at the counter in the kitchen with our coffee when Cordelia comes rushing out of the bedroom, setting down a pair of binoculars on her way and heading down the stairs.

I look at Jason to ask what that was, and he interrupts before I can even get words out, "She will be back in a minute. I'm gonna go ahead and make a call, be proactive." He pulls his phone out of his pocket and types a few things before he puts it up to his ear. "Yeah, hey, I was wondering if you have two paddle boards available to rent for the day?... Yep, experienced, we don't need a tutorial. Honestly, I should just buy one already," he says with a laugh.

"Alright, cool, thanks. Yeah, I will be up shortly to pick them up. Thank you."

Just as he hangs up, Cordelia comes back up the stairs, breathing hard, no doubt from running up all the stairs.

"The water." Gasp. "The sound." Gasp. "Is like." Gasp. "Glass," she gulps out.

"Already called in the paddleboard reservation for Dean and me. You have Brian's, I'm assuming?"

She nods her head.

We spend the majority of the day out on the sound, behind the house, on the paddleboards. Pointing out fish, stingrays, and a starfish to each other. I'm incredibly surprised by the depth of the water. In almost all of the spots we are in, you can see the bottom, and it's only a couple of feet deep. Cordelia uses her watch, which has built-in GPS, to track most of what we paddle. We did close to five miles on the water, not really going anywhere, and keeping the houses in sight so that we don't have to think about where we are going when we head back.

I haven't seen Cordelia as relaxed this whole trip as she is today. She is sitting on her board, never opting to stand up as Jason and I do; she has one leg bent at the knee in front of her across the board, and the other is over the side, dangling in the water. Her hair is pulled back in a ponytail through her hat, and while she has a bathing suit on, her top half is covered in a white and blue long-sleeved SPF shirt to keep her from getting burned. She's slowly pushing her paddle through the water while she looks at the sand below. Her face is relaxed, and there's a hint of a smile on her lips.

This is the Cordelia I want to bring to life again.

I will do whatever it takes to make it happen.

We all pull our boards up next to each other about one hundred yards offshore, sliding our paddles across all the boards. We each keep a leg on one as we recline back. We don't want to drift away from each other as we take in the sunset.

"One day, I brought all the new guys in to have a little chat with them," Jason starts from his board on the other side of Cordelia. "We were having some issues, and this was before the pressure to join the vendetta against me, but I think it might have been the catalyst. I wanted to talk to them for a bit about what I saw as the problem. They all just started bullshitting," he weaves a hand through the water next to his board, "just running their mouths to run their mouths. Then Brian just let loose on them. He said, 'All y'all are Marines, right? So fucking act like it. You are not in charge of us, so stop trying to supervise and just do the work because the NCOs and Gunny will supervise.'" Cordelia lets out a laugh and smiles as she looks down at her board, running a hand over it.

Jason laughs and goes on, "Then he added, 'None of you will just fucking work, y'all just bitch and fuck off.' That was the moment I knew he had what it took and would go so far. I started putting him in charge after that, and then everyone else slowly got the hint."

Cordelia turns her head to Jason, "You never told me that before."

He shrugs, "I guess I liked having something that was mine, but you deserve to know that story too."

We sit in silence as we watch the last of the sun disappear into the water.

* * *

The drive home the next day is quiet, neither of us really wanting to break the silence. It's as if we both know that we are going back to reality and need to take the time to absorb and process everything from this week.

Jason and I exchanged numbers, with him telling me to keep in touch, and he would do the same.

I texted the guys that Cordelia and I want to talk to them, and she told the girls. We have everyone coming over tomorrow for a late Sunday lunch. Madison will be there as well, but I know we can keep her busy in the pool and close one side of the windows if it will make Cordelia feel more comfortable not having those details said in front of her. I'm sure Graham is going to have a hard time figuring out what to tell her if she asks.

When we pull onto my street a little before six o'clock, Cordelia lets out a sigh and stretches her arms above her head, arching her back, as she gets the kinks out from the long drive.

"Now the fun of doing laundry and unpacking starts," she says around a yawn.

"Are you staying tonight? I don't really want you to be alone right now."

"I'd like that. I didn't want to assume," she's quiet, and her voice sounds unsure.

I reach over, grabbing her hand, "Please, assume."

She gives me the kind of smile that I will make my life's mission to see on her face.

After we get everything out of the truck and into my house, I grab her, pulling her into me. "We need to have a talk. Get one thing straight right now. If you think anything you told me over this past week is going to do anything to change the way I feel about you, the plans I have for us, you couldn't be more wrong. I love you, and just because you have had this awful thing happen to you, it doesn't define you. Only you can do that. You are who you choose to be. I know there will be harder days than others, and I know there may be times that you need to be alone with your thoughts or disappear into a book where someone decides to molest different foods, and that's okay. I will always be here when you need me. If you call me, if you need me, I will already be on my way." I cradle her face in my hands and use my thumbs to wipe away the tears that are falling.

"Thank you," she says around a shaky breath. "I'm going to struggle with things, Dean. It's just part of me now. Every time there's happiness for me, it reminds me that I can't share it with him. I don't think that will ever change. I don't know how to live in the moments without the weight of the past pulling me down."

"No one is telling you that you need to cut the strings. I'm not going to hold it against you when I take you to Italy in the future, if it makes you a little sad. That's just the way it is." I bring her hand up, pressing a kiss just above the blue diamond to her knuckles. "We have a whole world to show him."

* * *

The following day, when our friends and family are over, Sebastian and I take the lead along with Harper, not wanting to put all of that on Cordelia again after she just went through it.

Bast knew a great deal more than both Cordelia and I thought he did. Sure, he knew what happened, but he knew details that only someone who was there, like Cordelia, would know.

"Where's Gwen?" I ask as Cordelia helps me in the kitchen to get the chicken and spices out to the grill area.

"Oh, she had an episode today. None of us wanted to push her to come out. It's okay, though. She knows, and what is learned today, I'm sure Faye will fill her in on later," Cordelia explains.

"Ok, I'm going to need you to explain exactly *how* you knew all of that," Harper says, pointing the knife at Bast.

"Yes, Sebastian, please enlighten the rest of us," Faye says across the table from him. "I barely knew the details, and I have been friends with her longer than you have."

Bast lifts a shoulder and shrugs in response, "Let's just say that certain people still in the Corps owe me a few favors. I called them in a few years ago."

Cordelia's eyes bounce from mine and back to Bast's. "Um, are you going to tell me why you called those in a *couple of years* ago?"

Bast leans back in his chair, crossing his arms over his chest, "It was nothing more than my own curiosity. I never said anything because I figured when you were ready, you'd tell me. Didn't know it was going to take that one," he jerks his head in my direction, "to get you to open up though."

Graham is on the other side of me, extremely silent. "Hey, you ok?" I ask, which gets everyone's attention on him.

"I don't know," Graham sighs, scrubbing a hand down his face. "I just can't fathom it. I couldn't imagine—" his voice breaks and he closes his eyes. When he opens them, he seeks out Madison, who we sent inside with her food to watch a movie. "That kid is my whole world. I can't imagine it without her. Fuck, Cordelia, I'm so fucking sorry." Graham bats at a tear that rolls down his face.

I knew that out of everyone here, it would hit him the hardest. He always comes off as a goofball, but he's such an incredibly emotional person. He doesn't often show this side, though.

Cordelia pushes back from the table, going to Graham, who stands up as he wraps his arms around her. "Don't hold her back because of this, Graham. She still has to live her life. You can't keep her in bubble wrap. Brian was playing video games in his own room. You can't keep her on a short leash because of that. You gotta let her live," Cordelia's voice is quiet. I doubt the others can hear her much. Her words are just for Graham, one parent to another.

Graham nods, "Maybe in like twenty years I will think about it."

I smile at his words, knowing he's probably not really kidding about that.

I watch as Faye slides out of her chair and wraps her arms around both of them. "You two are making me feel all of the feels and I just need to hug you both."

The three of them stay that way in their hug for a minute before Lachlan clears his throat, breaking the silence and tender moment.

"Well, I just Googled her. Usually, it's just social media hits. I was not expecting what I found, though. But it got me thinking. I don't know the rules on this, with different states and all that, and since you already had a road dedication done back in Ohio. But I would be more than happy to take it to the mayor and get you in touch with the right people. The road that Glass is on is a state route, which would qualify it for a road dedication. It could be the portion right in front of Glass." He leans forward, grabbing his beer and taking a drink.

Cordelia has tears in her eyes. The soft gasp that leaves her lips as her hand flies to her throat is all the indication I need.

"Do it," I tell him. I turn to Cordelia, and she's nodding her head.

"Consider it done," Lachlan says.

After dinner, Cordelia and Bast start taking dishes in. I know there's no point in telling her to stop, so I let her. But the real reason is for a minute with Harper.

"Harper," I dart my eyes to the open French doors, tilting my head to indicate I want to talk to her.

Harper's eyes twinkle with mischief as she smiles. She follows me out of the doors on the opposite side of the pool and kitchen. "What's up? Are we about to be plotting something together?"

"It's not a plot. It's a question."

She pouts at me. "Well, that's no fun."

I exhale and pinch the bridge of my nose, "Cordelia told me about her ring. I don't think it's a secret that I have every intention of marrying her. I want to propose with a ring made the same way."

Harper lets out an ear-piercing squeal, and I have to shush her. "Oh! Yes. Do that. That's exactly what you should do." Then her elated face morphs into, I kid you not, the smile the Grinch gets when he decides to steal Christmas. That is the exact look on her face, and I have to say, I don't think I've ever been more terrified of a barely five-foot female in my life. "I think we are about to be plotting together, aren't we, Dean-O?"

Fuck.

"I'm going to regret this, but yeah, I guess we are."

She claps her hands and bounces up on her toes. "Excellent. I will graciously help you pull this off. And only because I can tell that, had you been there when she went through this, you would have burned the world to the ground for her."

I smile at her, "If I could make it right for her, I would. I think I have to resign myself to the fact that nothing ever will, and there's nothing I can do but be here for her now."

"You're a good man, Dean." Harper grabs my arm and squeezes it, her eyes going soft. "You're exactly what she's needed for a while. I'm really glad she finally let you in."

I duck my head, mumbling out a thanks as Harper walks back into the house.

After everyone leaves that night, I pull Cordelia into my arms, with her back to my chest, as I walk her forward into the hallway.

"Dean, what are you doing?" she chuckles as I come to a stop right in front of the end of the hallway.

"I'm thinking, I can build a shelf or two. Maybe a nice gloss black with some gold trim. We can make this wall a whole special spot for Brian. A couple of flameless candles. We hang a picture under the shelf." She's really quiet, and I'm wondering if I pushed too far too soon. "Or, I can build you a whole craft shed out back."

Cordelia turns in my arms. Her eyes have been red-rimmed all day, and they are filled with fresh tears again. She lifts her arms, wrapping them around my neck, "I would love both of those options." She lifts up onto her toes, pressing a kiss to my lips. "Thank you for wanting to make him a part of your home and wanting him to have a special place in it."

I brush a couple of loose strands of hair back from her face, tucking them behind her ear. "I will always make space for the things and people that are important to you."

"I love you, Dean."

"I love you too, Rosebud." I dip my head, pressing another kiss to her lips. "Now, I'm going to take you in that bedroom and do incredibly dirty things to you." I bend my knees, grab her ass, and lift her so she wraps her legs around my waist.

Epilogue One

DEAN - 11 MONTHS LATER

I'm lighting the candles on the table when I hear Cordelia's car in the driveway. She moved in officially six months ago, and to say that I'm ecstatic is an understatement. I love having her in my home and watching her decorate everything, bringing in warmth that my house has desperately been missing for years.

It finally feels like a real home now.

I smile, knowing that tonight marks the start of a new chapter for us. The box in my pocket presses against my thigh.

I've been waiting for this day for almost a year. It took some time for the ring to be made, and now that I have it, I couldn't wait even a day longer to ask this woman to be my wife.

I hear the door from the garage open, followed by her voice, "Hey, handsome. What's the special occasion?" she asks when she walks in and sees candles all over the kitchen, the dining room, and the living room.

I stride the few steps to her and quirk an eyebrow, "Do I need to have a reason to want to do something nice for the woman I love?" I wonder if she will catch that she said the same words to me the night she told me she loved me.

"I suppose not," she smiles as she wraps her arms around me.

I take her face in my hands, noticing the green in her eyes

sparkling in the candlelight. It brings out the gold flakes that are peppered through them, giving her an ethereal look. I bring my lips down to hers, and when my tongue seeks entrance, she parts her lips and groans as we both deepen the kiss.

I'm incredibly nervous to ask this question right now. I know how close we are to yet another year she has had to live her life without her son. I'm hoping I'm not making a huge mistake asking just a few weeks shy of the six-year mark.

But I also know just how much she will want another diamond and piece of him on her finger again.

Breaking the kiss, I breathe deeply and start, "Rosebud, you came into my life when I was just about ready to give up on ever finding love. You came into my world and turned everything upside down. I knew from the moment I met you that day at Glass, when you opened those doors and stepped into the sunlight, that you were going to be the one. I knew how guarded you were and how much you kept things locked up, and all I ever wanted to be was a safe place for you to land." I can see the question in her eyes and the slight smile at my words that dances across her pink lips. "When you finally let me fully in and told me about Brian and allowed yourself to feel love again, and more than that, you accepted how much I love you, I knew that it was only a matter of time before we took the next step." I can see the tears starting to fill her eyes, and she's trying to blink them away.

When I take a step back and reach into my pocket, wrapping my fingers around the box, I start to kneel down. She sucks in a sharp breath as she realizes what is happening.

When I pull the box from my pocket, and she sees the blue and white box with the logo on it, I know she knows, and that's when the tears start to spill over.

"I know I should have asked you, but I didn't want to ruin the surprise, so I asked Harper," I say sheepishly. "She fully agreed and told me that you would love that I did this for you." I take a breath and open the box to reveal the diamond set in a rose gold band with metal work around the diamond to mimic the petals of a rose, along with four smaller green diamonds in the leaves surrounding the rose. I wanted to mimic the ring she had made but still make this one a little more unique.

"I couldn't ask you to marry me without Brian being a part of this. So, I sent in the ashes to the same company you used to make your ring. When I told them I wanted this to be your engagement ring, they were so excited to start this with me." The tears are gently flowing down her face now. "Cordelia Scarlett Rivers, will you marry me?"

She lets out a sob before she throws her arms around me and whispers, "Yes, a thousand times, yes." I stand up, taking her with me, and when she pulls back, I take the ring from the box and place it on her left ring finger, smiling when it fits perfectly.

"I love this ring so much, Dean. And I love that you made sure to make Brian a part of this. I can't wait to marry you. You are the kind of man I always hoped my son would be, and I only wish I had found you sooner, so that he could have met you." She presses a kiss to my lips before murmuring against them, "I love you."

I take her face in my hands, "I cannot wait to call you my wife."

She pulls back, looking into my eyes, "What did you have engraved on the diamond?"

I smirk, "That was tricky to come up with, I had them put 'My Love My Home' with the appropriate spaces. Exactly fifteen characters." I raise my eyebrow in a silent question.

Cordelia brings her hands next to each other, admiring the rings that adorn her hands. "That's perfect, Dean." Her eyes bounce back to mine, "I had them put 'I Love You 3000', also with the spaces, exactly fifteen characters. It was meant to be."

I see the sadness creep into her eyes as she studies her new diamond.

"You know, Rosebud, it's okay to always be a little sad. It just reminds you that he was real, he was here. You will always walk with the grief, Cordelia, but you don't have to do it alone anymore. I will share that burden with you, however I can."

Tears fall from her eyes, "I love you, Dean. Thank you for never once making me feel like I'm a broken person. Thank you for pushing me to let love in." She presses a kiss to my lips. And I know in that moment that every single moment in my life has led me here, to her.

Epilogue Two

Amalfi Coast, Italy

I stand on the balcony of our hotel, overlooking the Mediterranean Sea. The setting sun is sparkling off the small waves, and the air smells like salt and flowers, and I swear I can smell wine and fresh pasta, but that might just be my imagination playing tricks on me.

Our wedding was at Glass, naturally, surrounded by all of our friends and family. Including my mother, who flew in from Alaska. Harper was the maid of honor, and Graham was the best man. I almost didn't even want to do that much, but the things Harper has been by my side through, it wouldn't have felt right to not have her by my side for a good memory. Gwen designed my dress, a simple chiffon A-line dress with a square neckline. But the part that really made it unique was the red and yellow roses through the bodice and the bottom of the skirt. It looked stunning with the rose bushes flowering under the lanai that Dean built. Faye wouldn't let me do any of the decorations, and she made Glass feel even more like a fairytale than it ever had before. Twinkle lights were everywhere, and everything was draped in white chiffon and flowering vines. I hear the faint click of Dean's dress shoes on the ceramic floor as he comes closer, pulling me out of my reverie.

His arms wrap around my waist as he kisses my neck, "Mmmm, my wife looks stunning." We've been married two weeks and are on the first night of our three-week trip around Italy. And I have yet to tire of hearing him call me his wife. "I think I would rather eat you than go to dinner."

I try to stifle the giggle, "It's our first night in Italy. As much as I would love to have your hands on my body, you have about twelve minutes before I go from hungry to hangry."

"I can't have a hangry wife on my hands," he chuckles as he loosens his grip and threads his fingers with mine before pulling me along.

"Dean!" I laugh, "I have to grab my bag!"

He stops in his tracks, casting a glance around the room when his eyes land on my small clutch bag on the edge of the dresser. He scoops it up and goes back to pulling me along behind him again. The man is determined to make this the best trip for both of us, and if that means he has to sacrifice his favorite way to spend his time since we got married to ensure I don't get grumpy, he will.

I will admit that I did enjoy it when he wouldn't let me wear a single piece of clothing for three days after the wedding, only letting me leave the bed to use the bathroom and shower. The man is insatiable.

"Buonasera signore e signora," the hostess says as we walk into the rooftop restaurant. *"Benvenuto a Senzafine,"* she continues in gorgeous Italian.

"Buonasera," I reply before Dean says, "We have a reservation for two under Campbell."

"Ah, *si*, the newlyweds. *Per favore*, follow me," she says, switching to English for my husband, as she leads us to a table close to the edge, with a perfect view of the sea below.

There is a chilled bottle of wine in a bucket next to the table that our hostess opens for us, pouring each of us a glass of wine.

"Please, enjoy your meals and your stay with us here at the Hotel Santa Caterina," she says as she sets the bottle back in the ice bucket.

Dean picks up his glass, prompting me to do the same, "To us, and our new chapter."

Despite the sadness that always creeps in with new beginnings and chapters in my life, this is one of the first times the happiness I feel isn't overshadowed by it. I still have to clear the emotion from my throat before I speak, but my voice doesn't break this time. "Thank you for giving me a reason to find real happiness in this life again, Dean."

"I will give you anything and everything to make sure you always find happiness."

* * *

Afterword

As I mentioned at the beginning of this book, not all experiences within the UCMJ will be the same, and not all Gold Star Mothers are made in the same way either.

We all have our own stories to tell, and none are any more or less painful.

We can do the hard things; it will never be easy for us, but we can do them. And some days, the hard things are just continuing to breathe.

We need to remember to be there for each other.

From this MoM to others, *Semper Fi*.

Acknowledgments

When you get that knock on the door as a Marine Mom or MoM (Mothers of Marines), it changes your whole life. And not only my life, but this whole book, because of that singular event. This was supposed to be a completely different story, and now... well, you read it. You know how life influenced this book.

Thank you for reading this story. Thank you for taking a chance on this book. I will never be able to fully put into words how much it really means to have you read this.

I wouldn't wish this life on anyone, but if you ever find yourself in a similiar situation, please find the one thing that will bring you peace. Writing this book was that for me. I won't lie and say it was easy, and there were countless tears shed during the writing of this, (the bootcamp hug, the dream, let's be honest, the whole Outer Banks trip).

To my husband, you stood by me and read an entire book. For someone who doesn't read at all, I can't begin to express what that meant to me. The way you never left my side and never once wavered during our hardest and darkest moments, I will love you forever.

To my amazing editor, Emma, and the team at Scott Editorial, thank you for believing in this story and me. Thank you for the endless advice and for helping me shape this into what it is today. I couldn't have done it without you.

To my beta readers - thank you for helping me to keep the plot plotting, and for all the passive-aggressive memes and gifs that were sent while I waited on y'all. You the real MVP's for putting up with me.

To my sister - I'm sorry I gave your character a low pain tolerance. I will make it up to you, I promise. Thank you for being my reading buddy and for the countless books recs.

To ADV - thank you for inspiring so many things for this story and the next one (The Pepsi Bottle IYKYK and if you don't you will!). You have been the best friend I could have ever asked for and there is not day that goes by that I am not thankful for you.

To my Oldest Son - Thank you for being my fantasy reading buddy and understanding my love for Dragons. I can only hope that you continue to do amazing things and keep making me proud of you. Life isn't and hasn't been the easiest for us, but you have kept pushing though, and some days, that's more than enough to keep going.

To Rob and Patricia, thank you for being the grandparents you are and the best ex-in-laws a girl could ask for. You are truly some of my most favorite people in this world and I'm so thankful to still have you both in my life.

To Kevin, thank you for being the role model and Marine that Austin looked up to more than he may have even realized. And thank you for seeing his potential, even if it was never fully realized. You helped him see what he was truly capable of, and for that, you have my deepest thanks.

To Austin, saying thank you doesn't feel right. So to you I say, I miss you every day, and I love you 3000. You know I will never ever let anyone touch my copy of the Mindf*ck Series, you will forever be the only one to touch every page of that book. I hope you are cruising around in your Mustang, just like Dean Winchester with Baby.

Requiesce in pace
dilectum filium meum
semper fidelis

About the Author

K.L. Austin writes romance with heart, hope, and a deep love for happy endings.

An only child with an overactive imagination, she's been making up

stories for as long as she can remember—long before she ever thought she'd write them down.

As a Gold Star Marine Mom, she draws on her life experience to shape the emotional depth of her work, while her stories always center on love, connection, and fulfillment.

She lives in Northeast Ohio and believes a good romance should leave readers feeling happier, softer, and a little more hopeful than when they started.

* * *

instagram.com/authorklaustin

tiktok.com/@klaustinauthor

www.ingramcontent.com/pod-product-compliance
Lightning Source LLC
LaVergne TN
LVHW091955080526
838231LV00033B/346